LIFE, HERE AND THERE:

OR

SKETCHES OF SOCIETY AND ADVENTURE

AT

FAR-APART TIMES AND PLACES.

BY

N. P. WILLIS.

NEW YORK:
BAKER AND SCRIBNER, 145 NASSAU STREET.
1850.

C. W. BENEDICT,
Stereotyper,
201 William st., N. Y.

PREFACE.

So imperceptibly is one stage of life shaded into the next—so gradual and easy are the transitions, through the changes worked by experience and observation—that we refer back to what we "always said," and "always thought," as if we had always looked through the same eyes and judged by the same standards. Yet, if we could recal the Past, with the backward-waving wand of the magician, and could see, together, the two pictures—life as it seemed then, and life as it seems now—how startling, to any mind, would be the comparison! An author who has chronicled his impressions, and preserved pictures of society, as he saw it at earlier and later stages of observation, has almost this magical privilege. He can look again at the scenes which he has copied and treasured up, and judge, as few others can, with what different eyes men look around them at far-apart times and places.

In the following sketches, the writer records much in which he had a personal share, though the narratives, even when told in the first person, are, by no means, intended to be strictly autobiographic. The characters are all drawn from life, however, and several of them are portraits, done with studied faithfulness, of celebrated men and women whom he has had the opportunity to know; while the scenes of the different stories are minutely true to the manners of the countries, and the style of the society, in which they are laid. If the two parts of the book do not seem to the reader to be written by the same pen, it but strengthens the remark with which this preface commences. But if, from these contrasted pictures, any knowledge can be drawn, as to the tendencies of a varied life, and as to the comparative value of the different spheres and relations of society, here and abroad, he will not feel that even so sketchy a work is without its uses.

CONTENTS.

PAGE

EDITH LINDSEY.

SCENES OF FEAR.

INCIDENTS ON THE HUDSON

EARLIER DAYS.

EDITH LINSEY.

PART I.

FROST AND FLIRTATION.

" Oh yes—for you're in love with *me!*
(I'm very glad of it, I'm sure;)
But then you are not rich, you see,
And I—— you know *I'm very* poor!
'Tis true that I can drive a tandem—
'Tis true that I can turn a sonnet—
'Tis true I leave the law at random,
When I *should* study—plague upon it!
But this is not—excuse me!—money!
(A thing they give for house and land;)
And we must eat in matrimony—
And love is neither bread nor honey—
And so——you understand?"

" Thou art spotless as the snow, lady mine, lady mine!
Thou art spotless as the snow, lady mine!
But the noon will have its ray,
And snow-wreaths melt away—
And hearts—why should not they?—
Why not thine?"

It began to snow. The air softened; the pattering of the horse's hoofs was muffled with the impeded vibration; the sleigh glided on with a duller sound; the large loose flakes fell soft and fast; and the low and just audible murmur, like the tread of a fairy host, melted on the ear with a drowsy influence, as if it were a descent of palpable sleep upon the earth. You may talk of falling water—of the running of a brook—of the humming song of an old crone on a sick vigil—or of the *levi susurro* of the bees of Hybla—but there is nothing like the falling of the snow, for soft and soothing music. You hear it, or not, as you will, but it melts into your soul unaware. If you have ever a heartache, or feel the need of " poppy or mandragora," or, like myself, grow sometimes a-weary of the stale repetitions of this unvaried world, seek me out in Massachusetts, when the wind softens and veers south, after a frost—say in January. There shall have been a long-lying snow on the ground, well-trodden. The road shall be as smooth as the paths to our first sins—of a seeming perpetual declivity, as it were—and never a jot or jar between us and the edge of the horizon; but all onward and down apparently, with an insensible ease. You sit beside me in my spring-sleigh, hung with the lightness of a cob-web cradle for a fairy's child in the trees. Our horse is, in the harness, of a swift and even pace, and around his neck is a string of fine small bells, that ring to his measured step in a kind of muffled music, softer and softer as the snow-flakes thicken in the air. Your seat is of the shape of the *fauteuil* in your library, cushioned and deep, and with a backward and gentle slope, and you are enveloped to the eyelids in warm furs. You settle down, with every muscle in repose, the visor of your ermine cap just shedding the snow from your forehead, and, with a word, the groom stands back, and the horse speeds on, steady, but beautifully fast. The bells, which you hear loudly at first, begin to deaden, and the low hum of the alighting flakes steals gradually on your ear; and soon the hoof-strokes are as silent as if the steed were shod with wool, and away you flee through the white air, like birds asleep upon the wing diving through the feathery fleeces of the noon. Your eyelids fall—forgetfulness steals upon the senses—a delicious torpor takes possession of the uneasy blood—and brain and thought yield to an intoxicating and trance-like slumber. It were perhaps too much to ask that any human bosom may go scathless to the grave; but, in my own unworthy petitions, I usually supplicate that my heart may be broken about Christmas. I know an anodyne o' that season.

Fred Fleming and I occupied one of the seven long seats in a stage-sleigh, flying at this time twelve miles in the hour, (yet not fast enough for our impatience), westward from the university gates. The sleighing had been perfect for a week, and the cold keen air had softened for the first time that morning, and assumed the warm and woolly complexion that foretokened snow. Though not very cheerful in its aspect, this is an atmosphere particularly pleasant to breathe; and Fred, who was making his first move after a six weeks' fever, sat with the furs away from his mouth, nostrils expanded, lips parted, and the countenance altogether of a man in a high state of physical enjoyment. I had nursed him through his illness, by-the-way, in my own rooms, and hence our position as fellow-travellers. A pressing invitation from his father to come home with him to Skaneateles, for the holydays, had diverted me from my usual winter journey to the North; and, for the first time in my life, I was going upon a long visit to a strange roof. My imagination had never more business upon its hands.

Fred had described to me, over and over again, every person I was to meet—brothers, sisters, aunts, cousins, and friends—a household of thirty people, guests included; but there was one person among them of whom his descriptions, amplified as they were, were very unsatisfactory.

"Is she so *very* plain?" I asked, for the twentieth time.

"Abominably!"

"And immense black eyes?'

"Saucers!"

"And large mouth?"

"Huge!"

"And very dark?"

"Like a squaw!"

"And skinny hands, did you say?"

"Lean, long, and pokerish!"

"And so *very* clever?"

"Knows everything, Phil!"

"But a sweet voice?"

"Um! everybody says so."

"And high temper?"

"She's the devil, Phil! don't ask any more questions about her."

"You don't like her, then?"

"She never condescends to speak to me; how should I."

And thereupon I put my head out of the sleigh, and employed myself with catching the snow-flakes on my nose, and thinking whether Edith Linsey would like me or no; for, through all Fred's derogatory descriptions, it was clearly evident that she was the ruling spirit of the hospitable household of the Flemings.

As we got farther on, the new snow became deeper, and we found that the last storm had been heavier here than in the country from which we had come. The occasional farm-houses were almost wholly buried, the black chimney alone appearing above the ridgy drifts, while the tops of the doors and windows lay below the level of the trodden road, from which a descending passage was cut to the threshold, like the entrance to a cave in the earth. The fences were quite invisible. The fruit-trees looked diminished to shrubberies of snow-flowers, their trunks buried under the visible surface, and their branches loaded with the still falling flakes, till they bent beneath the burden. Nothing was abroad, for nothing could stir out of the road without danger of being lost, and we dreaded to meet even a single sleigh, lest, in turning out, the horses should " slump" beyond their depth, in the untrodden drifts. The poor animals began to labor severely, and sunk at every step over their knees in the clogging and wool-like substance; and the long and cumbrous sleigh rose and fell in the deep pits like a boat in a heavy sea. It seemed impossible to get on. Twice we brought up with a terrible plunge and stood suddenly still, for the runners had struck in too deep for the strength of the horses; and, with the snow-shovels, which formed a part of the furniture of the vehicle, we dug them from their concrete beds. Our progress at last was reduced to scarce a mile in the hour, and we began to have apprehensions that our team would give out between the post-houses. Fortunately it was still warm, for the numbness of cold would have paralyzed our already flagging exertions.

We had reached the summit of a long hill with the greatest difficulty. The poor beasts stood panting and reeking with sweat; the runners of the sleigh were clogged with hard cakes of snow, and the air was close and dispiriting. We came to a stand-still, with the vehicle lying over almost on its side, and I stepped out to speak to the driver and look forward. It was a discouraging prospect; a long deep valley lay before us, closed at the distance of a couple of miles by another steep hill, through a cleft in the top of which lay our way. We could not even distinguish the line of the road between. Our disheartened animals stood at this moment buried to their breasts, and to get forward without rearing at every step seemed impossible. The driver sat on his box looking uneasily down into the valley. It was one undulating ocean of snow, not a sign of a human habitation to be seen, and even the trees indistinguishable from the general mass by their whitened and overladen branches. The storm had ceased, but the usual sharp cold that succeeds a warm fall of snow had not yet lightened the clamminess of the new-fallen flakes, and they clung around the foot like clay, rendering every step a toil.

"Your leaders are quite blown," I said to the driver, as he slid off his uncomfortable seat.

"Pretty nearly, sir!"

"And your wheelers are not much better."

"Sca'cely."

"And what do you think of the weather?"

"It'll be darnation cold in an hour." As he spoke, he looked up to the sky, which was already peeling off its clouds in long stripes, like the skin of an orange, and looked as hard and cold as marble between the widening rifts. A sudden gust of a more chilling temperature followed immediately upon his prediction, and the long cloth curtains of the sleigh flew clear off their slight pillars, and shook off their fringes of icicles.

"Could you shovel a little, mister?" said the driver, handing me one of the broad wooden utensils from his foot-board, and commencing, himself, after having thrown off his box-coat, by heaving up a solid cake of the moist snow at the side of the road.

" It's just to make a place to rub down them creturs," said he, as I looked at him, quite puzzled to know what he was going to do.

Fred was too weak to assist us, and having righted the vehicle a little, and tied down the flapping curtains, he wrapped himself in his cloak, and I set heartily to work with my shovel. In a few minutes, taking advantage of the hollow of a drift, we had cleared a small area of frozen ground, and, releasing the tired animals from their harness, we rubbed them well down with the straw from the bottom of the sleigh. The persevering driver then cleared the runners of their iced and clinging masses, and, a half hour having elapsed, he produced two bottles of rum from his box, and, giving each of the horses a dose, put them again to their traces.

We heaved out of the pit into which the sleigh had settled, and for the first mile it was down-hill, and we got on with compara tive ease. The sky was by this time almost bare, a dark, slaty mass of clouds alone settling on the horizon in the quarter of the wind, while the sun, as powerless as moonlight, poured with dazzling splendor on the snow, and the gusts came keen and bitter across the sparkling waste, rimming the nostrils as if with bands of steel, and penetrating to the innermost nerve with their pungent iciness. No protection seemed of any avail. The whole surface of the body ached as if it were laid against a slab of ice. The throat closed instinctively, and contracted its unpleasant respiration—the body and limbs drew irresistibly together, to economize, like a hedge-hog, the exposed surface—the hands and feet felt transmuted to lead—and across the forehead, below the pressure of the cap, there was a binding and oppressive ache, as if a bar of frosty iron had been let into the scull. The mind, meantime, seemed freezing up—unwillingness to stir, and inability to think of anything but the cold, becoming every instant more decided.

From the bend of the valley our difficulties became more serious. The drifts often lay across the road like a wall, some feet above the heads of the horses, and we had dug through one or two, and had been once upset, and often near it, before we came to the steepest part of the ascent. The horses had by this time begun to feel the excitement of the rum, and bounded on through the snow with continual leaps, jerking the sleigh after them with a violence that threatened momently to break the traces. The steam from their bodies froze instantly, and covered them with a coat like hoar-frost; and, spite of their heat, and the unnatural and violent exertions they were making, it was evident by the pricking of their ears, and the sudden crouch of the body when a stronger blast swept over, that the cold struck through even their hot and intoxicated blood.

We toiled up, leap after leap, and it seemed miraculous to me that the now infuriated animals did not burst a blood-vessel or crack a sinew with every one of those terrible springs. The sleigh plunged on after them, stopping dead and short at every other moment, and reeling over the heavy drifts, like a boat in a surging sea. A finer crystallization had meantime taken place upon the surface of the moist snow, and the powdered particles flew almost insensibly on the blasts of wind, filling the eyes and hair, and cutting the skin with a sensation like the touch of needle-points. The driver, and his maddened but almost exhausted team, were blinded by the glittering and whirling eddies, the cold grew intenser every moment, the forward motion gradually less and less, and when, with the very last effort apparently, we reached a spot on the summit of the hill, which, from its exposed situation, had been kept bare by the wind, the patient and persevering whip brought his horses to a stand, and despaired, for the first time, of his prospects of getting on. I crept out of the sleigh, the iron-bound runners of which now grated on the bare ground, but found it impossible to stand upright.

" If you can use your hands," said the driver, turning his back to the wind, which stung the face like the lash of a whip, " I'll trouble you to untackle them horses."

I set about it, while he buried his hands and face in the snow to relieve them for a moment from the agony of cold. The poor animals staggered stiffly as I pushed them aside, and every vein stood out from their bodies like ropes under the skin.

" What are you going to do ?" I asked, as he joined me again, and taking off the harness of one of the leaders, flung it into the snow.

" Ride for life !" was his ominous answer.

" Good God ! and what is to become of my sick friend ?"

" The Almighty knows—if he can't ride to the tavern !"

I sprang instantly to poor Fred, who was lying in the bottom of the sleigh almost frozen to death, informed him of the driver's decision, and asked him if he thought he could ride one of the horses. He was beginning to grow drowsy, the first symptom of death by cold, and could with difficulty be roused. With the driver's assistance, however, I lifted him out of the sleigh, shook him soundly, and, making stirrups of the traces, set him upon one of the horses, and started him off before us. The poor beasts seemed to have a presentiment of the necessity of exertion, and, though stiff and sluggish, entered willingly upon the deep drift which blocked up the way, and toiled exhaustedly on. The cold in our exposed position was agonizing. Every small fibre in the skin of my own face felt splitting and cracked, and my eyelids seemed made of ice. Our limbs soon lost all sensation. I could only press with my knees to the horse's side, and the whole collected energy of my frame seemed expended in the exertion. Fred held on wonderfully. The driver had still the use of his arm, and rode behind, flogging the poor animals on, whose every step seemed to be the last summons of energy. The sun set, and it was rather a relief, for the glitter upon the snow was exceedingly painful to the sight, and there was no warmth in its beams. I could see my poor friend drooping gradually to the neck of his horse, but, until he should drop off, it was impossible to assist him, and his faithful animal still waded on. I felt my own strength fast ebbing away. If I had been alone, I should certainly have lain down, with the almost irresistible inclination to sleep; but the thought of my friend, and the shouting of the energetic driver, nerved me from time to time—and, with hands hanging helplessly down, and elbows fastened convulsively to my side, we plunged and struggled painfully forward. I but remember being taken afterward to a fire, and shrinking from it with a shriek—the suffering of reviving consciousness was so intolerable. We had reached the tavern literally frozen upon our horses.

II.

I was balancing my spoon on the edge of a cup at the breakfast-table, the morning after our arrival, when Fred stopped in the middle of an eulogium on my virtues as a nurse, and a lady entering at the same moment, he said simply in parenthesis, "My cousin Edith, Mr. Slingsby," and went on with his story. I rose and bowed, and, as Fred had the *parole*, I had time to collect my courage, and take a look at the enemy's camp—for, of that considerable household, I felt my star to be in conjunction or opposition with her's only, who was at that moment my *vis-à-vis* across a dish of stewed oysters.

In about five minutes of rapid mental portrait-painting, I had taken a likeness of Edith Linsey, which I see at this moment (I have carried it about the world ever since) as distinctly as the incipient lines of care in this thin-wearing hand. My feelings changed in that time from dread or admiration, or something between these, to pity; she was so unscrupulously and hopelessly plain—so wretchedly ill and suffering in her aspect—so spiritless and unhappy in every motion and look. "I'll win her heart," thought I, "by being kind to her. Poor thing! it will be something new to her, I dare say!" Oh, Philip Slingsby! what a doomed donkey thou wert for that silly soliloquy!

And yet, even as she sat there, leaning over her untasted breakfast, listless, ill, and melancholy—with her large mouth, her protruding eyes, her dead and sallow complexion, and not one redeeming feature—there was something in her face which produced a phantom of beauty in my mind—a glimpse, a shadowing of a countenance that Beatrice Cenci might have worn at her last innocent orison—a loveliness moulded and exalted by superhuman and overpowering mind—instinct through all its sweetness with energy and fire. So strong was this phantom portrait, that in all my thoughts of her, as an angel in heaven, (for I supposed her dying for many a month, and a future existence was her own most frequent theme), she always rose to my fancy with a face half Niobe, half Psyche, radiantly lovely. And this, too, with a face of her own, a *bonâ fide* physiognomy, that must have made a mirror an unpleasant article of furniture in her bed-room.

I have no suspicion, in my own mind, whether Time was drunk or sober during the succeeding week of those Christmas holydays. The second Saturday had come round, and I just remember that Fred was very much out of humor with me for having appeared to his friends to be everything he said I was *not*, and nothing he said I *was*. He had described me as the most uproarious, noisy, good-humored, and agreeable dog in the world. And I was not that, at all—particularly the last. The old judge told him he had not improved in his penetration at the university.

A week ! and what a life had been clasped within its brief calendar, for me ! Edith Linsey was two years older than I, and I was considered a boy. She was thought to be dying slowly, but irretrievably, of consumption ; and it was little matter whom she loved, or how. They would only have been pleased, if, by a new affection, she could beguile the preying melancholy of illness ; for, by that gentle name, they called, in their kindness, a caprice and a bitterness of character that, had she been less a sufferer, would not have been endured for a day. But she was not capricious, or bitter to *me !* Oh, no ! And from the very extreme of her impatience with others—from her rudeness, her violence, her sarcasm—she came to me with a heart softer than a child's, and wept upon my hands, and weighed every word that might give me offence, and watched to anticipate my lighest wish, and was humble, and generous, and passionately loving and dependent. Her heart sprang to me with a rebound. She gave herself up to me with an utter and desperate abandonment, that owed something to her peculiar character, but more to her own solemn conviction that she was dying—that her best hope of life was not worth a week's purchase.

We had begun with books, and upon them her past enthusiasm

had hitherto been released. She loved her favorite authors with a passion. They had relieved her heart; and there was nothing of poetry or philosophy, that was deep, or beautiful, in which she had not steeped her very soul. How well I remember her repeating to me from Shelley those glorious lines to the soaring swan:—

> " Thou hast a home,
> Beautiful bird! Thou voyagest to thy home—
> Where thy sweet mate will twine her downy neck
> With thine, and welcome thy return with eyes
> Bright with the lustre of their own fond joy!
> And what am I, that I should linger here,
> With voice far sweeter than thy dying notes,
> Spirit more vast than thine, frame more attuned
> To beauty, wasting these surpassing powers
> To the deaf air, to the blind earth, and heaven
> That echoes not my thoughts!"

There was a long room in the southern wing of the house, fitted up as a library. It was a heavily-curtained, dim old place, with deep-embayed windows, and so many nooks, and so much furniture, that there was that hushed air, that absence of echo within it, which is the great charm of a haunt for study or thought. It was Edith's kingdom. She might lock the door, if she pleased, or shut or open the windows; in short, when she was there, no one thought of disturbing her, and she was like a " spirit in its cell," invisible and inviolate. And here I drank, into my very life and soul, the outpourings of a bosom that had been locked till (as we both thought) the last hour of its life—a flow of mingled intellect and passion that overran my heart like lava, sweeping everything into its resistless fire, and (may God forgive her!) leaving it scorched and desolate when its mocking brightness had gone out.

I remember that "Elia"—Charles Lamb's Elia—was the favorite of favorites among her books; and, partly, that the late death of this most-to-be-loved author reminded me to look it up, and, partly, to have time to draw back my indifference over a subject that it something stirs me to recall, you shall read an imitation (or continuation, if you will) that I did for Edith's eye, of his "Essay on Books and Reading." I sat with her dry and fleshless hand in mine while I read it to her, and the fingers of Psyche were never fairer to Canova than they to me.

"It is a little singular," I began (looking into her eyes as long as I could remember what I had written), "that, among all the elegancies of sentiment for which the age is remarkable, no one should ever have thought of writing a book upon 'Reading.' The refinements of the true epicure in books are surely as various as those of the gastronome and the opium-eater; and I can conceive of no reason why a topic of such natural occurrence should have been so long neglected, unless it is that that the taste itself, being rather a growth of indolence, has never numbered among its votaries one of the busy craft of writers.

"The great proportion of men read, as they eat, for hunger. I do not consider them readers. The true secret of the thing is no more adapted to their comprehension, then the sublimations of Louis Eustace Ude for the taste of a day-laborer. The refined reading-taste, like the palate of *gourmanderie*, must have got beyond appetite—gross appetite. It shall be that of a man who, having fed through childhood and youth on simple knowledge, values now, only, as it were, the apotheosis of learning—the spiritual *nare*. There are, it is true, instances of a keen natural relish: a boy, as you will sometimes find one, of a premature thoughtfulness, will carry a favorite author in his bosom, and feast greedily on it in his stolen hours. Elia tells the exquisite story:

'I saw a boy, with eager eye,
Open a book upon a stall,
And read as he'd devour it all;
Which, when the stall-man did espy,
Soon to the boy I heard him call,
"You, sir, you never buy a book,
Therefore in one you shall not look!"
The boy passed slowly on, and with a sigh,
He wished he had never been taught to read—
Then of the old churl's books he should have had no need.'

"The pleasure as well as the profit of reading depends as much upon time and manner, as upon the book. The mind is an opal—changing its color with every shifting shade. Ease of position is especially necessary. A muscle strained, a nerve unpoised, an admitted sunbeam caught upon a mirror, are slight circumstances; but a feather may tickle the dreamer from paradise to earth. 'Many a froward axiom,' says a refined writer, 'many an inhumane thought, hath arisen from sitting uncomfortably, or from a want of symmetry in your chamber.' Who has not felt, at times, an unaccountable disrelish for a favorite author? Who has not, by a sudden noise in the street, been startled from a reading dream, and found, afterward, that the broken spell was not to be rewound? An ill-tied cravat may unlink the rich harmonies of Taylor. You would not think Barry Cornwall the delicious heart he is, reading him in a tottering chair.

"There is much in the mood with which you come to a book. If you have been vexed out of doors, the good humor of an author seems unnatural. I think I should scarce relish the 'gentle spiriting' of Ariel with a pulse of ninety in the minute. Or, if I had been touched by the unkindness of a friend, Jack Falstaff would not move me to laughter as easily as he is wont. There are tones of the mind, however, to which a book will vibrate with a harmony than which there is nothing more exquisite in nature. To go abroad at sunrise in June, and admit all the holy influences of the hour—stillness, and purity, and balm—to a mind subdued and dignified, as the mind will be by the sacred tranquillity of sleep, and then to come in with bathed and refreshed senses, and a temper of as clear joyfulness as the soaring lark's, and sit down to Milton or Spenser, or, almost loftier still, the divine 'Prometheus' of Shelley, has seemed to me a harmony of delight almost too heavenly to be human. The great secret of such pleasure is sympathy. You must climb to the eagle poet's eyry. You must have senses, like his, for the music that is only audible to the fine ear of thought, and the beauty that is visible only to the spirit-eye of a clear, and, for the time, unpolluted fancy. The stamp and pressure of the magician's own time and season must be upon you. You would not read Ossian, for example, in a bath, or sitting under a tree in a sultry noon; but after rushing into the eye of the wind with a fleet horse, with all his gallant pride and glorious strength and fire obedient to your rein, and so mingling, as it will, with his rider's consciousness, that you feel as if you were gifted in your own body with the swiftness and energy of an angel, after this, to sit down to Ossian, is to read him with a magnificence of delusion, to my mind scarce less than reality. I never envied Napoleon till I heard it was his habit, after a battle, to read Ossian.

"You cannot often read to music. But I love, when the voluntary is pealing in church—every breath in the congregation suppressed, and the deep-volumed notes pouring through the arches of the roof with the sublime and almost articulate praise of the organ—to read, from the pew Bible, the book of Ecclesiastes. The solemn stateliness of its periods is fitted to music like a hymn. It is to me a spring of the most thrilling devotion—though I shame to confess that the richness of its eastern imagery, and, above all, the inimitable beauty of its philosophy, stand out somewhat definitely in the reminiscences of the hour.

"A taste for reading comes comparatively late. 'Robinson Crusoe' will turn a boy's head at ten. The 'Arabian Nights' are taken to bed with us at twelve. At fourteen, a forward boy will read the 'Lady of the Lake,' 'Tom Jones,' and 'Peregrine Pickle;' and at seventeen (not before) he is ready for Shakspere, and, if he is of a thoughtful turn, Milton. Most men do not read these last with a true relish till after this period. The hidden beauties of standard authors break upon the mind by surprise. It is like discovering a secret spring in an old jewel. You take up the book in an idle moment, as you have done a thousand times before, perhaps wondering, as you turn over the leaves, what the world finds in it to admire, when, suddenly as you read, your fingers press close upon the covers, your frame thrills, and the passage you have chanced upon, chains you like a spell—it is so vividly true and beautiful. Milton's 'Comus' flashed upon me in this way. I never could read the 'Rape of the Lock' till a friend quoted some passages from it during a walk. I know no more exquisite sensation than this warming of the heart to an old author; and it seems to me that the most delicious portion of intellectual existence is the brief period in which, one by one, the great minds of old are admitted with all their time-mellowed worth to the affections. With what delight I read, for the first time, the 'kind-hearted' plays of Beaumont and Fletcher! How I doated on Burton! What treasures to me were the 'Fairy Queen' and the Lyrics of Milton!

"I used to think, when studying the Greek and Latin poets in my boyhood, that, to be made a school-author, was a fair offset against immortality. I would as lief, it seemed to me, have my verses handed down by the town-crier. But latterly, after an interval of a few years, I have taken up my classics (the identical school copies with the hard places all thumbed and pencilled) and have read them with no little pleasure. It is not to be believed with what a satisfaction the riper eye glides smoothly over the once difficult line, finding the golden cadence of poetry beneath what once seemed only a tangled chaos of inversion. The associations of hard study, instead of reviving the old distaste, added wonderfully to the interest of a re-perusal. I could see now what brightened the sunken eye of the pale and sickly master, as he took up the hesitating passage, and read on, forgetful of the delinquent, to the end. I could enjoy now, what was a dead letter to me then, the heightened fullness of Herodotus, and the strong-woven style of Thucydides, and the magnificent invention of Æschylus. I took an aversion to Homer from hearing a classmate in the next room scan it perpetually through his nose. There is no music for me in the 'Iliad.' But, spite of the recollections scored alike upon my palm and the margin, I own to an Augustan relish for the smooth melody of Virgil, and freely forgive the sometime troublesome ferule—enjoying by its aid the raciness of Horace and Juvenal, and the lofty philosophy of Lucretius. It will be a dear friend to whom I put down, in my will, that shelf of defaced classics.

"There are some books that bear reading pleasantly once a

year. 'Tristram Shandy' is an annual with me—I read him regularly about Christmas. Jeremy Taylor (not to mingle things holy and profane) is a good table-book, to be used when you would collect your thoughts and be serious a while. A man of taste need never want for Sunday reading while he can find the sermons of Taylor, and South, and Fuller—writers of good theological repute—though, between ourselves, I think one likelier to be delighted with the poetry and quaint fancifulness of their style, than edified by the piety it covers. I like to have a quarto edition of Sir Thomas Brown, on a near shelf, or Milton's prose works, or Bacon. There are healthful moods of the mind when lighter nütriment is distasteful.

"I am growing fastidious in poetry, and confine myself more and more to the old writers. Castaly of late runs shallow. Shelley's (peace to his passionate heart!) was a deep draught, and Wordsworth and Wilson sit near the well, and Keats and Barry Cornwall have been to the fountain's lip, feeding their imaginations (the latter his *heart* as well), but they have brought back little for the world. The 'small silver stream' will, I fear, soon cease to flow down to us, and, as it dries back to its source, we shall close nearer and nearer upon the 'pure English undefiled.' The dabblers in muddy waters (tributaries to Lethe) will have Parnassus to themselves.

"The finest pleasures of reading come unbidden. You cannot, with your choicest appliances for the body, always command the many-toned mind. In the twilight alcove of a library, with a time-mellowed chair yielding luxuriously to your pressure, a June wind laden with idleness and balm floating in at the window, and, in your hand, some Russia-bound, rambling old author, as Izaak Walton, good-humored and quaint, one would think the spirit could scarce fail to be conjured. Yet often, after spending a morning hour restlessly thus, I have risen with my mind unhinged, and strolled off with a book in my pocket to the woods; and, as I live, the mood has descended upon me under some chance tree, with a crooked root under my head; and I have lain there, reading and sleeping by turns, till the letters were blurred in the dimness of twilight. It is the evil of refinement that it breeds caprice. You will sometimes stand unfatigued for hours on the steps of a library; or, in a shop, the eye will be arrested, and the jostling of customers and the looks of the jealous shopman will not divert you till you have read out the chapter.

"I do not often indulge in the supernatural, for I am an unwilling believer in ghosts, and the topic excites me. But, for its connexion with the subject upon which I am writing, I must conclude these rambling observations with a late mysterious visitation of my own.

"I had, during the last year, given up the early summer tea-parties, common in the town in which the university stands; and having, of course, three or four more hours than usual on my hands, I took to an afternoon habit of imaginative reading. Shakspeare came first, naturally; and I feasted for the hundredth time upon what I think his (and the world's) most delicate creation—the 'Tempest.' The twilight of the first day overtook me at the third act, where the banquet is brought in with solemn music, by the fairy troop of Prospero, and set before the shipwrecked king and his followers. I closed the book, and, leaning back in my chair, abandoned myself to the crowd of images which throng always upon the traces of Shakspeare. The *fancy* music was still in my mind, when an apparently *real* strain of the most solemn melody came to my ear, dying, it seemed to me, as it reached it, the tones were so expiringly faint and low. I was not startled, but lay quietly, holding my breath, and more fearing when the strain would be broken, than curious whence it came. The twilight deepened, till it was dark, and it still played on, changing the tune at intervals, but always of the same melancholy sweetness; till, by-and-by, I lost all curiosity, and, giving in to the charm, the scenes I had been reading began to form again in my mind; and Ariel, with his delicate ministers, and Prospero, and Miranda, and Caliban, came moving before me to the measure, as bright and vivid as the reality. I was disturbed in the midst of it by Alfonse, who came in at the usual hour with my tea; and, on starting to my feet, I listened in vain for the continuance of the music. I sat thinking of it a while, but dismissed it at last, and went out to enjoy, in a solitary walk, the loveliness of the summer night. The next day I resumed my book, with a smile at my previous credulity, and had read through the last scenes of the 'Tempest,' when the light failed me. I again closed the book, and presently again, as if the sympathy were instantaneous, the strain broke in, playing the same low and solemn melodies, and falling with the same dying cadence upon the ear. I listened to it, as before, with breathless attention; abandoned myself once more to its irresistible spell; and, half-waking, half-sleeping, fell again into a vivid dream, brilliant as fairy-land, and creating itself to the measures of the still audible music. I could not now shake off my belief in its reality; but I was so rapt with its strange sweetness, and the beauty of my dream, that I cared not whether it came from earth or air. My indifference, singularly enough, continued for several days; and, regularly at twilight, I threw aside my book, and listened with dreamy wakefulness for the music. It never failed me, and its results were as constant as its coming. Whatever I had read—sometimes a canto of

Spenser, sometimes an act of a play, or a chapter of romance—the scene rose before me with the stately reality of a pageant. At last I began to think of it more seriously; and it was a relief to me one evening when Alfonse came in earlier than usual with a message. I told him to stand perfectly still; and, after a minute's pause, during which I heard distinctly an entire passage of a funeral hymn, I asked him if he heard any music? He said he did not. My blood chilled at his positive reply, and I bade him listen once more. Still he heard nothing. I could endure it no longer. It was to me as distinct and audible as my own voice; and I rushed from my room as he left me, shuddering to be left alone.

"The next day I thought of nothing but death. Warnings by knells in the air, by apparitions, by mysterious voices, were things I had believed in, speculatively, for years, and now their truth came upon me like conviction. I felt a dull, leaden presentiment about my heart, growing heavier and heavier with every passing hour. Evening came at last, and with it, like a summons from the grave, a 'dead march' swelled clearly on the air. I felt faint and sick at heart. This could not be fancy; and why was it, as I thought I had proved, audible to my ear alone? I threw open the window, and the first rush of the cool north wind refreshed me; but, as if to mock my attempts at relief, the dirge-like sounds rose, at the instant, with treble distinctness. I seized my hat and rushed into the street, but, to my dismay, every step seemed to bring me nearer to the knell. Still I hurried on, the dismal sounds growing distractingly louder, till, on turning a corner that leads to the lovely burying-ground of New Haven, I came suddenly upon—a bell foundry! In the rear had lately been hung, for trial, the chiming bells just completed for the new

Trinity church, and the master of the establishment informed me that one of his journeymen was a fine player, and every day, after his work, he was in the habit of amusing himself with the 'Dead March in Saul,' the 'Marsellois Hymn,' and other melancholy and easy tunes, muffling the hammers that he might not disturb the neighbors."

I have had my reward for these speculations, dear reader—a smile that is lying at this instant, *perdu*, in the innermost recess of memory—and I care not much (without offence) whether you like it or no. *She* thanked me—*she* thought it well done—*she* laid her head on my bosom while I read it in the old library of the Flemings, and every word has been "paid for in fairy gold."

I have taken up a thread that lengthens as I unravel it, and I cannot well see how I shall come to the end, without trespassing on your patience. We will cut it here, if you like, and resume it after a pause; but, before I close, I must give you a little instance of how love makes the dullest earth poetical. Edith had given me a *portefeuille* crammed with all kinds of embossed and curious note-paper, all quite too pretty for use, and what I would show you are my verses on the occasion. For a hand unpractised, then, in aught save the "Gradus ad Parnassum," I must own I have fished them out of that same old fortfolio (faded now from its glory, and worn with travel—but O how cherished!) with a pleasant feeling of paternity:

"Thanks for thy gift! But heardst thou ever
  A story of a wandering fay,
Who, tired of playing sylph for ever,
  Came romping to the earth one day
And, flirting like a little Love
  With everything that flew and flirted,

Made captive of a sober dove,
  Whose pinions (so the tale asserted),
Though neither very fresh nor fair,
  Were well enough for common wear?

"The dove, though plain, was gentle bred,
  And cooed agreeably, though low;
But still the fairy shook her head,
  And, patting with her foot, said '*No!*'
'Twas true that he was rather fat:
  But that was living in an abbey;—
And solemn—but it was not that—
  'What then?' '*Why, sir, your wings are shabby.*'

"The dove was dumb: he drooped, and sidled
  In shame along the abbey-wall;
And then the haughty fay unbridled,
  And blew her snail-shell trumpet-call;
And summoning her waiting-sprite,
  Who bore her wardrobe on his back,
She took the wings she wore at night,
  (Silvery stars on plumes of black,)
And, smiling, begged that he would take
And wear them for his lady's sake.

"He took them; but he could not fly!
  A fay-wing was too fine for him;
And when she pouted, by-and-by,
  And left him for some other whim,
He laid them softly in his nest,
  And did his flying with his own,
And they were soft upon his breast,
  When many a night he slept alone;
And many a thought those wings would stir,
And many a dream of love and her."

PART II.

LOVE AND SPECULATION.

Edith Linsey was religious. There are many *intensifiers* (a new word, that I can't get on without: I submit it for admission into the language);—there are many intensifiers, I say, to the passion of love: such as pride, jealousy, poetry (money, sometimes, *Dio mio!*) and idleness:* but, if the experience of one who first studied the Art of Love in an "evangelical" country is worth a penny, there is nothing within the bend of the rainbow that deepens the tender passion like religion. I speak it not irreverently. The human being that loves us throws the value of its existence into the crucible, and it can do no more. Love's best alchymy can only turn into affection what is in the heart. The vain, the proud, the poetical, the selfish, the weak, can and do fling their vanity, pride, poetry, selfishness, and weakness, into a first passion; but these are earthly elements, and there is an antagonism in their natures that is forever striving to resolve them back to their original earth. But religion is of the soul as well as the heart—the mind as well as the affections—and, when it mingles in love, it is the infusion of an immortal essence into an unworthy and else perishable mixture.

Edith's religion was equally without cant, and without hesitation or disguise. She had arrived at it by elevation of mind, aided by the habit of never counting on her tenure of life beyond the setting of the next sun, and, with her, it was rather an intellectual exaltation than a humility of heart. She thought of God because the subject was illimitable, and her powerful imagination found in it

* "La paresse dans les femmes est le présage de l'amour."—La Bruyere.

the scope for which she pined. She talked of goodness, and purity, and disinterestedness, because she found them easy virtues with a frame worn down with disease, and she was removed by the sheltered position of an invalid from the collision which tries so shrewdly, in common life, the ring of our metal. She prayed, because the fullness of her heart was loosed by her eloquence when on her knees, and she found that an indistinct and mystic unburthening of her bosom, even to the Deity, was a hush and a relief. The heart does not always require rhyme and reason of language and tears.

There are many persons of religious feeling, who, from a fear of ridicule or misconception, conduct themselves as if to express a devout sentiment were a want of taste or good-breeding. Edith was not of these. Religion was to her a powerful enthusiasm, applied without exception to every pursuit and affection. She used it as a painter ventures on a daring color, or a musician on a new string in his instrument. She felt that she aggrandized botany, or history, or friendship, or love, or what you will, by making it a stepping-stone to heaven, and she made as little mystery of it as she did of breathing and sleep, and talked of subjects which the serious usually enter upon with a suppressed breath, as she would comment upon a poem or define a new philosophy. It was surprising what an impressiveness this threw over her in everything; how elevated she seemed above the best of those about her; and with what a worshipping and half-reverent admiration she inspired all whom she did not utterly neglect or despise. For myself, my soul was drank up in hers as the lark is taken into the sky, and I forgot there was a world beneath me in my intoxication. I thought her an angel unrecognized on earth. I believed her as pure from worldliness, and as spotless from sin, as a cherub with his breast upon his lute; and I knelt by her when she prayed, and held her upon my bosom in her fits of faintness and exhaustion, and sat at her feet, with my face in her hands, listening to her wild speculations (often till the morning brightened behind the curtains) with an utter and irresistible abandonment of my existence to hers, which seems to me, *now*, like a recollection of another life—it were, with this conscious body and mind, a self-relinquishment so impossible!

Our life was a singular one. Living in the midst of a numerous household, with kind and cultivated people about us, we were as separated from them as if the ring of Gyges encircled us from their sight. Fred wished me joy of my *giraffe*, as he offensively called his cousin; and his sisters, who were quite too pretty to have been left out of my story so long, were more indulgent, I thought, to the indigenous beaux of Skaneateles than those aboriginal specimens had a right to expect; but I had no eyes, ears, sense, or civility, for anything but Edith. The library became a forbidden spot to all feet but ours; we met at noon after our late vigils and breakfasted together; a light sleigh was set apart for our *tête-à-tête* drives over the frozen lake, and the world seemed to me to revolve on its axle with a special reference to Philip Slingsby's happiness. I wonder whether an angel out of heaven would have made me believe that I should ever write the story of those passionate hours with a smile and a sneer! I tell thee, Edith! (for thou wilt read every line that I have written, and feel it, as far as thou *canst* feel anything), that I have read "Faust" since, and thought thee Mephistopheles! I have looked on thee since, with the cheek rosy dark, thy lip filled with the blood of health, and curled with thy contempt of the world and thy yet wild ambition to be its master-spirit and idol, and struck my breast with instinctive self-questioning if thou hadst given back my soul that was thine own! I fear thee, Edith. Thou hast grown beautiful that wert so hideous—the wonder-wrought miracle of health and intellect, filling thy veins, and breathing almost a newer shape over form and feature; but it is not thy beauty; no, nor thy enthronement in the admiration of thy woman's world. These are little to me; for I saw thy loveliness from the first, and I worshipped thee more in the duration of a thought than a hecatomb of these worldlings in their lifetime. I fear thy mysterious and unaccountable power over the human soul! I can scorn thee here, in another atmosphere, with sufficient distance between us, and anatomize the character that I alone have read truly and too well, for the instruction of the world (its amusement, too, proud woman—thou wilt writhe at that)—but I confess to a natural and irresistible obedience to the mastery of thy spirit over mine. I would not willingly again touch the radius of thy sphere. I would come out of Paradise to walk alone with the devil as soon.

How little even the most instructed women know the secret of this power! They make the mistake of cultivating only *their own* minds. They think that, by *self*-elevation, they will climb up to the intellects of men, and win them by seeming their equals. Shallow philosophers! You never remember, that, to subdue a human being to your will, it is more necessary to know *his* mind than your own—that, in conquering a heart, vanity is the first outpost—that, while you are employing your wits in thinking how most effectually to dazzle *him*, you should be sounding his character for its undeveloped powers to assist him to dazzle *you*—that love is a reflected light, and, to be pleased with others, we must be first pleased with ourselves!

Edith (it has occurred to me in my speculations since) seemed to me always an echo of myself. She expressed my thought as it sprang into my brain. I thought that in her I had met my double and counterpart, with the reservation that I was a little the stronger spirit, and that in *my* mind lay the material of the eloquence that flowed from her lips—as the almond, that you endeavor to split equally, leaves the kernel in the deeper cavity of its shell. Whatever the topic, she seemed using *my* thoughts, anticipating *my* reflections, and, with an unobtrusive but thrilling flattery, referring me to myself for the truth of what I must know was but a suggestion of my own! O! Lucrezia Borgia! if Machiavelli had but practised that subtle cunning upon thee, thou wouldst have had little space in thy delirious heart for the passion that, in the history of crime, has made thee the marvel and the monster.

The charm of Edith to most people was that she was no *sublimation.* Her mind seemed of any or no stature. She was as natural, and earnest, and as satisfied to converse, on the meanest subject as on the highest. She overpowered nobody. She (apparently) eclipsed nobody. Her passionate and powerful eloquence was only lavished on the passionate and powerful. She *never misapplied herself:* and what a secret of influence and superiority is contained in that single phrase! We so hate him who out-measures us, as we stand side by side before the world!

I have in my portfolio several numbers of a manuscript "Gazette," with which the Flemings amused themselves during the deep snows of the winter in which I visited them. It was contributed to, by everybody in the house, and read aloud at the breakfast table on the day of its weekly appearance; and, quite *apropos* to these remarks upon the universality of Edith's mind, there is in one of them an essay of hers on what she calls *minute philosophies.* It is curious, as showing how, with all her loftiness of speculation, she descended sometimes to the examination of the smallest machinery of enjoyment.

" The principal sources of everyday happiness," (I am copying out a part of the essay, dear reader), " are too obvious to need a place in a chapter of breakfast-table philosophy. Occupation and a clear conscience, the very truant in the fields will tell you, are craving necessities. But when these are secured, there are lighter matters, which, to the sensitive and educated at least, are to happiness what foliage is to the tree. They are refinements which add to the beauty of life without diminishing its strength; and, as they spring only from a better use of our common gifts, they are neither costly nor rare. I have learned secrets under the roof of a poor man, which would add to the luxury of the rich. The blessings of a cheerful fancy and a quick eye come from nature, and the trailing of a vine may develop them as well as the curtaining of a king's chamber.

" Riding and driving are such stimulating pleasures, that, to talk of any management in their indulgence, seems superfluous. Yet we are, in motion or at rest, equally liable to the caprices of feeling, and, perhaps, the gayer the mood the deeper the shade cast on it by untoward circumstances. The time of riding should never be regular. It then becomes a habit, and habits, though sometimes comfortable, never amount to positive pleasure. I would ride when nature prompted—when the shower was past, or the air balmy, or the sky beautiful—whenever and wherever the significant finger of Desire pointed. Oh! to leap into the saddle when the west wind blows freshly, and gallop off into its very eye, with an undrawn rein, careless how far or whither; or, to spring up from a book when the sun breaks through, after a storm, and drive away under the white clouds, through light and shadow, while the trees are wet and the earth damp and spicy ; or, in the clear sunny afternoons of autumn, with a pleasant companion on the seat beside you, and the glorious splendor of the decaying foliage flushing in the sunshine, to loiter up the valley, dreaming over the thousand airy castles that are stirred by such shifting beauty—these are pleasures indeed, and such as he, who rides regularly after his dinner, knows as little of as the dray-horse of the exultation of the courser.

"There is a great deal in the choice of a companion. If he is an indifferent acquaintance, or an indiscriminate talker, or has a coarse eye for beauty, or is insensible to the delicacies of sensation or thought—if he is sensual, or stupid, or practical constitutionally—he will never do. He must be a man who can detect a rare color in a leaf, or appreciate a peculiar passage in scenery, or admire a grand outline in a cloud ; he must have accurate and fine senses, and a heart, noble at least by nature, and subject still to her direct influences ; he must be a lover of the beautiful in whatever shape it come ; and, above all, he must have read and thought like a scholar, if not like a poet. He will then ride by your side without crossing your humor ; if talkative, he will talk well, and if silent, you are content, for you know that the same grandeur or beauty, which has wrought the silence in your own thoughts, has given a color to his.

"There is much in the manner of driving. I like a capricious rein—now fast through a hollow, and now loiteringly on the edge of a road or by the bank of a river. There is a singular delight in quickening your speed in the animation of a climax, and in coming down gently to a walk with a digression of feeling, or a sudden sadness.

"An important item in household matters is the management of light. A small room well-lighted is much more imposing than a large one lighted ill. Cross lights are painful to the eye, and they destroy, besides, the cool and picturesque shadows of the furniture and figures. I would have a room always partially darkened: there is a repose in the twilight dimness of a drawing-room which affects one with the proper gentleness of the place: the out-of-door humor of men is too rude, and the secluded light subdues them fitly as they enter. I like curtains—heavy, and of the richest material: there is a magnificence in large crimson folds which nothing else equals, and the color gives everything a beautiful tint as the light streams through them. Plants tastefully arranged are pretty; flowers are always beautiful. I would have my own room like a painter's—one curtain partly drawn; a double shadow has a nervous look. The effect of a proper disposal of light upon the feelings is by most people surprisingly neglected. I have no doubt that as an habitual thing it materially affects the character; the disposition for study and thought is certainly dependent on it in no slight degree. What is more contemplative than the twilight of a deep alcove in a library? What more awakens thought than the dim interior of an old church, with its massive and shadowy pillars?

"There may be the most exquisite luxury in furniture. A crowded room has a look of comfort, and suspended lamps throw a mellow depth into the features. Descending light is always the most becoming; it deepens the eye, and distributes the shadows in the face judiciously. Chairs should be of different and curious fashions, made to humor every possible weariness. A spice-lamp should burn in the corner, and the pictures should be colored of a pléasant tone, and the subjects should be subdued and dreamy. It should be a place you would live in for a century without an uncomfortable thought. I hate a neat room. A dozen of the finest old authors should lie about, and a new novel, and the last new prints. I rather like the French fashion of a *bonbonnière*, though that perhaps is an extravagance.

"There is a management of one's own familiar intercourse, which is more neglected, and at the same time more important to happiness, than every other; it is particularly a pity that it is not oftener understood by newly-married people; as far as my own experience goes, I have rarely failed to detect, far too early, signs of ill-disguised and disappointed weariness. It was not the reaction of excitement—not the return to the quiet ways of home—but a new manner—a forgetful indifference, believing itself concealed, and yet betraying itself continually by unconscious and irrepressible symptoms. I believe it resulted oftenest from the same causes: partly that they saw each other too much; and partly that when the *form* of etiquette was removed, they forgot to retain its invaluable *essence*—an assiduous and minute disinterestedness. It seems nonsense to lovers, but absence is the secret of respect, and therefore of affection. Love is divine, but its flame is too delicate for a perpetual household lamp; it should be burned only for incense, and even then trimmed skilfully. It is wonderful how a slight neglect, or a glimpse of weakness, or a chance defect of knowledge, dims its new glory. Lovers, married or single, should have separate pursuits—they should meet to respect each other for new and distinct acquisitions. It is the weakness of human affections that they are founded on pride, and waste with over-much familiarity. And oh, the delight to meet

2*

after hours of absence—to sit down by the evening lamp, and, with a mind unexhausted by the intercourse of the day, to yield to the fascinating freedom of conversation, and clothe the rising thoughts of affection in fresh and unhackneyed language! How richly the treasures of the mind are colored—not doled out, counter by counter, as the visible machinery of thought coins them, but heaped upon the mutual altar in lavish and unhesitating profusion! And how a bold fancy assumes beauty and power—not traced up through all its petty springs till its dignity is lost by association, but flashing full-grown and suddenly on the sense! The gifts of no one mind are equal to the constant draught of a lifetime; and even if they were, there is no one taste which could always relish them. It is an humiliating thought that immortal mind must be husbanded like material treasure!

"There is a remark of Godwin, which, in rather too strong language, contains a valuable truth: 'A judicious and limited voluptuousness,' he says, 'is necessary to the cultivation of the mind, to the polishing of the manners, to the refinement of the sentiment, and to the development of the understanding; and a woman deficient in this respect may be of use in the government of our families, but cannot add to the enjoyment, nor fix the partiality of a man of taste!' Since the days when 'St. Leon' was written, the word by which the author expressed his meaning is grown perhaps into disrepute, but the remark is still one of keen and observant discrimination. It refers (at least so I take it) to that susceptibility to delicate attentions, that fine sense of the nameless and exquisite tendernesses of manner and thought, which constitute in the minds of its possessors the deepest undercurrent of life—the felt and treasured, but unseen and inexpressible richness of affection. It is rarely found in the characters of men, but it outweighs, when it is, all grosser qualities—for its possession implies a generous nature, purity, fine affections, and a heart open to all the sunshine and meaning of the universe. It belongs more to the nature of woman ; but, indispensable as it is to her character, it is oftener than anything else, wanting. And without it, what is she ? What is love, to a being of such dull sense that she hears only its common and audible language, and sees nothing but what it brings to her feet, to be eaten, and worn, and looked upon ? What is woman, if the impassioned language of the eye, or the deepened fullness of the tone, or the tenderness of a slight attention, are things unnoticed and of no value ?—one who answers you when you speak, smiles when you tell her she is grave, assents barely to the expression of your enthusiasm, but has no dream beyond—no suspicion that she has not felt and reciprocated your feelings as fully as you could expect or desire ? It is a matter too little looked to. Sensitive and ardent men too often marry with a blindfold admiration of mere goodness or loveliness. The *abandon* of matrimony soon dissipates the gay dream, and they find themselves suddenly unsphered, linked indissolubly with affections strangely different from their own, and lavishing their only treasure on those who can neither appreciate nor return it. The after-life of such men is a stifling solitude of feeling. Their avenues of enjoyment are their maniform sympathies, and, when these are shut up or neglected, the heart is dark, and they have nothing to do thenceforward but to forget.

" There are many, who, possessed of the capacity for the more elevated affections, waste and lose it by a careless and often unconscious neglect. It is not a plant to grow untended. The breath of indifference, or a rude touch, may destroy forever its delicate texture. To drop the figure, there is a daily attention to the slight courtesies of life, and an artifice in detecting the passing shadows of feeling, which alone can preserve, through life, the first freshness of passion. The easy surprises of pleasure, and earnest cheerfulness of assent to slight wishes, the habitual respect to opinions, the polite abstinence from personal topics in the company of others, the assiduous and unwavering attention to her comfort, at home and abroad, and, above all, the absolute preservation, in private, of those proprieties of conversation and manner which are sacred before the world—are some of the thousand secrets of that rare happiness which age and habit alike fail to impair or diminish."

Of course, a "periodical," though issued for one fireside only, could not be popular with merely such abstract and intangible matter as the foregoing; and I must redeem its character, in this its only history, by copying one of its more practical articles, furnished from my own pen and my own college experience, viz: —the story of

ALBINA McLUSH.

I HAVE a passion for fat women. If there is anything I hate in life, it is what dainty people call a *spirituelle*. Motion—rapid motion—a smart, quick, squirrel-like step, a pert, voluble tone—in short, a lively girl—is my exquisite horror! I would as lief have a *diable petit* dancing his infernal hornpipe on my cerebellum as to be in the room with one. I have tried before now to school myself into liking these parched peas of humanity. I have followed them with my eyes, and attended to their rattle till I was as crazy as a fly in a drum. I have danced with them, and romped with them in the country, and perilled the salvation of my "white tights" by sitting near them at supper. I swear off from this moment. I do. I won't—no—bang me if ever I show another small, lively, *spry* woman a civility.

Albina McLush is divine. She is like the description of the Persian beauty by Hafiz: "her heart is full of passion and her eyes are full of sleep." She is the sister of Lurly McLush, my old college chum, who, as early as his sophomore year, was chosen president of the *Dolce-far-niente* Society—no member of which was ever known to be surprised at anything—(the college law of rising before breakfast excepted.) Lurly introduced me to his sister one day, as he was lying upon a heap of turnips, leaning on his elbow with his head in his hand, in a green lane in the suburbs. He had driven over a stump, and been tossed out of his gig, and I came up just as he was wondering how in the d—l's name he got there! Albina sat quietly in the gig, and when I was presented, requested me, with a delicious drawl, to say nothing about the adventure—"it would be so troublesome to relate it to everybody!" I loved her from that moment. Miss McLush was tall, and her shape, of its kind, was perfect. It was not a *fleshy* one, exactly, but she was large and full. Her skin was clear, fine-grained, and transparent: her temples and forehead perfectly rounded and polished, and her lips and chin swelling into a ripe and tempting pout, like the cleft of a bursted apricot. And then her eyes—large, liquid and sleepy—they languished beneath their long, black fringes as if they had no business with daylight—like two magnificent dreams, surprised in their jet embryos by some bird-nesting cherub. Oh! it was lovely to look into them!

She sat, usually, upon a *fauteuil*, with her large, full arm embedded in the cushion, sometimes for hours without stirring. I have seen the wind lift the masses of dark hair from her shoulders when it seemed like the coming to life of a marble Hebe—she had been motionless so long. She was a model for a goddess of sleep, as she sat with her eyes half closed, lifting up their superb lids slowly as you spoke to her, and dropping them again with the deliberate motion of a cloud, when she had murmured out her syllable of assent. Her figure, in a sitting posture, presented a gentle declivity from the curve of her neck to the instep of the small round foot lying on its side upon the ottoman. I remember a fellow's bringing her a plate of fruit one evening. He was one of your lively men—a horrid monster, all right angles and activity. Having never been accustomed to hold her own plate, she had not well extricated her whole fingers from her handkerchief, before he set it down in her lap. As it began slowly to slide towards her feet, her hand relapsed into the muslin folds, and she fixed her eye upon it with a kind of indolent surprise, drooping her lids gradually, till as the fruit scattered over the ottoman, they closed entirely, and a liquid jet line was alone visible through the heavy lashes. There was an imperial indifference in it worthy of Juno.

Miss McLush rarely walks. When she does, it is with the deliberate majesty of a Dido. Her small, plump feet melt to the ground like snow-flakes, and her figure sways to the indolent motion of her limbs with a glorious grace and yieldingness quite indescribable. She was idling slowly up the Mall one evening just at twilight, with a servant at a short distance behind her, who, to while away the time between her steps, was employing himself in throwing stones at the cows feeding upon the Common. A gentleman, with a natural admiration for her splendid person, addressed her. He might have done a more eccentric thing. Without troubling herself to look at him, she turned to her servant and requested him, with a yawn of desperate *ennui*, to knock that fellow down! John obeyed his orders; and, as his mistress resumed her lounge, picked up a new handful of pebbles, and tossing one at the nearest cow, loitered lazily after.

Such supreme indolence was irresistible. I gave in—I—who never before could summon energy to sigh—I—to whom a declaration was but a synonym for perspiration—I—who had only thought of love as a nervous complaint, and of women but to pray for a good deliverance—I—yes—I—knocked under. Albina McLush! Thou wert too exquisitely lazy. Human sensibilities cannot hold out forever!

I found her one morning sipping her coffee at twelve, with her eyes wide open. She was just from the bath, and her complexion had a soft, dewy transparency, like the cheek of Venus rising from the sea. It was the hour Lurly had told me, when she would be at the trouble of thinking. She put away with her dimpled forefinger, as I entered, a cluster of rich curls that had fallen over her face, and nodded to me like a water-lily swaying to the wind when its cup is full of rain.

"Lady Albina," said I, in my softest tone, "how are you to-day?"

"Bettina," said she, addressing her maid in a voice as clouded and rich as a south wind on an Æolian, "how am I to-day?"

The conversation fell into short sentences. The dialogue became a monologue. I entered upon my declaration. With the assistance of Bettina, who supplied her mistress with cologne, I kept her attention alive through the incipient circumstances. Symptoms were soon told. I came to the avowal. Her hand lay reposing on the arm of the sofa, half buried in a muslin *foulard*,

I took it up and pressed the cool, soft fingers to my lips—unforbidden. I rose and looked into her eyes for confirmation. Delicious creature! she was asleep!

I never have had courage to renew the subject. Miss McLush seems to have forgotten it altogether. Upon reflection, too, I'm convinced she would not survive the excitement of the ceremony unless, indeed, she should sleep between the responses and the prayer. I am still devoted, however, and if there should come a war or an earthquake, or if the millenium should commence, as it is expected, in 1833, or if anything happens that can keep her waking so long, I shall deliver a declaration, abbreviated for me by a scholar-friend of mine, which, he warrants, may be articulated in fifteen minutes—without fatigue.

II.

Vacation was over, but Fred and myself were still lingering at Fleming Farm. The roads were impassable, with a premature THAW. Perhaps there is nothing so peculiar in American meteorology as the phenomenon which I alone, probably, of all the imprisoned inhabitants of Skaneateles, attributed to a kind and "special Providence." Summer had come back, like Napoleon from Elba, and astonished usurping Winter in the plenitude of apparent possession and security. No cloud foreboded the change, as no alarm preceded the apparition of "the child of destiny." We awoke on a February morning, with the snow lying chin-deep on the earth, and it was June! The air was soft and warm—the sky was clear, and of the milky cerulean of chrysoprase—the south wind (the same, save his unperfumed wings, who had crept off like a satiated lover in October,) stole back suddenly from the tropics, and found his flowery mistress asleep and insensible to his kisses beneath her snowy mantle. The sunset warmed back from its wintry purple to the golden tints of heat, the stars burned with a less vitreous sparkle, the meteors slid once more lambently down the sky, and the house-dove sat on the eaves, washing her breast in the snow-water, and thinking (like a neglected wife at a capricious return of her truant's tenderness) that the sunshine would last for ever!

The air was now full of music. The water trickled away under the snow, and, as you looked around and saw no change or motion in the white carpet of the earth, it seemed as if a myriad of small bells were ringing under ground—fairies, perhaps, startled in mid-revel with the false alarm of summer, and hurrying about with their silver anklets, to wake up the slumbering flowers. The mountain-torrents were loosed, and rushed down upon the valleys like the Children of the Mist; and the hoarse war-cry, swelling and falling upon the wind, maintained its perpetual undertone, like an accompaniment of bassoons; and occasionally, in a sudden lull of the breeze, you would hear the click of the undermined snow-drifts dropping upon the earth, as if the chorister of spring were beating time to the reviving anthem of nature.

The snow sunk perhaps a foot in a day, but it was only perceptible to the eye where you could measure its wet mark against a tree from which it had fallen away, or by the rock, from which the dissolving bank shrunk and separated, as if rocks and snow were as heartless as ourselves, and threw off *their* friends, too, in their extremity! The low-lying lake, meantime, surrounded by melting mountains, received the abandoned waters upon its frozen bosom, and, spreading them into a placid and shallow lagoon, separate by a crystal plane from its own lower depths, gave them the repose denied in the more elevated sphere in which lay their birthright. And thus—(oh, how full is nature of these gentle moralities!)—and thus sometimes do the lowly, whose bosom, like the frozen lake, is at first cold and unsympathetic to the rich and noble, still receive them in adversity, and—when neighborhood and dependence have convinced them that they are made of the same common element—as the lake melts its dividing and icy plane, and mingles the strange waters with its own, do *they* dissolve the unnatural barrier of prejudice, and take the humbled wanderer to their bosom!

The face of the snow lost its dazzling whiteness as the thaw went on—as disease steals away the beauty of those we love—but it was only in the distance, where the sun threw a shadow into the irregular pits of the dissolving surface. Near to the eye (as the dying one pressed to the bosom), it was still of its original beauty, unchanged and spotless. And now you are tired of my loitering speculations, gentle reader, and we will return (please Heaven, only on paper!) to Edith Linsey.

The roads were at last reduced to what is expressively called, in New England, *slosh*, (in New York, *posh*, but equally descriptive), and Fred received a hint from the judge that the mail had arrived in the usual time, and his *beaux jours* were at an end.

A slighter thing than my departure would have been sufficient to stagger the tottering spirits of Edith. We were sitting at table when the letters came in, and the dates were announced that proved the opening of the roads; and I scarce dared to turn my eyes upon the pale face that I could just see had dropped upon her bosom. The next instant there was a general confusion, and she was carried lifeless to her chamber.

A note, scarcely legible, was put into my hand in the course of the evening, requesting me to sit up for her in the library. She would come to me, she said, if she had strength.

It was a night of extraordinary beauty. The full moon was high in the heavens at midnight, and there had been a slight shower soon after sunset, which, with the clearing-up wind, had frozen thinly into a most fragile rime, and glazed everything, open to the sky, with transparent crystal. The distant forest looked serried with metallic trees, dazzlingly and unspeakably gorgeous; and, as the night-wind stirred through them and shook their crystal points in the moonlight, the aggregated stars of heaven springing from their Maker's hand to the spheres of their destiny, or the march of the host of the archangel Michael with their irradiate spear-points glittering in the air, or the diamond beds of central earth thrust up to the sun in some throe of the universe, would, each or all, have been well bodied forth by such similitude.

It was an hour after midnight when Edith was supported in by her maid, and, choosing her own position, sunk into the broad window-seat, and lay with her head on my bosom, and her face turned outward to the glittering night. Her eyes had become, I thought, unnaturally bright, and she spoke with an exhausted faintness that gradually strengthened to a tone of the most thrilling and melodious sweetness. I shall never get that music out of my brain!

"Philip!" she said.

"I listen, dear Edith!"

"I am dying."

And she looked it, and I believed her; and my heart sunk to its deepest abyss of wretchedness with the conviction.

She went on to talk of death. It was the subject that pressed most upon her mind, and she could scarce fail to be eloquent on any subject. She was very eloquent on this. I was so impressed with the manner in which she seemed almost to rhapsodize between the periods of her faintness, as she lay in my arms that night, that every word she uttered is still fresh in my memory. She seemed to forget my presence, and to commune with her own thoughts aloud.

"I recollect," she said, "when I was strong and well, (years ago, dear Philip!) I left my books, on a morning in May, and looking up to find the course of the wind, started off alone for a walk into its very eye. A moist steady breeze came from the southwest, driving before it fragments of the dispersed clouds. The air was elastic and clear; a freshness that entered freely at every pore was coming up, mingled with the profuse perfume of grass and flowers; the colors of the new, tender foliage were particularly soothing to an eye pained with close attention—and the just perceptible murmur of the drops shaken from the trees, and the peculiarly soft rustle of the wet leaves, made as much music as an ear accustomed to the silence of solitude could well relish. Altogether, it was one of those rarely-tempered days when every sense is satisfied, and the mind is content to lie still, with its common thoughts, and simply enjoy.

"I had proceeded perhaps a mile—my forehead held up to the wind, my hair blowing back, and the blood glowing in my cheeks with the most vivid flush of exercise and health—when I saw, coming toward me, a man apparently in middle life, but wasted by illness to the extremest emaciation. His lip was colorless, his skin dry and white, and his sunken eyes had that expression of inquiring earnestness which comes always with impatient sickness. He raised his head, and looked steadily at me as I came on. My lips were open, and my whole air must have been that of a person in the most exulting enjoyment of health. I was just against him, gliding past with an elastic step, when, with his eye still fixed on me, he half turned, and, in a voice of inexpressible meaning, exclaimed, 'Merciful Heaven! *how well she is!*' I passed on, with his voice still ringing in my ear. It haunted me like a tone in the air. It was repeated in the echo of my tread—in the panting of my heart. I felt it in the beating of the strong pulse in my temples. As if it were strange that I should be so well! I had never before realized that it could be otherwise. It seemed impossible to me that my strong limbs should fail me, or the pure blood I felt bounding so bravely through my veins could be reached and tainted by disease. How should it come? If I ate, would it not nourish me? If I slept, would it not refresh me? If I came out in the cool, free air, would not my lungs heave, and my muscles spring, and my face feel its grateful freshness? I held out my arm, for the first time in my life, with a doubt of its strength. I closed my hand unconsciously, with a fear it would not obey. I drew a deep breath, to feel if it was difficult to breathe; and even my bounding step, that was elastic then as a fawn's, seemed to my excited imagination already to have become decrepit and feeble.

"I walked on, and thought of death. I had never before done so definitely; it was like a terrible shape that had always pursued me dimly, but which I had never before turned and looked steadily on. Strange! that we can live so constantly with that threatening hand hung over us, and not think of it always! Strange! that we can use a limb, or enter with interest into any pursuit of time, when we know that our continued life is almost a daily miracle!

"How difficult it is to realize death! How difficult it is to believe that the hand with whose every vein you are familiar, will ever lose its motion and its warmth? That the quick eye, which is so restless now, will settle and grow dull? That the refined lip, which now shrinks so sensitively from defilement, will not feel the earth lying upon it, and the tooth of the feeding worm? That the free breath will be choked, and the forehead be pressed heavily on by the decaying coffin, and the light and air of heaven be shut quite out; and this very body, warm, and breathing, and active as it is now, will not feel uneasiness or pain? I could not help looking at my frame, as these thoughts crowded on me; and I confess I almost doubted my own convictions—there was so much strength and quickness in it—my hand opened so freely, and my nostrils expanded with such a satisfied thirst to the moist air. Ah! it is hard to believe at first that we must die! harder still to believe and realize the repulsive circumstances that follow that terrible change! It is a bitter thought, at the lightest. There is little comfort in knowing that the *soul* will not be there—that the sense and the mind, that feel and measure suffering, will be gone. The separation is too great a mystery to satisfy fear. It is the body that we *know*. It is this material frame in which the affections have grown up. The spirit is a mere thought—a presence that we are told of, but do not see. Philosophize as we will, the idea of existence is connected indissolubly with the visible body, and its pleasant and familiar senses. We talk of, and believe, the soul's ascent to its Maker; but it is not ourselves—it is not our own conscious breathing identity that we send up in imagination through the invisible air. It is some phantom, that is to issue forth mysteriously, and leave us gazing on it in wonder. We do not understand, we cannot realize it.

"At the time I speak of, my health had been always unbroken. Since then, I have known disease in many forms, and have had, of course, more time and occasion for the contemplation of death. I have never, till late, known resignation. With my utmost energy, I was merely able, in other days, to look upon it with quiet despair; as a terrible, unavoidable evil. I remember, once, after severe suffering for weeks, I overheard the physician telling my mother that I must die, and from that moment the thought never left me. A thin line of light came in between the shutters of the south window; and, with this one thought fastened on my mind, like the vulture of Prometheus, I lay and watched it, day after day, as it passed with its imperceptible progress over the folds of my curtains. The last faint gleam of sunset never faded from its damask edge, without an inexpressible sinking of my heart, and a belief that I should see its pleasant light no more. I turned from the window when even imagination could find the daylight no longer there, and felt my pulse and lifted my head to try my remaining strength. And then every object, yes, even the meanest, grew unutterably dear to me; my pillow, and the cup with which my lips were moistened, and the cooling amber which I had held in my hand, and pressed to my burning lips when the fever was on me—everything that was connected with life, and that would remain among the living when I was gone.

"It is strange, but, with all this clinging to the world, my affection for the living decreased sensibly. I grew selfish in my weakness. I could not bear that they should go from my chamber into the fresh air, and have no fear of sickness and no pain. It seemed unfeeling that they did not stay and breathe the close atmosphere of my room—at least till I was dead. How could they walk round so carelessly, and look on a fellow-creature dying helplessly and unwillingly, and never shed a tear! And then the passing courtesies exchanged with the family at the door, and the quickened step on the sidewalk, and the wandering looks about my room, even while I was answering with my difficult breath their cold inquiries! There was an inhuman carelessness in all this that stung me to the soul.

"I craved sympathy as I did life; and yet I doubted it all. There was not a word spoken, by the friends who were admitted to see me, that I did not ponder over when they were gone, and always with an impatient dissatisfaction. The tone, and the manner, and the expression of face, all seemed forced; and often, in my earlier sickness, when I had pondered for hours on the expressed sympathy of some one I had loved, the sense of utter helplessness, which crowded on me with my conviction of their insincerity, quite overcame me. I have lain, night after night, and looked at my indifferent watchers: and oh, how I hated them for their careless ease, and their snatched moments of repose! I could scarce keep from dashing aside the cup they came to give me so sluggishly.

"It is singular that, with all our experience of sickness, we do not attend more to these slight circumstances. It can scarce be conceived how an ill-managed light, or a suppressed whispering, or a careless change of attitude, in the presence of one whose senses are so sharpened, and whose mind is so sensitive as a sick person's, irritate and annoy. And, perhaps, more than these to bear, is the affectedly subdued tone of condolence. I remember nothing which I endured so impatiently.

"Annoyances like these, however, scarcely diverted for a moment the one great thought of death. It became at last familiar, but, if possible, more dreadfully horrible from that very fact. It was giving it a new character. I realized it more. The minute circumstances became nearer and more real—I tried the position in which I should lie in my coffin—I lay, with my arms to my side, and my feet together, and, with the cold sweat standing in large drops on my lip, composed my features into a forced expression of tranquillity.

"I awoke on the second morning after the hope of my recovery had been abandoned. There was a narrow sunbeam lying in a clear crimson line across the curtain, and I lay and watched the specks of lint sailing through it, like silver-winged insects, and the thin dust, quivering and disappearing on its definite limit, in a dream of wonder. I had thought not to see another sun, and my mind was still fresh with the expectation of an immediate change; I could not believe that I was alive. Ths dizzy throb in my temples was done; my limbs felt cool and refreshed; my mind had that feeling of transparency which is common after healthful and sweet sleep; and an indefinite sensation of pleasure trembled in every nerve. I thought that this might be death, and that, with this exquisite feeling of repose, I was to linger thus consciously with the body till the last day; and I dwelt on it pleasantly, with my delicious freedom from pain. I felt no regret for life—none for a friend even: I was willing—quite willing—to lie thus for ages. Presently the physician entered; he came and laid his fingers on my pulse, and his face brightened. 'You will get well,' he said, and I heard it almost without emotion. Gradually, however, the love of life returned; and, as I realized it fully, and all the thousand cords which bound me to it vibrated once more, the tears came thickly to my eyes, and a crowd of delightful thoughts pressed cheerfully and glowingly upon me. No language can do justice to the pleasure of convalescence from extreme sickness. The first step upon the living grass—the first breath of free air—the first unsuppressed salutation of a friend—my fainting heart, dear Philip, rallies and quickens even now with the recollection."

I have thrown into a continuous strain what was murmured to me between pauses of faintness, and with difficulty of breath that seemed overpowered only by the mastery of the eloquent spirit apparently trembling on its departure. I believed Edith Linsey would die that night; I believed myself listening to words spoken almost from heaven; and if I have wearied you, dear reader, with what must be more interesting to me than to you, it is because every syllable was burnt like enamel into my soul, in my boundless reverence and love.

It was two o'clock, and she still lay breathing painfully in my arms. I had thrown up the window, and the soft south wind, stirring gently among the tinkling icicles of the trees, came in, warm and genial, and she leaned over to inhale it, as if it came from the source of life. The stars burned gloriously in the heavens; and, in a respite of her pain, she laid back her head, and gazed up at them with an inarticulate motion of her lips, and eyes so unnaturally kindled, that I thought reason had abandoned her.

"How beautiful are the stars to-night, Edith!" I said, with half a fear that she would answer me in madness.

"Yes," she said, putting my hand (that pressed her closer, involuntarily, to my bosom) first to her lips—"Yes; and, beautiful as they are, they are all accurately numbered and governed, and, just as they burn now, have they burned since the creation, never 'faint in their watches,' and never absent from their place. How glorious they are! How thrilling it is to see them stand with such a constant silence in the sky, unsteadied and unsupported, obeying the great law of their Maker! What pure and silvery light it is! How steadily it pours from those small fountains, giving every spot of earth its due portion! The hovel and the palace are shone upon equally, and the shepherd gets as broad a beam as the king, and these few rays that are now streaming into my feverish eyes were meant and lavished only for me! I have often thought —has it never occurred to you, dear Philip?—how ungrateful we are, to call ourselves poor, when there is so much that no poverty can take away! Clusters of silver rays from every star in these heavens are *mine*. Every breeze that breaks on my forehead was sent for *my* refreshment. Every tinkle and ray from those stirring and glistening icicles, and the invigorating freshness of this unseasonable and delicious wind, and moonlight, and sunshine, and the glory of the planets, are all gifts that poverty could not take away; it is not often that I forget these treasures; for I have loved nature, and the skies of night and day, in all their changes, from my childhood, and they have been unspeakably dear to me; for, in them, I see the evidence of an Almighty Maker, and, in the excessive beauty of the stars and the unfading and equal splendor of their steadfast fires, I see glimpses of an immortal life, and find an answer to the eternal questioning within me!

"Three! The village clock reaches us to-night. Nay, the wind can not harm me now. Turn me more to the window, for I would look nearer upon the stars: it is the last time—I am sure of it—the very last! Yet to-morrow night those stars will all be there—not one missing from the sky, nor shining one ray the less because I am dead! It is strange that this thought should be so bitter—strange that the companionship should be so close between our earthly affections and those spiritual worlds—and stranger yet, that, satisfied as we must be that we shall know them nearer and better when released from our flesh, we still cling so fondly to our earthly and imperfect vision. I feel, Philip, that I shall traverse hereafter every star in those bright heavens. If the course of that career of knowledge, which I believe in my soul it will be the reward of the blessed to run, be determined in any degree by the strong desires that yearn so sickeningly within us, I see the thousand gates of my future heaven shining at this instant above me. There they are! the clustering Pleiades, with 'their sweet influences;' and the morning star, melting into the east with its transcendent lambency and whiteness; and the broad galaxy, with its myriads of bright spheres, dissolving into each other's light, and belting the heavens like a girdle. I shall see them all! I shall know them and their inhabitants as the angels of God know them; the mystery of their order, and the secret of their wonderful harmony, and the duration of their appointed courses—all will be made clear!"

I have trespassed again, most indulgent reader, on the limits of these Procrustean papers. I must defer the "change" that "came o'er the spirit of my dream" till another mood and time. Meanwhile, you may consider Edith, if you like, the true heart she thought herself, (and I thought her,) during her nine deaths in the library; and you will have leisure to imagine the three years over which we shall skip with this *finale*, during which I made a journey to the north, and danced out a winter in John Bull's territories at Quebec—a circumstance I allude to, no less to record the hospitalities of the garrison of that time, (this was in '27—were you there?) than to pluck forth, from Time's hindermost wallet, a modest copy of verses I addressed thence to Edith. She sent them back to me considerably mended; but I give you the original draught, scorning her finger in my poesies:—

TO EDITH, FROM THE NORTH.

As, gazing on the Pleiades,
  We count each fair and starry one,
Yet wander from the light of these
  To muse upon the 'Pleiad gone;'—
As, bending o'er fresh-gathered flowers,
  The rose's most enchanting hue
Reminds us but of other hours,
  Whose roses were all lovely, too;—
So, dearest, when I rove among
  The bright ones of this northern sky,
And mark the smile, and list the song,
  And watch the dancers gliding by—
The fairer still they seem to be,
  The more it stirs a thought of thee.

The sad, sweet bells of twilight chime,
  Of many hearts may touch but one,
And so this seeming careless rhyme
  Will whisper to thy heart alone,
I give it to the winds. The bird,
  Let loose, to his far nest will flee,
And love, though breathed but on a word,
  Will find thee, over land and sea.
Though clouds across the sky have driven,
  We trust the star at last will shine;
And, like the very light of heaven,
  I trust thy love—*trust thou in mine.*

PART III.

A DIGRESSION.

"*Boy.* Will you not sleep, sir?
Knight. Fling the window up!
I'll look upon the stars. Where twinkle now
The Pleiades?
Boy. Here, master!
Knight. Throw me now
My cloak upon my shoulders, and good night!
I have no mind to sleep! * * *
* * * * She bade me look
Upon this band of stars when other eyes
Beamed on me brightly, and remember her
By the lost Pleiad.
Boy. Are you well, sir?
Knight. Boy!
Love you the stars?
Boy When they first spring at eve
Better than near to morning.
Knight. Fickle child!
Are they more fair in twilight?
Boy. Master, no!
Brighter, as night wears on—*but I forget*
Their beauty, looking on them long!"

"Sir Fabian," *an unpublished Poem.*

It was a September night at the university. On the morrow I was to appear upon the stage as the winner of the first honors of my year. I was the envy—the admiration—in some degree the wonder, of the collegiate town in which the university stands; for I had commenced my career as the idlest and most riotous of freshmen. What it was that had suddenly made me enamored of my chambers and my books—that had saddened my manners and softened my voice—that had given me a disgust to champagne and my old allies, in favor of cold water and the Platonists—that, in short, had metamorphosed, as Bob Wilding would have said, a gentleman-like rake and *vaurien* into so dull a thing as an exemplary academician—was past the divining of most of my acquaintances. Oh, once-loved Edith! hast thou any inkling, in thy downward metempsychosis, of the philosophy of this marvel?

If you were to set a poet to make a town, with *carte blanche* as to trees, gardens, and green blinds, he would probably turn out very much such a place as New Haven. (Supposing your education in geography to have been neglected, dear reader, this is the second capital of Connecticut, a half-rural, half-metropolitan town, lying between a precipice that makes the fag-end of the Green Mountains and a handsome bay in Long-Island Sound.) The first thought of the inventor of New Haven was to lay out the streets in parallelograms, and the second was to plant them, from suburb to water-side, with the magnificent elms of the country. The result is, that, at the end of fifty years, the town is buried in leaves. If it were not for the spires of the churches, a bird, flying over on his autumn voyage to the Floridas, would never mention having seen it in his travels. It is a glorious tree, the elm—and those of the place I speak of are famous, even in our land of trees, for their surprising size and beauty. With the curve of their stems in the sky, the long weepers of their outer and lower branches drop into the street, fanning your face as you pass under with their geranium-like leaves; and close overhead, interwoven like the trellis of a vine, they break up the light of the sky into golden flecks, and make you, of the common highway, a bower of the most approved secludedness and beauty. The houses are something between an Italian palace and an English cottage—built of wood, but, in the dim light of those overshadowing trees, as fair to the eye as marble, with their triennial coats of paint; and each stands in the midst of its own encircling grass-plot, half buried in vines and flowers, and facing outwards from a cluster of gardens divided by slender palings, and filling up, with fruit-trees and summer-houses, the square on whose limit it stands. Then, like the vari-colored parallelograms upon a chessboard, green openings are left throughout the town, fringed with triple and interweaving elm-rows, the long and weeping branches sweeping downward to the grass, and, with their enclosing shadows, keeping moist and cool the road they overhang ; and fair forms (it is the garden of American beauty—New Haven) flit about in the green light in primitive security and freedom, and you would think the place, if you alit upon it in a summer's evening—what it seems to me now in memory, and what I have made it in this Rosa-Matilda description—a scene from Boccacio, or a vision from long-lost Arcady.

New Haven may have eight thousand inhabitants. Its steamers run to New York in six hours (or did, in my time—I have ceased to be astonished on *that* subject, and should not wonder if they did it soon in *one*—a trifle of seventy miles up the Sound), and the ladies go up in the morning for a yard of bobbin, and return at night, and the gentlemen the same for a stroll in Broadway ; and it is to this circumstance that, while it preserves its rural exterior, it is a very metropolitan place in the character of its society. The Amaryllis of the pretty cottage you admire wears the fashion twenty days from Paris, and her shepherd has a coat from Nugee, the divine peculiarity of which is not yet suspected east of Bond street ; and, in the newspaper, hanging out of the window, there is news, red-hot with the velocity of its arrival, from Russia and the Rocky Mountains, from the sources of the Mississippi and the brain of Monsieur Herbault. Distance is an imaginary quantity, and Time, that used to give everything the go-by, has come to a standstill, in his astonishment. There will be a proposition in Congress, ere long, to do without him altogether—every new thing "saves time" so marvellously.

Bright as seems to me this seat of my Alma Mater, however, and gayly as I describe it, it is to me, if I may so express it, a picture of memory glazed and put away; if I see it ever again, it will be but to walk through its embowered streets by a midnight moon. It is vain and heart-breaking to go back, after absence, to any spot of earth of which the interest was the human love whose home and cradle it had been. But there is a period in our lives when the heart fuses and compounds with the things about it, and the close enamel with which it overruns and binds, in the affections, and which hardens in the lapse of years, till the immortal germ within is not more durable and unwasting, warms never again, nor softens; and there is nothing on earth so mournful and unavailing as to return to the scenes which are unchanged, and look to return to ourselves and others as we were when we thus knew them.

Yet we think (I judge you by my own soul, gentle reader!) that it is others—not we—who are changed! We meet the friend that we loved in our youth, and it is ever *he* who is cold and altered! We take the hand that we bent over with our passionate kisses in boyhood, and our raining tears when we last parted, and it is ever hers that returns not the pressure, and *her* eyes, and not ours—oh, *not ours!*—that look back the moistened and once familiar regard with a dry lid and a gaze of stone! Oh, God! it is ever *he*—the friend you have worshipped—for whom you would have died—who gives you the tips of his fingers, and greets you with a phrase of fashion, when you would rush into his bosom, and break your heart with weeping out the imprisoned tenderness of years! I could carve out the heart from my bosom, and fling it with a malison into the sea, when I think how utterly and worse than useless it is, in this world of mocking names! Yet "love" and "friendship" are words that read well. You could scarce spare them in poetry.

II.

It was, as I have said, a moonlight night of unparalleled splendor. The morrow was the college anniversary—the day of the departure of the senior class—and the town, which is, as it were, a part of the university, was in the usual tumult of the gayest and saddest evening of the year. The night was warm, and the houses, of which the drawing-rooms are all on a level with the gardens in the rear, and through which a long hall stretches like a ball-room, were thrown open, doors and windows, and the thousand students of the university, and the crowds of their friends, and the hosts of strangers drawn to the place at this season by the annual festivities, and the families, every one with a troop of daughters, (as the leaves on our trees, compared with those of old countries—three to one—so are our sons and daughters,) were all sitting without lamps in the moon-lit rooms, or strolling together, lovers and friends, in the fragrant gardens, or looking out upon the street, returning the greetings of the passers-by, or, with heads uncovered, pacing backward and forward beneath the elms before the door—the whole scene one that the angels in heaven might make a holy-day to see.

There were a hundred of my fellow-seniors—young men of from eighteen to twenty-four—every one of whom was passing the last evening, of the four most impressible and attaching years of his life, with the family in which he had been most intimate, in a town where refinement and education had done their utmost upon the society, and which was renowned throughout America for the extraordinary beauty of its women. They had come from every State in the Union, and the Georgian and the Vermontese, the Kentuckian and the Virginian, were to start alike on the morrow-night with a lengthening chain for home, each bearing away the hearts he had attached to him, (one or more !) and leaving his own, till, like the magnetized needle, it should drop away with the weakened attraction ; and there was probably but *one* that night in the departing troop who was not whispering, in some throbbing ear, the passionate, but vain and mocking avowal of fidelity in love ! And yet I had had *my* attachments, too ; and there was scarce a house in that leafy and murmuring paradise of friendship and trees, that would not have hailed me with acclamation had I entered the door ; and I make this record of kindness and hospitality, (unforgotten after busy years of vicissitude and travel,) with the hope that there may yet live some memory as constant as mine, and that some eye will read it with a warmth in its lid, and some lip —some *one* at least—murmur, "*I* remember him !" There are trees in that town whose drooping leaves I could press to my lips with an affection as passionate as if they were human, though the lips and voices that have endeared them to me are as changed as the foliage upon the branch, and would recognise my love as coldly.

There was one, I say, who walked the thronged pavement alone that night, or but with such company as Uhland's ;* yet the heart

* Almost the sweetest thing I remember is the German poet's thought when crossing the ferry to his wife and child :—

"Take, O boatman ! thrice thy fee,
Take, I give it willingly ;
For, *invisibly to thee,*
Spirits twain have crossed with **me.**"

of that solitary senior was far from lonely. The palm of years of ambition was in his grasp—the reward of daily self-denial and midnight watching—the prize of a straining mind and a yearning desire; and there was not one of the many who spoke of him that night in those crowded rooms, either to rejoice in his success or to wonder at its attainment, who had the shadow of an idea what spirit sat uppermost in his bosom. Oh! how common is this ignorance of human motives! How distant, and slight, and unsuspected, are the springs often of the most desperate achievement! How little the world knows for what the poet writes, the scholar toils, the politician sells his soul, and the soldier perils his life! And how insignificant and unequal to the result would seem these invisible wires, could they be traced back from the hearts whose innermost resource and faculty they have waked and exhausted! It is a startling thing to question even your own soul for its motive. Ay, even in trifles. Ten to one you are surprised at the answer. I have asked myself, while writing this sentence, whose eye it is most meant to please; and, as I live, the face that is conjured up at my bidding is one of whom I have not had a definite thought for years. I would lay my life she thinks at this instant I have forgotten her very name. Yet I know she will read this page with an interest no other could awaken, striving to trace in it the changes that have come over me since we parted. I know, (and I knew *then*, though we never exchanged a word save in friendship,) that she devoted her innermost soul, when we strayed together by that wild river in the West, (dost thou remember it, dear friend? for now I speak to thee!) to the study of a mind and character of which she thought better than the world or their possessor; and I know—oh, how *well* I know!—that, with husband and children around her, whom she loves and to whom she is devoted, the memory of me is laid away in her heart, like a fond, but incomplete dream, of what once seemed possible—the feeling with which the mother looks on her witless boy, and loves him more for what he *might* have been, than his brothers for what they *are!*

I scarce know what thread I dropped to take up this *improvista* digression (for, like "Opportunity and the Hours," I "never look back;"*) but let us return to the shadow of the thousand elms of New Haven.

The Gascon thought his own thunder and lightning superior to that of other countries, but I must run the hazard of your incredulity as well, in preferring an American moon. In Greece and Asia Minor, perhaps (*ragione*—she was first worshipped there), Cytheris shines as brightly; but the Ephesian of Connecticut sees the flaws upon the pearly buckler of the goddess, as does the habitant of no other clime. His eye lies close to the moon. There is no film, and no visible beam, in the clarified atmosphere. Her light is less an emanation than a presence—the difference between the water in a thunder-shower and the depths of the sea. The moon struggles to you in England—she is all about you, like an element of the air, in America.

The night was breathless, and the fragmented light lay on the pavement in motionless stars, as clear and definite in their edges as if the "patines of bright gold" had dropped through the trees, and lay glittering beneath my feet. There was a kind of darkness visible in the streets, overshadowed as they were by the massy and leaf-burthened elms, and, as I looked through the houses, standing in obscurity myself, the gardens seemed full of

* Walter Savage Landor.

daylight—the unobstructed moon poured with such a flood of radiance on the flowery alleys within, and their gay troops of promenaders. And, as I distinguished one and another familiar friend, with a form as familiar clinging to his side, and, with drooping head and with faltering step, listening or replying, (I well knew), to the avowals of love and truth, I murmured in thought, to my own far away, but never-forgotten Edith, a vow as deep—ay, deeper than theirs, as my spirit and hers had been sounded by the profounder plummet of sorrow and separation. How the very moonlight—how the stars of heaven—how the balm in the air, and the languor of summer night in my indolent frame, seemed, in those hours of loneliness, ministers at the passionate altar-fires of my love! Forsworn and treacherous Edith! do I live to write this for thine eye?

I linger upon these trifles of the past—these hours for which I would have borrowed wings when they were here—and, as *then* they seemed but the flowering promise of happiness, they seem *now* like the fruit, enjoyed and departed. *Past* and *future* bliss there would seem to be in the world—knows any one of such a commodity in the *present?* I have not seen it in my travels.

III.

I was strolling on, through one of the most fashionable and romantic streets (when did these two words ever before find themselves in a sentence together?) when a drawing-room with which I was very familiar, lit, unlike most others on that bright night, by a suspended lamp, and crowded with company, attracted my attention for a moment. Between the house and the street there was a slight shrubbery, shut in by a white paling, just sufficient to give an air of seclusion to the low windows without concealing them from the passer-by, and, with the freedom of an old visiter, I unconsciously stopped, and looked unobserved into the rooms. It was the residence of a magnificent girl, who was generally known as the Connecticut beauty—a singular instance in America of what is called in England a *fine* woman. (With us that word applies wholly to moral qualities.) She was as large as Juno, and a great deal handsomer, if the painters have done that much-snubbed goddess justice. She was a "book of beauty" printed with virgin type; and that, by the way, suggests to me what I have all my life been trying to express—that some women seem wrought of *new* material altogether, apropos to others who seem mortal *réchauffés*—as if every limb and feature had been used, and got out of shape, in some other person's service. The lady I speak of looked *new*—and her name was Isidora.

She was standing just under the lamp, with a single rose in her hair, listening to a handsome coxcomb of a classmate of mine with evident pleasure. She was a great fool, (did I mention that before?) but weak, and vacant, and innocent of an idea as she was, Faustina was not more naturally majestic, nor Psyche (*soit elle en grande*) more divinely and meaningly graceful. Loveliness and fascination came to her as dew and sunshine to the flowers, and she obeyed her instinct, as they theirs, and was helplessly, and without design, the loveliest thing in nature. I do not see, for my part, why all women should not be so. They are as useful as flowers; they perpetuate our species.

I was looking at her with irresistible admiration, when a figure stepped out from the shadow of a tree, and my chum, monster, and ally, Job Smith (of whom I have before spoken of in certain historical papers), laid his hand on my shoulder.

"Do you know, my dear Job," I said, in a solemn tone of admonition, "that blind John was imprisoned for looking into people's windows?"

But Job was not in the vein for pleasantry. The light fell on his face as I spoke to him, and a more haggard, almost blasted expression of countenance, I never saw even in a madhouse. I well knew he had loved the splendid girl who stood unconsciously in our sight, since his first year in college; but, that it would ever so master him, or that he could link his monstrous deformity, even in thought, with that radiant vision of beauty, was a thing that I thought as probable as that hirsute Pan would tempt from her sphere the moon that kissed Endymion.

"I have been standing here, looking at Isidora, ever since you left me," said he. (We had parted three hours before, at twilight.)

"And why not go in, in the name of common sense?"

"Oh! Heavens, Phil!—with this demon in my heart? Can you see my face in this light?"

It was too true—he would have frightened the household gods from their pedestals.

"But what would you do, my dear Job? Why come here to madden yourself with a sight you must have known you would see"

"Phil?"

"What, my dear boy?"

"Will you do me a kindness?"

"Certainly."

"Isidora would do anything you wished her to do."

"Um! with a reservation, my dear chum!"

"But she would give you the rose that is in her hair."

"Without a doubt."

"And for me—if you told her it was for me. Would she not?"

"Perhaps. But will that content you?"

"It will soften my despair. I will never look on her face more; but I should like my last sight of her to be associated with kindness?"

Poor Job! how true it is that "affection is a fire which kindleth as well in the bramble as in the oak, and catcheth hold where it first lighteth, not where it may best burn." I do believe in my heart that the soul in thee was designed for a presentable body—thy instincts were so invariably mistaken. When didst thou ever think a thought, or stir hand or foot, that it did not seem prompted, monster though thou wert, by conscious good-looking-ness! What a lying similitude it was that was written on every blank page in thy Lexicon: "Larks that mount in the air, build their nests below in the earth; and women who cast their eyes upon kings, may place their hearts upon vassals." Apelles must have been better looking than Alexander, when Campaspe said that!

As a general thing you may ask a friend freely to break any three of the commandments, in your service, but you should hesitate to require of friendship a violation of etiquette. I was in a round jacket and boots, and it was a dress evening throughout New Haven. I looked at my dust-covered feet, when Job asked me to enter a soirée upon his errand, and passed my thumb and finger around the edge of my white jacket; but I loved Job, as the Arabian loves his camel, and for the same reason, with a difference—the imperishable well-spring he carried in his heart through the desert of the world, and which I well knew he would give up his life to offer at need, as patiently as the animal whose construction (inner and outer) he so remarkably resembled. When I hesitated, and looked down at my boots, therefore, it was less to seek for an excuse to evade the sacrificing office required of me, than to beat about in my unprepared mind for a preface to my request. If she had been a women of sense, I should have had no difficulty; but it requires caution and skill to go out of the beaten track with a fool.

"Would not the rose do as well," said I, in desperate embarrassment, "if she does not know that it is for *you*, my dear Job?" It would have been very easy to have asked for it for myself.

Job laid his hand upon his side, as if I could not comprehend the pang my proposition gave him.

"Away, prop, and down, scaffold," thought I, as I gave my jacket a hitch, and entered the door.

"Mr. Slingsby," announced the servant.

"Mr. Slingsby?" inquired the mistress of the house, seeing only a white jacket in the *clair obscur* of the hall.

"Mr. Slingsby!!!" cried out twenty voices in amazement, as I stepped over the threshold into the light.

It has happened, since the days of Thebet Ben Khorat, that scholars have gone mad, and my sanity was evidently the uppermost concern in the minds of all present. (I should observe, that in those days, I relished rather of dandyism.) As I read the suspicion in their minds, however, a thought struck me. I went straight up to Miss Higgins, and, *sotto voce*, asked her to take a turn with me in the garden.

"Isidora," I said, "I have long known your superiority of mind," (when you want anything of a woman, praise her for that in which she is most deficient, says La Bruyère), "and I have great occasion to rely on it, in the request I am about to make of you."

She opened her eyes, and sailed along the gravel-walk with heightened majesty. I had not had occasion to pay her a compliment before, since my freshman year.

"What is it, Mr. Slingsby?"

"You know Smith—my chum."

"Certainly."

"I have just come from him."

"Well!"

"He is gone mad!"

"Mad! Mr. Slingsby?"

"Stark and furious!"

"Gracious goodness!"

"And all for you!"

"For me!!"

"For you!" I thought her great blue eyes would have become what they call in America "sot," at this astounding communication.

"Now, Miss Higgins," I continued, "pray listen; my poor friend has such extraordinary muscular strength, that seven men cannot hold him."

"Gracious!"

"And he has broken away, and is here at your door."

"Good Gracious!"

"Don't be afraid! He is as gentle as a kitten when I am present. And now, hear my request. He leaves town to-morrow, as you well know, not to return. I shall take him home to Vermont with keepers. He is bent upon one thing, and in that you must humor him."

Miss Higgins began to be alarmed.

"He has looked through the window, and seen you with a rose in your hair, and, despairing even in his madness, of your love, he says, that if you would give him that rose, with a kind word, and a farewell, he should be happy. You will do it, will you not?"

"Dear me! I should be *so* afraid to speak to him!"

"But will you? and I'll tell you what to say."

Miss Higgins gave a reluctant consent, and I passed ten minutes in drilling her upon two sentences, which, with her fine manner and sweet voice, really sounded like the most interesting thing in the world. I left her in the summer-house at the end of the garden, and returned to Job.

"You have come without it!" said the despairing lover, falling back against the tree.

"Miss Higgins's compliments, and begs you will go round by the gate, and meet her in the summer-house. She prefers to manage her own affairs."

"Good God! are you mocking me?"

"I will accompany you, my dear boy."

There was a mixture of pathos and ludicrousness in that scene, which starts a tear and a laugh together, whenever I recall it to my mind. The finest heart in the world, the most generous, the most diffident of itself, yet the most self-sacrificing and delicate, was at the altar of its devotion, offering its all in passionate abandonment for a flower and a kind word; and she, a goose in the guise of an angel, repeated a phrase of kindness, of which she could not comprehend the meaning or the worth, but which was to be garnered up by that half-broken heart, as a treasure that repaid him for years of unrequited affection! She recited it really very well. I stood at the latticed door, and interrupted them the instant there was a pause in the dialogue ; and, getting Job away as fast as possible, I left Miss Higgins with a promise of secrecy, and resumed my midnight stroll.

Apropos—among Job's letters is a copy of verses, which, spite of some little inconsistencies, I think were written on this very occasion :—

I.

Nay—smile not on me—I have borne
  Indifference and repulse from thee ;
With my heart sickening, I have worn
  A brow, as thine own cold one, free ;
My lip has been as gay as thine,
  Ever thine own light mirth repeating,
Though, in this burning brain of mine,
  A throb the while, like death, was beating:
My spirit did not shrink or swerve—
  Thy look—I thank thee !—froze the nerve !

II.

But now again, as when I met
  And loved thee in my happier days,
  A smile upon thy bright lip plays,
And kindness in thine eye is set—
    And this I cannot bear !
It melts the manhood from my pride,
It brings me closer to thy side—
    Bewilders—chains me there—
There—where my dearest hope was crushed and died !

III.

Oh, if thou couldst but know the deep
  Of love that hope has nursed for years—
How in the heart's still chambers sleep
  Its hoarded thoughts, its trembling fears—
Treasure that love has brooded o'er

Till life, than this, has nothing more—
  And couldst thou—but 'tis vain !—
I will not, cannot tell thee, how
That hoard consumes its coffer now—
    I may not write of pain
That sickens in the heart, and maddens in the brain !

IV.

Then smile not on me ! pass me by
  Coldly, and with a careless mien—
'Twill pierce my heart, and fill mine eye,
  But I shall be as I have been—
    Quiet in my despair !
'Tis better than the throbbing fever,
That else were in my brain for ever,
    And easier to bear !
I'll not upbraid the coldest look—
The bitterest word thou hast, in my sad pride I'll brook !

If Job had rejoiced in a more euphonious name, I should have bought a criticism in some review, and started him fairly as a poet. But " Job Smith !"—" Poems by Job Smith !"—It would never do ! If he wrote like a seraph, and printed the book at his own expense, illustrated and illuminated, and half-a-crown to each person that would take one away, the critics would damn him all the same ! Really, one's father and mother have a great deal to answer for !*

But Job is a poet who should have lived in the middle ages, no less for the convenience of the *nom de guerre*, fashionable in those days, than because his poetry, being chiefly the mixed product of feeling and courtesy, is particularly susceptible to ridicule. The philosophical and iron-wire poetry of our day stands an attack like a fortification, and comes down upon the besieger with reason and

* Charles Lamb writes to a friend, on the subject of naming his child:— " For God's sake, *don't Nicodemus him* into nothing !"

logic as good as his own. But the more delicate offspring of tenderness and chivalry, intending no violence, and venturing out to sea upon a rose-leaf, is destroyed and sunk beyond diving-bells by half a breath of scorn. I would subscribe liberally, myself, to a private press and court of honor in poetry—critics, if admitted, to be dumb upon a penalty. Will no Howard or Wilberforce act upon this hint? Poets now-a-days are more slaves and felons than your African, or your culprit at the old Bailey!

I would go a great way, privately, to find a genuine spark of chivalry, and Job lit his every-day lamp with it. See what a redolence of old time there is in these verses, which I copied long ago from a lady's album. Yet, you may ridicule them if you like!—

There is a story I have met,
  Of a high angel, pure and true,
With eyes that tears had never wet,
  And lips that pity never knew;
But ever on his throne he sate,
  With his white pinions proudly furled,
And, looking from his high estate,
  Beheld the errors of a world:
Yet, never, as they rose to heaven,
Plead ev'n for one to be forgiven.

God looked at last upon his pride,
  And bade him fold his shining wing,
And o'er a land where tempters bide,
  He made the heartless angel king.

'Tis lovely, reading in the tale,
  The glorious spells they tried on him,
Ere grew his heavenly birth-star pale,
  Ere grew his frontlet jewel dim—
Cups of such rare and ravishing wines

As ev'n a god might drink and bless,
Gems from unsearched and central mines,
Whose light than heaven's was scarcely less—
Gold of a sheen like crystal spars,
And silver whiter than the moon's,
And music like the songs of stars,
And perfume like a thousand Junes,
And breezes, soft as heaven's own air,
Like fingers playing in his hair!
He shut his eyes—he closed his ears—
He bade them, in God's name, begone!
And, through the yet eternal years,
Had stood, the tried and sinless one:
But there was yet one untried spell—
A woman tempted—and he fell!

And I—if semblance I may find
Between such glorious sphere and mine—
Am not to the high honor blind,
Of filling this fair page of thine—
Writing my unheard name among
Sages and sires and men of song—
But honor, though the best e'er given,
And glory, though it were a king's,
And power, though loving it like heaven,
Were, to my seeming, lesser things,
And less temptation, far, to me,
Than *half a hope of serving thee!*

I am mounted upon my hobby now, dear reader; for Job Smith, though as hideous an idol as ever was worshipped on the Indus, was still my idol. Here is another touch of his quality:

I look upon the fading flowers
Thou gav'st me, lady, in thy mirth,
And mourn, that, with the perishing hours,

Such fair things perish from the earth—
For thus, I know, the moment's feeling
Its own light web of life unweaves,
The deepest trace from memory stealing,
Like perfume from these dying leaves—
The thought that gave it, and the flower
Alike the creatures of an hour.

And thus it better were, perhaps,
For feeling is the nurse of pain,
And joys, that linger in their lapse,
Must die at last, and so are vain!
Could I revive these faded flowers,
Could I call back departed bliss,
I would not, though this world of ours
Were ten times brighter than it is!
They must—and let them—pass away!
We are forgotten—ev'n as they!

I think I must give Edith another reprieve. I have no idea why I have digressed, this time, from the story which (you may see by the motto at the beginning of the paper) I have not yet told. I can conceive easily how people, who have nothing to do, betake themselves to autobiography—it is so pleasant rambling about over the past, and re-gathering only the flowers. Why should pain and mortification be unsepultured? The world is no wiser for these written experiences. "The best book," said Southey, "does but little good to the world, and much harm to the author." I shall deliberate whether to enlighten the world, as to Edith's metempsychosis, or no.

PART IV.

SCENERY AND A SCENE.

"Truth is no doctoresse ; she takes no degrees at Paris or Oxford, among great clerks, disputants, subtle Aristotles, men *nodosi ingenii*, able to take Lully by the chin ; but oftentimes, to such a one as myself, an *idiota* or common person, no great things, melancholizing in woods where waters are, quiet places by rivers, fountains ; whereas the silly man, expecting no such matter, thinketh only how best to delectate and refresh his mynde continually with nature, her pleasant scenes, woods, waterfalls : on a sudden the goddess herself, Truth has appeared with a shining light and a sparkling countenance, so as ye may not be able lightlv to resist her."—BURTON.

Ever thus
Drop from us treasures one by one ;
They who have been from youth with us,
Whose every look, whose every tone,
Is linked to us like leaves to flowers—
They who have shared our pleasant hours—
Whose voices, so familiar grown,
They almost seem to us our own—
The echoes of each breath of ours—
They who have ever been our pride,
Yet in their hours of triumph dearest—
They whom we must have known and tried,
And loved the most when tried the nearest—
They pass from us, like stars that wane,
The brightest still before,
Or gold links broken from a chain
That can be joined no more !

JOB SMITH and myself were on the return from Niagara. It was in the slumberous and leafy midst of June. Lake Erie had lain with a silver glaze upon its bosom for days ; the ragged trees upon its green shore dropping their branches into the stirless water, as if it were some rigid imitation—the lake glass, and the leaves emerald ; the sky was of an April blue, as if a night-rain had washed out its milkiness, till you could see through its clarified depths to the gates of heaven ; and yet, breathless and sunny as was the face of the earth, there was a nerve and a vitality in the air that exacted of every pulse its full compass—searched every pore for its capacity of the joy of existence.

No one can conceive, who has not had his imagination stretched at the foot of Niagara, or in the Titanic solitudes of the West, the vastness of the unbroken phases of nature ; where every tree looks a king, and every flower a marvel of glorious form and color—where the rocks are rent, every one, as by the "tenth" thunder-bolt—and lake, mountain, or river, ravine or waterfall, cave or eagle's nest, whatever it may be that feeds the eye or the fancy, is as the elements have shaped and left it—where the sculpture, and the painting, and the poetry, and the wonderful alchymy of nature, go on under the naked eye of the Almighty, and by his own visible and uninterrupted hand—and where the music of nature, from the anthem of the torrent and storm, broken only by the scream of the vulture, to the trill of the rivulet with its accompaniment of singing birds and winds, is for ever ringing its changes, as if for the stars to hear—in such scenes, I say, and in such scenes only, is the imagination overtasked, or stretched to the capacity of a seraph's; and, while common minds sink beneath them to the mere inanition of their animal senses, the loftier spirit takes their color and stature, and outgrows the common and pitiful standards of the world. Cooper and Leatherstocking thus became what they are—the one a high-priest of imagination and poetry, and the other a simple-hearted but mere creature of instinct; and Cooper is no more a living man, and liable to the common laws of human nature, than Leatherstocking a true and life-like transcript of the more common effect of those overpowering solitudes on the character.

We got on board the canal-boat at noon, and Job and myself, seated on the well-cushioned seats, with the blinds half-turned, to give us the prospect and exclude the sun, sat disputing in our usual amicable way. He was the only man I ever knew with whom I could argue without losing my temper; and the reason was, that I always had the last word, and thought myself victorious.

"We are about to return into the bosom of society, my dear Job," said I, looking with unctuous good nature on the well-shaped boot I had put on for the first time in a month that morning. (It is an unsentimental fact that hob-nailed shoes are indispensable on the most poetical spots of earth.)

"Yes," said Job; "but how superior is the society we leave behind! Niagara and Erie! What, in your crowded city, is comparable to these?"

"Nothing, for size!—but, for society—you will think me a pagan, dear chum—but, on my honor, straight from Niagara as I come, I feel a most dissatisfied yearning for the society of Miss Popkins!"

"Oh, Phil!"

"On my honor!"

"You, who were in such raptures at the Falls!"

"And real ones—but I wanted a woman at my elbow to listen to them. Do you know, Job, I have made up my mind on a great principle since we have been on our travels? Have you observed that I was pensive?"

"Not particularly—but what is your principle?"

"That a man is a much more interesting object than a mountain."

"A man! did you say?"

"Yes—but I meant a woman!"

"I don't think so."

"I do!—and I judge by myself. When did I ever see wonder of nature—tree, sunset, waterfall, rapid, lake, or river—that I would not rather have been talking to a woman the while? Do you remember the three days we were tramping through the forest without seeing the sun, as if we had been in the endless aisle of a cathedral? Do you remember the long morning when we lay on the moss at the foot of Niagara, and it was a divine luxury only to breathe? Do you remember the lunar rainbows at midnight on Goat Island? Do you remember the ten thousand glorious moments we have enjoyed between weather and scenery since the bursting of these summer leaves? Do you?

"Certainly, my dear boy!"

"Well, then, much as I love nature and you, there has not been an hour since we packed our knapsacks, that, if I could have distilled a charming girl out of a mixture of you and any mountain, river, or rock, that I have seen, I would not have flung you, without remorse, into any witch's caldron that was large enough, and would boil at my bidding."

"Monster!"

"And I believe I should have the same feelings in Italy or Greece, or wherever people go into raptures with things you can neither eat nor make love to."

"Would not even the Venus fill your fancy for a day?"

"An hour, perhaps, it might; for I should be studying, in its cold Parian proportions, the structure of some living Musidora—but I should soon tire of it, and long for my lunch or my love; and, I give you my honor, I would not lose the three meals of a single day to see Santa Croce and St. Peter's."

"Both?"

"Both."

Job disdained to argue against such a want of sentimental principle, and, pulling up the blind, he fixed his eyes on the slowly-gliding panorama of rock and forest, and I mounted for a promenade upon the deck.

Mephistopheles could hardly have found a more striking amusement for Faust than the passage of three hundred miles in the canal from Lake Erie to the Hudson. As I walked up and down the deck of the packet-boat, I thought to myself, that, if it were not for thoughts of things that come more home to one's "business and bosom" (particularly "bosom"), I could be content to re-take my berth at Schenectady, and return to Buffalo for amusement. The Erie canal-boat is a long and very pretty drawing-room afloat. It has a library, sofas, a tolerable cook, curtains or Venetian blinds, a civil captain, and no smell of steam or perceptible motion. It is drawn generally by three horses at a fair trot, and gets you through about a hundred miles a day, as softly as if you were witched over the ground by Puck and Mustard-seed. The company (say fifty people) is such as pleases Heaven; though I must say (with my eye all along the shore, collecting the various dear friends I have made and left on that long canal) there are few highways on which you will meet so many lovely and loving fellow-passengers. On this occasion my star was bankrupt—Job Smith being my only civilized companion—and I was left to the unsatisfactory society of my own thoughts and the scenery.

Discontented as I may seem to have been, I remember, through a number of years of stirring and thickly-sown manhood, every moment of that lovely evening. I remember the progression of the sunset, from the lengthening shadows and the first gold upon the clouds, to the deepening twilight and the new-sprung star hung over the wilderness. And I remember what I am going to describe—a twilight anthem in the forest—as you remember an air of Rossini's, or a transition in the half-fiendish, half-heavenly creations of Meyerbeer. I thought time dragged heavily, then, but I wish I had as light a heart and could feel as vividly now!

The Erie canal is cut a hundred or two miles through the heart of the primeval wilderness of America, and the boat was gliding on silently and swiftly; and, never sailed a lost cloud through the abyss of space on a course more apparently new and untrodden. The luxuriant soil had sent up a rank grass that covered the horse-path like velvet; the Erie water was clear as a brook in the winding canal; the old shafts of the gigantic forest spurred into the sky by thousands, and the yet unscared eagle swung off from the dead branch of the pine, and skimmed the tree-tops for another perch, as if he had grown to believe that gliding spectre a harmless phenomenon of nature. The horses drew steadily and unheard, at the end of the long line; the steersman stood motionless at the tiller, and I lay on a heap of baggage in the prow, attentive to the slightest breathing of nature, but thinking, with an ache at my heart, of Edith Linsey, to whose feet (did I mention it?) I was hastening with a lover's proper impatience. I might as well have taken another turn in my "fool's paradise."

The gold of the sunset had glided up the the dark pine tops and disappeared, like a ring taken slowly from an Ethiop's finger; the whip-poor-will had chanted the first stave of his lament; the bat was abroad, and the screech-owl, like all bad singers, commenced without waiting to be importuned, though we were listening for the nightingale. The air, as I said before, had been all day breathless; but, as the first chill of evening displaced the warm atmosphere of the departed sun, a slight breeze crisped the mirrored bosom of the canal, and then commenced the night anthem of the forest, audible, I would fain believe, in its soothing changes, by the dead tribes whose bones whiten amid the perishing leaves. First, whisperingly yet articulately, the suspended and wavering foliage of the birch was touched by the many-fingered wind, and, like a faint prelude, the silver-lined leaves rustled in the low branches; and, with a moment's pause, when you could hear the moving of the vulture's claws upon the bark, as he turned to get his breast to the wind, the increasing breeze swept into the pine-tops, and drew forth, from their fringe-like and myriad tassels, a low monotone like the refrain of a far-off dirge; and still as it murmured, (seeming to you sometimes like the confused and heart-broken responses of the penitents on a cathedral floor), the blast strengthened and filled, and the rigid leaves of the oak, and the swaying fans and chalices of the magnolia, and the rich cups of the tulip trees, stirred and answered with their different voices like many-toned harps; and when the wind was fully abroad, and every moving thing on the breast of the earth was roused from its daylight repose, the irregular and capricious blast, like a player on an organ of a thousand stops, lulled and strengthened by turns; and, from the hiss in the rank grass, low as the whisper of fairies, to the thunder of the impinging and groaning branches of the larch and the fir, the anthem went ceaselessly through its changes, and the harmony (though the owl broke in with his scream, and though the over-blown monarch of the wood came crashing to the earth), was still perfect and without a jar. It is strange that there is no sound of nature out of tune. The roar of the waterfall comes into this anthem of the forest like an accompaniment of bassoons, and the occasional bark of the wolf, or the scream of a night-bird, or even the deep-throated croak of the frog, is no more discordant than the outburst of an octave flute above the even melody of an orchestra; and it is surprising how the large rain-drops, pattering on the leaves, and the small voice of the nightingale (singing, like nothing but himself, sweetest in the darkness) seems an intensitive and a low burthen to the general anthem of the earth—as it were, a single voice among instruments.

I had what Wordsworth calls a "couchant ear" in my youth, and my story will wait, dear reader, while I tell you of another harmony that I learned to love in the wilderness.

There will come sometimes in the Spring—say in May, or whenever the snow-drops and sulphur butterflies are tempted out by the first timorous sunshine—there will come, I say, in that yearning and youth-renewing season, a warm shower at noon. Our tent shall be pitched on the skirts of a forest of young pines, and the evergreen foliage, if foliage it may be called, shall be a daily refreshment to our eye while watching, with the west wind upon our cheeks, the unclothed branches of the elm. The rain descends softly and warm; but, with the sunset, the clouds break away, and it grows suddenly cold enough to freeze. The next morning you shall come out with me to a hill-side looking upon the south, and lie down with your ear to the earth. The pine tassels hold, in every four of their fine fingers, a drop of rain frozen like a pearl in a long ear-ring, sustained in their loose grasp by the rigidity of the cold. The sun grows warm at ten, and the slight green fingers begin to relax and yield, and, by eleven, they are all dropping their icy pearls upon the dead leaves, with a murmur through the forest like the swarming of the bees of Hybla. There is not much variety in its music, but it is a pleasant monotone for thought; and if, you have a restless fever in your bosom (as I had, when I learned to love it, for the travel which has corrupted the heart and the ear that it soothed and satisfied then) you may lie down with a crooked root under your head, in the skirts of the forest, and thank Heaven for an anodyne to care. And it is better than the voice of your friend, or the song of your lady-love, for it exacts no gratitude, and will not desert you ere the echo dies upon the wind.

Oh, how many of these harmonies there are!—how many that we hear, and how many that are "too constant to be heard!" I could go back to my boyhood, now, with this thread of recollection, and unsepulture a hoard of simple and long-buried joys, that would bring the blush upon my cheek to think how my senses are dulled since such things could give me pleasure! Is there no "well of Kanathos" for renewing the youth of the soul?—no St. Hilary's cradle? no elixir to cast the slough of heart-sickening and heart-tarnishing custom? Find me an alchymy for *that*, with your alembic and crucible, and you may resolve to dross again your philosopher's stone!

II.

Everybody who makes the passage of the Erie canal, stops at the half-way town of Utica, to visit a wonder of nature fourteen miles to the west of it, called Trenton Falls. It would be becoming in me, before mentioning the Falls, however, to sing the praises of Utica and its twenty thousand inhabitants—having received much hospitality from the worthy burghers, and philandered up and down their well-flagged *trottoir* very much to my private satisfaction. I should scorn any man's judgment who should attempt to convince me that the Erie water, which comes down the canal a hundred and fifty miles, and passes through the market-place of that pleasant town, has not communicated, to the hearts of its citizens, the expansion and depth of the parent lake from which it is drawn. I have a theory on that subject with which I intend to surprise the world, whenever politics and Mr. Bulwer draw less engrossingly on its attention. Will any one tell me that the dark eyes I knew there, and whose like, for softness and meaning, I inquired for in vain through Italy, and the voice that accompanied their gaze—(that Pasta, in her divinest out-gush of melody and soul, alone recalls to me)—that these, and the noble heart, and high mind, and even the genius, that were other gifts of the same marvel among women—that these were born of common parentage, and nursed by the air of a demi-metropolis? We were but the kindest of friends, that bright creature and myself, and I may say, without charging myself with the blindness of love, that I believe in my heart she was the foster-child of the water-spirits on whose wandering streamlet she lived—that the thousand odors that swept down from the wilderness upon Lake Erie, and the unseen but wild and innumerable influences of nature, or whatever you call that which makes the Indian a believer in the Great Spirit —that these came down with those clear waters, ministering to the mind and watching over the budding beauty of this noble and most high-hearted woman! If you do not believe it, I should like you to tell me how else such a creature was "raised," as they phrase it in Virginia. I shall hold to my theory till you furnish me with a more reasonable.

We heard at the hotel that there were several large parties at Trenton Falls, and, with an abridgment of our toilets in our pockets, Job and I galloped out of Utica about four o'clock of as bright a summer's afternoon as was ever promised in the almanac. We drew rein a mile or two out of town, and dawdled along the wild road more leisurely, Job's Green Mountain proportions fitting to the saddle something in the manner and relative fitness of a skeleton on a poodle. By the same token, he rode safely, the looseness of his bones accommodating itself with singular facility to the irregularities in the pace of the surprised animal beneath him

I dislike to pass over the minutest detail of a period of my life that will be rather interesting in my biography, (it is my intention to be famous enough to merit that distinction, and I would recommend to my friends to be noting my "little peculiarities"), and, with this posthumous benevolence in my heart, I simply record, that our conversation on the road turned upon Edith Linsey—at this time the lady of my constant love—for whose sake, and at whose bidding, I was just concluding (with success I presumed) a probation of three years of absence, silence, hard study, and rigid morals; and upon whose parting promise (God forgive her!) I had built my uttermost gleaning and sand of earthly hope and desire. I tell you, in the tail of this mocking paragraph, dear reader, that the bend of the rainbow spans not the earth more perfectly than did the love of that woman my hopes of future bliss; and the ephemeral arc does not sooner melt into the clouds—but I am anticipating my story.

Job's extraordinary appearance, as he extricated himself from his horse, usually attracted the entire attention of the by-standers at a strange inn; and, under cover of this, I usually contrived to get into the house and commit him by ordering the dinner as soon as it could be got ready. Else, if it was in the neighborhood of scenery, he was off till Heaven knew when, and, as I had that delicacy for his feelings never to dine without him, you may imagine the necessity of my hungry manœuvre.

We dined upon the trout of the glorious stream we had come to see; and, as our host's eldest daughter waited upon us (recorded, in Job's journal, in my possession at this moment, as "the most comely and gracious virgin" he had seen in his travels), we felt bound to adapt our conversation to the purity of her mind, and discussed only the philosophical point, whether the beauty of the stream could be tasted in the flavor of the fish—Job for it, I against it. The argument was only interrupted by the entrance of an apple-pudding, so hot that our tongues were fully occupied in removing it from place to place as the mouth felt its heat inconvenient; and then, being in a country of liberty and equality, and the damsel in waiting, as Job smilingly remarked, as much a lady as the President's wife, he requested permission to propose her health in a cool tumbler of cider, and we adjourned to the moonlight.

III.

Ten or fifteen years ago, the existence of Trenton Falls was not known. It was discovered, like Pæstum, by a wandering artist, when there was a town of ten thousand inhabitants, a canal, a theatre, a liberty-pole, and forty churches, within fourteen miles of it. It may be mentioned to the credit of the Americans, that in the "hardness" of character of which travellers complain, there is the soft trait of a passion for scenery; and, before the fact of its discovery had got well into the "Cahawba Democrat" and "Go-the-whole-hog-Courier," there was a splendid wooden hotel on the edge of the precipice, with a French cook, soda-water, and olives; and a law was passed by the Kentucky Travellers' Club, requiring a hanging-bird's nest from the trees "frowning down the awful abysm," (so expressed in the regulation), as a qualification for membership. Thenceforward, to the present time, it has been a place of fashionable resort during the summer solstice, and the pine woods, in which the hotel stands, being impervious to the sun, it is prescribed by oculists for gentlemen and ladies with weak eyes. If the luxury of corn-cutters had penetrated to the United States, it might be prescribed for tender feet as well—the soft floor of pine-tassels spread under the grassless woods, being considered an improvement upon Turkey carpets and green-sward.

Trenton Falls is rather a misnomer. I scarcely know what you would call it, but the wonder of nature which bears the name is a tremendous torrent, whose bed, for several miles, is sunk fathoms deep into the earth—a roaring and dashing stream, so far below the surface of the forest in which it is lost, that you would think, as you come suddenly upon the edge of its long precipice, that it was a river in some inner world (coiled within ours, as we in the outer circle of the firmament), and laid open by some Titanic throe that had cracked clear asunder the crust of this shallow earth. The idea is rather assisted if you happen to see below you, on its abysmal shore, a party of adventurous travellers; for, at that vast depth, and in contrast with the gigantic trees and rocks, the same number of well-shaped pismires, dressed in the last fashions, and philandering upon your parlor floor, would be about of their apparent size and distinctness.

They showed me at Eleusis the well by which Proserpine ascends to the regions of day on her annual visit to the plains of Thessaly—but, with the *genius loci* at my elbow in the shape of a Greek girl as lovely as Phryné, my memory reverted to the bared axle of the earth in the bed of this American river, and I was persuaded (looking the while at the *feronière* of gold sequins on the Phidian forehead of my Katinka) that, supposing Hades in the centre of the earth, you are nearer to it by some fathoms at Trenton. I confess, I have had, since my first descent into those depths, an uncomfortable doubt of the solidity of the globe—how the deuce it can hold together with such a crack in its bottom !

It was a night to play Endymion, or do any Tom-foolery that could be laid to the charge of the moon, for, a more omnipresent and radiant atmosphere of moonlight never sprinkled the wilderness with silver. It was a night in which to wish it might never be day again—a night to be enamored of the stars, and bid God bless them like human creatures on their bright journey—a night to love in, to dissolve in—to do everything but what night is made for—sleep ! Oh heaven ! when I think how precious is life in such moments ; how the aroma—the celestial bloom and flower of the soul—the yearning and fast-perishing enthusiasm of youth—waste themselves, in the solitude of such nights, on the senseless and unanswering air ; when I wander alone, unloving and unloved, beneath influences that could inspire me with the elevation of a seraph, were I at the ear of a human creature that could summon forth and measure my limitless capacity for devotion—when I think this, and feel this, and so waste my existence in vain yearnings—I could extinguish the divine spark within me, like a lamp on an unvisited shrine, and thank Heaven for an assimilation to the animals I walk among ! And that is the substance of a speech I made to Job, as a sequitur of a well-meant remark of his own, that "it was a pity Edith Linsey was not there." He took the clause about the "animals" to himself, and I made an apology for the same, a year after. We sometimes give our friends, quite innocently, such terrible knocks in our rhapsodies !

Most people talk of the *sublimity* of Trenton, but I have haunted it by the week together for its mere loveliness. The river, in the heart of that fearful chasm, is the most varied and beautiful assemblage of the thousand forms and shapes of running water, that I know in the world. The soil, and the deep-striking roots of the forest, terminate far above you, looking like a black rim on the enclosing precipices; the bed of the river and its sky-sustaining walls are of solid rock, and, with the tremendous descent of the stream—forming for miles one continuous succession of falls and rapids—the channel is worn into curves and cavities which throw the clear waters into forms of inconceivable brilliancy and variety. It is a sort of half twilight below, with here and there a long beam of sunshine reaching down to kiss the lip of an eddy, or form a rainbow over a fall, and the reverberating and changing echoes:—

> "Like a ring of bells whose sound the wind still alters,"

maintain a constant and most soothing music, varying at every step with the varying phase of the current. Cascades of from twenty to thirty feet, over which the river flies with a single and hurrying leap (not a drop missing from the glassy and bending sheet), occur frequently as you ascend; and it is from these that the place takes its name. But the falls, though beautiful, are only peculiar from the dazzling and unequalled rapidity with which the waters come to the leap. If it were not for the leaf which drops wavering down into the abysm from trees apparently painted on the sky, and which is caught away by the flashing current as if the lightning had suddenly crossed it, you would think the vault of the steadfast heavens a flying element as soon. The spot, in that long gulf of beauty, that I best remember, is a smooth descent of some hundred yards, where the river in full and undivided volume skims over a plane as polished as a table of scagliola, looking, in its invisible speed, like one mirror of gleaming but motionless crystal. Just above, there is a sudden turn in the glen, which sends the water like a catapult against the opposite angle of the rock, and, in the action of years, it has worn out a cavern of unknown depth, into which the whole mass of the river plunges, with the abandonment of a flying fiend into hell, and, reappearing like the angel that has pursued him, glides swiftly but with divine serenity on its way. (I am indebted for that last figure to Job, who travelled with a Milton in his pocket, and had a natural redolence of "Paradise Lost" in his conversation.)

Much as I detest water in small quantities, (to drink), I have a hydromania in the way of lakes, rivers, and waterfalls. It is, by much, the *belle* in the family of the elements. *Earth* is never tolerable unless disguised in green. *Air* is so thin as only to be visible when she borrows drapery of water; and *Fire* is so staringly bright as to be unpleasant to the eyesight; but *Water!* soft, pure, graceful water! there is no shape into which you can throw her that she does not seem lovelier than before. She can borrow nothing of her sisters. Earth has no jewels in her lap so brilliant as water's spray pearls and emeralds; Fire has no rubies like what she steals from the sunset; Air has no robes like the grace of her fine-woven and ever-changing drapery of silver. A health (in wine!) to WATER!

Who is there, who did not love some stream in his youth? Who is there, in whose vision of the past there does not sparkle up, from every picture of childhood, a spring or a rivulet, woven through the darkened and torn woof of first affections like a thread of unchanged silver? How do you interpret the instinctive yearning with which you search for the river-side or the fountain in every scene of nature—the clinging unaware to the river's course when a truant in the fields of June—the dull void you find in every landscape of which it is not the ornament and the centre? For myself, I hold with the Greek: "Water is the first principle of all things: we were made from it and we shall be resolved into it."*

IV.

The awkward thing in all story-telling is transition. Invention, you do not need if you have experience; for fact is stranger than fiction. A beginning in these days of startling abruptness is as simple as open your mouth; and when you have once begun you can end whenever you like, and leave the sequel to the reader's imagination: but the hinges of a story—the turning gracefully *back* from a digression (it is easy to turn *into* one)—is the *pas qui coûte.* My education on that point was neglected.

It was, as I said before, a moonlight night, and Job and myself having, like Sir Fabian, "no mind to sleep," followed the fashion and the rest of the company at the inn, and strolled down to see the falls by moonlight. I had been there before, and I took Job straight to the spot, in the bed of the river, which I have described above as my favorite, and, after watching it for a few minutes, we turned back to a dark cleft in the rock which afforded a rude seat, and sat musing in silence.

Several parties had strolled past without seeing us in our recess, when two female figures, with their arms around each other's waists, sauntered slowly around the jutting rock below, and approached us, eagerly engaged in conversation. They came on to the very verge of the shadow which enveloped us, and turned to look back at the scene. As the head nearest me was raised to the light, I started half to my feet: it was Edith! In the same instant her voice of music broke on my ear, and an irresistible

* The Ionic philosophy, supported by Thales.

impulse to listen unobserved drew me down again upon my seat, and Job, with a similar instinct, laid his hand on my arm.

"It was his favorite spot!" said Edith. (We had been at Trenton together years before.) "I stood here with him, and I wish he stood here now, that I might tell him what my hand hesitates to write."

"Poor Philip!" said her companion, whom, by the voice, I recognised as the youngest of the Flemings, "I cannot conceive how you can resolve so coldly to break his heart."

I felt a dagger entering my bosom, but still I listened. Edith went on.

"Why, I will tell you, my dear little innocent. I loved Philip Slingsby when I thought I was going to die. It was a fitting attachment, for I never thought to need, of the goods of this world, more than a sick chamber and a nurse; and Phil was kind-hearted and devoted to me, and I lived at home. But, with returned health, a thousand ambitious desires have sprung up in my heart, and I find myself admired by whom I will, and every day growing more selfish and less poetical. Philip is poor, and love in a cottage, though very well for you if you like it, would never do for me. I should like him very well for a friend, for he is gentlemanlike and devoted, but, with my ideas, I should only make him miserable, and so—I think I had better put him out of misery at once—don't you think?"

A half-smothered groan of anguish escaped my lips; but it was lost in the roar of the waters, and Edith's voice, as she walked on, lessened and became inaudible to my ear. As her figure was lost in the shadow of the rocks beyond, I threw myself on the bosom of my friend, and wept in the unutterable agony of a crushed heart. I know not how that night was spent, but I awoke at noon of the next day, in my bed, with Job's hand clasped tenderly in my own.

V.

I kept my tryst. I was to meet Edith Linsey at Saratoga in July—the last month of the probation by which I had won a right to her love. I had not spoken to her, or written, or seen her (save, unknown to her, in the moment I have described), in the three long years to which my constancy was devoted. I had gained the usual meed of industry in my profession, and was admitted to its practice. I was on the threshold of manhood ; and she had promised, before heaven, here to give me heart and hand.

I had parted from her at twelve on that night three years, and as the clock struck, I stood again by her side in the crowded ballroom of Saratoga.

"Good God ! Mr. Slingsby !" she exclaimed, as I put out my hand.

" Am I so changed that you do not know me, Miss Linsey ?" I asked, as she still looked with a wondering gaze into my face—pressing my hand, however, with real warmth, and evidently under the control, for the moment, of the feelings with which we had parted.

" Changed, indeed ! Why, you have studied yourself to a skeleton ! My dear Philip, you are ill !"

I was—but it was only for a moment. I asked her for a waltz, and never before or since came wit or laughter so freely to my lip. I was collected, but, at the same time, I was the gayest of the gay ; and, when everybody had congratulated me, in her hearing, on the school to which I had put my wits in my long apprenticeship to the law, I retired to the gallery looking down upon the garden, and cooled my brow and rallied my sinking heart.

The candles were burning low, and the ball was nearly over, when I entered the room again, and requested Edith to take a turn with me on the colonnade. She at once assented, and I could feel, by her arm in mine, and see by the fixed expression on her lip, that she did so with the intention of revealing to me what she little thought I could so well anticipate.

"My probation is over," I said, breaking the silence which she seemed willing to prolong, and which had lasted till we had twice measured the long colonnade.

"It was three years ago to-night, I think, since we parted." She spoke in an absent and careless tone, as if trying to work out another more prominent thought in her mind.

"Do you find me changed?" I asked.

"Yes—oh, yes! very!"

"But I am more changed than I seem, dear Edith!"

She turned to me, as if to ask me to explain myself.

"Will you listen to me while I tell you how?"

"What can you mean? Certainly.'

"Then listen, for I fear I can scarce bring myself to repeat what I am going to say. When I first learned to love you, and when I promised to love you for life, you were thought to be dying, and I was a boy. I did not count on the future, for I despaired of your living to share it with me, and, if I had done so, I was still a child, and knew nothing of the world. I have since grown more ambitious, and, I may as well say at once, more selfish and less poetical. You will easily divine my drift. You are poor, and I find myself, as you have seen to-night, in a position which will enable me to marry more to my advantage; and, with these views, I am sure I should only make you miserable by fulfilling my contract with you, and you will agree with me that I consult our mutual happiness by this course—don't you think?"

At this instant I gave a signal to Job, who approached and made some sensible remarks about the weather; and, after another turn or two, I released Miss Linsey's arm, and cautioning her against the night air, left her to finish her promenade and swallow her own projected speech and mine, and went to bed.

And so ended my first love!

SCENES OF FEAR.

NO. I.

THE DISTURBED VIGIL.

'*Antonio.*—Get me a conjurer, I say! Inquire me out a man that lets out devils.''—OLD PLAY.

SUCH a night! It was like a festival of Dian. A burst of a summer shower at sunset, with a clap or two of thunder, had purified the air to an intoxicating rareness, and the free breathing of the flowers, and the delicious perfume from the earth and grass, and the fresh foliage of the new Spring, showed the delight and sympathy of inanimate Nature in the night's beauty. There was no atmosphere—nothing between the eye and the pearly moon—and she rode through the heavens without a veil, like a queen as she is, giving a glimpse of her nearer beauty for a festal favor to the worshipping stars.

I was a student at the famed university of Connecticut, and the bewilderments of philosophy and poetry were strong upon me, in a place where exquisite natural beauty, and the absence of all other temptation, secure to the classic neophite an almost supernatural wakefulness of fancy. I contracted a taste for the horrible in those days, which still clings to me. I have travelled since then with no object but general observation, and have dawdled my hour at courts and operas with little interest, while the sacking and drowning of a woman in the Bosphorus, the impalement of a robber on the Nile, and the insane hospitals, from Liverpool to Cathay, are described in my capricious journal with the vividness of the most stirring adventure.

There is a kind of *crystallization* in the circumstances of one's life. A peculiar turn of mind draws to itself events fitted to its particular nucleus, and it is frequently a subject of wonder why one man meets with more remarkable things than another, when it is owing merely to a difference of natural character.

It was, as I was saying, a night of wonderful beauty. I was watching a corpse. In that part of the United States, the dead are never left alone till the earth is thrown upon them; and, as a friend of the family, I had been called upon for this melancholy service on the night preceding the interment. It was a death which had left a family of broken hearts; for, beneath the sheet which sank so appallingly to the outline of a human form, lay a wreck of beauty and sweetness whose loss seemed to the survivors to have darkened the face of the earth. The ethereal and touching loveliness of that dying girl, whom I had known only a hopeless victim of consumption, springs up in my memory even yet, and mingles with every conception of female beauty.

Two ladies, friends of the deceased, were to share my vigils. I knew them but slightly, and, having read them to sleep an hour after midnight, I performed my half-hourly duty of entering the room where the corpse lay, to look after the lights, and then strolled into the garden to enjoy the quiet of the summer night. The flowers were glittering in their pearl-drops, and the air was breathless.

The sight of the long, sheeted corpse, the sudden flare of lights as the long snuffs were removed from the candles, the stillness of the close-shuttered room, and my own predisposition to invest death with a supernatural interest, had raised my heart to my throat. I walked backward and forward in the garden-path; and the black shadows beneath the lilacs, and even the glittering of the glow-worms within them, seemed weird and fearful.

The clock struck, and I re-entered. My companions still slept, and I passed on to the inner chamber. I trimmed the lights, and stood and looked at the white heap lying so fearfully still within the shadow of the curtains; and my blood seemed to freeze. At the moment when I was turning away with a strong effort at a more composed feeling, a noise like a flutter of wings, followed by a rush and a sudden silence, struck on my startled ear. The street was as quiet as death, and the noise, which was far too audible to be a deception of the fancy, had come from the side toward an uninhabited wing of the house. My heart stood still. Another instant, and the fire-screen was dashed down, and a *white cat* rushed past me, and, with the speed of light, sprang like a hyena upon the corpse. The flight of a vampyre into the chamber would not have more curdled my veins. A convulsive shudder ran cold over me, but recovering my self-command, I rushed to the animal (of whose horrible appetite for the flesh of the dead I had read incredulously), and attempted to tear her from the body. With her claws fixed in the breast, and a *yowl* like the wail of an infernal spirit, she crouched fearlessly upon it, and the stains already upon the sheet convinced me that it would be impossible to remove her without shockingly disfiguring the corpse. I seized her by the throat, in the hope of choking her; but, with the first pressure of my fingers, she flew into my face, and the infuriated animal seemed persuaded that it was a contest for life. Half blinded by the fury of her attack, I loosed her for a moment, and she immediately leaped again upon the corpse, and had covered her feet and face with blood before I could recover my hold upon her. The body was no longer in a situation to be spared, and I seized her with a desperate grasp to draw her off; but, to my horror, the half-covered and bloody corpse rose upright in her fangs, and, while I paused in fear, sat with drooping arms, and head fallen with ghastly helplessness over the shoulder. Years have not removed that fearful spectacle from my eyes.

The corpse sank back, and I succeeded in throttling the monster, and threw her at last, lifeless, from the window. I then composed the disturbed limbs, laid the hair away once more smoothly on the forehead, and, crossing the hands over the bosom, covered the violated remains, and left them again to their repose. My companions, strangely enough, slept on, and I paced the garden-walk alone, till the day, to my inexpressible relief, dawned over the mountains.

NO. II.

THE MAD SENIOR.

I WAS called upon in my senior year to watch with an insane student. He was a man who had attracted a great deal of attention in college. He appeared in an extraordinary costume at the beginning of our freshman term, and wrote himself down as Washington Greyling, of ——, an unheard-of settlement somewhere beyond the Mississippi. His coat and other gear might have been the work of a Chickasaw tailor, aided by the superintending taste of some white huntsman, who remembered faintly the outline of habiliments he had not seen for half a century. It was a body of green cloth, eked out with wampum and otter-skin, and would have been ridiculous if it had not encased one of the finest models of a manly frame that ever trod the earth. With close-curling black hair, a fine weather-browned complexion, Spanish features (from his mother—a frequent physiognomy in the countries bordering on Spanish America), and the port and lithe motion of a lion, he was a figure to look upon in any disguise with warm admiration. He was soon put into the hands of a tailor-proper, and, with the facility which belongs to his countrymen, became in a month the best-dressed man in college. His manners were of a gentleman-like mildness, energetic, but courteous and chivalresque, and unlike most savages and all coins, he polished without "losing his mark." At the end of his first term, he would have been called a high-bred gentleman at any court in Europe.

The opening of his mind was almost as rapid and extraordinary. He seized everything with an ardor and freshness that habit and difficulty never deadened. He was like a man who had tumbled into a new star, and was collecting knowledge for a world to which he was to return. The first in all games, the wildest in all adventure, the most distinguished even in the elegant society for which the town is remarkable, and unfailingly brilliant in his recitations and college performances, he was looked upon as a sort of admirable phenomenon, and neither envied nor opposed in anything. I have often thought, in looking on him, that his sensations, at coming fresh from a wild, western prairie, and, at the first measure of his capacities with men of better advantages, finding himself so uniformly superior, must have been stirringly delightful. It is a wonder he never became arrogant; but it was the last foible of which he could have been accused.

We were reading hard for the honors in the senior year, when Greyling suddenly lost his reason. He had not been otherwise ill, and had, apparently in the midst of high health, gone mad at a moment's warning. The physicians scarce knew how to treat him. The confinement to which he was at first subjected, however, was thought inexpedient, and he seemed to justify their lenity by the gentlest behavior when at liberty. He seemed oppressed by a heart-breaking melancholy. We took our turns in guarding and watching with him, and it was upon my first night of duty that the incident happened which I have thus endeavored to introduce.

It was scarce like a vigil with a sick man, for our patient went regularly to bed, and usually slept well. I took my "Lucretius" and the "Book of the Martyrs," which was just then my favorite reading, and, with hot punch, a cold chicken, books, and a fire, I looked forward to it as merely a studious night; and, as the wintry wind of January rattled in at the old college windows, I thrust my feet into slippers, drew my dressing-gown about me, and congratulated myself on the excessive comfortableness of my position. The Sybarite's bed of roses would have been no temptation.

It had snowed all day, but the sun had set with a red rift in the clouds, and the face of the sky was swept in an hour to the clearness of—I want a comparison—your own blue eye, dear Mary! The all-glorious arch of heaven was a mass of sparkling stars.

Greyling slept, and I, wearied of the cold philosophy of the Latin poet, took to my "Book of Martyrs." I read on, and read on. The college clock struck, it seemed to me, the quarters rather than the hours. Time flew: it was three.

"Horrible! most horrible!" I started from my chair with the exclamation, and felt as if my scalp were self-lifted from my head. It was a description, in the harrowing faithfulness of the language of olden time, painting almost the articulate groans of an impaled Christian. I clasped the old iron-bound book, and rushed to the window as if my heart were stifling for fresh air.

Again at the fire. The large walnut fagots had burnt to a bed of bright coals, and I sat gazing into it, totally unable to shake off the fearful incubus from my breast. The martyr was there—on the very hearth—with the stakes scornfully crossed in his body; and, as the large coal cracked asunder and revealed the brightness within, I seemed to follow the nerve-rending instrument from hip to shoulder, and suffer with him, pang for pang, as if the burning redness were the pools of his fevered blood.

"Aha!"

It struck on my ear like the cry of an exulting fiend.

"Aha!"

I shrunk into the chair as the awful cry was repeated, and looked slowly and with difficult courage over my shoulder. A single fierce eye was fixed upon me from the mass of bed-clothes, and, for a moment, the relief from the fear of some supernatural presence was like water to a parched tongue. I sank back, relieved, into the chair.

There was a rustling immediately in the bed, and, starting again, I found the wild eyes of my patient fixed steadfastly upon me. He was creeping stealthily out of bed. His bare foot touched the floor, and his toes worked upon it as if he was feeling its strength, and in a moment he stood upright on his feet, and, with his head forward and his pale face livid with rage, stepped toward me. I looked to the door. He observed the glance, and in the next instant he sprung clear over the bed, turned the key, and dashed it furiously through the window.

"Now!" said he.

"Greyling!" I said. I had heard that a calm and fixed gaze would control a madman, and, with the most difficult exertion of nerve, I met his lowering eye, and we stood looking at each other for a full minute, like men of marble.

"Why have you left your bed?" I mildly asked.

"To kill you!" was the appalling answer; and, in another moment, the light stand was swept from between us, and he struck me down with a blow that would have felled a giant. Naked as he was, I had no hold upon him, even if in muscular strength I had been his match; and, with a minute's struggle, I yielded, for resistance was vain. His knee was now upon my breast and his left hand in my hair, and he seemed, by the tremulousness of his clutch, to be hesitating whether he should dash my brains out on the hearth. I could scarce breathe with his weight upon my chest, but I tried, with the broken words I could command, to move his pity. He laughed, as only maniacs can, and placed his hand on my throat. Oh God! shall I ever forget the fiendish deliberation with which he closed those feverish fingers?

"Greyling! for God's sake! Greyling!"

"Die! curse you!"

In the agonies of suffocation I struck out my arm, and almost buried it in the fire upon the hearth. With an expiring thought, I grasped a handful of the red-hot coals, and had just strength sufficient to press them hard against his side.

"Thank God!" I exclaimed with my first breath, as my eyes recovered from their sickness, and I looked upon the familiar objects of my chamber once more.

The madman sat crouched like a whipped dog in the farthest corner of the room, gibbering and moaning, with his hands upon his burnt side. I felt that I had escaped death by a miracle.

The door was locked, and, in dread of another attack, I threw up the broken window, and, to my unutterable joy, the figure of a man was visible upon the snow near the out-buildings of the college. It was a charity-student, risen before day to labor in the wood-yard. I shouted to him, and Greyling leaped to his feet.

"There is time yet!" said the madman; but, as he came toward me again with the same panther-like caution as before, I seized a heavy stone pitcher standing in the window-seat, and, hurling it at him with a fortunate force and aim, he fell stunned and bleeding on the floor. The door was burst open at the next moment, and, calling for assistance, we tied the wild Missourian into his bed, bound up his head and side, and committed him to fresh watchers. * * * * *

We have killed bears together at a Missouri salt-lick since then; but I never see Wash. Greyling with a smile off his face, without a disposition to look around for the door.

NO. III.

THE LUNATIC'S SKATE.

I HAVE only, in my life, known one *lunatic*—properly so called. In the days when I carried a satchel on the banks of the Shawsheen (a river whose half-lovely, half-wild scenery is tied like a silver thread about my heart), Larry Wynn and myself were the farthest boarders from school, in a solitary farm-house on the edge of a lake of some miles square, called by the undignified title of Pomp's Pond. An old negro, who was believed by the boys to have come over with Christopher Columbus, was the only other human being within anything like a neighborhood of the lake (it took its name from him), and the only approaches to its waters, girded in as it was by an almost impenetrable forest, were the path through old Pomp's clearing, and that by our own door. Out of school, Larry and I were inseparable. He was a pale, sad-faced boy, and, in the first days of our intimacy, he had confided a secret to me which, from its uncommon nature, and the excessive caution with which he kept it from every one else, bound me to him with more than the common ties of school-fellow attachment. We built wigwams together in the woods, had our tomahawks made of the same fashion, united our property in fox-traps, and played Indians with perfect contentment in each other's approbation.

I had found out, soon after my arrival at school, that Larry never slept on a moonlight night. With the first slender horn that dropped its silver and graceful shape behind the hills, his uneasiness commenced, and, by the time its full and perfect orb poured a flood of radiance over vale and mountain, he was like one haunted by a pursuing demon. At early twilight he closed the shutters, stuffing every crevice that could admit a ray; and then, lighting as many candles as he could beg or steal from our thrifty landlord, he sat down with his book in moody silence, or paced the room with an uneven step, and a solemn melancholy in his fine countenance, of which, with all my familiarity with him, I was almost afraid. Violent exercise seemed the only relief, and when the candles burnt low after midnight, and the stillness around the lone farm-house became too absolute to endure, he would throw up the window, and, leaping desperately out into the moonlight, rush up the hill into the depths of the wild forest, and walk on with supernatural excitement till the day dawned. Faint and pale, he would then creep into his bed, and, begging me to make his very common and always credited excuse of illness, sleep soundly till I returned from school. I soon became used to his way, ceased to follow him, as I had once or twice endeavored to do, into the forest, and never attempted to break in on the fixed and rapt silence which seemed to transform his lips to marble And for all this Larry loved me.

Our preparatory studies were completed, and, to our mutual despair, we were destined to different universities. Larry's father was a disciple of the great Channing, and mine a Trinitarian of uncommon zeal; and the two institutions of Yale and Harvard were in the hands of most eminent men of either persuasion, and few are the minds that could resist a four years' ordeal in either. A student was as certain to come forth a Unitarian from one, as a Calvinist from the other; and, in the New England States, these two sects are bitterly hostile. So, to the glittering atmosphere of Channing and Everett went poor Larry, lonely and dispirited; and I was committed to the sincere zealots of Connecticut, some two hundred miles off, to learn Latin and Greek, if it pleased Heaven, but the mysteries of "election and free grace," whether or no.

Time crept, ambled, and galloped, by turns, as we were *in* love or *out*, moping in term-time, or revelling in vacation, and gradually, I know not why, our correspondence had dropped, and the four years had come to their successive deaths, and we had never met. I grieved over it; for in those days I believed, with a schoolboy's fatuity,

> "That two, or one, are almost what they seem;"

and I loved Larry Wynn, as I hope I may never love man or woman again—with a pain at my heart. I wrote one or two reproachful letters in my senior years, but his answers were overstrained, and too full of protestations by half; and, seeing that absence had done its usual work on him, I gave it up, and wrote an epitaph on a departed friendship. I do not know, by the way, why I am detaining you with all this, for it has nothing to do with my story; but, let it pass as an evidence that it is a true one. The climax of things in real life has not the regular procession of incidents in a tragedy.

Some two or three years after we had taken "the irrevocable yoke" of life upon us, (not matrimony, but money-making,) a winter occurred of uncommonly fine sleighing—*sledging* they call it in England. At such times the American world is all abroad, either for business or pleasure. The roads are passable, at any rate of velocity of which a horse is capable; smooth as *montagnes Russes*, and hard as is good for hoofs; and a hundred miles is diminished to ten, in facility of locomotion. The hunter brings down his venison to the cities, the western trader takes his family a hundred leagues to buy calicoes and tracts, and parties of all kinds scour the country, drinking mulled wine and "flip," and shaking the very nests out of the fir-trees with the ringing of their horses' bells. You would think death and sorrow were buried in the snow with the leaves of the last autumn.

I do not know why I undertook, at this time, a journey to the West; certainly not for scenery, for it was a world of waste, desolate and dazzling whiteness, for a thousand unbroken miles. The trees were weighed down with snow, and the houses were thatched and half buried in it, and the mountains and valleys were like the vast waves of an illimitable sea, congealed with its yeasty foam in the wildest hour of a tempest. The eye lost its power in gazing on it. The "spirit-bird," that spread his refreshing green wings before the pained eyes of Thalaba, would have been an inestimable fellow traveller. The worth of the eyesight lay in the purchase of a pair of green goggles.

In the course of a week or too, after skimming over the buried scenery of half a dozen States, each as large as Great Britain, (more or less,) I found myself in a small town on the border of one of our western lakes. It was some twenty years since the bears had found it thinly settled enough for their purposes, and now it contained, perhaps, twenty thousand souls. The oldest inhabitant, born in the town, was a youth in his minority. With the usual precocity of new settlements, it had already most of the peculiarities of an old metropolis. The burnt stumps still stood about among the houses; but there was a fashionable circle, at the head of which were the lawyer's wife and the member of Congress's daughter; and people ate their peas with silver forks, and drank their tea with scandal, and forgave men's *many* sins and refused to forgive women's *one*, very much as in towns whose history is written in black letter. I dare say there were not more than one or two offences against the moral and Levitical law, fashionable in Europe, which had not been committed, with the authentic aggravations, in the town of ——; I would mention the name if this were not a true story.

Larry Wynn (now Lawrence Wynn, Esq.,) lived here. He had, as they say in the United States, "hung out a shingle" (*Londonice*, put up a sign) as attorney-at-law, and, to all the twenty thousand innocent inhabitants of the place, he was the oracle and the squire. He was besides colonel of militia, church-warden, and canal commissioner; appointments which speak volumes for the prospects of "rising young men" in our flourishing republic.

Larry was glad to see me—very. I was more glad to see *him*. I have a soft heart, and forgive a wrong generally, if it touches neither my vanity nor my loves. I forgot his neglect, and called him "Larry." By the same token he did *not* call me "Phil." (There are very few that love me, patient reader; but those who do, thus abbreviate my pleasant name of Philip. I was called after the Indian sachem of that name, whose blood runs in this tawny hand.) Larry looked upon me as a *man*. I looked on him, with all his dignities and changes, through the sweet vista of memory—as a *boy*. His mouth had acquired the pinched corners of caution and mistrust common to those who know their fellow-men; but I never saw it, unless when speculating as I am now. He was to me the pale-faced and melancholy friend of my boyhood; and I could have slept, as I used to do, with my arm around his neck, and feared to stir lest I should wake him. Had my last earthly hope lain in the palm of my hand, I could have given it to him, had he needed it, but to make him sleep; and yet he thought of me but as a stranger under his roof, and added, in his warmest moments, a "Mr." to my name! There is but one circumstance in my life that has wounded me more. Memory avaunt!

Why should there be no unchangeableness in the world? why no friendship? or why am I, and you, gentle reader, (for by your continuing to pore over these idle musings, you have a heart too,) gifted with this useless and restless organ beating in our bosoms, if its thirst for love is never to be slaked, and its aching self-fulness never to find flow or utterance? I would positively sell my whole stock of affections for three farthings. Will you say "*two?*"

"You are come in good time," said Larry, one morning, with a half-smile, " and shall be groomsman to me. I am going to be married."

" Married ?"

" Married."

I repeated the word after him, for I was surpised. He had never opened his lips about his unhappy lunacy, since my arrival, and I had felt hurt at this apparent unwillingness to renew our ancient confidence, but had felt a repugnance to any forcing of the topic upon him, and could only hope that he had outgrown or overcome it. I argued, immediately on this information of his intended marriage, that it must be so. No man, in his senses, I thought, would link an impending madness to the fate of a confiding and lovely woman.

He took me into his sleigh, and we drove to her father's house. She was a flower in the wilderness. Of a delicate form, as all my countrywomen are, and lovely, as *quite* all certainly are not, large-eyed, soft in her manners, and yet less timid than confiding and sister-like—with a shade of melancholy in her smile, caught, perhaps, with the " trick of sadness" from himself, and a patrician slightness of reserve, or pride, which nature sometimes, in very mockery of high birth, teaches her most secluded child—the bride elect was, as I have said before, a flower in the wilderness. She was one of those women we sigh to look upon as they pass by—as if there went a fragment of the wreck of some blessed dream.

The day arrived for the wedding, and the sleigh-bells jingled merrily into the village. The morning was as soft and genial as June, and the light snow on the surface of the lake melted, and lay on the breast of the solid ice beneath, giving it the effect of one white silver mirror, stretching to the edge of the horizon. It was exquisitely beautiful, and I was standing at the window in the afternoon, looking off upon the shining expanse, when Larry approached, and laid his hand familiarly on my shoulder.

"What glorious skating we shall have," said I, "if this smooth water freezes to-night!"

I turned the next moment to look at him; for we had not skated together since I went out, at his earnest entreaty, at midnight, to skim the little lake where we had passed our boyhood, and drive away the fever from his brain, under the light of a full moon.

He remembered it, and so did I; and I put my arm behind him, for the color fled from his face, and I thought he would have sunk to the floor.

"The moon is full to-night," said he, recovering instantly to a cold self-possession.

I took hold of his hand firmly, and, in as kind a tone as I could summon, spoke of our early friendship, and, apologizing thus for the freedom, asked if he had quite overcome his melancholy disease. His face worked with emotion, and he tried to withdraw his hand from my clasp, and evidently wished to avoid an answer.

"Tell me, dear Larry," said I.

"Oh God! *no!*" said he, breaking violently from me, and throwing himself with his face downward upon the sofa. The tears streamed through his fingers upon the silken cushion.

"Not cured? And does *she* know it?"

"No! no! thank God! not yet!"

I remained silent a few minutes, listening to his suppressed moans, (for he seemed heart-broken with the confession,) and pitying while I inwardly condemned him. And then the picture of that lovely and fond woman rose up before me, and the impossibility of concealing his fearful malady from his wife, and the fixed insanity in which it must end, and the whole wreck of her hopes and his own prospects and happiness—and my heart grew sick.

I sat down by him, and, as it was too late to remonstrate on the injustice he was committing toward her, I asked how he came to appoint the night of a full moon for his wedding. He gave up his reserve, calmed himself, and talked of it at last as if he were relieved by the communication. Never shall I forget the doomed pallor, the straining eye, and feverish hand, of my poor friend during that half hour.

Since he had left college he had striven with the whole energy of his soul against it. He had plunged into business—he had kept his bed, resolutely, night after night, till his brain seemed on the verge of phrensy with the effort—he had taken opium to secure to himself an artificial sleep ; but he had never dared to confide it to any one, and he had no friend to sustain him in his fearful and lonely hours ; and it grew upon him rather than diminished. He described to me, with the most touching pathos, how he had concealed it for years—how he had stolen out like a thief to give vent to his insane restlessness in the silent streets of the city at midnight, and in the more silent solitudes of the forest—how he had prayed, and wrestled, and wept over it—and finally, how he had come to believe that there was no hope for him, except in the assistance and constant presence of some one who would devote life to him in love and pity. Poor Larry! I put up a silent prayer in my heart that the desperate experiment might not end in agony and death.

The sun set, and, according to my prediction, the wind changed suddenly to the north, and the whole surface of the lake, in a couple of hours, became of the lustre of polished steel. It was intensely cold.

The fires blazed in every room of the bride's paternal mansion, and I was there early, to fulfil my office of master of ceremonies at the bridal. My heart was weighed down with a sad boding, but I shook off at least the appearance of it, and superintended the concoction of a huge bowl of punch, with a merriment which communicated itself, in the shape of most joyous hilarity, to a troop of juvenile relations. The house resounded with their shouts of laughter.

In the midst of our noise in the small inner room, entered Larry. I started back, for he looked more like a demon possessed than a Christian man. He had walked to the house alone in the moonlight, not daring to trust himself in company. I turned out the turbulent troop about me, and tried to dispel his gloom, for a face like his, at that moment, would have put to flight the rudest bridal party ever assembled on holy ground. He seized on the bowl of strong spirits which I had mixed for a set of hardy farmers, and, before I could tear it from his lips, had drank a quantity which, in an ordinary mood, would have intoxicated him helplessly in an hour. He then sat down with his face buried in his hands, and, in a few minutes, rose, his eyes sparkling with excitement, and the whole character of his face utterly changed. I thought he had gone wild.

"Now, Phil," said he, "now for my bride!" And, with an unbecoming levity, he threw open the door, and went half dancing into the room where the friends were already assembled to witness the ceremony.

I followed with fear and anxiety. He took his place by the side of the fair creature on whom he had placed his hopes of life, and, though sobered somewhat by the impressiveness of the scene, the wild sparkle still danced in his eyes, and I could see that every nerve in his frame was excited to the last pitch of tension. If he had fallen a gibbering maniac on the floor, I should not have been astonished.

The ceremony proceeded, and the first tone of his voice in the response startled even the bride. If it had rung from the depths of a cavern, it could not have been more sepulchral. I looked at him with a shudder. His lips were curled with an exulting expression, mixed with an indefinable fear ; and all the blood in his face seemed settled about his eyes, which were so bloodshot and fiery, that I have ever since wondered he was not, at the first glance, suspected of insanity. But oh ! the heavenly sweetness with which that loveliest of creatures promised to love and cherish him, in sickness and in health ! I never go to a bridal but it half breaks my heart ; and, as the soft voice of that beautiful girl fell with its eloquent meaning on my ear, and I looked at her, with lips calm and eyes moistened, vowing a love which I knew to be stronger than death, to one who, I feared, was to bring only pain and sorrow into her bosom, my eyes warmed with irrepressible tears, and I wept.

The stir in the room as the clergyman closed his prayer, seemed to awake him from a trance. He looked around with a troubled face for a moment ; and then, fixing his eyes on his bride, he suddenly clasped his arms about her, and, straining her violently to his bosom, broke into an hysterical passion of tears and laughter. Then suddenly resuming his self-command, he apologized for the over-excitement of his feelings, and behaved with forced and gentle propriety till the guests departed.

There was an apprehensive gloom over the spirits of the small bridal party left in the lighted rooms; and, as they gathered round the fire, I approached, and endeavored to take a gay farewell. Larry was sitting with his arm about his wife, and he wrung my hand in silence, as I said, "Good-night," and dropped his head upon her shoulder. I made some futile attempt to rally him, but it jarred on the general feeling, and I left the house.

It was a glorious night. The clear piercing air had a vitreous brilliancy, which I have never seen in any other climate, the rays of the moonlight almost visibly splintering with the keenness of the frost. The moon herself was in the zenith, and there seemed nothing between her and the earth but palpable and glittering cold.

I hurried home: it was but eleven o'clock; and, heaping up the wood in the large fireplace, I took a volume of "Ivanhoe," which had just then appeared, and endeavored to rid myself of my unpleasant thoughts. I read on till midnight; and then, in a pause of the story, I rose to look out upon the night, hoping, for poor Larry's sake, that the moon was buried in clouds. The house was near the edge of the lake; and, as I looked down upon the glassy waste, spreading away from the land, I saw the dark figure of a man kneeling directly in the path of the moon's rays. In another moment he rose to his feet, and the tall, slight form of my poor friend was distinctly visible, as, with long and powerful strokes, he sped away upon his skates along the shore.

To take my own Hollanders, put a collar of fur around my mouth, and hurry after him, was the work of but a minute. My straps were soon fastened; and, following in the marks of the sharp irons at the top of my speed, I gained sight of him in about half an hour, and, with great effort, neared him sufficiently to shout his name with a hope of being heard.

"Larry! Larry!"

The lofty-mountain shore gave back the cry in repeated echoes —but he redoubled his strokes, and sped on faster than before. At my utmost speed I followed on; and when, at last, I could almost lay my hand on his shoulder, I summoned my strength to my breathless lungs, and shouted again—"Larry! Larry!"

He half looked back, and the full moon at that instant streamed full into his eyes. I have thought since that he could not have seen me for its dazzling brightness; but I saw every line of *his* features with the distinctness of daylight, and I shall never forget them. A line of white foam ran through his half-parted lips; his hair streamed wildly over his forehead, on which the perspiration glittered in large drops; and every lineament of his expressive face was stamped with unutterable and awful horror. He looked back no more; but, increasing his speed with an energy of which I did not think his slender frame capable, he began gradually to outstrip me. Trees, rocks, and hills, fled back like magic. My limbs began to grow numb; my fingers had lost all feeling, but a strong northeast wind was behind us, and the ice smoother than a mirror; and I struck out my feet mechanically, and still sped on

For two hours we had kept along the shore. The branches of the trees were reflected in the polished ice, and the hills seemed hanging in the air, and floating past us with the velocity of storm-clouds. Far down the lake, however, there glimmered the just visible light of a fire, and I was thanking God that we were probably approaching some human succor, when, to my horror, the retreating figure before me suddenly darted off to the left, and made, swifter than before, toward the centre of the icy waste.

Oh, God! what feelings were mine at that moment! Follow him far I dared not; for, the sight of land once lost, as it would be almost instantly with our tremendous speed, we perished, without a possibility of relief.

He was far beyond my voice, and to overtake him was the only hope. I summoned my last nerve for the effort, and, keeping him in my eye, struck across at a sharper angle, with the advantage of the wind full in my back. I had taken note of the mountains, and knew that we were already forty miles from home, a distance it would be impossible to retrace against the wind; and the thought of freezing to death, even if I could overtake him, forced itself appallingly upon me.

Away I flew, despair giving new force to my limbs, and soon gained on the poor lunatic, whose efforts seemed flagging and faint. I neared him. Another struggle! I could have dropped down where I was, and slept, if there were death in the first minute, so stiff and drowsy was every muscle in my frame.

"Larry!" I shouted. "Larry!"

He started at the sound, and I could hear a smothered and breathless shriek, as, with supernatural strength, he straightened up his bending figure, and, leaning forward again, sped away from me, like a phantom on the blast.

I could follow no longer. I stood stiff on my skates, still going on rapidly before the wind, and tried to look after him, but the frost had stiffened my eyes, and there was a mist before them, and they felt like glass. Nothing was visible around me but moonlight and ice, and, dimly and slowly, I began to retrace the slight path of semicircles toward the shore. It was painful work. The wind seemed to divide the very fibres of the skin upon my face. Violent exercise no longer warmed my body, and I felt the cold shoot sharply into my loins, and bind across my breast like a chain of ice; and, with the utmost strength of mind at my command, I could just resist the terrible inclination to lie down and sleep. I forgot poor Larry. Life—dear life!—was now my only thought! So selfish are we in our extremity!

With difficulty I at last reached the shore, and then, unbuttoning my coat, and spreading it wide for a sail, I set my feet together, and went slowly down before the wind, till the fire which I had before noticed began to blaze cheerily in the distance. It seemed an eternity, in my slow progress. Tree after tree threw the shadow of its naked branches across the way; hill after hill glided slowly backward; but my knees seemed frozen together, and my joints fixed in ice; and, if my life had depended on striking out my feet, I should have died powerless. My jaws were locked, my shoulders drawn half down to my knees, and, in a few minutes more, I am well convinced, the blood would have thickened in my veins, and stood still, for ever.

I could see the tongues of the flames—I counted the burning fagots—a form passed between me and the fire—I struck, and fell prostrate on the snow; and I remember no more.

The sun was darting a slant beam through the trees when I awoke. The genial warmth of a large bed of embers played on my cheek, a thick blanket enveloped me, and beneath my head was a soft cushion of withered leaves. On the opposite side of the fire lay four Indians wrapped in their blankets, and, with her head on her knees, and her hands clasped over her ankles, sat an Indian woman, who had apparently fallen asleep upon her watch. The stir I made aroused her, and, as she piled on fresh fagots, and kindled them to a bright blaze with a handful of leaves, drowsiness came over me again, and I wrapped the blanket about me more closely, and shut my eyes to sleep.

I awoke refreshed. It must have been ten o'clock, by the sun. The Indians were about, busy in various occupations, and the woman was broiling a slice of deer's flesh on the coals. She offered it to me as I rose ; and, having eaten part of it with a piece of cake made of meal, I requested her to call in the men, and, with offers of reward, easily induced them to go with me in search of my lost friend.

We found him, as I had anticipated, frozen to death, far out on the lake. The Indians tracked him by the marks of his skate-irons, and, from their appearance, he had sunk quietly down, probably drowsy and exhausted, and had died of course without pain. His last act seemed to have been under the influence of his strange madness, for he lay on his face, turned from the quarter of the setting moon.

We carried him home to his bride. Even the Indians were affected by her uncontrollable agony. I cannot describe that scene, familiar as I am with pictures of horror.

I made inquiries with respect to the position of his bridal chamber. There were no shutters, and the moon streamed broadly into it : and, after kissing his shrieking bride with the violence of a madman, he sprang out of the room, with a terrific scream, and she saw him no more till he lay dead on his bridal bed.

INCIDENTS ON THE HUDSON.

M. Chabert, the fire-eater, would have found New York uncomfortable. I would mention the height of the thermometer, but for an aversion I have to figures. Broadway, at noon, had been known to *fry soles*.

I had fixed upon the first of August for my annual trip to Saratoga—and, with a straw hat, a portmanteau and a black boy, was huddled into the "rather-faster-than-lightning" steamer, "North America," with about seven hundred other people, like myself, just in time. Some hundred and fifty gentlemen and ladies, thirty seconds too late, stood "larding" the pine chips upon the pier, gazing after the vanishing boat through showers of perspiration. Away we "streaked" at the rate of twelve miles in the hour against the current, and, by the time I had penetrated to the baggage-closet, and seated William Wilberforce upon my portmanteau, with orders not to stir for eleven hours and seven minutes, we were far up the Hudson, opening into its hills and rocks, like a witches' party steaming through the Hartz in a cauldron.

A North-river steamboat, as a Vermont boy would phrase it, is *another guess sort o' thing from a Britisher*. A coal-barge and an eight-oars on the Thames are scarce more dissimilar. Built for smooth water only, our river boats are long, shallow, and graceful, of the exquisite proportions of a pleasure-yacht, and painted as brilliantly and fantastically as an Indian shell. With her bow just leaning up from the surface of the stream, her cut-water throwing off a curved and transparent sheet from either side, her white awnings, her magical speed, and the gay spectacle of a thousand well-dressed people on her open decks, I know nothing prettier than the vision that shoots by your door, as you sit smoking in your leaf-darkened portico on the bold shores of the Hudson.

The American edition of Mrs. Trollope (several copies of which are to be found in every boat, serving the same purpose to the feelings of the passengers as the escape-valve to the engine) lay on a sofa beside me, and taking it up, as to say, "I will be let alone," I commenced dividing my attention, in my usual quiet way, between the varied panorama of rock and valley flying backward in our progress, and the as varied multitude about me.

For the mass of the women, as far as satin slippers, hats, dresses and gloves could go, a Frenchman might have fancied himself in the midst of a transplantation from the Boulevards. In London, French fashions are in a manner Anglified: but an American woman looks on the productions of Herbault, Boivin, and Maneuri, as a translator of the Talmud on the inspired text. The slight figure and small feet of the race rather favor the resemblance; and a French milliner, who would probably come to America expecting to see bears and buffaloes prowling about the landing-place, would rub her eyes in New York, and imagine she was still in France, and had crossed, perhaps, only the broad part of the Seine.

The men were a more original study. Near me sat a Kentuckian on three chairs. He had been to the metropolis, evidently for the first time, and had "looked round sharp." In a fist of no very delicate proportions, was crushed a pair of French kid-gloves, which, if they fulfilled to him a glove's destiny, would flatter "the rich man" that "the camel" might yet give him the required precedent. His hair had still the traces of having been astonished with curling-tongs, and across his Atlantean breast was looped, in a complicated zig-zag, a chain that must have cost him a wilderness of racoon-skins. His coat was evidently the production of a Mississippi tailor, though of the finest English material; his shirt-bosom was ruffled like a swan with her feathers full spread, and a black silk cravat, tied in a kind of a curse-me-if-I-care sort of a knot, flung out its ends like the arms of an Italian *improvisatore.* With all this he was a man to look upon with respect. His under jaw was set up to its fellow with an habitual determination that would throw a hickory-tree into a shiver; but frank good-nature, and the most absolute freedom from suspicion, lay at large on his Ajacean features, mixed with an earnestness that commended itself at once to your liking.

In a retired corner, near the wheel, stood a group of Indians, as motionless by the hour together as figures carved in *rosso antico.* They had been on their melancholy annual visit to the now-cultivated shores of Connecticut, the burial place, but unforgotten and once wild home of their fathers. With the money given them by the romantic persons whose sympathies are yearly moved by these stern and poetical pilgrims, they had taken a passage in the "fire-canoe," which would set them two hundred miles on their weary journey back to the prairies. Their Apollo-like forms loosely dressed in blankets, their gaudy wampum belts and feathers, the muscular arm and close clutch upon the rifle, the total absence of surprise at the unaccustomed wonders about them, and the lowering and settled scorn and dislike expressed in their copper faces, would have powerfully impressed a European. The only person on whom they deigned to cast a glance was the Kentuckian, and at him they occasionally stole a look, as if, through all his metropolitan finery, they recognized metal with whose ring they were familiar.

There were three foreigners on board, two of them companions, and one apparently alone. With their coats too small for them, their thick-soled boots and sturdy figures, collarless cravats, and assumed unconsciousness of the presence of another living soul, they were recognizable at once as Englishmen. To most of the people on board they probably appeared equally well-dressed, and of equal pretensions to the character of gentlemen; but any one who has made observations between Temple Bar and the steps of Crockford's, would easily resolve them into two Birmingham bagmen "sinking the shop," and a quiet gentleman on a tour of information.

The only other persons I particularly noted were a southerner, probably the son of a planter from Alabama, and a beautiful girl, dressed in singularly bad taste, who seemed his sister. I knew the "specimen" well. The indolent attitude, the thin, but powerfully-jointed frame, the prompt politeness, the air of superiority acquired from constant command over slaves, the mouth habitually flexible and looking eloquent even in silence, and the eye in which slept a volcano of violent passions, were the marks that showed him of a race that I had studied much, and preferred to all the many and distinct classes of my countrymen. His sister was of the slightest and most fragile figure, graceful as a fawn, but with no trace of the dancing master's precepts in her motions, vivid in her attention to everything about her, and amused with all she saw; a copy of Lalla Rookh sticking from the pocket of her French apron, a number of gold chains hung outside her travelling habit, and looped to her belt, and a glorious profusion of dark curls broken loose from her combs and floating unheeded over her shoulders.

Toward noon we rounded West Point, and shot suddenly into the overshadowed gorge of the mountains, as if we were dashing into the vein of a silver mine, laid open and molten into a flowing river by a flash of lightning. (The figure should be Montgomery's; but I can in no other way give an idea of the sudden darkening of the Hudson, and the underground effect of the sharp over-hanging mountains as you sweep first into the Highlands.)

The solitary Englishman, who had been watching the Southern beauty with the greatest apparent interest, had lounged over to her side of the boat, and, with the instinctive knowledge that women have of character, she had shrunk from the more obtrusive attempts of the Brummagems to engage her in conversation, and had addressed some remark to him, which seemed to have advanced them at once to acquaintances of a year. They were admiring the stupendous scenery together, a moment before the boat stopped for a passenger, off a small town above the point. As the wheels were checked, there was a sudden splash in the water, and a cry of "a lady overboard!" I looked for the fair creature who had been standing before me, and she was gone. The boat was sweeping on, and, as I darted to the railing, I saw the gurgling eddy where something had just gone down; and, in the next minute, the Kentuckian and the youngest of the Indians rushed together to the stern, and clearing the taffrail with tremendous leaps, dived side by side into the very centre of the foaming circle. The Englishman had coolly seized a rope, and, by the time they reappeared, stood on the railing with a coil in his hand, and flung it with accurate calculation directly over them. With immovably grave faces, and eyes blinded with water, the two divers rose, holding high between them—a large pine fagot! Shouts of laughter pealed from the boat, and the Kentuckian, discovering his error, gave the log an indignant fling behind, and, taking hold of the rope, lay quietly to be drawn in: while the Indian, disdaining assistance, darted through the wake of the boat with arrowy swiftness, and sprang up the side with the agility of a tiger-cat. The lady reappeared from the cabin as they jumped dripping upon the deck; the Kentuckian shook himself, and sat down in the sun to dry; and the graceful and stern Indian, too proud even to put the wet hair away from his forehead, resumed his place, and folded his arms, as indifferent and calm, save the suppressed heaving of his chest, as if he had never stirred from his stone-like posture.

An hour or two more brought us to the foot of the Catskills, and here the boat lay alongside the pier, to discharge those of her passengers who were bound to the House on the mountain. A hundred or more moved to the gangway, at the summons to get ready, and among them the Southerners and the Kentuckian. I had begun to feel an interest in our fair fellow-passenger, and I suddenly determined to join their party—a resolution which the Englishman seemed to come to, at the same moment, and probably for the same reason.

We slept at the pretty village on the bank of the river, and, the next day, made the twelve hours' ascent, through glen and forest, our way skirted with the most gorgeous and odorent flowers, and turned aside and towered over by the trees whose hoary and moss-covered trunks would have stretched the conceptions of the "Savage Rosa.' Everything that was not lovely was gigantesque and awful. The rocks were split with the visible impress of the Almighty Power that had torn them apart, and the daring and dizzy crags spurred into the sky, as if the arms of a buried and phrensied Titan were thrusting them from the mountain's bosom. It gave one a kind of maddening desire to shout and leap—the energy with which it filled the mind so out-measured the power of the frame.

Near the end of our journey, we stopped together on a jutting rock, to look back on the obstacles we had overcome. The view extended over forty or fifty miles of vale and mountain, and, with a half-shut eye, it looked, in its green and lavish foliage, like a near and unequal bed of verdure, while the distant Hudson crept through it like a half-hid satin riband, lost as if in clumps of moss among the bryken banks of the highlands. I was trying to fix the eye of my companion upon West Point, when a steamer, with its black funnel and retreating line of smoke, issued as if from the bosom of the hills into an open break of the river. It was as small, apparently, as the white hand that pointed to it so rapturously.

"Oh!" said the half-breathless girl, "is it not like some fairy bark on an eastern stream, with a spice-lamp alight in its prow?"

"More like an old shoe afloat, with a cigar stuck in it," interrupted Kentucky.

As the sun began to kindle into a blaze of fire,—the tumultuous masses, so peculiar to an American sky, turning every tree and rock to a lambent and rosy gold,—we stood on the broad platform on which the house is built, braced even beyond weariness by the invigorating and rarified air of the mountain. A hot supper and an early pillow, with the feather beds and blankets of winter, were unromantic circumstances, but I am not aware that any one of the party made any audible objection to them; I sat next the Kentuckian at table, and can answer for two.

A mile or two back from the Mountain-House, on nearly the same level, the gigantic forest suddenly sinks two or three hundred feet into the earth, forming a tremendous chasm, over which a bold stag might almost leap, and above which the rocks hang on either side with the most threatening and frowning grandeur. A mountain-stream creeps through the forest to the precipice, and leaps as suddenly over, as if, Arethusa-like, it fled into the earth from the pursuing steps of a satyr. Thirty paces from its brink, you would never suspect, but for the hollow reverberation of the plunging stream, that anything but a dim and mazy wood was within a day's journey. It is visited as a great curiosity in scenery, under the name of Cauterskill Falls.

We were all on the spot by ten the next morning, after a fatiguing tramp through the forest; for the Kentuckian had rejected the offer of a guide, undertaking to bring us to it in a straight line by only the signs of the water-course. The caprices of the little stream had misled him, however, and we arrived half-dead with the fatigue of our cross-marches.

I sat down on the bald edge of the precipice, and suffered my more impatient companions to attempt the difficult and dizzy descent before me. The Kentuckian leaped from rock to rock, followed daringly by the Southerner; and the Englishman, thoroughly enamored of the exquisite child of nature, who knew no reserve beyond her maidenly modesty, devoted himself to her assistance, and compelled her with anxious entreaties to descend more cautiously. I lay at my length as they proceeded, and, with my head over the projecting edge of the most prominent crag, watched them in a giddy dream, half-stupified by the grandeur of the scene, half-interested in their motions.

They reached the bottom of the glen at last, and shouted to the two who had gone before, but they had followed the dark passage of the stream to find its vent, and were beyond sight or hearing.

After sitting a minute or two, the restless, but over-fatigued girl, rose to go nearer the fall, and I was remarking to myself the sudden heaviness of her steps, when she staggered, and, turning toward her companion, fell senseless into his arms. The closeness of the air below, combined with over-exertion, had been too much for her.

The small hut of an old man who served as a guide stood a little back from the glen, and I had rushed into it, and was on the first step of the descent with a flask of spirits, when a cry from the opposite crag, in the husky and choking scream of infuriated passion, suddenly arrested me. On the edge of the yawning chasm, gazing down into it with a livid and death-like paleness, stood the Southerner. I mechanically followed his eye. His sister lay on her back upon a flat rock immediately below him, and over her knelt the Englishman, loosening the dress that pressed close upon her throat, and with his face so near to hers as to conceal it entirely from the view. I felt the brother's misapprehension at a glance, but my tongue clung to the roof of my mouth ; for in the madness of his fury he stood stretching clear over the brink, and every instant I looked to see him plunge headlong. Before I could recover my breath, he started back, gazed wildly round, and seizing upon a huge fragment of rock, heaved it up with supernatural strength, and hurled it into the abyss. Giddy and sick with horror, I turned away and covered up my eyes. I felt assured he had dashed them to atoms.

The lion roar of the Kentuckian was the first sound that followed the thundering crash of the fragments.

"Hallo, youngster! what in tarnation are you arter? You've killed the gal, by gosh!"

The next moment I heard the loosened stones as he went plunging down into the glen, and, hurrying after him with my restorative, I found the poor Englishman lying senseless on the rocks, and the fainting girl, escaped miraculously from harm, struggling slowly to her senses.

On examination, the new sufferer appeared only stunned by a small fragment which had struck him on the temple, and the Kentuckian, taking him up in his arms like a child, strode through the spray of the fall, and held his head under the descending torrent till he kicked lustily for his freedom. With a draught from a flask, the pale Alabamian was soon perfectly restored, and we stood on the rock together, looking at each other like people who had survived an earthquake.

We climbed the ascent and found the brother lying with his face to the earth, beside himself with his conflicting feelings. The rough tongue of the Kentuckian to whom I had explained the apparent cause of the rash act, soon cleared up the tempest, and he joined us presently, and walked back by his sister's side in silence.

We made ourselves into a party to pass the remainder of the summer on the Lakes, unwillingly letting off the Kentuckian, who was in a hurry to get back to propose himself for the Legislature.

PEDLAR KARL.

" Which manner of digression, however, some dislike as frivolous and impertinent, yet I am of Beroaldus his opinion, such digressions do mightily delight and refresh a weary reader: they are like sawce to a bad stomach, and I therefore do most willingly use them."—BURTON.

" Bienheureuses les imparfaites ; à elles appartient le royaume de l'amour.—L'EVANGILE DES FEMMES.

I AM not sure whether Lebanon Springs, the scene of a romantic story I am about to tell, belong to New York or Massachusetts. It is not very important, to be sure, in a country where people take Vermont and Patagonia to be neighboring States; but I have a natural looseness in geography, which I take pains to mortify by exposure. Very odd that I should not remember more of the spot where I took my first lessons in philandering!—where I first saw you, brightest and most beautiful, A. D., (not *Anno Domini*,) in your white morning frocks and black French aprons!

Lebanon Springs are the rage about once in three years. I must let you into the secret of these things, gentle reader; for, perhaps I am the only individual existing, who has penetrated the mysteries of the four dynasties of American fashion. In the fourteen millions of inhabitants in the United States, there are precisely four authenticated and undisputed aristocratic families. There is one in Boston, one in New York, one in Philadelphia, and one in Baltimore. By a blessed Providence, they are not all in one State, or we should have a civil war and a monarchy in no time. With two hundred miles' interval between them, they agree passably, and generally meet at one or another of the three watering-places of Saratoga, Ballston, or Lebanon. Their meeting is as mysterious as the process of crystallization, for it is not by agreement. You must explain it by some theory of homœopathy or magnetism. As it is not known till the moment they arrive, there is, of course, great excitement among the hotel-keepers in these different parts of the country; and a village that has ten thousand transient inhabitants one summer, has, for the next, scarcely as many score. The vast and solitary temples of Pæstum, are gay in comparison with these halls of disappointment.

As I make a point of dawdling away July and August in this locomotive metropolis of pleasure, and rather prefer Lebanon, it is always agreeable to me to hear that the nucleus is formed in that valley of hemlocks. Not for its scenery; for really, my dear eastern hemispherian! you that are accustomed to what is called nature in England, (to wit, a soft park, with a gray ruin in the midst,) have little idea how wearily upon heart and mind presses a waste wilderness of mere forest and water, without stone or story. Trees in England have characters and tongues; if you see a fine one, you know whose father planted it, and for whose pleasure it was designed, and about what sum the man must possess to afford to let it stand. They are statistics, as it were—so many trees, *ergo*, so many owners, so rich. In America, on the contrary, trees grow, and waters run, as the stars shine—quite unmeaningly. There may be ten thousand princely elms, and not a man within a hundred miles worth "five pounds five." You ask, in England, who has the privilege of this water? or you say of an oak, that it stood in such a man's time: but, with us, water is an element unclaimed and unrented; and a tree dabbles in the clouds as they go over, and is like a great idiot, without soul or responsibility.

If Lebanon *had* a history, however, it would have been a spot for a pilgrimage, for its *natural* beauty. It is shaped like a lotus, with one leaf laid back by the wind. It is a great green cup, with a scoop for a drinking-place. As you walk in the long porticoes of the hotel, the dark forest mounts up before you like a leafy wall, and the clouds seem just to clear the pine-tops, and the eagles sail across from horizon to horizon, without lifting their wings, as if you saw them from the bottom of a well. People born there, think the world about two miles square, and hilly.

The principal charm of Lebanon to me, is the village of "Shakers," lying in a valley about three miles off. As Glaucus wondered at the inert tortoise of Pompeii, and loved it for its antipodal contrast to himself, so do I *affection* (a French verb that I beg leave to introduce to the English language) the Shaking Quakers. That two thousand men could be found in the New World, who would embrace a religion enjoying a frozen and unsympathetic intercouse with the diviner sex; and that an equal number of females could be induced to live in the same community, without locks or walls, in the cold and rigid observance of a creed of celibacy, is to me an inexplicable and grave wonder. My delight is to get into my stanhope after breakfast, and drive over and spend the forenoon in contemplating them at their work in the fields. They have a peculiar and most expressive physiognomy. The women are pale, or of a wintry redness in the cheek, and are all attenuated and spare. Gravity, deep and habitual, broods in every line of their thin faces. They go out to their labor in company with those serious men, and are never seen to smile; their eyes are all hard and stony, their gait is precise and stiff, their voices are of a croaking hoarseness, and nature seems dead in them. I would bake you such men and women in a brick kiln.

Do they think the world is coming to an end? Are there to be no more children? Is Cupid to be thrown out of business, like a coach-proprietor on a railroad? What can the Shakers mean, I should be pleased to know?

The oddity is that most of them are young. Men of from twenty to thirty, and women from sixteen to twenty-five, and often, spite of their unbecoming dress, good-looking and shapely, meet you at every step. Industrious, frugal, and self-denying, they certainly are; and there is every appearance that their tenets of difficult abstinence are kept, to the letter. There is little temptation beyond principle to remain; and they are free to go and come as they list: yet there they live on, in peace and unrepining industry, and a more thriving community does not exist in the Republic. Many a time have I driven over, on a Sunday, and watched those solemn virgins, dropping in, one after another, to the church; and when the fine-limbed and russet-faced brotherhood were swimming round the floor in their fanatical dance, I have watched their countenances for some look of preference, some betrayal of an ill-suppressed impulse, till my eyes ached again. I have selected the youngest and fairest, and have not lost sight of her for two hours; and she might have been made of cheese-parings, for any trace of emotion. There is food for speculation in it. Can we do without matrimony? Can we "strike," and be independent of these dear, delightful tyrants, for whom we "live, and move, and have our being?" Will it ever be no blot on our escutcheon, to have attained thirty-five as an unfructifying unit? Is that fearful campaign, with all its embarrassments and awkwardnesses, and inquisitions into your money and morals, its bullyings and backings-out, is it inevitable?

Lebanon has one other charm. Within a morning drive of the Springs, lies the fairest village it has ever been my lot to see. It is English in its character, except that there is really nothing in this country so perfect of its kind. There are many towns in the United States more picturesquely situated; but this, before I had been abroad, always seemed to me the very ideal of English rural scenery, and the kind of place to set apart for either love or death—for one's honeymoon or burial: the two periods of life which I have always hoped would find me in the loveliest spot of nature. Stockbridge lies in a broad, sunny valley, with mountains at exactly the right distance, and a river in its bosom, that is as delicate in its windings, and as suited to the charms it wanders among, as a vein in the transparent neck of beauty. I am not going into a regular description, but I have carried myself back to Lebanon; and the remembrance of the leafy mornings of summer, in which I have driven to that fair earthly paradise, and loitered under its elms, imagining myself amid the scenes of song and story in distant England, has a charm for me now. I have seen the mother-land; I have rambled through park, woodland, and village, wherever the name was old and the scene lovely; and it pleases me to go back to my dreaming days, and compare the reality with the anticipation. Most small towns in America have traces of *newness* about them. The stumps of a clearing, or freshly-boarded barns—something that is the antipodes of romance—meets your eye from every aspect. Stockbridge, on the contrary, is an old town, and the houses are of a rural structure; the fields look soft and genial, the grass is swardlike, the bridges picturesque, the hedges old, and the elms, nowhere so many and so luxuriant, are full-grown and majestic. The village is embowered in foliage.

Greatest attraction of all, the authoress of "Redwood" and "Hope Leslie," a novelist of whom America has the good sense to be proud, is the Miss Mitford of Stockbridge. A *man*, though a distinguished one, may have little influence on the town he lives in; but a remarkable *woman* is the invariable cynosure of a community, and irradiates it all. I think I could divine the presence of one almost by the growing of the trees and flowers. "Our Village" does not look like other villages.

II.

You will have forgotten that I had a story to tell, dear reader. I was at Lebanon in the summer of ——, (perhaps you don't care about knowing exactly when it was, and, in that case, I would rather keep shy of dates. I please myself with the idea, that time gets on faster than I.) The Springs were thronged. The President's lady was there, (this was under *our* administration, the Adams',) and all the four *cliques*, spoken of above, were amicably united—each other's beaux dancing with each other's belles, and so on. If I were writing merely for American eyes, I should digress once more to describe the distinctive characters of the south, north, and central representations of beauty; but it would scarcely interest the general reader. I may say, in passing, that the Boston belles were *à l'Anglaise*, rosy and *riantes;* the New-Yorkers, like Parisians, cool, dangerous, and dressy; and the Baltimoreans, (and so south,) like Ionians or Romans, indolent, passionate, lovely, and languishing. Men, women, and pine-apples, I am inclined to think, flourish with a more kindly growth in the fervid latitudes.

The campaign went on, and a pleasant campaign it was; for the parties concerned had the management of their own affairs—that is, they who had hearts to sell, made the bargain for themselves, (this was the greater number;) and they who disposed of this commodity gratis, though necessarily young and ignorant of the world, made the transfer in the same manner—in person. This is your true Republic. The trading in affections by reference—the applying to an old and selfish heart for the purchase of a young and ingenuous one—the swearing to your rents, and not to your faithful passion—to your settlements, and not your constancy—the cold distance between yourself and the young creature who is to lie in your bosom, till the purchase-money is secured, and the hasty marriage and sudden abandonment of a nature thus chilled, and put on its guard, to a freedom with one almost a stranger, that cannot but seem licentious, and cannot but break down that sense of propriety in which modesty is most strongly intrenched—this seems to me the *one* evil of your old worm-eaten monarchies that side the water, which touches the essential happiness of the well-bred individual. Taxation and oppression are but things he reads of in the morning paper.

This freedom of intercourse between unmarried people, has a single disadvantage—one gets so desperately soon to the end of the chapter! There shall be two hundred young ladies at the Springs in a given season, and, by the difference in taste, so wisely arranged by Providence, there will scarcely be, of course, more than four in that number, whom any one gentleman, at all difficult, will find within the range of his *beau ideal*. With these four he may converse freely, twelve hours in the day—more, if he particularly desires it. They may ride together, drive together, ramble together, sing together, be together from morning till night; and, at the end of a month passed in this way, if he escape a committal, as is possible, he will know all that are agreeable, in one large circle, at least, as well as he knows his sisters—a state of things that is very likely to end in his going abroad soon, from a mere dearth of amusement. I have imagined, however, the case of an unmarrying idle man—a character too rare, as yet, in America, to affect the general question. People marry as they die, in that country—when their time comes. *We must all marry*, is as much an axiom as *we must all die*, and eke as melancholy.

Shall we go on with the story? I had escaped for two blessed weeks, and was congratulating the susceptible gentleman under my waistcoat-pocket that we should never be in love with less than the whole sex again, when a German Baron Von ——— arrived at the Springs with a lame daughter. She was eighteen, transparently fair, and, at first sight, so shrinkingly dependent, so delicate, so childlike, that attention to her assumed the form almost of pity, and sprang as naturally and unsuspectingly from the heart. The only womanly trait about her was her voice, which was so deeply soft and full, so earnest and yet so gentle, so touched with subdued pathos and yet so melancholy calm, that, if she spoke after a long silence, I turned to her involuntarily with the feeling that she was not the same—as if some impassioned and eloquent woman had taken unaware the place of the simple and petted child.

I am inclined to think there is a particular tenderness in the human breast for lame women. Any other deformity in the gentler sex is monstrous; but lameness (the devil's defect) is "the devil." I picture myself, to my own eye, now—pacing those rickety colonnades at Lebanon with the gentle Meeta hanging heavily, and with the dependence inseparable from her infirmity, on my arm, while the moon (which was the moon of the Rhine to *her*, full of thrilling and unearthly influences) rode solemnly up above the mountain-tops. And that strange voice, filling like a flute with sweetness as the night advanced, and that irregular pressure of the small wrist in her forgotten lameness, and my own (I thought) almost paternal feeling as she leaned more and more heavily, and turned her delicate and fair face confidingly up to mine, and that dangerous mixture altogether of childlikeness and womanly passion, of dependence and superiority, of reserve on the one subject of love, and absolute confidence on every other—if I had not a story to tell, I could prate of those June nights and their witcheries till you would think

> "Tutti gli alberi del mondo
> Fossero penne,"

and myself "bitten by the dipsas."

We were walking one night late in the gallery running around the second story of the hotel. There was a ball on the floor below, and the music, deadened somewhat by the crowded room, came up softened and mellowed to the dark and solitary colonnade, and added to other influences in putting a certain lodger in my bosom beyond my temporary control. I told Meeta that I loved her.

The building stands against the side of a steep mountain high up above the valley, and the pines and hemlocks, at that time, hung in their primeval blackness almost over the roof. As the most difficult and embarrassed sentence of which I had ever been delivered died on my lips, and Meeta, lightening her weight on my arm, walked in apparently offended silence by my side, a deep-toned guitar was suddenly struck in the woods, and a clear, manly voice broke forth in a song. It produced an instant and startling effect on my companion. With the first word she quickly withdrew her arm; and, after a moment's pause, listening with her hands raised in an attitude of the most intense eagerness, she sprang to the extremity of the balustrade, and gazed breathlessly into the dark depths of the forest. The voice ceased, and she started back, and laid her hand hastily upon my arm.

"I must go," she said, in a voice of hurried feeling; "if you are generous, stay here and await me!" and in another moment she sprang along the bridge connecting the gallery with the rising ground in the rear, and was lost in the shadows of the hemlocks.

"I have made a declaration," thought I, "just five minutes too soon."

I paced up and down the now *too* lonely colonnade, and picked up the fragments of my dream with what philosophy I might. By the time Meeta returned—perhaps a half hour, perhaps an age, as you measure by her feeling or mine—I had hatched up a very pretty and heroical magnanimity. She would have spoken, but was breathless.

"Explain nothing," I said, taking her arm within mine, "and let us mutually forget. If I can serve you better than by silence, command me entirely. I live but for your happiness—even," I added after a pause, "though it spring from another."

We were at her chamber-door. She pressed my hand with a strength of which I did not think those small, slight fingers capable, and vanished, leaving me, I am free to confess, less resigned than you would suppose from my last speech. I had done the dramatic thing, thanks to much reading of you, dear Barry Cornwall! but it was not in a play. I remained killed after the audience was gone!

III.

The next day a new character appeared on the stage.

"*Such* a handsome pedlar!" said magnificent Helen ——— to me, as I gave my horse to the groom after a ride in search of hellebore, and joined the promenade at the well: "and what do you think? he sells only by raffle! It's so nice! All sorts of Berlin iron ornaments, and everything German and sweet; and the pedlar's smile's worth more than the prizes; and *such* a mustache! See! there he is!—and now, if he has sold all his tickets—will you come, Master Gravity?"

"I hear a voice you cannot hear," thought I, as I gave the beauty my arm, and joined a crowd of people gathered about a pedlar's box in the centre of the parterre.

The itinerant vender spread his wares in the midst of the gay assemblage, and the raffle went on. He was excessively handsome. A head of the sweet gentleness of Raphael's, with locks flowing to his shoulders in the fashion of German students, a soft brown mustache curving on a short Phidian upper lip, a large blue eye expressive of enthusiasm rather than passion, and features altogether purely intellectual—formed a portrait of which even jealousy might console itself. Through all the disadvantages of a dress suited to his apparent vocation, an eye the least on the alert for a disguise would have penetrated his in a moment. The gay and thoughtless crowd about him, not accustomed to impostors who were *more* than they pretended to be, trusted him for a pedlar, but treated him with a respect far above his station, insensibly.

Whatever his object was, so it were honorable, I inly determined to give him all the assistance in my power. A single glance at the face of Meeta, who joined the circle as the prizes were drawn—a face so changed since yesterday, so flushed with hope and pleasure, and yet so saddened by doubt and fear, the small lips compressed, the soft black eye kindled and restless, and the red leaf on her cheek deepened to a feverish beauty—left me no shadow of hesitation. I exchanged a look with her that I intended should say as much.

IV.

I know nothing that gives one such an elevated idea of human nature (in one's own person) as helping another man to a woman one loves. Oh last days of minority or thereabout! oh primal manhood! oh golden time, when we have let go all but the enthusiasm of the boy, and seized hold of all but the selfishness of the man! oh blessed interregnum of the evil and stronger genius! why can we not bottle up thy hours like the wine of a better vintage, and enjoy them in the parched world-weariness of age? In the tardy honeymoon of a bachelor (as mine will be, if it come ever, alas!) with what joy of paradise should we bring up, from the cellars of the past, a hamper of that sunny Hyppocrene!

Pedlar Karl and the "gentleman in No. 10" would have been suspected in any other country of conspiracy. (How odd, that the highest crime of a monarchy—the attempt to supplant the existing ruler—becomes in a republic a creditable profession!

You are a *traitor* here, a *politician* there!) We sat together from midnight onward, discoursing in low voices over sherry and sandwiches; and, in that crowded Babylon, his entrances and exits required a very conspirator-like management. Known as my friend, his trade and his disguise were up. As a pedlar, wandering about where he listed when not employed over his wares, his interviews with Meeta were easily contrived, and his lover's watch, gazing on her through the long hours of the ball from the crowd of villagers at the windows, hovering about her walks, and feeding his heart on the many, many chance looks of fondness given him every hour in that out-of-doors society, kept him comparatively happy.

"The baron looked hard at you to-day," said I, as he closed the door in my little room, and sat down on the bed.

"Yes; he takes an interest in me as a countryman, but he does not know me. He is a dull observer, and has seen me but once in Germany."

"How, then, have you known Meeta so long?"

"I accompanied her brother home from the university, when the baron was away, and for a long month we were seldom parted. Riding, boating on the Rhine, watching the sunset from the bartizan of the old castle-towers, reading in the old library, rambling in the park and forest—it was a heaven, my friend, than which I can conceive none brighter."

"And her brother?"

"Alas! changed! We were both boys then, and a brother is slow to believe his sister's beauty dangerous. He was the first to shut the doors against me, when he heard that the poor student had dared to love his highborn Meeta."

Karl covered his eyes with his hand, and brooded for a while in silence on the remembrances he had awakened.

"Do you think the baron came to America purposely to avoid you?"

"Partly, I have no doubt, for I entered the castle one night in my despair, when I had been forbidden entrance, and he found me at her feet in the old corridor. It was the only time he ever saw me, if, indeed, he saw me at all in the darkness; and he immediately hastened his preparations for a long-contemplated journey, I knew not whither."

"Did you follow him soon?"

"No, for my heart was crushed at first, and I despaired. The possibility of following them in my wretched poverty, did not even occur to me for months."

"How did you track them hither, of all places in the world?"

"I sought them first in Italy. It is easy, on the continent, to find out where persons are *not*, and after two years' wanderings, I heard of them in Paris. They had just sailed for America. I followed; but in a country where there are no passports, and no *espionage*, it is difficult to trace the traveller. It was probable only that they would be at a place of general resort, and I came here with no assurance but hope. Thanks to God, the first sight that greeted my eyes was my dear Meeta, whose irregular step, as she walked back and forth with you in the gallery, enabled me to recognize her in the darkness."

Who shall say the days of romance are over? The plot is not brought to the catastrophe, but we hope it is near.

V.

My aunt, Isabella Slingsby (now in heaven, with the "eleven thousand virgins," God rest her soul!) was at this time, as at all others, under my respectable charge. She would have said I was under hers—but it amounts to the same thing—we lived together in peace and harmony. She said what she pleased, for I loved her—and I *did* what I pleased, for she loved me. When Karl told me that Meeta's principal objection to an elopement was the want of a matron, I shut the teeth of my resolution, as they say in Persia, and inwardly vowed my unconscious aunt to this exigency. You should have seen Miss Isabella Slingsby to know what a desperate man may be brought to resolve on.

On a certain day, Count Von Raffle-off (as my witty friend and ally, Tom Fane, was pleased to call the handsome pedlar) departed with his pack and the hearts of all the dressing-maids and some of their mistresses, on his way to New York. I drove down the road to take my leave of him out of sight, and give him my last instructions.

How to attack my aunt was a subject about which I had many unsatisfactory thoughts. If there was one thing she disapproved of more than another, it was an elopement; and with what face to propose to her to run away with a baron's only daughter, and leave her in the hands of a pedlar, taking upon herself, as she must, the whole sin and odium, was an enigma I ate, drank, and slept upon, in vain. One thing at last became very clear—she would do it for nobody but *me*. *Sequitur*, I must play the lover myself.

I commenced with a fit of illness. What *was* the matter? For two days I was invisible. Dear Isabella! it was the first time I had ever drawn seriously on thy fallow sympathies, and, how freely they flowed at my affected sorrows, I shame to remember! Did ever woman so weep? Did ever woman so take antipathy to man as she to that innocent old baron for his supposed refusal of his daughter to Philip Slingsby? This revival of the remembrance shall not be in vain. The mignonette and roses planted above thy grave, dearest aunt, shall be weeded anew!

Oh that long week of management and hypocrisy! The day came at last.

"Aunt Bel!'

"What, Philip, dear?"

"I think I feel better to-day."

"Yes?"

"Yes. What say you to a drive? There is the stanhope."

"My dear Phil, don't mention that horrid stanhope. I am sure, if you valued my life—"

"Precisely, aunt—(I had taken care to give her a good fright the day before)—but Tom Fane has offered me his ponies and Jersey wagon, and that, you know, is the most quiet thing in the world, and holds four. So, perhaps——ehem!——you'll ask Meeta?"

"Um! Why, you see, Philip—"

I saw at once, that, if it got to an argument, I was *perdu*. Miss Slingsby, though a sincere Christian, never *could* keep her temper when she tried to reason. I knelt down on her footstool, smoothed away the false hair on her forehead, and kissed her. It was a fascinating endearment of mine, that I only resorted to on great emergencies. The hermit tooth, in my aunt's mouth, became gradually visible, heralding what in youth had been a smile; and, as I assisted her in rolling up her embroidery, she looked on me with an unsuspecting affection, that touched my heart. I made a silent vow, that if she survived the scrape into which she was being inveigled, I would be to her and her dog Whimsiculo, (the latter my foe and my aversion,) the soul of exemplary kindness for the remainder of their natural lives. I lay the unction to my soul, that this vow was kept. My aunt blessed me shortly before she was called to " walk in white," (she had, hitherto, walked in yellow;) and, as it would have been unnatural in Whimsiculo to survive her, I considered his " natural life" as ended with hers, and had him peacefully strangled on the same day. He lies at her feet, as usual—a delicate attention, of which (I trust in Swedenborg) her spirit is aware.

With the exception of " Tom Thumb" and " Rattler," who were of the same double-jointed family, of interminable wind and bottom, there was never, perhaps, such a pair of goers as Tom Fane's ponies. My aunt had a lurking hope, I believe, that the baron would refuse Meeta permission to join us; but either he did not think me a dangerous person, (I have said before he was a dull man,) or he had no objection to me as a son-in-law; which my aunt and myself (against the world) would have thought the natural construction upon his indifference. He came to the end of the colonnade to see us start; and, as I eased the ribands, and let the ponies off, like a shot from a crossbow, I stole a look at Meeta. The color had fled from cheek and lip, and the tears streamed over them like rain. Aunt Bel was on the back seat, *grace à Dieu*.

We met Tom at the foot of the hill, and I pulled up. He was the *best* fellow, that Tom Fane!

" Ease both the bearing reins," said I; " I am going up the mountain."

" The devil, you are!" said Tom, doing my bidding, however; " you'll find the road to the Shakers much pleasanter. What an odd whim! It's a perpendicular three miles, Miss Slingsby. I would as lief be hoisted up a well, and let down again. Don't go that way, Phil, unless you are going to run away with Miss Von——"

"Many a shaft at random sent,"

thought I; and waving the tandem lash over the ears of the ponies, I brought up the silk on the cheek of their malaprop master, and spanked away up the hill, leaving him in a range likely to get a fresh supply of fuel by dinner-time. Tom was of a plethoric habit; and if I had not thought he could afford to burst a blood-vessel better than two lovers to break their hearts, I should not have ventured on the bold measure of borrowing his horses for an hour, and keeping them a week. We have shaken hands upon it since; but it is my private opinion, that he has never forgiven me in his heart.

As we wound slowly up the mountain, I gave Meeta the reins, and jumped out to gather some wild flowers for my aunt. Dear old soul! the attention reconciled her to what she considered a very unwarrantable caprice of mine. What I *could* wish to toil up that steep mountain for? Well! the flowers *are* charming in these high regions!

"Don't you see my reason for coming, then, aunt Bella?"

"*Was* it for that, dear Philip?" said she, putting the wild flowers affectionately into her bosom, where they bloomed like broidery on saffron tapestry; "How considerate of you!" And she drew her shawl around her, and was at peace with all the world. So easily are the old made happy by the young! Reader, I scent a moral in the air!

We were at the top of the hill. If I was sane, my aunt was probably thinking I should turn here and go back. To descend the other side, and re-ascend and descend again to the Springs, was hardly a sort of thing one would do for pleasure.

"Here's a good place to turn, Philip," said she, as we entered a smooth, broad hollow, on the top of the mountain.

I dashed through it, as if the ponies were shod with *talaria*. My aunt said nothing, and luckily the road was very narrow for a mile, and she had a horror of a short turn. A new thought struck me.

"Did you ever know, aunt, that there was a way back around the foot of the mountain?"

"Dear, no; how delightful! Is it far?"

"A couple of hours, or so; but I can do it in less. We'll try;" and I gave the sure-footed Canadians the whip, and scampered down the hills, as if the rock of Sisyphus had been rolling after us.

We were soon over the mountain-range, and the road grew better and more level. Oh, how fast pattered those little hoofs, and how full of spirit and excitement looked those small ears, catching the lightest chirrup I could whisper, like the very spell of swiftness! Pines, hemlocks, and cedars—farmhouses and milestones, flew back like shadows. My aunt sat speechless in the middle of the back seat, holding on with both hands, in apprehensive resignation! She expected soon to come in sight of the Springs, and had, doubtless, taken a mental resolution, that if, please God, she once more found herself at home, she would never "tempt Providence," (it was a favorite expression of hers,) by trusting herself again behind such a pair of fly-away demons. As I read this thought in her countenance, by a stolen glance over my shoulder, we rattled into a village distant from Lebanon twenty miles.

"There, aunt," said I, as I pulled up at the door of the inn, "we have very nearly described a circle. Now, don't speak! if you do, you'll start the horses. There's nothing they are so much afraid of as a woman's voice. Very odd, isn't it? We'll just sponge their mouths now, and be home in the crack of a whip. Five miles more, only. Come!"

Off we sped again, like the wind, aunt Bel just venturing to wonder whether the horses wouldn't *rather* go slower. Meeta had hardly spoken; she had thoughts of her own to be busy with, and I pretended to be fully occupied with my driving. The nonsense I talked to those horses, to do away the embarrassment of her silence, would convict me of insanity before any jury in the world.

The sun began to throw long shadows, and the short-legged ponies figured like flying giraffes along the retiring hedges. Luckily, my aunt had very little idea of conjecturing a course by the points of the compass. We sped on gloriously.

"Philip, dear! hav'n't you lost your way? It seems to me we've come more than five miles since you stopped"—(ten, at least)—"and I don't see the mountains about Lebanon, at all!"

"Don't be alarmed, aunty, dear! We're very high, just here, and shall *drop down* on Lebanon, as it were. Are *you* afraid, Meeta?"

"*Nein!*" she answered. She was thinking in German, poor girl, and heart and memory were wrapped up in the thought.

I drove on almost cruelly. Tom's incomparable horses justified all his eulogiums; they were indefatigable. The sun blazed a moment through the firs, and disappeared; the gorgeous changes of eve came over the clouds; the twilight stole through the damp air, with its melancholy gray; and the whippoorwills—

birds of evening—came abroad, like gentlemen in debt, to flit about in the darkness. Everything was saddening. My own volubility ceased; the whiz of the lash, as I waved it over the heads of my foaming ponies, and an occasional "Steady!" as one or the other broke into a gallop, were the only interruptions to the silence. Meeta buried her face in the folds of her shawl, and sat closer to my side; and my aunt, soothed and flattered by turns, believed and doubted, and was, finally, persuaded, by my ingenious and well-inserted fibs, that it was only somewhat farther than I anticipated, and we should arrive "presently."

Somewhere about eight o'clock, the lights of a town appeared in the distance, and, straining every nerve, the gallant beasts whirled us in through the streets, and I pulled up, suddenly, at the door of an hotel.

"Why, Philip!" said my aunt, in a tone of unutterable astonishment, looking about her as if she had awoke from a dream, "this is Hudson!"

It was too clear to be disputed. We were upon the North River, forty miles from Lebanon, and the steamer would touch at the pier in half an hour. My aunt was to be one of the passengers to New York, but she was yet to be persuaded of it; the only thing now was, to get her into the house, and enact the scene as soon as possible.

I helped her out as tenderly as I knew how, and, as we went up stairs, I requested Meeta to sit down in a corner of the room, and cover her face with her handkerchief. When the servant was locked out, I took my aunt into the recess of the window, and informed her, to her very great surprise, that she had run away with the baron's daughter.

"Philip Slingsby!"

My aunt was overcome. I had nothing for it, but to be over come too. She sunk into one chair, and I into the other; and burying my face in my hands, I looked through my fingers to watch the effect. Five mortal minutes lasted my aunt's wrath; gradually, however, she began to steal a look at me, and the expression of resentment about her thin lips, softened into something like pity.

"Philip!" said she, taking my hand.

"My dear aunt!"

"What is to done?"

I pointed to Meeta, who sat with her head on her bosom, pressed my hand to my heart, as if to suppress a pang, and proceeded to explain. It seemed impossible for my aunt to forgive the deception of the thing. Unsophisticated Isabella! If thou hadst known that thou wert, even yet, one fold removed from the truth—if thou couldst have divined, that it was not for the darling of thy heart, that thou wert yielding a point only less dear to thee than thy maiden reputation—if it could have entered thy region of possibilities, that thine own house, in town, had been three days aired for the reception of a bride, run away with by thy ostensible connivance, and all for a German pedlar, in whose fortunes and loves thou hadst no shadow of interest—I think the brain in thee would have turned, and the dry heart in thy bosom have broken with surprise and grief!

I wrote a note to Tom, left his horses at the inn, and, at nine o'clock, we were steaming down the Hudson, my aunt in bed, and Meeta pacing the deck with me, and pouring forth her fears and her gratitude in a voice of music that made me almost repent my self-sacrificing enterprise. I have told the story gaily, gentle reader!

but there was a nerve ajar in my heart, while its little events went on.

How we sped, thereafter, dear reader!—how the consul of his majesty of Prussia was persuaded by my aunt's respectability, to legalize the wedding by his presence—how my aunt fainted dead away when the parson arrived, and she discovered who was *not* to be the bridegroom and who *was*—how I persuaded her she had gone too far to recede, and worked on her tenderness once more—how the weeping Karl, and his lame and lovely bride, lived with us till the old baron thought it fit to give Meeta his blessing and some money—how Tom Fane wished no good to the pedlar's eyes—and, lastly, how Miss Isabella Slingsby lived and died, wondering what earthly motive I could have for my absurd share in these events, are matters of which I spare you the particulars.

NIAGARA—LAKE ONTARIO—THE ST. LAWRENCE.

NO. I.—NIAGARA.

"He was born when the crab was ascending, and all his affairs go backward."—LOVE FOR LOVE.

It was in my senior vacation, and I was bound to Niagara for the first time. My companion was a specimen of the human race, found rarely in Vermont, and never elsewhere. He was nearly seven feet high, walked as if every joint in his body was in a hopeless state of dislocation, and was hideously, ludicrously, and painfully ugly. This whimsical exterior contained the conscious spirit of Apollo, and the poetical susceptibility of Keats. He had left his plough in the Green Mountains, at the age of twenty-five, and entered as a poor student at the university, where, with the usual policy of the college government, he was allotted to me as a compulsory chum, on the principle of breaking in a colt with a cart-horse. I began with laughing at him, and ended with loving him. He rejoiced in the common appellation of Job Smith—a synonymous soubriquet, as I have elsewhere remarked, which was substituted by his classmates for his baptismal name of Forbearance.

Getting Job away, with infinite difficulty, from a young Indian girl, who was selling moccasins in the streets of Buffalo, (a straight, slender creature, of eighteen, stepping about like a young leopard, cold, stern, and beautiful,) we crossed the outlet of Lake Erie, at the ferry, and took horses on the northern bank of Niagara River, to ride to the Falls. It was a noble stream—as broad as the Hellespont, and as blue as the sky; and I could not look at it, hurrying on headlong to its fearful leap, without a feeling almost of dread.

There was only one thing to which Job was more susceptible, than to the beauties of nature, and that was the beauty of woman. His romance had been stirred by the lynx-eyed Sioux, who took her money for the moccasins, with such haughty and thankless *superbia;* and full five miles of the river, with all the gorgeous flowers and rich shrubs upon its rim, might as well have been Lethe for his admiration. He rode along, like the man of rags you see paraded on an ass, in the carnival, his legs and arms dangling about in ludicrous obedience to the sidelong hitch of his pacer.

The roar of the Falls was soon audible; and Job's enthusiasm, and my own, if the increased pace of our Narraganset ponies meant anything, were fully aroused. The river broke into rapids, foaming furiously on its course; and the subterranean thunder increased, like a succession of earthquakes, each louder than the last. I had never heard a sound so broad and universal. It was impossible not to suspend the breath, and feel absorbed, to the exclusion of all other thoughts, in the great phenomenon with which the world seemed trembling to its centre. A tall, misty cloud, changing its shape continually, as it felt the shocks of the air, rose up before us; and, with our eyes fixed upon it, and our horses at a hard gallop, we found ourselves, unexpectedly, in front of a vast, white —— hotel! which suddenly interposed between the cloud and our vision. Job slapped his legs against the sides of his panting beast, and urged him on; but a long fence, on either side of the immense building, cut him off from approach; and, having assured ourselves that there was no access to Niagara, except through the back-door of the gentleman's house, who stood with hat off to receive us, we wished no good to his majesty's province of Upper Canada, and dismounted.

"Will you visit the Falls before dinner, gentlemen?" asked mine host.

"No, sir!" thundered Job, in a voice that, for a moment, stopped the roar of the cataract.

He was like an improvisatore who had been checked by some rude *birbone* in the very crisis of his eloquence. He would not have gone to the Falls that night to have saved the world. We dined.

As it was the first meal we had ever eaten under a monarchy, I proposed the health of the King; but Job refused it. There was an impertinent profanity, he said, in fencing up the entrance to Niagara, that was a greater encroachment on natural liberty than the 'stamp act.' He would drink to no King or parliament under which such a thing could be conceived possible. I left the table and walked to the window.

"Job, come here! Miss ——, by all that is lovely!"

He flounced up like a snake touched with a torpedo, and sprang to the window. Job had never seen the lady whose name produced such a sensation, but he had heard more of her than of Niagara. So had every soul of the fifteen millions of inhabitants between us and the Gulf of Mexico. She was one of those miracles of nature that occur, perhaps once, in the rise and fall of an empire—a woman of the perfect beauty of an angel, with the most winning human sweetness of character and manner. She was kind, playful, unaffected, and radiantly, gloriously beautiful. I am sorry I may not mention her name, for in more chivalrous times she would have been a character of history. Everybody who has been in America, however, will know whom I am describing, and I am sorry for those who have not. The country of Washington will be in its decadence before it sees such another.

She had been to the Fall, and was returning, with her mother, and a troop of lovers, who, I will venture to presume, brought away a very imperfect impression of the scene. I would describe her as she came laughing up that green bank, unconscious of everything but the pleasure of life in a summer sunset; but I leave it for a more skilful hand. The authoress of "Hope Leslie" will, perhaps, mould her image into one of her inimitable heroines.

I presented my friend, and we passed the evening in her dangerous company. After making an engagement to accompany her in the morning behind the sheet of the Fall, we said "Good-night" at twelve—one of us at least as many "fathoms deep in love" as a thousand Rosalinds. My poor chum! The roar of the cataract that shook the very roof over thy head was less loud to thee that night than the beating of thine own heart, I warrant me!

I rose at sunrise to go alone to the Fall, but Job was before me, and the angular outline of his gaunt figure, stretching up from Table Rock in strong relief against the white body of the spray, was the first object that caught my eye as I descended.

As I came nearer the Fall, a feeling of disappointment came over me. I had imagined Niagara a vast body of water descending as if from the clouds. The approach to most falls is *from below*, and we get an idea of them as of rivers pitching down to the plain from the brow of a hill or mountain. Niagara River, on the contrary, comes out from Lake Erie through a flat plain. The top of the cascade is ten feet, perhaps, below the level of the country around—consequently invisible from any considerable distance. You walk to the bank of a broad and rapid river, and look over the edge of a rock, where the outlet flood of an inland sea seems to have broken through the crust of the earth, and, by its mere weight, plunged with an awful leap into an immeasurable and resounding abyss. It seems to strike and thunder upon the very centre of the world, and the ground beneath your feet quivers with the shock till you feel unsafe upon it.

Other disappointment than this I cannot conceive at Niagara. It is a spectacle so awful, so beyond the scope and power of every other phenomenon in the world, that, I think, people who are disappointed there mistake the incapacity of their own conception for the want of grandeur in the scene.

The " hell of waters" below needs but a little red ochre to out Phlegethon Phlegethon. I can imagine the surprise of the gentle element, after sleeping away a se'nnight of moonlight in the peaceful bosom of Lake Erie, at finding itself of a sudden in such a coil! A Mediterranean sea-gull, which had tossed out the whole of a January in the infernal " yeast" of the Archipelago, (was I not all but wrecked every day between Troy and Malta in a score of successive hurricanes?)—I say, the most weather-beaten of sea-birds would look twice before he ventured upon the roaring cauldron below Niagara. It is astonishing to see how far the descending mass is driven under the surface of the stream. As far down towards Lake Ontario as the eye can reach, the immense volumes of water rise like huge monsters to the light, boiling and flashing out in rings of foam, with an appearance of rage and anger that I have seen in no other cataract in the world.

"A *nice* fall, as an Englishman would say, my dear Job"

"Awful!"

Halleck, the American poet (a better one never "strung pearls"), has written some admirable verses on Niagara, describing its effect on the different individuals of a mixed party, among whom was a tailor. The sea of incident that has broken over me in the years of travel, has washed out of my memory all but the two lines descriptive of its impression upon Snip:—

"The tailor made one single note—
'Gods! what a place to sponge a coat!'"

"Shall we go to breakfast, Job?"

"How slowly and solemnly they drop into the abysm!"

It was not an original remark of Mr. Smith's Nothing is so surprising to the observer as the extraordinary deliberateness with which the waters of Niagara take their tremendous plunge. All hurry and foam and fret, till they reach the smooth limit of the curve—and then the laws of gravitation seem suspended, and, like Cæsar, they pause, and determine, since it is inevitable, to take the death-leap with becoming dignity.

"Shall we go to breakfast, Job?" I was obliged to raise my voice, to be heard, to a pitch rather exhausting to an empty stomach.

His eyes remained fixed upon the shifting rainbows bending and vanishing in the spray. There was no moving him, and I gave in for another five minutes.

"Do you think it probable, Job, that the waters of Niagara strike on the axis of the world?"

No answer.

"Job!"

"What?"

"Do you think His Majesty's half of the cataract is finer than ours?"

"Much."

"For *water*, merely, perhaps. But look at the delicious verdure on the American shore, the glorious trees, the massed foliage, the luxuriant growth even to the very rim of the ravine! By Jove! it seems to me things grow better in a republic. Did you ever see a more barren and scraggy shore than the one you stand upon?"

"How exquisitely," said Job, soliloquizing, "that small green island divides the Fall! What a rock it must be founded on, not to have been washed away in the ages that these waters have split against it!"

"I'll lay you a bet it is washed away before the year two thousand—payable in any currency with which we may then be conversant."

"Don't trifle!"

"With time, or geology, do you mean? Isn't it perfectly clear from the looks of that ravine, that Niagara has *backed up* all the way from Lake Ontario? These rocks are not adamant, and the very precipice you stand on has cracked, and looks ready for the plunge.* It must gradually wear back to Lake Erie, and then there will be a sweep, I should like to live long enough to see. The instantaneous junction of two seas, with a difference of two hundred feet in their levels, will be a spectacle—eh, Job?"

* It has since fallen into the abyss—fortunately in the night, as visitors were always upon it during the day. The noise was heard at an incredible distance.

"Tremendous!"

"Do you intend to wait and see it, or will you come to breakfast?"

He was immovable. I left him on the rock, went up to the hotel and ordered mutton-chops and coffee, and, when they were on the table, gave two of the waiters a dollar each to bring him up *nolens-volens.* He arrived in a great rage, but with a good appetite, and we finished our breakfast just in time to meet Miss ——, as she stepped like Aurora from her chamber.

It is necessary to a reputation for prowess in the United States to have been behind the sheet of the Fall (supposing you to have been to Niagara). This achievement is equivalent to a hundred shower-baths, one severe cold, and being drowned twice—but most people do it.

We descended to the bottom of the precipice, at the side of the Fall, where we found a small house, furnished with coarse linen dresses for the purpose, and, having arranged ourselves in habiliments not particularly improving to our natural beauty, we reappeared—only three out of a party of ten having had the courage to trust their attractions to such a trial. Miss —— looked like a fairy in disguise, and Job like the most ghostly and diabolical monster that ever stalked unsepultured abroad. He would frighten a child, in his best black suit—but, with a pair of wet linen trowsers scarcely reaching to his knees, a jacket with sleeves shrunk to the elbows, and a white cap, he was something supernaturally awful. The guide hesitated about going under the Fall with him.

It looked rather appalling. Our way lay through a dense, descending sheet of water, along a slender pathway of rocks, broken into small fragments, with an overhanging wall on one side, and the boiling cauldron of the cataract on the other. A false step, and you were a subject for the "shocking accident" maker.

The guide went first, taking Miss ——'s right hand. She gave me her left, and Job brought up the rear, as they say in Connecticut, "on his own hook." We picked our way boldly up to the water. The wall leaned over so much, and the fragmented declivity was so narrow and steep, that, if it had not been done before, I should have turned back at once. Two steps more, and the small hand in mine began to struggle violently, and, in the same instant, the torrent beat into my eyes, mouth, and nostrils, and I felt as if I were drowning. I staggered a blind step onward, but still the water poured into my nostrils, and the conviction rushed for a moment on my mind that we were lost. I struggled for breath, stumbled forward, and, with a gasp that I thought was my last, sunk upon the rocks within the descending waters. Job tumbled over me the next instant, and, as soon as I could clear my eyes sufficiently to look about me, I saw the guide sustaining Miss —— who had been as nearly drowned as most of the subjects of the Humane Society, but was apparently in a state of resuscitation. None but the half-drowned know the pleasure of breathing.

Here we were, within a chamber that Undine might have coveted, a wall of rock at our back, and a transparent curtain of shifting water between us and the world, having entitled ourselves *à peu près* to the same reputation with Hylas and Leander, for seduction by the Naiads.

Whatever sister of Arethusa inhabits there, we could but congratulate her on the beauty of her abode. A lofty and well-lighted hall, shaped like a long pavilion, extended as far as we could see through the spray, and, with the two objections, that you could not have heard a pistol at your ear for the noise, and that the floor was somewhat precipitous, one could scarce imagine a more agreeable retreat for a gentleman who was disgusted with the world, and subject to dryness of the skin. In one respect it resembled the enchanted dwelling of the Witch of Atlas, where, Shelley tells us—

> "the invisible rain did ever sing
> A silver music on the mossy lawn."

It is lucky for Witches and Naiads that they are not subject to rheumatism.

The air was scarcely breathable—(if air it may be called, which streams down the face with the density of a shower from a watering-pot), and our footing upon the slippery rocks was so insecure, that the exertion of continually wiping our eyes was attended with imminent danger. Our sight was valuable, for surely, never was such a brilliant curtain hung up to the sight of mortals, as spread apparently from the zenith to our feet, changing in thickness and lustre, but with a constant and resplendent curve. It was what a child might imagine the arch of the sky to be where it bends over the edge of the horizon.

The sublime is certainly very much diluted when one contemplates it with his back to a dripping and slimy rock, and his person saturated with a continual supply of water. From a dry window, I think the infernal writhe and agony of the abyss into which we were continually liable to slip, would have been as fine a thing as I have seen in my travels; but I am free to admit, that, at the moment, I would have exchanged my experience and all the honor attached to it, for a dry escape. The idea of *drowning back* through that thick column of water, was at least a damper to enthusiasm. We seemed cut off from the living. There was a death between us and the vital air and sunshine.

I was screwing up my courage for the return, when the guide seized me by the shoulder. I looked around, and what was my horror to see Miss —— standing far in, behind the sheet, upon the last visible point of rock, with the water pouring over her in torrents, and a gulf of foam between us, which I could in no way understand how she had passed over.

She seemed frightened and pale; and the guide explained to me, by signs, (for I could not distinguish a syllable, through the roar of the cataract,) that she had walked over a narrow ledge, which had broken with her weight. A long, fresh mark, upon the rock, at the foot of the precipitous wall, made it sufficiently evident: her position was most alarming.

I made a sign to her, to look well to her feet; for the little island on which she stood was green with slime, and scarce larger than a hat; and an abyss, of full six feet wide, foaming and unfathomable, raged between it and the nearest foothold. What was to be done? Had we a plank, even, there was no possible hold for the further extremity; and the shape of the rock was so conical, that its slippery surface, evidently, would not hold a rope for a moment. To jump to her, even if it were possible, would endanger her life; and when I was smiling, and encouraging the beautiful creature, as she stood trembling and pale on her dangerous foothold, I felt my very heart sick within me.

The despairing guide said something, which I could not hear, and disappeared through the watery wall; and I fixed my eyes upon the lovely form, standing, like a spirit, in the misty shroud of the spray, as if the intensity of my gaze could sustain her upon her dangerous foothold. I would have given ten years of my life, at that moment, to have clasped her hand in mine.

I had scarce thought of Job, until I felt him trying to pass behind me. His hand was trembling, as he laid it on my shoulder, to steady his steps; but there was something, in his ill-hewn features, that shot an indefinable ray of hope through my mind. His sandy hair was plastered over his forehead, and his scant dress clung to him like a skin; but, though I recall his image *now*, with a smile, I looked upon him with a feeling far enough from amusement *then*. God bless thee, my dear Job! wherever, in this unfit world, thy fine spirit may be fulfilling its destiny!

He crept down carefully to the edge of the foaming abyss, till he stood with the breaking bubbles at his knees. I was at a loss to know what he intended. She, surely, would not dare to attempt a jump to his arms, from that slippery rock; and to reach her, in any way, seemed impossible.

The next instant he threw himself forward; and, while I covered my eyes in horror, with the flashing conviction that he had gone mad, and flung himself into the hopeless whirlpool, to reach her, she had crossed the awful gulf, and lay trembling and exhausted at my feet! He had thrown himself over the chasm, caught the rock barely with the extremities of his fingers, and, with certain death if he missed his hold, or slipped from his uncertain tenure, had sustained her with supernatural strength, as she walked over his body!

The guide, providentially, returned with a rope, in the same instant, and fastening it around one of his feet, we dragged him back through the whirlpool; and, after a moment or two to recover from the suffocating immersion, he fell on his knees, and we joined him, I doubt not, devoutly, in his inaudible thanks to God.

II.—LAKE ONTARIO.

The next bravest achievement to venturing behind the sheet of Niagara, is to cross the river, in a small boat, at some distance below the Phlegethon of the abyss. I should imagine it were something like riding in a howdah, on a swimming elephant. The immense masses of water, driven under by the Fall, rise, splashing and fuming, far down the river; and they are as unlike a common wave, *to ride*, as a horse and a camel. You are, perhaps, ten or fifteen minutes pulling across, and you may get two or three of these lifts, which shove you straight into the air, about ten feet, and then drop you into the cup of an eddy, as if some long-armed Titan had his hand under the water, and were tossing you up and down for his amusement. It imports lovers to take heed how their mistresses are seated; as all ladies, on these occasions, throw themselves into the arms of the nearest "hose and doublet."

Job and I went over to dine on the American side, and refresh our patriotism. We dined under a hickory-tree, on Goat Island, just over the glassy curve of the cataract; and, as we grew joyous, with our champagne, we strolled up to the point where the waters divide for the American and British Falls; and Job harangued the "mistaken gentleman on his right," in eloquence that would have turned a division in the House of Commons. The deluded multitude, however, rolled away in crowds, for the monarchy; and, at the close of his speech, the British Fall was still, by a melancholy majority, the largest. We walked back to our bottle, like foiled patriots; and soon after, hopeless of our principles, went over to the other side, too!

I advise all people, going to Niagara, to suspend making a note in their journal, till the last day of their visit. You might as well teach a child the magnitude of the heavens, by pointing to the sky with your finger, as comprehend Niagara in a day. It has to create its own mighty place in your mind. You have no comparison, through which it can enter. It is too vast. The imagination shrinks from it. It rolls in gradually, thunder upon thunder, and plunge upon plunge; and the mind labors with it, to an exhaustion such as is created only by the extremest intellectual effort. I have seen men sit and gaze upon it, in a cool day of autumn, with the perspiration standing on their foreheads, in large beads, from the unconscious, but toilsome agony of its conception. After haunting its precipices, and looking on its solemn waters, for seven days, sleeping with its wind-played monotony in your ears, dreaming, and returning to it, till it has grown the one object, as it will, of your perpetual thought, you feel, all at once, like one who has compassed the span of some almighty problem. It has stretched itself within you. Your capacity has attained the gigantic standard, and you feel an elevation, and breadth of nature, that could measure girth and stature with a seraph. We had fairly "done" Niagara. We had seen it by sunrise, sunset, and moonlight—from top and bottom—fasting and full—alone and together. We had learned, by heart, every green path on the island of perpetual dew, which is set like an imperial emerald, on its front, (a poetical idea of my own, much admired by Job;) we had been grave, gay, tender, and sublime, in its mighty neighborhood; we had become so accustomed to the base of its broad thunder, that it seemed to us like a natural property in the air, and we were unconscious of it for hours; our voices had become so tuned to its key, and our thoughts so tinged by its grand and perpetual anthem, that I almost doubted if the air, beyond the reach of its vibrations, would not agonize us with its unnatural silence, and the common features of the world seem of an unutterable and frivolous littleness.

We were eating our last breakfast there, in tender melancholy —mine for the Falls, and Job's for the Falls and Miss ——, to whom I had a half suspicion, that he had made a declaration.

"Job!" said I.

He looked up from his egg.

"My dear Job!"

"Don't allude to it, my dear chum," said he, dropping his spoon, and rushing to the window, to hide his agitation. It was quite clear.

I could scarce restrain a smile. Psyche, in the embrace of a respectable giraffe, would be the first thought, in anybody's mind, who should see them together. And yet, why should he not woo her—and win her, too? He had saved her life in the extremest peril, at the most extreme hazard of his own; he had a heart as high and worthy, and as capable of an undying worship of her, as she would find in a wilderness of lovers; he felt like a graceful man, and acted like a brave one, and was *sans peur et sans reproche*; and why should he not love like other men? My dear Job! I fear thou wilt go down to thy grave, and but one woman in this wide world will have loved thee—thy mother! Thou art the soul of a *preux chevalier*, in the body of some worthy gravedigger, who is strutting about the world, perhaps, in thy more proper carcass. These angels are o'er hasty in packing!

We got upon our horses, and had a pleasant amble before us, of fifteen miles, on the British side of the river. We cantered off stoutly for a mile, to settle our regrets; and then I pulled up, and requested Job to ride near me, as I had something to say to him.

"You are entering," said I, "my dear Job, upon your first journey in a foreign land. You will see other manners than your own, which are not, therefore, laughable, and hear a different pronunciation from your own, which is not, therefore, vulgar. You are to mix with British subjects, whom you have attacked vigorously in your school declamations, as "the enemy," but who are not, therefore, to be bullied in their own country, and who have certain tastes of their own, upon which you had better reserve your judgment. We have no doubt that we are the greatest country that ever was, is, or ever shall be; but, as this is an unpalatable piece of information to other nations, we will not stuff it into their teeth, unless by particular request. John Bull likes his coat too small. Let him wear it. John Bull prefers his beefsteak to a fricandeau. Let him eat it. John Bull will leave no stone unturned to serve you, in his own country, if you will let him. Let him. John Bull will suffer you to find fault, for ever, with king, lords, and commons, if you do not compare them invidiously with other governments. Let the comparison alone. In short, my dear chum, as we insist that foreigners should adopt our manners while they are travelling in the United States, we had better adopt theirs when we return the visit. They are, doubtless, quite wrong throughout; but it is not worth while to bristle one's back against the opinions of some score millions."

The foam disappeared from the stream, as we followed it on, and the roar of the Falls—

* * * "Now loud, now calm again,
Like a ring of bells, whose sound the wind still alters,"

was soon faint on our ears, and, like the regret of parting, lessened with the increasing distance, till it was lost. Job began to look around him, and see something else besides a lovely face in the turnings of the road; and the historian of this memorable journey, who never had but one sorrow that "would not budge with a filip," rose in his stirrups, as he descried the broad blue bosom of Lake Ontario, and gave vent to his feelings in (he begs the reader to believe) the most suitable quotation.

Seeing any celebrated water, for the first time, was always, to me, an event. River, waterfall, or lake, if I have heard of it, and thought of it, for years, has a sensible *presence*, that I feel, like the approach of a human being, in whom I am interested. My heart flutters to it. It is, thereafter, an acquaintance; and I defend its beauty, or its grandeur, as I would the fair fame and worth of a woman who had shown me a preference. My dear reader, do you love *water?* Not to drink—for, I own, it is detestable in small quantities; but water, running or falling, sleeping or gliding, tinged by the sunset glow, or silvered by the gentle alchymist of the midnight heaven? Do you love a lake? Do you love a river? Do you "affect" any one laughing and sparkling brook, that has flashed on your eye like a fay overtaken by the cock-crowing, and tripping away slily to dream-land? As you see four sisters, and but one to love; so, in the family of the elements, I have a tenderness for water.

Lake Ontario spread away to the horizon, glittering in the summer sun, boundless to the eye as the Atlantic; and, directly beneath us, lay the small town of Fort Niagara, with the steamer at the pier, in which we promised ourselves a passage down the St. Lawrence. We rode on to the hotel, which we found, to our surprise, crowded with English officers; and, having disposed of our Narragansets, we inquired the hour of departure, and what we could eat meantime, in as nearly the same breath as possible.

"Cold leg of mutton, and the steamboat's engaged, sir!"

The mercury, in Job's Britishometer, fell plump to zero. The idea of a monopoly of the whole steamer, by a Colonel and his staff, and no boat again for a week!

There was a government to live under!

We sat down to our mutton, and presently enter the waiter.

"Colonel ——'s compliments; hearing that two gentlemen have arrived, who expected to go by the steamer, he is happy to offer them a passage, if they can put up with rather crowded accommodations."

"Well, Job! what do you think now of England, politically, morally, and religiously? Has not the gentlemanlike courtesy, of one individual, materially changed your opinions upon every subject connected with the united kingdom of Great Britain?"

"It has."

"Then, my dear Job, I recommend you, never again to read a book of travels, without writing down on the margin of every bilious chapter, "probably lost his passage in the steamer," or, "had no mustard to his mutton," or, "could find no ginger-nuts for the interesting little traveller," or some similar annotation. Depend upon it, that dear, delightful Mrs. Trollope, would never have written so agreeable a book, if she had thriven with her bazaar in Cincinnati."

We paid our respects to the Colonel, and, at six o'clock in the evening, got on board. Part of an Irish regiment was bivouacked on the deck, and happier fellows I never saw. They had completed their nine years' service on the three Canadian stations, and were returning to the *ould* country, wives, children, and all

A line was drawn across the deck, reserving the after-quarter for the officers; the sick were disposed of, among the women in the bows of the boat; and the band stood ready to play the farewell air, to the cold shores of Upper Canada.

The line was cast off, when a boy of thirteen rushed down to the pier, and springing on board with a desperate leap, flew from one end of the deck to the other, and flung himself, at last, upon the neck of a pretty girl sitting on the knee of one of the privates.

"Mary, dear Mary!" was all he could utter. His sobs choked him.

"Avast with the line, there!" shouted the captain, who had no wish to carry off this unexpected passenger. The boat was again swung to the wharf, and the boy very roughly ordered ashore. His only answer was to cling closer to the girl, and redouble his tears; and by this time the Colonel had stepped aft, and the case seemed sure of a fair trial. The pretty Canadian dropped her head on her bosom, and seemed divided between contending emotions; and the soldier stood up, and raised his cap to his commanding officer, but held firmly by her hand. The boy threw himself on his knees to the colonel, but tried in vain to speak.

"Who's this, O'Shane?" asked the officer.

"Sure, my sweetheart, your honor."

"And, how dare you bring her on board, sir?"

"Och, she'll go to ould Ireland wid us, your honor."

"No, no, no!" cried the convulsed boy, clasping the Colonel's knees, and sobbing, as if his heart would break; "she's my sister! She isn't his wife! Father'll die, if she does! She can't go with him! She *sha'n't* go with him!"

Job began to snivel, and I felt warm about the eyes, myself.

"Have you got a wife, O'Shane?" asked the Colonel.

"Plase your honor, never a bit," said Paddy. He was a tight, good-looking fellow, by the way, as you would wish to see.

"Well; we'll settle this thing at once. Get up, my little fellow! Come here, my good girl! Do you love O'Shane well enough to be his wife?"

"Indeed I do, sir!" said Mary, wiping her eyes with the back of her hand, and stealing a look at the "six feet one," that stood as straight as a pike beside her.

"O'Shane! I allow this girl to go with us, only on condition that you marry her at the first place where we can find a priest. We will make her up a bit of a dowry, and I will look after her comfort as long as she follows the regiment. What do you say, sir? Will you marry her!"

O'Shane began to waver in his military position—from a full front face, getting to very nearly a right-about. It was plain he was taken by surprise. The eyes of the company were on him, however, and public opinion, which, in most human breasts, is considerably stronger than conscience, had its effect.

"I'll do it, your honor!" said he, bolting it out, as a man volunteers upon a "forlorn hope."

Tears might as well have been bespoken for the whole company. The boy was torn from his sister's neck, and set ashore, in the arms of two sailors; and poor Mary, very much in doubt whether she was happy or miserable, sank upon a heap of knapsacks, and buried her eyes in a cotton handkerchief, with a map of London upon it—probably a *gage d'amour* from the *desaving* O'Shane. I did the same myself, with a silk one, and Job *item*. *Item* the Colonel and several officers.

The boat was shoved off, and the wheels spattered away; but, as far as we could hear his voice, the cry came following on, "Mary, Mary!"

It rung in my ears all night, "Mary, Mary!"

I was up in the morning at sunrise, and was glad to escape from the confined cabin, and get upon deck. The steamer was booming on through a sea as calm as a mirror, and no land visible. The fresh dewiness of the morning air ashore played in my nostrils, and the smell of grass was perceptible in the wind; but, in all else, it was like a calm in mid ocean. The soldiers were asleep along the decks, with their wives and children, and the pretty runaway lay with her head on O'Shane's bosom, her red eyes, and soiled finery, showing too plainly how she had passed the night. Poor Mary! she has enough of following a soldier, by this, I fear.

I stepped forward, and was not a little surprised to see standing against the railing, on the larboard bow, the motionless figure of an Indian girl of sixteen. Her dark eye was fixed on the line of the horizon we were leaving behind, her arms were folded on her bosom, and she seemed not even to breathe. A common shawl was wrapped carelessly around her, and another glance betrayed to me, that she was in a situation soon to become a mother. Her feet were protected by a pair of once gaudy, but now shabby and torn moccasins, singularly small; her hands were of a delicate thinness, unusual to her race; and her hollow cheeks, and forehead marked with an expression of pain, told all I could have prophesied of the history of a white man's tender mercies. I approached very near, quite unperceived. A small burning spot, was just perceptible in the centre of her dark cheek; and, as I looked at her steadfastly, I could see a working of the muscles of her dusky brow, which betrayed, in one of a race so trained to stony calmness, an unusual fever of feeling. I looked around for the place in which she must have slept. A mantle of wampum-work, folded across a heap of confused baggage, partly occupied as a pillow by a brutal-looking and sleeping soldier, told, at once, the main part of her story. I felt for her, from my soul!

"You can hear the great waterfall no more," I said, touching her arm.

"I hear it, when I think of it," she replied, turning her eyes upon me as slowly, and with as little surprise, as if I had been talking to her an hour.

I pointed to the sleeping soldier. "Are you going with him to his country?"

"Yes."

"Are you his wife?"

"My father gave me to him."

"Has he sworn before the priest, in the name of the Great Spirit, to be your husband?"

"No." She looked intently into my eyes, as she answered, as if she tried, in vain, to read my meaning.

"Is he kind to you?"

She smiled, bitterly.

"Why, then, did you follow him?"

Her eyes dropped upon the burden she bore at her heart. The answer could not have been clearer if written with a sunbeam. I said a few words of kindness, and left her, to turn over in my mind how I could better interfere for her happiness.

III.—THE ST. LAWRENCE.

On the third evening we had entered upon the St. Lawrence, and were winding cautiously into the channel of the Thousand Isles. I think there is not, within the knowledge of the "all-beholding sun," a spot so singularly and exquisitely beautiful. Between the Mississippi and the Cimmerian Bosphorus, I *know* there is not, for I have pic-nicked from the Symplegades westward. The Thousand Isles of the St. Lawrence are as imprinted on my mind, as the stars of heaven. I could forget them as soon.

The river is here as wide as a lake, while the channel just permits the passage of a steamer. The islands, more than a thousand in number, are a singular formation of flat, rectangular rock, split, as it were, by regular mathematical fissures, and overflowed nearly to the tops, which are loaded with a most luxuriant vegetation. They vary in size, but the generality of them would about accommodate a tea-party of six. The water is deep enough to float a large steamer directly at the edge, and an active deer would leap across from one to the other, in any direction. What is very singular, these little rocky platforms are covered with a rich loam, and carpeted with moss and flowers, while immense trees take root in the clefts, and interlace their branches with those of the neighboring islets, shadowing the water with the unsunned dimness of the wilderness. It is a very odd thing to glide through in a steamer. The luxuriant leaves sweep the deck, and the black funnel parts the drooping sprays as it keeps its way; and you may pluck the blossoms of the acacia, or the rich chestnut flowers, sitting on the taffrail; and, really, a magic passage in a witch's steamer, beneath the tree-tops of an untrodden forest, could not be more novel and startling. Then the solitude and silence of the dim and still waters, are continually broken by the plunge and leap of the wild deer springing or swimming from one island to another, and the swift and shadowy canoe of the Indian glides out from some unseen channel, and, with a single stroke of his broad paddle, he vanishes, and is lost again, even to the ear. If the beauty-sick and nature-searching spirit of Keats is abroad in the world, "my basnet to a 'prentice cap," he passes his summers amid the Thousand Isles of the St. Lawrence! I would we were there, with our tea-things, sweet Rosa Matilda!

We had dined on the quarter-deck, and were sitting over the Colonel's wine, pulling the elm-leaves from the branches, as they swept saucily over the table, and listening to the band—who were playing waltzes, that, probably, ended in the confirmed insanity of every wild heron and red deer, that happened, that afternoon, to come within ear-shot of the good steamer Queenston. The paddles began to slacken in their spattering, and the boat came to, at the sharp side of one of the largest of the shadowy islands. We were to stop an hour or two, and take in wood.

Everybody was soon ashore for a ramble, leaving only the Colonel, who was a cripple from a score of Waterloo tokens, and your servant, reader, who had something on his mind.

"Colonel! will you oblige me, by sending for Mahoney? Steward, call me that Indian girl, sitting with her head on her knees, in the boat's bow."

They stood before us.

"How is this?" exclaimed the Colonel; "another! good God! these Irishmen! Well, sir! what do you intend to do with this girl, now that you have ruined her?"

Mahoney looked at her out of a corner of his eye, with a libertine contempt, that made my blood boil. The girl watched for his answer, with an intense but calm gaze into his face, that, if he had had a soul, would have killed him. Her lips were set firmly, but not fiercely, together; and, as the private stood looking from one side to the other, unable, or unwilling to answer, she suppressed a rising emotion in her throat, and turned her look on the commanding officer, with a proud coldness that would have become Medea.

"Mahoney!" said the Colonel, sternly, "will you marry this poor girl?"

"Never, I hope, your honor!"

The wasted and noble creature raised her burdened form to its fullest height, and, with an inaudible murmur bursting from her lips, walked back to the bow of the vessel. The Colonel pursued his conversation with Mahoney, and the obstinate brute was still refusing the only reparation he could make the poor Indian, when she suddenly reappeared. The shawl was no longer around her shoulders. A coarse blanket was bound below her breast, with a belt of wampum, leaving her fine bust entirely bare, her small feet trod the deck with the elasticity of a leopard about to leap on his prey, and her dark, heavily-fringed eyes, glowed like coals of fire. She seized the Colonel's hand, and imprinted a kiss upon it, another upon mine, and, without a look at the father of her child, dived, with a single leap, over the gangway. She rose directly in the clear water, swam with powerful strokes to one of the most distant islands; and, turning once more to wave her hand, as she stood on the shore, strode on, and was lost in the tangles of the forest.

THE CHEROKEE'S THREAT.

"Notre bonheur, mon cher, se tiendra toujours entre la plante de nos pieds et notre occiput ; et qu'il coûte un million par an ou cent louis, la perception intrinsique est la même au-dedans de nous."—LE PÈRE GORIOT.

THERE were a hundred students in the new class matriculated at Yale College, in Connecticut, in the year 18—. They were young men of different ages, and of all conditions in life, but less various in their mien and breeding, than in the characteristics of the widely-separate States from which they came. It is not thought extraordinary in Europe, that the French and English, the German and the Italian, should possess distinct national traits; yet one American is supposed to be like every other, though the two, between whom the comparison is drawn, were born and bred as far apart, and in as different latitudes, as the Highland cateran and the brigand of Calabria.

I looked around me with some interest, when, on the first morning of the term, the president, professors, and students of the university, assembled in the college chapel, at the sound of the prayer-bell, and, with my brother freshmen, I stood in the side aisle, closing up, with our motley, and, as yet, unclassical heads and habiliments, the long files of the more initiated classes. The berry-brown tan of the sun of Georgia, unblanched by study, was still dark and deep on the cheek of one; the look of command, breathing through the indolent attitude, betrayed, in another, the young Carolinian and slave-master; a coat of green, garnished with fur and bright buttons, and shaped less by the tailor than by the Herculean and expansive frame over which it was strained, had a taste of Kentucky in its complexion; the white skin, and red or sandy hair, cold expression, stiff black coat, and serious attention to the service, told of the Puritan son of New Hampshire or Vermont; and, perked up in his well-fitted coat, the exquisite of the class, stood the slight and metropolitan New-Yorker, with a firm belief in his tailor and himself written on his effeminate lip, and an occasional look at his neighbors' coats and shoulders, that might have been construed into wonder, upon what western river or mountain dwelt the builders of such coats and men!

Rather annoyed, at last, by the glances of one or two seniors, who were amusing themselves with my simple gaze of curiosity, I turned my attention to my more immediate neighborhood. A youth, with close, curling, brown hair, rather under-sized, but with a certain decision and nerve in his lip which struck me immediately, and which seemed to express, somehow, a confidence in himself which his limbs scarce bore out, stood with his back to the pulpit, and, with his foot on the seat, and his elbow on his knee, he seemed to have fallen, at once, into the habit of the place, and to be beyond surprise or interest. As it was the custom of the college to take places at prayers and recitation alphabetically, and he was likely to be my neighbor in chapel and hall for the next four years, I speculated rather more than I should else have done, on his face and manner; and, as the president came to his "Amen," I came to the conclusion, that, whatever might be Mr.

"S.'s" capacity for friendship, his ill-will would be very demonstrative and uncomfortable.

The term went on, the politics of the little republic fermented, and, as first appearances wore away, or peculiarities wore off by collision, or developed by intimacy, the different members of the class rose or fell in the general estimation, and the graduation of talent and spirit became more just and definite. The "Southerners and Northerners," as they are called, soon discovered, like the classes that had gone before them, that they had no qualities in common, and, of the secret societies which exist among the students in that university, joined each that of his own compatriots. The Carolianian or Georgian, who had passed his life on a plantation, secluded from the society of his equals, soon found out the value of his chivalrous deportment and graceful indolence, in the gay society for which the town is remarkable; while the Vermontese, or White-Mountaineer, "made unfashionably," and ill at ease on a carpet, took another line of ambition, and sat down with the advantage of constitutional patience and perseverance, to the study which he would find, in the end, a "better continuer," even in the race for a lady's favor.

It was the only republic I have ever known—that class of freshmen. It was a fair arena; and neither in politics, nor society, nor literature, nor love, nor religion, have I, in much searching through the world, found the same fair play or good feeling. Talk of our own republic!—its society is the very core and gall of the worst growth of aristocracy. Talk of the republic of letters!—the two graves by the pyramid of Caius Cestius laugh it to scorn. Of love!—of religion. What is bought and sold like that which has the name of the first? What is made a snare and a tool by the designing like the last? But here—with a government over us ever kindly and paternal, no favor shown, and no privilege denied; every equality in the competitors at all possible—age, previous education, and, above all, worldly position—it was an arena in which a generous spirit would wrestle, with an *abandon* of heart and limb he might never know in the world again. Every individual rising or falling by the estimation he exacts of his fellows, there is no such school of honor; each, of the many palms of scholarship, from the severest to the lightest, aiming at that which best suits his genius, and as welcome as another to the goal—there is no apology for the laggard. Of the feelings that stir the heart in our youth—of the few, the *very* few, which have no recoil, and leave no repentance—this leaping from the start-post of mind, this first spread of the encouraged wing in the free heaven of thought and knowledge, is recorded in my own slender experience as the most joyous and the most unmingled. He who has soiled his bright honor with the tools of political ambition—he who has leant his soul upon the charity of a sect in religion—he who has loved, hoped, and trusted, in the greater arena of life and manhood—must look back on days like these as the broken-winged eagle to the sky—as the Indian's subdued horse to the prairie.

II.

New Haven is not alone the seat of a university. It is a kind of metropolis of education. The excessive beauty of the town, with its embowered streets and sunny gardens, the refinement of its society, its central position and accessibility, and the facilities for attending the lectures of the college professors, render it a most desirable place of instruction in every department. Among others, the female schools of the place have a great reputation, and this, which, in Europe, or with a European state of society, would probably be an evil, is, from the simple and frank character of manners in America, a mutual and decided advantage. The daughters of the first families of the country are sent here, committed for two, three, and four years, to the exclusive care of the head of the establishment, and (as one of the privileges and advantages of the school) associating freely with the general society of the town, the male part, of course, composed principally of students. A more easy and liberal intercourse exists in no society in the world, and, in no society that I have ever seen, is the tone of morals and manners so high and unexceptionable. Attachments are often formed, and little harm is thought of it; and, unless it is a very strong case of disparity or objection, no obstacle is thrown in the way of the common intercourse between lovers; and the lady returns to her family, and the gentleman senior disappears with his degree, and they meet and marry—if they like. If they do not, the lady stands as well in the matrimonial market as ever, and the gentleman (unlike his horse) is not damaged by having been on his knees.

Like "Le Noir Fainéant," at the tournament, my friend St. John seemed more a looker-on than an actor in the various pursuits of the university. A sudden interference in a quarrel, in which a brother freshman was contending against odds, enlightened the class as to his spirit and personal strength; he acquitted himself at recitations with the air of self-contempt for such easy excellence; he dressed plainly, but with instinctive taste; and, at the end of the first term, having shrunk from all intimacy, and lived alone with his books and a kind of trapper's dog he had brought with him from the west, he had acquired an ascendancy in the opinion of the class for which no one could well account, but to which every one unhesitatingly assented.

We returned after our first short vacation, and of my hundred classmates there was but one whom I much cared to meet again. St. John had passed the vacation in his rooms, and my evident pleasure at meeting him, for the first time, seemed to open his heart to me. He invited me to breakfast with him. By favor seldom granted to a freshman, he had a lodging in the town—the rest of the class being compelled to live with a chum in the college buildings. I found his rooms—(I was the first of the class who had entered them)—more luxuriously furnished than I had expected from the simplicity of his appearance, but his books, not many, but select, and (what is in America an expensive luxury) in the best English editions and superbly bound, excited most my envy and surprise. How he should have acquired tastes of such ultra-civilization in the forests of the west was a mystery that remained to be solved.

III.

At the extremity of a green lane in the outer skirt of the fashionable suburb of New Haven stood a rambling old Dutch house, built probably when the cattle of Mynheer grazed over the present site of the town. It was a wilderness of irregular rooms, of no describable shape in its exterior, and, from its southern balcony, to use an expressive Gallicism, "gave upon the bay." Long Island Sound, the great highway frôm the northern Atlantic to New York, weltered in alternate lead and silver (oftener like the brighter metal, for the climate is divine), between the curving lip of the bay and the interminable and sandy shore of the island some six leagues distant; the procession of ships and steamers stole past with an imperceptible progress; the ceaseless bells of the college chapel came deadened through the trees from behind, and (the day being one of golden autumn, and myself and St. John waiting while black Agatha answered the door-bell) the sun-steeped precipice of East Rock, with its tiara of blood-red maples flushing like a Turk's banner in the light, drew from us, both, a truant wish for a ramble and a holyday. I shall have more to say anon of the foliage of an American October: but just now, while I remember it, I wish to record a belief of my own, that if, as philosophy supposes, we have lived other lives—(if

"our star
Hath had elsewhere its setting,
And cometh from afar")—

it is surely in the days tempered like the one I am remembering and describing—profoundly serene, sunny as the top of Olympus, heavenly pure, holy, and more invigorating and intoxicating than luxurious or balmy; the sort of air that the visiting angels might have brought with them to the tents of Abraham—it is on such days, I would record, that my own memory steps back over the dim threshold of life (so it seems to me), and on such days only. It is worth the translation of our youth and our household gods to a sunnier land, if it were alone for those immortal revelations.

In a few minutes from this time were assembled, in Mrs. Ilfrington's drawing-room, the six or seven young ladies of my more particular acquaintance among her pupils, of whom one was a new-comer, and the object of my mingled curiosity and admiration. It was the one day of the week when morning visitors were admitted, and I was there, in compliance with an unexpected request from my friend, to present him to the agreeable circle of Mrs. Ilfrington. As an *habitué* in her family, this excellent lady had taken occasion to introduce to me, a week or two before, the newcomer of whom I have spoken above—a departure from the ordinary rule of the establishment, which I felt to be a compliment, and which gave me, I presumed, a tacit claim to mix myself up in that young lady's destiny as deeply as I should find agreeable. The newcomer was the daughter of an Indian chief, and her name was Nunu.

The wrongs of civilization to the noble aborigines of America are a subject of much poetical feeling in the United States, and will ultimately become the poetry of the nation. At present the sentiment takes occasionally a tangible shape, and the transmission of the daughter of a Cherokee chief to New Haven, to be educated at the expense of the government, and of several young men of the same high birth to different colleges, will be recorded among the evidences in history that we did not plough the bones of their fathers into our fields without some feelings of compunction. Nunu had come to the seaboard under the charge of a female missionary, whose pupil she had been in one of the native schools of the west, and was destined, though a chief's daughter, to return as a teacher to her tribe when she should have mastered some of the higher accomplishments of her sex. She was an apt scholar, but her settled melancholy, when away from her books, had determined Mrs. Ilfrington to try the effect of a little society upon her, and hence my privilege to ask for her appearance in the drawing-room.

As we strolled down in the alternate shade and sunshine of the road, I had been a little piqued at the want of interest, and the manner-of-course, with which St. John had received my animated descriptions of the personal beauty of the Cherokee.

"I have hunted with the tribe," was his only answer, "and know their features."

"But she is not like them," I replied, with a tone of some im patience; "she is the beau ideal of a red skin, but it is with the softened features of an Arab or an Egyptian. She is more wil lowy than erect, and has no higher cheek-bones than the plaster Venus in your chambers. If it were not for the lambent fire in her eye, you might take her, in the sculptured pose of her attitudes, for an immortal bronze of Cleopatra. I tell you she is divine."

St. John called to his dog, and we turned along the green bank above the beach, with Mrs. Ilfrington's house in view, and so opens a new chapter in my story.

IV.

In the united pictures of Paul Veronese and Raphael, steeped as their colors seem to have been in the divinest age of Venetian and Roman female beauty, I have scarcely found so many lovely women, of so different models and so perfect, as were assembled during my sophomore year under the roof of Mrs. Ilfrington. They went about in their evening walks, graceful and angelic, but, like the virgin pearls of the sea, they poured the light of their loveliness on the vegetating oysters about them, and no diver of fashion had yet taught them their value. Ignorant myself, in those days, of the scale of beauty, their features are enamelled in my memory, and I have tried insensibly by that standard, (and found wanting), of every court in Europe the dames most worshipped and highest born. Queen of the Sicilies, loveliest in your own realm of sunshine and passion! Pale and transpaparent Princess—pearl of the court of Florence—than whom the creations on the immortal walls of the Pitti less discipline our eye for the shapes of heaven! Gipsy of the Pactolus! Jewess of the Thracian Gallipolis! Bright and gifted cynosure of the aristocracy of England!—ye are five women I have seen in as many years' wandering over the world, lived to gaze upon, and live to remember and admire—a constellation, I almost believe, that has absorbed all the intensest light of the beauty of a hemisphere—yet, with your pictures colored to life in my memory, and the pride of rank and state thrown over most of you like an elevating charm, I go back to the school of Mrs. Ilfrington, and (smile if you will!) they were as lovely, and stately, and as worthy of the worship of the world.

I introduced St. John to the young ladies as they came in. Having never seen him, except in the presence of men, I was a little curious to know whether his singular *aplomb* would serve him as well with the other sex, of which I was aware he had had very slender experience. My attention was distracted, at the moment of mentioning his name to a lovely little Georgian (with eyes full of the liquid sunshine of the south), by a sudden bark of joy from the dog, who had been left in the hall; and, as the door opened, and the slight and graceful Indian girl entered the room, the usually unsocial animal sprang bounding in, lavishing caresses on her, and seemingly wild with the delight of a recognition.

In the confusion of taking the dog from the room, I had again lost the moment of remarking St. John's manner, and, on the entrance of Mrs. Ilfrington, Nunu was sitting calmly by the piano, and my friend was talking in a quiet undertone with the passionate Georgian.

"I must apologize for my dog," said St. John, bowing gracefully to the mistress of the house; "he was bred by Indians, and the sight of a Cherokee reminded him of happier days—as it did his master."

Nunu turned her eyes quickly upon him, but immediately resumed her apparent deep study of the abstruse figures in the Kidderminster carpet.

"You are well arrived, young gentlemen," said Mrs. Ilfrington; "we press you into our service for a botanical ramble. Mr. Slingsby is at leisure, and will be delighted, I am sure. Shall I say as much for you, Mr. St. John?"

St. John bowed, and the ladies left the room for their bonnets—Mrs. Ilfrington last. The door was scarcely closed when Nunu reappeared, and, checking herself with a sudden feeling at the first step over the threshold, stood gazing at St. John, evidently under very powerful emotion.

"Nunu!" he said, smiling slowly and unwillingly, and holding out his hand with the air of one who forgives an offence.

She sprang upon his bosom with the bound of a leveret, and, between her fast kisses, broke the endearing epithets of her native tongue, in words that I only understood by their passionate and thrilling accent. The language of the heart is universal.

The fair scholars came in, one after another, and we were soon on our way through the green fields to the flowery mountain-side of East Rock; Mrs. Ilfrington's arm and conversation having fallen to my share, and St. John rambling at large with the rest of the party, but more particularly beset by Miss Temple, whose Christian name was Isabella, and whose Christian charity had no bowels for broken hearts.

The most sociable individuals of the party for a while were Nunu and Lash; the dog's recollections of the past, seeming, like those of wiser animals, more agreeable than the present. The Cherokee astonished Mrs. Ilfrington by an abandonment to joy and frolic which she had never displayed before—sometimes fairly outrunning the dog at full speed, and sometimes sitting down breathless upon a green bank, while the rude creature overpowered her with his caresses. The scene gave origin to a grave discussion between that well-instructed lady and myself, upon the singular force of childish association—the extraordinary intimacy between the Indian and the trapper's dog being explained satisfactorily (to her, at least) on that attractive principle. Had she but seen Nunu spring into the bosom of my friend, half an hour before, she might have added a material corollary to her proposition. If the dog and the chief's daughter were not old friends, the chief's daughter and St. John certainly *were.*

As well as I could judge by the motions of two people walking before me, St. John was advancing fast in the favor and acquaintance of the graceful Georgian. Her southern indolence was probably an apology in Mrs. Ilfrington's eyes for leaning heavily on her companion's arm; but, in a momentary halt, the capricious beauty disembarrassed herself of the bright scarf that had floated over her shoulders, and bound it playfully around his waist. This was rather strong, on a first acquaintance, and Mrs. Ilfrington was of that opinion.

"Miss Temple!" said she, advancing to whisper a reproof in the beauty's ear.

Before she had taken a second step, Nunu bounded over the low hedge, followed by the dog, with whom she had been chasing a butterfly, and, springing upon St. John with eyes that flashed fire, she tore the scarf into shreds, and stood trembling and pale, with her feet on the silken fragments.

"Madam!" said St. John, advancing to Mrs. Ilfrington, after

casting on the Cherokee a look of surprise and displeasure, " I should have told you before that your pupil and myself are not new acquaintances. Her father is my friend. I have hunted with the tribe, and have hitherto looked upon Nunu as a child. You will believe me, I trust, when I say her conduct surprises me, and I beg to assure you that any influence I may have over her will be in accordance with your own wishes exclusively.

His tone was cold, and Nunu listened with fixed lips and frowning eyes.

" Have you seen her since her arrival?" asked Mrs. Ilfrington.

" My dog brought me yesterday the first intelligence that she was here: he returned from his morning ramble with a string of wampum about his neck, which had the mark of the tribe. He was her gift," he added, patting the head of the dog, and looking with a softened expression at Nunu, who dropped her head upon her bosom, and walked on in tears.

V.

The chain of the Green Mountains, after a gallop of some five hundred miles, from Canada to Connecticut, suddenly pulls up on the shore of Long-Island Sound, and stands rearing with a bristling mane of pine-trees, three hundred feet in air, as if checked in mid career by the sea. Standing on the brink of this bold precipice, you have the bald face of the rock in a sheer perpendicular below you; and, spreading away from the broken masses at its feet, lies an emerald meadow, inlaid with a crystal and rambling river, across which, at a distance of a mile or two, rise the spires of the university, from what, else, were a thick-serried wilderness of elms. Back from the edge of the precipice extends a wild forest of hemlock and fir, ploughed on its northren side by a mountain-torrent, whose bed of marl, dry and overhung with trees in the summer, serves as a path and a guide from the plain to the summit. It were a toilsome ascent but for that smooth and hard pavement, and the impervious and green thatch of pine tassels overhung.

Antiquity in America extends no farther back than the days of Cromwell, and East Rock is traditionary ground with us—for there harbored the regicides Whalley and Goffe, and many a breath-hushing tale is told of them over the smouldering log-fires of Connecticut. Not to rob the historian, I pass on to say, that this cavernous path to the mountain-top was the resort, in the holyday summer afternoons, of most of the poetical and otherwise well-disposed gentlemen sophomores; and, on the day of which I speak, of Mrs. Ilfrington and her seven-and-twenty lovely scholars. The kind mistress ascended with the assistance of my arm, and St. John drew stoutly between Miss Temple and a fat young lady with an incipient asthma. Nunu had not been seen since the first cluster of hanging flowers had hidden her from our sight, as she bounded upward.

The hour or two of slanting sunshine, pouring in upon the summit of the precipice from the west, had been sufficient to induce a fine and silken moss to show its fibres and small blossoms above the carpet of pine-tassels; and, emerging from the brown shadow of the wood, you stood on a verdant platform, the foliage of sighing trees overhead, a fairies' velvet beneath you, and a view below that you may as well (if you would not die in your ignorance) make a voyage or journey to see.

We found Nunu lying thoughtfully near the brink of the precipice, and gazing off over the waters of the Sound, as if she watched the coming or going of a friend under the white sails that spotted its bosom. We recovered our breath in silence, I alone, perhaps, of that considerable company, gazing with admiration at the lithe and unconscious figure of grace lying in the attitude of the Grecian Hermaphrodite on the brow of the rock before us. Her eyes were moist and motionless with abstraction, her lips just perceptibly curved in an expression of mingled pride and sorrow, her small hand buried and clinched in the moss, and her left foot and ankle, models of spirited symmetry, escaping carelessly from her dress, the high instep strained back as if recovering from a leap, with the tense control of emotion.

The game of the coquettish Georgian was well played. With a true woman's pique, she had redoubled her attentions to my friend from the moment that she found it gave pain to another of her sex; and St. John, like most men, seemed not unwilling to see a new altar kindled to his vanity, though a heart he had already won was stifling with the incense. Miss Temple was very lovely. Her skin, of that teint of opaque and patrician white which is found oftenest in Asian latitudes, was just perceptibly warmed toward the centre of the cheek with a glow like sunshine through the thick white petal of a magnolia; her eyes were hazel, with those inky lashes which enhance the expression a thousand-fold, either of passion or melancholy; her teeth were like strips from the lily's heart; and she was clever, captivating, and graceful, and a thorough coquette. St. John was mysterious, romantic-looking, superior, and, just now, the only victim in the way. He admired, as all men do, those qualities which, to her own sex, rendered the fair Isabella unamiable; and yielded himself, as all men will, a satisfied prey to enchantments of which he knew the springs were the pique and vanity of the enchantress. How singular it is that the highest and best qualities of the female heart are those with which men are most rarely captivated!

A rib of the mountain formed a natural seat a little back from the pitch of the precipice, and here sat Miss Temple, triumphant in drawing all eyes upon herself and her tamed lion ; her lap full of flowers, which he had found time to gather on the way, and her white hands employed in arranging a bouquet, of which the destiny was yet a secret. Next to their own loves, ladies like nothing on earth like mending or marring the loves of others ; and, while the violets and already drooping wild flowers were coquettishly chosen or rejected by those slender fingers, the sun might have swung back to the east like a pendulum, and those seven-and-twenty misses would have watched their lovely schoolfellow the same. Nunu turned her head slowly around, at last, and silently looked on. St. John lay at the feet of the Georgian, glancing from the flowers to her face, and from her face to the flowers, with an admiration not at all equivocal. Mrs. Ilfrington sat apart, absorbed in finishing a sketch of New Haven ; and I, interested painfully in watching the emotions of the Cherokee, sat with my back to the trunk of a hemlock—the only spectator who comprehended the whole extent of the drama.

A wild rose was set in the heart of the bouquet at last, a spear of riband-grass added to give it grace and point, and nothing was wanting but a string. Reticules were searched, pockets turned inside out, and never a bit of riband to be found. The beauty was in despair.

"Stay," said St. John, springing to his feet. "Lash ! Lash !"

The dog came coursing in from the wood, and crouched to his master's hand.

"Will a string of wampum do ?" he asked, feeling under the long hair on the dog's neck, and untying a fine and variegated thread of many-colored beads, worked exquisitely.

The dog growled, and Nunu sprang into the middle of the circle with the fling of an adder, and, seizing the wampum as he handed it to her rival, called the dog, and fastened it once more around his neck.

The ladies rose in alarm; the belle turned pale, and clung to St. John's arm; the dog, with his hair bristling upon his back, stood close to her feet in an attitude of defiance; and the superb Indian, the peculiar genius of her beauty developed by her indignation, her nostrils expanded, and her eyes almost showering fire in their flashes, stood before them like a young Pythoness, ready to strike them dead with a regard.

St. John recovered from his astonishment, after a moment, and, leaving the arm of Miss Temple, advanced a step, and called to his dog.

The Cherokee patted the animal on his back, and spoke to him in her own language; and, as St. John still advanced, Nunu drew herself to her fullest height, placed herself before the dog, who slunk growling from his master, and said to him, as she folded her arms, "The wampum is mine."

St. John colored to the temples with shame.

"Lash!" he cried, stamping with his feet, and endeavoring to fright him from his protectress.

The dog howled and crept away, half crouching with fear, toward the precipice; and St. John, shooting suddenly past Nunu, seized him on the brink, and held him down by the throat.

The next instant, a scream of horror from Mrs. Ilfrington, followed by a terrific echo from every female present, started the rude Kentuckian to his feet.

Clear over the abyss, hanging with one hand by an ashen sapling, the point of her tiny foot just poising on a projecting ledge of rock, swung the desperate Cherokee, sustaining herself with perfect ease, but with all the determination of her iron race collected in calm concentration on her lips.

"Restore the wampum to his neck," she cried, with a voice that thrilled the very marrow with its subdued fierceness, "or my blood rest on your soul!"

St. John flung it toward the dog, and clasped his hands in silent horror.

The Cherokee bore down the sapling till its slender stem cracked with the tension, and, rising lightly with the rebound, alit like a feather upon the rock. The subdued student sprang to her side; but with scorn on her lip, and the flush of exertion already vanished from her cheek, she called to the dog, and with rapid strides took her way alone down the mountain.

VI.

Five years had elapsed. I had put to sea from the sheltered river of boyhood—had encountered the storms of a first entrance into life—had trimmed my boat, shortened sail, and, with a sharp eye to windward, was laying fairly on my course. Among others from whom I had parted company was Paul St. John, who had shaken hands with me at the university gate, leaving me, after four years' intimacy, as much in doubt as to his real character and history as the first day we met. I had never heard him speak of either father or mother, nor had he, to my knowledge, received a letter, from the day of his matriculation. He passed his vacations at the university; he had studied well, yet refused one of the highest college honors offered him with his degree; he had shown many good qualities, yet some unaccountable faults; and, all in all, was an enigma to myself and the class. I knew him clever, accomplished, and conscious of superiority; and my knowledge went no farther. The coach was at the gate, and I was there to see him off; and, after four years' constant association, I had not an idea where he was going, or to what he was destined. The driver blew his horn.

"God bless you, Slingsby!"

"God bless you, St. John!"

And so we parted.

It was five years from this time, I say, and, in the bitter struggles of first manhood, I had almost forgotten there was such a being in the world. Late in the month of October, in 1829, I was on my way westward, giving myself a vacation from the law. I embarked, on a clear and delicious day, in the small steamer which plies up and down the Cayuga Lake, looking forward to a calm feast of scenery, and caring little who were to be my fellow-passengers. As we got out of the little harbor of Cayuga, I walked astern for the first time, and saw the not very unusual sight of a group of Indians standing motionless by the wheel. They were chiefs, returning from a diplomatic visit to Washington.

I sat down by the companion-ladder, and opened soul and eye to the glorious scenery we were gliding through. The first severe frost had come, and the miraculous change had passed upon the leaves which is known only in America. The blood-red sugar maple, with a leaf brighter and more delicate than a Circassian lip, stood here and there in the forest like the Sultan's standard in a host—the solitary and far-seen aristocrat of the wilderness; the birch, with its spirit-like and amber leaves, ghosts of the departed summer, turned out along the edges of the woods like a lining of the palest gold; the broad sycamore and the fan-like catalpa flaunted their saffron foliage in the sun, spotted with gold like the wings of a lady-bird; the kingly oak, with its summit shaken bare, still hid its majestic trunk in a drapery of sumptuous dyes, like a stricken monarch, gathering his robes of state about him to die royally in his purple; the tall poplar, with its minaret of silver leaves, stood blanched like a coward in the dying forest, burthening every breeze with its complainings; the hickory paled through its enduring green; the bright berries of the mountain-ash flushed with a more sanguine glory in the unobstructed sun; the gaudy tulip-tree, the Sybarite of vegetation, stripped of its golden cups, still drank the intoxicating light of noonday, in leaves than which the lip of an Indian shell was never more delicately tinted; the still deeper-dyed vines of the lavish wilderness, perishing with the noble things whose summer they had shared, outshone them in their decline, as woman in her death is heavenlier than the being on whom in life she leaned; and, alone and unsympathizing in this universal decay, outlaws from Nature, stood the fir and the hemlock, their frowning and sombre heads darker and less lovely than ever, in contrast with the death-struck glory of their companions.

The dull colors of English autumnal foliage, give you no conception of this marvellous phenomenon. The change there is gradual; in America it is the work of a night—of a single frost!

Oh, to have seen the sun set on hills bright in the still green and lingering summer, and to wake in the morning to a spectacle like this!

It is as if a myriad of rainbows were laced through the tree-tops; as if the sunsets of a summer—gold, purple, and crimson—had been fused in the alembic of the west, and poured back in a new deluge of light and color over the wilderness. It is as if every leaf, in those countless trees, had been painted to outflush the tulip; as if, by some electric miracle, the dyes of the earth's heart had struck upward, and her crystals and ores, her sapphires, hyacinths, and rubies, had let forth their imprisoned colors, to mount through the roots of the forest, and, like the angels that in olden time entered the body of the dying, re-animate the perishing leaves, and revel an hour in their bravery.

I was sitting by the companion-ladder, thinking to what on earth these masses of foliage could be resembled, when a dog sprang upon my knees, and, the moment after, a hand was laid on my shoulder.

"St. John? Impossible!"

"Bodily!" answered my quondam classmate.

I looked at him with astonishment. The *soigné* man of fashion I had once known, was enveloped in a kind of hunter's frock, loose and large, and girded to his waist by a belt; his hat was exchanged for a cap of rich otter skin; his pantaloons spread with a slovenly carelessness over his feet; and, altogether, there was that in his air which told me, at a glance, that he had renounced the world. Lash had recovered his lameness, and, after wagging out his joy, he crouched between my feet, and lay looking into my face, as if he were brooding over the more idle days in which we had been acquainted.

"And where are *you* bound?" I asked, having answered the same question for myself.

"Westward, with the chiefs!"

"For how long?"

"For the remainder of my life."

I could not forbear an exclamation of surprise.

"You would wonder less," said he, with an impatient gesture, "if you knew more of me. And, by-the-way," he added, with a smile, "I think I never told you the first half of the story—my life up to the time I met you."

"It was not for want of a catechist" I answered, settling myself in an attitude of attention.

"No; and I was often tempted to gratify your curiosity. But, from the little intercourse I had with the world, I had adopted some precocious principles; and one was, that a man's influence, over others, was vulgarized and diminished by a knowledge of his history."

I smiled; and, as the boat sped on her way over the calm waters of the Cayuga, St. John went on leisurely with a story which is scarce remarkable enough for a repetition. He believed himself the natural son of a Western hunter; but only knew that he had passed his early youth on the borders of civilization, between whites and Indians, and that he had been more particularly indebted for protection to the father of Nunu. Mingled ambition and curiosity had led him Eastward, while still a lad; and a year or two of a most vagabond life in the different cities, had taught him the caution and bitterness for which he was so remarkable. A fortunate experiment in lotteries supplied him with the means of education; and, with singular application in a youth of such wandering habits, he had applied himself to study under a private master, fitted himself for the university in half the usual time, and cultivated, in addition, the literary taste which I have remarked upon.

"This," he said, smiling at my look of astonishment, "brings me up to the time when we met. I came to college at the age of eighteen, with a few hundred dollars in my pocket—some pregnant experience of the rough side of the world—great confidence in myself, and distrust of others, and, I believe, a kind of instinct of good manners, which made me ambitious of shining in society. You were a witness to my *début*. Miss Temple was the first highly-educated woman I had ever known, and you saw her effect on me."

"And—since we parted?"

"Oh, since we parted, my life has been vulgar enough. I have ransacked civilized life to the bottom, and found it a heap of unredeemed falsehoods. I do not say it from common disappointment; for I may say I succeeded in everything I undertook—"

"Except Miss Temple," I said, interrupting, at the hazard of wounding him.

"No; she was a coquette, and I pursued her till I had my turn. You see me in my new character now. But a month ago, I was the Apollo of Saratoga, playing my own game with Miss Temple. I left her for a woman worth ten thousand of her; and here she is."

As Nunu came up the companion-way from the cabin, I thought I had never seen breathing creature so exquisitely lovely. With the exception of a pair of brilliant moccasins on her feet, she was dressed in the usual manner, but with the most absolute simplicity. She had changed, in those five years, from the child to the woman, and, with a round, well-developed figure, additional height, and manners at once gracious and dignified, she walked and looked the chieftain's daughter. St. John took her hand, and gazed on her with moisture in his eyes.

"That I could ever have put a creature like this," he said, "into comparison with the dolls of civilization!"

We parted at Buffalo; St. John, with his wife and the chiefs, to pursue their way westward, by Lake Erie; and I, to go moralizing on my way to Niagara.

F. SMITH.

"Nature had made him for some other planet,
And pressed his soul into a human shape
By accident or malice."—COLERIDGE.

"I'll have you chronicled, and chronicled, and cut-and-chronicled, and sung in all-to-be-praised sonnets, and graved in new brave ballads, that all tongues shall troule you."—PHILASTER.

IF you can imagine a buried Titian, lying along the length of a continent, with one arm stretched out into the midst of the sea—the place to which I would transport you, reader mine!—would lie, as it were, in the palm of the giant's hands. The small promontory to which I refer, which becomes an island in certain states of the tide, is at the end of one of the long capes of Massachusets, and is still called by its Indian name, *Nahant.* Not to make you uncomfortable, I beg to introduce you, at once, to a pretentious hotel, "squat like a toad," upon the unsheltered and highest point of this citadel in mid sea, and a very great resort for the metropolitan New-Englanders. Nahant is, perhaps, liberally measured—a square half mile; and it is distant from what may fairly be called mainland, perhaps a league.

Road to Nahant there is none. The *oi polloi* go there by steam; but when the tide is down, you may drive there with a thousand chariots, over the bottom of the sea. As I suppose there is not such another place in the known world, my tale will wait while I describe it more fully. If the Bible had been a fiction (not to speak profanely), I should have thought the idea of the destruction of Pharaoh and his host, had its origin in some such wonder of nature.

Nahant is so far out into the ocean, that what is called the "ground swell," the majestic heave of its great bosom going on for ever like respiration (though its face may be like a mirror beneath the sun, and a wind may not have crisped its surface for days and weeks), is as broad and powerful within a rood of the shore, as it is a thousand miles at sea.

The promontory, itself, is never wholly left by the ebb; but, from its western extremity, there runs a narrow ridge, scarce broad enough for a horse-path, impassible for the rocks and sea-weed of which it is matted, and extending at just high-water mark from Nahant to the mainland. Seaward from this ridge, which is the only connection of the promontory with the Continent, descends an expanse of sand, left bare six hours out of the twelve by the retreating sea, as smooth and hard as marble, and as broad, and apparently as level, as the plain of the Hermus. For three miles it stretches away without shell or stone, a surface of white, fine-grained sand, beaten so hard by the eternal hammer of the surf that the hoof of a horse scarce marks it, and the heaviest wheel leaves it as printless as a floor of granite. This will be easily understood, when you remember the tremendous rise and fall of the ocean swell, from the very bosom of which, in all its breadth and strength, roll in the waves of the flowing tide, breaking down on the beach, every one, with the thunder of a host precipitated from the battlements of a castle. Nothing could be more solemn and anthem-like, than the succession of these plunging surges. And when the "tenth wave" gathers, far out at sea, and rolls onward to the shore—first with a glassy and heaving swell, as if some mighty monster were lurching inland beneath the water, and then, bursting up into foam, with a front like an endless and sparry crystal wall, advances and overwhelms everything in its progress, till it breaks with a centupled thunder on the beach—it has seemed to me, standing there, as if thus might have beaten the first surge on the shore after the fiat which "divided sea and land." I am no Cameronian, but the sea (myself on shore) always drives me to Scripture for an illustration of my feelings.

The promontory of Nahant must be based on the earth's axle, else I cannot imagine how it should have lasted so long. In the mildest weather, the ground-swell of the sea gives it a fillip at every heave, that would lay the "castled crag of Drachenfels" as low as Memphis. The wine trembles in your beaker of claret, as you sit after dinner at the hotel; and, if you look out at the eastern balcony, (for it is a wooden pagoda, with balconies, verandahs, and colonnades *ad libitum*,) you will see the grass breathless in the sunshine upon the lawn, and the ocean as polished and calm as *Miladi's* brow beyond, and yet the spray and foam dashing fifty feet into the air between, and enveloping the "Devil's Pulpit" (a tall rock, split off from the promontory's front) in a perpetual kaleidoscope of mist and rainbows. Take the trouble to transport yourself there! I will do the remaining honors on the spot. A cavern, as cool (not as silent) as those of Trophonius, lies just under the brow of yonder precipice, and the waiter shall come after us with our wine. You have dined with the Borromeo, in the grotto of Isola Bella, I doubt not, and know the perfection of *art*—I will show you that of *nature*. (I should like to transport you, for a similar contrast, from Terni to Niagara, or from San Giovanni Laterano to an aisle in a forest of Michigan; but the Dædalian mystery, alas! is unsolved. We "fly not yet."

Here we are, then, in the "Swallow's Cave." The floor descends by a gentle declivity to the sea, and, from the long, dark cleft, stretching outward, you look forth upon the broad Atlantic —the shore of Ireland, the first *terra firma* in the path of your eye. Here is a dark pool, left by the retreating tide for a refrigerator; and, with the champagne in the midst, we will recline about it like the soft Asiatics, of whom we learned pleasure in the East, and drink to the small-featured and purple-lipped "Mignons" of Syria—those fine-limbed and fiery slaves, adorable as Peris, and, by turns, languishing and stormy, whom you buy for a pinch of piastres (say, £5 5s.) in sunny Damascus. Your drowsy Circassian, faint and dreamy, or you crockery Georgian—fit dolls for the sensual Turk—is, to him who would buy *soul*, dear at a penny the hecatomb.

We recline, as it were, in an ebon pyramid, with a hundred feet of floor and sixty of wall, and the fourth side open to the sky. The light comes in, mellow and dim, and the sharp edges of the rocky portal seem let into the pearly arch of heaven. The tide is at half-ebb, and the advancing and retreating waves, which, at first, just lifted the fringe of crimson dulse at the lip of the cavern, now dash their spray-pearls on the rock below, the "tenth" surge alone rallying, as if in scorn of its retreating fellows, and, like the chieftain of Culloden Moor, rushing back singly to the contest. And now that the waters reach the entrance no more, come forward, and look on the sea! The swell lifts! Would you not think the bases of the earth rising beneath it? It falls? Would you not think the foundation of the deep had given way? A plain, broad enough for the navies of the world to ride at large, heaves up evenly and steadily, as if it would lie against the sky, rests a moment spell-bound in its place, and falls again as far—the respiration of a sleeping child not more regular and full of slumber. It is only on the shore that it chafes. Blessed emblem! it is at peace with itself! The rocks war with a nature so unlike their own, and the hoarse din, of their border onsets, resounds through the caverns they have rent open; but beyond, in the calm bosom of the ocean, what heavenly dignity! what godlike unconsciousness of alarm! I did not think we should stumble on such a moral in the cave!

By the deeper base of its hoarse organ, the sea is now playing upon its lowest stops, and the tide is down. Hear! how it rushes in beneath the rocks, broken and stilled in its tortuous way, till it ends with a washing and dull hiss among the sea-weed, and, like a myriad of small tinkling bells, the dripping from the crags is audible. There is fine music in the sea!

And now the beach is bare. The cave begins to cool and darken, and the first gold tint of sunset is stealing into the sky, and the sea looks of a changing opal, green, purple, and white, as if its floor were paved with pearl, and the changing light struck up through the waters. And there heaves a ship into the horizon, like a white-winged bird, lying with dark breast on the waves, abandoned of the sea-breeze within sight of port, and repelled even by the spicy breath that comes with a welcome off the shore. She comes from "merry England." She is freighted with more than merchandise. The home-sick exile will gaze on her snowy sail as she sets in with the morning breeze, and bless it; for the wind that first filled it on its way, swept through the green valley of his home! What links of human affection brings she over the sea? How much comes in her that is not in her "bill of lading," yet worth, to the heart that is waiting for it, a thousand times the purchase of her whole venture!

Mais montons nous! I hear the small hoofs of Thalaba; my stanhope waits; we will leave this half bottle of champagne, that "remainder biscuit," and the echoes of our philosophy, to the Naiads who have lent us their drawing-room. Undine, or Egeria! Lurly, or Arethusa! whatever thou art called, nymph of this shadowy cave! adieu!

Slowly, Thalaba! Tread gingerly down this rocky descent! So! Here we are, on the floor of the vasty deep! What a glorious race-course! The polished and printless sand spreads away before you, as far as the eye can see, the surf comes in below, breast-high ere it breaks, and the white fringe of the sliding wave shoots up the beach, but leaves room for the marching of a Persian phalanx on the sands it has deserted. Oh, how noiselessly runs the wheel, and how dreamily we glide along, feeling our motion but in the resistance of the wind, and in the trout-like pull of the ribands by the excited animal before us. Mark the color of the sand! White at high-water mark, and thence deepening to a silvery gray as the water has evaporated less—a slab of Egyptian granite in the obelisk of St. Peter's not more polished and unimpressible. Shell or rock, weed or quicksand, there is none; and, mar or deface its bright surface as you will, it is ever beaten down anew, and washed even of the dust of the foot of man, by the returning sea. You may write upon its fine-grained face with a crowquill—you may course over its dazzling expanse with a troop of chariots.

Most wondrous and beautiful of all, within twenty yards of the surf, or for an hour after the tide has left the sand, it holds the water without losing its firmness, and is like a gray mirror, bright as the bosom of the sea. (By your leave, Thalaba!) And now lean over the dasher, and see those small fetlocks striking up from beneath—the flying mane, the thorough-bred action, the small and expressive head, as perfect in the reflection as in the reality; like Wordsworth's swan, he

"*Trots* double, *horse* and shadow."

You would swear you were skimming the surface of the sea; and the delusion is more complete, as the white foam of the "tenth wave" skims in beneath wheel and hoof, and you urge on, with the treacherous element gliding away visibly beneath you.

We seem not to have driven fast, yet three miles, fairly measured, are left behind, and Thalaba's blood is up. Fine creature! I would not give him

"For the best horse the Sun has in his stable."

We have won champagne ere now, Thalaba, and I, trotting on this silvery beach; and if ever old age comes on me, and I intend it never shall, on aught save my mortal coil, (my spirit vowed to perpetual youth), I think these vital breezes, and a trot on these exhilarating sands, would sooner renew my prime than a rock in St. Hilary's cradle, or a dip in the well of Kanathos. May we try the experiment together, gentle reader!

I am not settled in my own mind whether this description of one of my favorite haunts in America was written most to introduce the story that is to follow, or the story to introduce the description. Possibly the latter, for, having consumed my callow youth in wandering "to and fro in the earth," like Sathanas of old, and looking on my country now with an eye from which all the minor and temporary features have gradually faded, I find my pride in it (after its glory as a republic) settling principally on the superior handiwork of nature in its land and water. When I talk of it now, it is looking through another's eyes—his who listens. I do not describe it after my own memory of what it *was once to me*, but according to my idea of what it will *seem now to a stranger*. Hence I speak not of the friends I made, rambling by lake or river. The lake and the river are there, but the friends are changed—to themselves and me. I speak not of the lovely and loving ones that stood by me, looking on glen or waterfall. The glen and the waterfall are romantic still, but the form and the heart that breathed through it are no longer lovely or loving. I should renew my joys by the old mountain and river, for, all they ever were I should find them still, and never seem to myself grown old, or cankered of the world, or changed in form or spirit, while they reminded me but of my youth, with their familiar sunshine and beauty. But the friends that I knew—*as* I knew them—are dead. They look no longer the same; they have another heart in them; the kindness of the eye, the smilingness of the lip, are no more there. Philosophy tells me, the material and living body changes and renews, particle by particle, with time; and experience—cold-blooded and stony monitor—tells me, in his frozen monotone, that heart and spirit change with it and renew! But the name remains, mockery that it is! and the memory sometimes; and so these apparitions of the past—that we almost fear to question when they encounter us, lest the change they have undergone should freeze our blood—stare coldly on us, yet call us by name, and answer, though coldly to their own, and have that terrible similitude to what they were, mingled with their unsympathizing and hollow mummery, that we wish the grave of the past, with all that it contained of kind or lovely, had been sealed for ever. The heart we have lain near before our birth (so read I the book of human life) is the only one that cannot forget that it has loved us. As we once wove the sentiment into a verse :—

"Mother! dear mother! the feelings nurst
As I hung at thy bosom, *clung round thee first*—
'Twas the earliest link in love's warm chain,
'Tis the only one that will long remain;
And as, year by year, and day by day,
Some friend, still trusted, drops away,
Mother! dear mother! *oh, dost thou see*
How the shortened chain brings me nearer thee!"

II.

I have observed that of all the friends one has in the course of his life, the truest and most attached is exactly the one who, from his dissimilarity to yourself, the world finds it very odd you should fancy. We hear sometimes of lovers who "are made for each other," but rarely of the same natural match in friendship. It is no great marvel. In a world like this, where we pluck so desperately at the fruit of pleasure, we prefer for company those who are not formed with precisely the same palate as ourselves. You will seldom go wrong, dear reader, if you refer any human question about which you are in doubt, to that icy oracle—selfishness.

My shadow for many years was a gentle monster, whom I have before mentioned, baptized by the name of *Forbearance Smith.* He was a Vermontese, a descendant of one of the Puritan Pilgrims, and the first of his family who had left the Green Mountains since the flight of the regicides to America. We assimilate to what we live among, and Forbearance was very *green*, and very like a *mountain*. He had a general resemblance to one of Thorwaldsen's unfinished apostles—larger than life, and just hewn into outline. My acquaintance with him commenced during my first year at the university. He stalked into my room one morning with a hair-trunk on his back, and handed me the following note from the tutor:—

"SIR: The Faculty have decided to impose upon you the fine of ten dollars and damages, for painting the president's horse, on Sabbath night, while grazing on the college green. They, moreover, have removed Freshman Wilding from your rooms, and appoint, as your future chum, the studious and exemplary bearer, Forbearance Smith, to whom you are desired to show a becoming respect.

"Your obedient servant,

"ERASMUS SNUFFLEGREEK.

"*To Freshman Slingsby.*"

Rather relieved by my lenient sentence (for, till the next shedding of his well-saturated coat, the sky-blue body and red mane and tail of the president's once gray mare would interfere with that esteemed animal's usefulness), I received Mr. Smith with more politeness than he expected. He deposited his hair-trunk in the vacant bedroom, and remarked with a good-humored smile that it was a cold morning; and seating himself in my easiest chair, opened his Euclid, and went to work upon a problem, as perfectly at home as if he had furnished the room himself, and lived in it from his matriculation. I had expected some preparatory apology at least, and was a little annoyed; but, being upon my good behavior, I bit my lips, and resumed the "Art of Love," upon which I was just then practising my nascent Latinity, instead of calculating logarithms for recitation. In about an hour, my new chum suddenly vociferated "*Eureka!*" shut up his book, and having stretched himself, (a very unnecessary operation), coolly walked to my dressing-table, selected my best hair-brush, redolent of Macassar, and used it with the greatest apparent satisfaction.

"Have you done with that hair-brush?" I asked, as he laid it in its place again.

"Oh yes!"

"Then, perhaps, you will do me the favor to throw it out of the window."

He did it without the slightest hesitation. He then resumed his seat by the fire, and I went on with my book in silence. Twenty minutes had elapsed, when he rose very deliberately, and, without a word of preparation, gave me a cuff that sent me flying into the wood-basket in the corner behind me. As soon as I could pick myself out, I flew upon him, but I might as well have grappled with a boa-constrictor. He held me off at arm's length till I was quite exhausted with rage, and, at last, when I could struggle no more, I found breath to ask him what the devil he meant.

"To resent what seemed to me, on reflection, to be an insult," he answered, in the calmest tone, "and now to ask your pardon for a fault of ignorance. The first was due to myself, the second to you."

Thenceforth, to the surprise of everybody and Bob Wilding and the tutor, we were inseparable. I took Bruin (by a double elision *Forbearance* became "*bear*," and by a paraphrase *Bruin*, and he answered to the name)—I took him, I say, to the omnium shop, and presented him with a dressing-case, and other appliances for his *outer* man ; and, as my *inner* man was relatively as much in need of his assistance, we mutually improved. I instructed him in poetry and politeness, and he returned the lesson in problems and politics. My star was never in more fortunate conjunction.

Four years had woven their threads of memory about us, and there was never woof more free from blemish. Our friendship was proverbial. All that much care and Macassar could do for Bruin had been done, but there was no abating his seven feet of stature, nor reducing the size of his feet proper, nor making the muscles of his face answer to their natural wires. At his most placid smile, a strange waiter would run for a hot towel and the doctor ; (colic was not more like itself than that like colic) ; and for his motions—oh Lord ! a skeleton, with each individual bone appended to its neighbor with a string, would execute a *pas seul* with the same expression. His mind, however, had none of the awkwardness of his body. A simplicity and truth, amounting to the greatest *naïveté*, and a fatuitous unconsciousness of the effect on beholders of his outer man, were its only approaches to fault or foible. With the finest sense of the beautiful, the most unerring judgment in literary taste, the purest romance, a fervid enthusiasm, constancy, courage, and good temper, he walked about the world in a mask—an admirable creature, in the guise and seeming of a ludicrous monster.

Bruin was sensitive on but one point. He never could forgive his father and mother for the wrong they had entailed on him at his baptism. "*Forbearance* Smith !" he would say to himself sometimes in unconscious soliloquy, "they should have given me the virtue as well as the name !" And then he would sit with a pen, and scrawl "F. Smith" on a sheet of paper by the hour together. To insist upon knowing his Christian name was the one impertinence he never forgave.

III.

My party at Nahant consisted of Thalaba, Forbearance, and myself. The place was crowded, but I passed my time very much between my horse and my friend, and was as certain to be found on the beach, when the tide was down, as the sea to have left the sands. Job (a synonyme for Forbearance which became, at this time, his common *sobriquet*) was, of course, in love. Not the least to the prejudice, however, of his last faithful passion—for he was as fond of the memory of an old love, as he was tender in the presence of the new. I intended to have had him dissected after his death, to see whether his organization was not peculiar. I strongly incline to the opinion that we should have found a mirror in the place of his heart. Strange! how the same man who is so fickle in love, will be so constant in friendship! But is it fickleness? Is it not rather a *superflu* of tenderness in the nature, which overflows to all who approach the fountain? I have ever observed that the most susceptible men are the most remarkable for the finer qualities of character. They are more generous, more delicate, and of a more chivalrous complexion altogether, than other men. It was surprising how reasonably Bruin would argue upon this point. "Because I was happy at Niagara," he was saying one day as we sat upon the rocks, "shall I take no pleasure in the Falls of Montmorenci? Because the sunset was glorious yesterday, shall I find no beauty in that of to-day? Is my fancy to be used but once, and the key turned upon it for ever? Is the heart like a *bonbon*, to be eaten up by the first favorite, and thought of no more? Are our eyes blind, save to one shape of beauty? Are our ears insensible to the music, save of one voice?"

"But do you not weaken the heart, and become incapable of a lasting attachment, by this habit of inconstancy?"

"How long, my dear Phil, will you persist in talking as if the heart were material, and held so much love, as a cup so much water, and had legs to be weary, or organs to grow dull? How is my sensibility lessened—how my capacity enfeebled? What would I have done for my first love, that I would not do for my last? I would have sacrificed my life to secure the happiness of one you wot of, in days gone by; I would jump into the sea, if it would make Blanche Carroll happier to-morrow."

"*Sautez-donc!*" said a thrilling voice behind; and, as if the utterance of her name had conjured her out of the ground, the object of all Job's admiration, and a little of my own, stood before us. She had a work-basket in her hand, a gipsy-hat tossed carelessly on her head, and had preceded a whole troop of belles and matrons, who were coming out to while away the morning, and breathe the invigorating sea-air, on the rocks.

Blanche Carroll was what the women would call "a little love;" but that phrase of endearment would not at all express the feeling with which she inspired the men. She was small, and her face and figure might have been framed in fairy-land for bewitching beauty; but, with the manner of a spoiled child, and, apparently, the most thoughtless playfulness of mind, she was as veritable a little devil as ever took the shape of a woman. Scarce seventeen at this time, she had a knowledge of character that was like an instinct, and was an accomplished actress in any part it was necessary for her purpose to play. No grave Machiavel ever managed his cards with more finesse, than that little *intriguante*, the limited world of which she was the star. She was a natural master-spirit and plotter; and the talent that would have employed itself in the deeper game of politics, had she been born a woman of rank in Europe, displayed itself, in the simple society of a Republic, in subduing to her power everything in the shape of a single man that ventured to her net. I have nothing to tell of her, at all commensurate with the character I have drawn; for the disposal of her own heart, (if she has one,) must, of course, be the most important event of her life; but, I merely pencil the outline of the portrait, in passing, as a specimen of the material that exists—even in the simplest society—for the *dramatis personæ* of a court.

We followed the light-footed beauty to the shelter of one of the caves opening on the sea, and seated ourselves about her upon the rocks. Some one proposed that Job or myself should read.

"Oh, Mr. Smith," interrupted the belle, "where is my bracelet? and where are my verses?"

At the ball the night before, she had dropped a bracelet in the waltz, and Job had been permitted to take care of the fragments, on condition of restoring them, with a sonnet, the next morning. She had just thought of it.

"Read them out! read them out!" she cried, as Job, blushing a deep blue, extracted a tri-colored pink document from his pocket, and tried to give it to her unobserved, with the packet of jewelry. Job looked at her imploringly, and she took the verses from his hand, and ran her eye through them.

Pretty well!" she said; "but the last line might be improved. Give me a pencil, some one!" And bending over it, till her luxuriant hair concealed her fairy fingers in their employment, she wrote a moment upon her knee, and, tossing the paper to me, bade me read it out with the emendation. Bruin had, meantime, modestly disappeared, and I read with the more freedom—

'Twas broken in the gliding dance,
When thou wert in thy dream of power;
When shape and motion, tone and glance,
Were glorious all—the woman's hour!
The light lay soft upon thy brow,
The music melted in thine ear,
And one, perhaps, forgotten now,
With 'wildered thoughts stood listening near
Marvelling not that links of gold
A pulse like thine had not controlled.

"'Tis midnight now. The dance is done,
And thou, in thy soft dreams, asleep,
And I, awake, am gazing on
The fragments given me to keep:
I think of every glowing vein
That ran beneath these links of gold,
And wonder if a thrill of pain
Made those bright channels ever cold!
With gifts like thine, I cannot think,
Grief ever chilled this broken link.

"Good night! 'Tis little now to thee,
That in my ear thy words were spoken
And thou wilt think of them and me,
As long as of the bracelet broken.
For thus is riven many a chain,
That thou hast fastened but to break;
And thus thou'lt sink to sleep again,
As careless that another wake:
The only thought thy heart can rend,
Is—*what the fellow'll charge to mend!*"

Job's conclusion was more pathetic, but, probably, less true

He appeared after the applause had ceased, and resumed his place at the lady's feet, with a look in his countenance of having deserved an abatement of persecution. The beauty spread out the fragments of the broken bracelet on the rock beside her.

"Mr. Smith!" said she, in her most conciliating tone.

Job leaned toward her, with a look of devoted inquiry.

"Has the tide turned?"

"Certainly. Two hours since."

"The beach is passable, then?"

"Hardly, I fear."

"No matter. How many hours' drive is it to Salem?"

"Mr. Slingsby drives it in two."

"Then you'll get Mr. Slingsby to lend you his stanhope, drive to Salem, have this bracelet mended, and bring it back in time for the ball. *I have spoken*, as the Grand Turk says. *Allez!*"

"But, my dear Miss Caroll——"

She laid her hand on his mouth, as he began to remonstrate; and while I made signs to him to refuse, she said something to him which I lost in a sudden dash of the waters. He looked at me for my consent.

"Oh! you can have Mr. Slingsby's horse," said the beauty, as I hesitated whether my refusal would not check her tyranny, "and I'll drive him out this evening for his reward, *N'est-ce pas?* you cross man!"

So, with a sun hot enough to fry the brains in his skull, and a quivering reflection on the sands, that would burn his face to a blister, *exit* Job, with the broken bracelet in his bosom

"Stop, Mr. Slingsby," said the imperious little belle, as I was making up a mouth, after his departure, to express my disapprobation of her measures—"no lecture, if you please. Give me that book of plays, and I'll read you a precedent. Because you are virtuous, shall we have no more cakes and ale? *Ecoutez!* And, with an emphasis and expression, that would have been perfect on the stage, she read the following passage from "The Careless Husband"—

"*Lady Betty.*—The men of sense, my dear, make the best fools in the world; their sincerity and good breeding throw them so entirely into one's power, and give one such an agreeable thirst of using them ill, to show that power—'tis impossible not to quench it."

"*Lady Easy.*—But, my Lord Morelove—"

"*Lady B.*—Pooh! my Lord Morelove's a mere Indian damask—one can't wear him out; o' my conscience, I must give him to my woman, at last. I begin to be known by him; had I not best leave him off, my dear?"

"*Lady E.*—Why did you ever encourage him?"

"*Lady B.*—Why, what would you have one do? For my part, I could no more choose a man by my eye than a shoe—one must draw them on a little, to see if they are right to one's foot."

"*Lady E.*—But I'd no more fool on with a man I could not like, than wear a shoe that pinched me."

"*Lady B.*—Ay; but then a poor wretch tells one he'll widen 'em, or do anything; and is so civil and silly, that one does not know how to turn such a trifle as a pair of shoes, or a heart, upon a fellow's hands again."

"*Lady E.*—And there's my Lord Foppington."

"*Lady B.*—My dear! fine fruit will have flies about it; but, poor things! they do it no harm; for, if you observe, people are

10

generally most apt to choose that the flies have been busy with Ha! ha!"

"*Lady E.*—Thou art a strange, giddy creature!"

"*Lady B.*—That may be from too much circulation of thought, my dear!"

"Pray, Miss Carroll,' said I, as she threw aside the book, with a theatrical air, "have you any precedent for broiling a man's brains, as well as breaking his heart? For, by this time, my friend Forbearance has a *coup de soliel*, and is hissing over the beach like a steam-engine."

"How tiresome you are! Do you really think it will kill him?"

"It might injure him seriously—let alone the danger of driving a spirited horse over the beach, with the tide quarter-down."

"What shall I do to be 'taken out of the corner,' Mr. Slingsby?"

"Order your horses an hour sooner, and drive to Lynn, to meet him half way on his return. I will resume my stanhope, and give him the happiness of driving back with you."

"And shall I be gentle Blanche Caroll, and no ogre, if I do?"

"Yes; Mr. Smith surviving."

"Take the trouble to give my orders, then; and come back immediately, and read to me till it is time to go. Meantime, I shall look at myself in this black mirror." And the spoilt, but most lovely girl, bent over a dark pool in the corner of the cave, forming a picture on its shadowy background, that drew a murmur of admiration even from the neglected group who had been the silent and disapproving witnesses of her caprice.

IV.

A thunder-cloud strode into the sky, with the rapidity which marks that common phenomenon of a breathless summer afternoon in America; darkened the air for a few minutes, so that the birds betook themselves to their nests; and then poured out its refreshing waters, with the most terrific flashes of lightning and crashes of thunder, which, for a moment, seemed to still even the eternal base of the sea. With the same fearful rapidity, the black roof of the sky tore apart, and fell back, in rolling and changing masses, upon the horizon; the sun darted with intense brilliancy through the clarified and transparent air; the light-stirring breeze came freighted with delicious coolness; and the heavy sea-birds, who had lain brooding on the waves, while the tumult of the elements went on, rose on their cimeter-like wings, and fled away, with incomprehensible instinct, from the beautiful and freshening land. The whole face of earth and sky had been changed in an hour.

Oh, of what fulness of delight are even the senses capable! What a nerve there is sometimes in every pore! What love, for all living and all inanimate things, may be born of a summer shower! How stirs the fancy, and brightens hope, and warms the heart, and sings the spirit within us, at the mere animal joy with which the lark flies into heaven! And yet, of this exquisite capacity for pleasure, we take so little care! We refine our taste—we elaborate and finish our mental perception—we study the beautiful, that we may know it when it appears; yet, the senses by which these faculties are approached, the stops by which this fine instrument is played, are trifled with and neglected. We forget that a single excess blurs and confuses the music written on our minds—we forget that an untimely vigil weakens and bewilders the delicate minister to our inner temple—we know not, or act as if we knew not, that the fine and easily-jarred harmony of health, is the only interpreter of Nature to our souls—in short, we drink too much claret, and eat too much *pâté fôie gras*. Do you understand me, *gourmand et gourmet*?

Blanche Carroll was a beautiful whip, and the two bay ponies in her phaeton were quite aware of it. La Bruyère says, with his usual wisdom, "Une belle femme qui a les qualités d'un honnête homme est ce qu'il y a au monde d'un commerce plus délicieux;" and, to a certain degree, masculine accomplishments, too, are very winning in a woman—if pretty; if plain, she is expected not only to be quite feminine, but quite perfect. Foibles are as hateful in a woman who does *not* possess beauty, as they are engaging in a woman who *does*. Clouds are only lovely when the heavens are bright.

She looked loveliest while driving, did Blanche Carroll; for she was born to rule, and the expression native to her lip was energy and nerve; and, as she sat with her little foot pressed against the dasher, and reined in those spirited horses, the finely-pencilled mouth, usually playful or pettish, was pressed together in a curve as warlike as Minerva's, and twice as captivating. She drove, too, as capriciously as she acted. At one moment her fleet ponies fled over the sand at the top of their speed; and, at the next, they were brought down to a walk, with a suddenness which threatened to bring them upon their haunches. Now far up on the dry sand, cutting a zigzag to lengthen the way; and again, below at the tide edge, with the waves breaking over her seaward wheel: all her powers, at one instant, engrossed in pushing them to their fastest trot; and, in another, the reins lying loose on their backs, while she discussed some sudden flight of philosophy. "Be his fairy, his page, his everything that love and poetry have invented," said Roger Ascham to Lady Jane Grey, just before her marriage; but Blanche Carroll was almost the only woman I ever saw, capable of the *beau ideal* of fascinating characters.

Between Miss Caroll and myself, there was a safe and cordial friendship. Besides loving another better, she was neither earnest, nor true, nor affectionate enough, to come at all within the range of my possible attachments; and, though I admired her, she felt that the necessary sympathy was wanting for love; and, the idea, of fooling me with the rest, once abandoned, we were the greatest of allies. She told me all her triumphs, and I listened and laughed, without thinking it worth while to burden her with my confidence in return; and you may as well make a memorandum, gentle reader, that *that* is a very good basis for a friendship. Nothing bores women or worldly persons so much, as to return their secrets with your own.

As we drew near the extremity of the beach, a boy rode up on horseback, and presented Miss Carroll with a note. I observed that it was written on a very dirty slip of paper, and was waiting to be enlightened as to its contents, when she slipped it into her belt, took the whip from the box, and, flogging her ponies through the heavy sand of the outer beach, went off, at a pace which seemed to engross all her attention, on her road to Lynn. We reached the hotel, and she had not spoken a syllable; and, as I made a point of never inquiring into anything that seemed odd in her conduct, I merely stole a glance at her face—which wore the expression of mischievous satisfaction, that I liked the least of its common expressions—and descended from the phaeton, with the simple remark, that Job could not have arrived, as I saw nothing of my stanhope in the yard.

"Mr. Slingsby." It was the usual preface to asking some particular favor.

"Miss Carroll."

"Will you be so kind as to walk to the library, and select me a book to your own taste, and ask no questions as to what I do with myself meantime?"

But, my dear Miss Carroll—your father——"

"Will feel quite satisfied when he hears that Cato was with me. Leave the ponies to the groom, Cato, and follow me." I looked after her as she walked down the village street with the old black behind her, not at all certain of the propriety of my acquiescence, but feeling that there was no help for it.

I lounged away a half hour at the library, and found Miss Carroll waiting for me on my return. There were no signs of Bruin; and, as she seemed impatient to be off, I jumped into the phaeton, and away we flew to the beach as fast as her ponies could be driven under the whip. As we descended upon the sands she spoke for the first time.

"It is *so* civil of you to ask no questions, Mr. Slingsby; but you are *not* offended with me?"

"If you have got into no scrape while under my charge, I shall certainly be too happy to shake hands upon it to-morrow."

"Are you *quite* sure?" she asked archly.

"Quite sure."

"So am *not* I," she said with a merry laugh; and in her excessive amusement she drove down to the sea, till the surf broke over the nearest poney's back, and filled the bottom of the phaeton with water. Our wet feet were now a fair apology for haste, and, taking the reins from her, I drove rapidly home, while she wrapped herself in her shawl, and sat apparently absorbed in the coming of the twilight over the sea.

I slept late after the ball, though I had gone to bed exceedingly anxious about Bruin, who had not yet made his appearance. The tide would prevent his crossing the beach after ten in the morning, however, and I made myself tolerably easy till the sands were passable with the evening ebb. The high-water mark was scarcely deserted by the waves, when the same boy who had delivered the note to Miss Carroll the day before, rode up from the beach on a panting horse, and delivered me the following note :—

"DEAR PHILIP: You will be surprised to hear that I am in the Lynn jail on a charge of theft and utterance of counterfeit money. I do not wait to tell you the particulars. Please come and identify.

"Yours truly,
"F. SMITH."

I got upon the boy's horse, and hurried over the beach with whip and spur. I stopped at the justice's office, and that worthy seemed uncommonly pleased to see me.

"We have got him, sir," said he.

"Got whom?" I asked rather shortly.

"Why, the fellow that stole your stanhope and Miss Carroll's bracelet, and passed a twenty dollar counterfeit bill—ha'n't you hear*n* on't?"

The justice's incredulity, when I told him it was probably the most intimate friend I had in the world, would have amused me at any other time.

"Will you allow me to see the prisoner?" I asked.

"Be sure I will. I let Miss Carroll have a peep at him yesterday, and what do you think? Oh, Lord! he wanted to make her believe she knew him! Good! wasn't it! Ha! ha! And *such* an ill-looking fellow! Why, I'd know him for a thief anywhere! *Your* intimate friend, Mr. Slingsby! Oh, Lord! when you come to see him! Ha! ha!"

We were at the prison-door. The grating bolts turned slowly, and the door swung rustily on its hinges as if it was not often used, and in the next minute I was enfolded in Job's arms, who sobbed and laughed, and was quite hysterical with his delight. I scarce wondered at the justice's prepossessions when I looked at the figure he made. His hat knocked in, his coat muddy, his hair full of the dust of straw—the natural hideousness of poor Job had every possible aggravation.

We were in the stanhope, and fairly on the beach, before he had sufficiently recovered to tell me the story. He had arrived quite overheated at Lynn, but, in a hurry to execute Miss Carroll's commission, he merely took a glass of soda-water, had Thalaba's mouth washed, and drove on. A mile on his way, he was overtaken by a couple of ostlers on horseback, who very roughly ordered him back to the inn. He refused, and a fight ensued, which ended in his being tied into the stanhope, and driven back as a prisoner. The large note, which he had given for his soda-water, it appeared, was a counterfeit, and placards, offering a reward for the detection of a villain, described in the usual manner as an ill-looking fellow, had been sticking up for some days in the village. He was taken before the justice, who declared at first sight that he answered the description in the advertisement. His stubborn refusal to give the whole of his name (he would rather have died, I suppose), his possession of my stanhope, which was immediately recognized, and, lastly, the bracelet found in his pocket, of which he refused indignantly to give any account, were circumstances enough to leave no doubt on the mind of the worthy justice. He made out his *mittimus* forthwith, granting Job's request that he might be allowed to write a note to Miss Carroll (who, he knew, would drive over the beach toward evening), as a very great favor. She arrived as he expected.

"And what in Heaven's name did she say?" said I, interested beyond my patience at this part of the story.

Expressed the greatest astonishment when the justice showed her the bracelet, and declared she *never saw me before in her life!*"

That Job forgave Blanche Carroll in two days, and gave her a pair of gloves with some verses on the third, will surprise only those who have not seen that lady. It would seem incredible, but here are the verses, as large as life:—

"Slave of the snow-white hand! I fold
  My spirit in thy fabric fair;
And, when that dainty hand is cold,
  And rudely comes the wintry air,
Press in thy light and straining form
Those slender fingers scft and warm;
  And, as the fine-traced veins within
Quicken their bright and rosy flow,
  And gratefully the dewy skin
Clings to the form that warms it so,
  Tell her my heart is hiding there,
Trembling to be so closely prest,
  Yet feels how brief its moments are,
And saddens even to be blest—
Fated to serve her for a day,
And then, like thee, *be flung away*."

PART II.

LATER DAYS.

OR,

SKETCHES OF PERSONS AND SCENES OF HIGH LIFE IN EUROPE.

LEAVES FROM THE HEART-BOOK OF ERNEST CLAY.

CHAPTER I.

In a small room, second floor, front, No. — South Audley street, Grosvenor square, on one of the latter days of May, five or six years ago, there stood an inkstand, of which you may buy the like for three halfpence, in most small shops in Soho. It was stuck in the centre of the table, like the largest of the Azores on a schoolboy's amateur map—a large blot, surrounded by innumerable smaller blotlings. On the top of a small leather portmanteau near by, stood two pair of varnished-leather boots, of a sumptuous expensiveness, slender, elegant, and without spot, except the leaf of a crushed orange blossom, clinging to one of the heels. Between the inkstand and the boots, sat the young and then fashionable author of ——— ; and the boots and the inkstand were tolerable exponents of his two opposite, but closely woven existences.

It was two o'clock, P. M., and the author was stirring his tea. He had been stirring it with the same velocity, three quarters of an hour; for, when that cup should be drank, *inevitably* the next thing was, to write the first sentence of an article for the New Month. Mag., and he was prolonging his breakfast, as a criminal his last prayer.

The "fatigued" sugar and milk were still flying round the edge of the cup in a whity blue concave, when the "maid of all work" of his landlord the baker, knocked at the door with a note.

"13 G—— M—— street.

"Dear Sir:

"Has there been any mistake in the two-penny post delivery, that I have not received your article for this month? If so, please send me the rough draught by the bearer (who waits), and the compositors will try to make it out. Yours, truly,

"——.

"P. S.—If the tale is not finished, please send me the title and motto, that we may print the 'contents' during the delay."

The tea, which, for some minutes, had turned off a decreasing ripple from the edge of the arrested spoon, came to a standstill, at the same moment, with the author's wits. He had seized his pen, and commenced:—

"Dear Sir:

"The tale of this month will be called—"

As it was not yet conceived, he found a difficulty in baptizing it. His eyebrows descended, like the bars of a knight's visor; his mouth, which had expressed only lassitude and melancholy, shut close, and curved downward, and he sat for some minutes dipping his pen in the ink, and, at each dip, adding a new shoal to the banks of the inky Azores.

A long sigh of relief, and an expansion of every line of his face into a look of brightening thought, gave token, presently, that the incubation had been successful. The gilded note-paper was pushed aside, a broad and fair sheet of "foreign post," was hastily drawn from his blotting-book, and, forgetful alike of the unachieved cup of tea, and the waiting "devil" of Marlborough street, the felicitous author dashed the first magic word on mid-page, and, without title or motto, traced rapidly line after line, his face clearing of lassitude, and his eyes of their troubled languor, as the erasures became fewer, and his punctuations farther between.

"Any answer to the note, sir?" said the maid-servant, who had entered unnoticed, and stood close at his elbow, wondering at the flying velocity of his pen.

He was at the bottom of the fourth page, and in the middle of a sentence. Handing the wet and blotted sheet to the servant, with an order for the messenger to call the following morning for the remainder, he threw down his pen, and abandoned himself to the most delicious of an author's pleasures—*revery in the mood of composition.* He forgot *work.* Work is to put such reveries into words. His imagination flew on like a horse without a rider—gloriously and exultingly, but to no goal. The very waste made his indolence sweeter—the very nearness of his task, brightened his imaginative idleness. The ink dried upon his pen. Some capricious association soon drew back his thoughts to himself. His eye dulled. His lips resumed their mingled expression of pride and voluptuousness. He started to find himself idle, remembered that he had sent off the sheet with a broken sentence, without retaining even the concluding word, and, with a sigh more of relief than vexation, *he drew on his boots.* Presto!—the world of which his penny-half-penny inkstand was the immortal centre—the world of heaven-born imagination—melted from about him! He stood in patent leather—human, handsome, and liable to debt!

And thus fugitive and easy of decoy—thus compulsory, irresolute, and brief, is the unchastised toil of genius—the earning of the "fancy-bread" of poets!

It would be hard if a man who has "made himself a name," (beside being paternally christened,) should want one in a story—so, if you please, I will name my hero in the next sentence. Ernest Clay was dressed to walk to Marlborough street—to apply for his "guinea-a-page" in advance, and find out the concluding word of his *MS.*—when there was heard a footman's rap at the street door. The baker on the ground floor ran to pick up his penny loaves, jarred from the shelves by the tremendous rat-a-tat-tat, and the maid ran herself out of her shoes, to inform Mr. Clay that Lady Mildred —— wished to speak with him. Neither maid nor baker were displeased at being put to inconvenience, nor was the baker's hysterical mother disposed to murmur at the outrageous clatter which shattered her nerves for a week. There is a spell, to a Londoner, in a coronetted carriage, which changes the noise and impudence of the unwhipped varlets who ride behind it, into music and condescension.

"You were going out," said Lady Mildred; "can I take you anywhere?"

"You can *take* me," said Clay, spreading out his hands in an attitude of surrender, "when and where you please; but I was going to my publisher's."

The chariot-steps rattled down, and his foot was on the crimson carpet, when a plain family carriage suddenly turned out of Grosvenor square, and pulled up, as near his own door as the obstruction permitted.

Ernest changed color slightly, and Lady Mildred, after a glance through the window behind her, stamped her little foot, and said, "Come!"

"One moment!" was his insufficient apology, as he sprang to the window of the other carriage, and, with a manner almost infantine in its cordial simplicity, expressed his delight at meeting the two ladies who sat within.

"Have you set up a chariot, Ernest?" said the younger, laying her hand upon the dark mass of curls on his temple, and pushing his head gently back, that she might see what equipage stopped the way.

He hesitated a moment, but there was no escape from the truth.

"It is Lady Mildred, who has just—"

"Is she alone?"

The question was asked by the elder lady, with a look that expressed a painfully sad wish to hear him answer, "No."

While he hesitated, the more forgiving voice next him hurriedly broke the silence.

"We are forgetting our errand, Ernest. Can you come to Ashurst to-morrow?"

"With all my heart."

"Do not fail! My uncle wishes to see you. Stay—I have brought you a note from him. Good-bye! Are you going to the rout at Mrs. Rothschild's to-night?"

"I *was* not—but, if you are going, I will."

"Till this evening, then?"

The heavy vehicle rolled away, and Ernest crushed the note in his hand unread, and, with a slower step than suited the impatience of Lady Mildred, returned to the chariot. The coachman, with that mysterious instinct that coachmen have, let fall his silk upon the backs of his spirited horses, and drove in time with his master's quickened pulses; and, at the corner of Chesterfield street, as the family carriage rolled slowly on its way to Howell and James's, (on an errand connected with bridal pearls), the lofty-stepping bays of Lady Mildred dashed by, as if all the anger and scorn of a whole descent of coronets were breathing from their arched nostrils.

What a boon, from nature to aristocracy, was the pride of the horse!

* * * * * * *

Lady Mildred was a widow, of two years' weeds, thirty-two, and of a certain kind of talent, which will be explained in the course of this story. She had no personal charms, except such as are indispensably necessary to lady-likeness—indispensably necessary, for that very reason, to any control over the fancy of a man of imagination. Her upper lip was short enough to express scorn, and her feet and hands were exquisitely small. Some men of fancy would exact these attractions, and a great many more. But, without these, no woman ever secured even the most transient homage of a poet. She had one of those faces you never find yourself at leisure to criticise, or, rather, she had one of those syren voices, that, if you heard her speak before you had found leisure to look at her features, you had lost your opportunity forever. Her voice expressed *the presence of beauty*, as much as a carol in a tree expresses the presence of a bird;

and, though you saw not the beauty, as you may not see the bird, it was impossible to doubt it was there. Yet, with all this enchantment in her voice, it was the most changeable music on earth; for, hear it when you would, if she were in earnest, you might be sure it was the softened echo of the voice to which she was replying. She never spoke first. She never led the conversation. She had not (or never used) the talent which many very common-place women have, of giving a direction to the feelings, and controlling even the course of thought, of superior men who may admire them. *In everything she played a second.* She was silent through all your greetings—through all your compliments; smiled and listened, if it were for hours, till your lighter spirits were exhausted, and you came down to the true under-tone of your heart; and, by the first-struck chord of feeling and earnest, (and her skill in detecting it was an infallible instinct,) she modulated her voice, and took up the strain; and, from the echo of your own soul, and the flow of the most throbbing vein in your own heart, she drew your enchantment and intoxication. Her manners were a necessary part of such a character. Her limbs seemed always enchanted into stillness. When you gazed at her more earnestly, her eyes gradually drooped; and again, her enlarged orbs brightened and grew eager, as your gaze retreated. With her slight forefinger laid upon her cheek, and her gloved hand supporting her arm, she sat stirless and rapt; and, by an indescribable magnetism, you felt that there was not a nerve in your eye, nor a flutter toward change in the expression of your face, that was not linked to hers, nerve for nerve, pulsation for pulsation. Whether this charm would work on common men, it is difficult to say; for Lady Mildred's passions were invariably men of genius.

You may not have seen such a woman as Lady Mildred—but you have seen girls like Eve Gore. There are many lilies, though each one, new-found, seems to the finder the miracle of nature. She was a pure, serene-hearted, and very beautiful girl, of seventeen. Her life had been, hitherto, the growth of love and care, as the lily she resembled is the growth of sunshine and dew; and, flower-like, all she had ever known, or felt, had turned to spotless loveliness. She had met the gifted author of her favorite romance, at a country house where they were guests together; and I could not, short of a chapter of metaphysics, tell you how natural it was for these two apparently uncongenial persons to mingle, like drops of dew. I will merely say now, that, strongly-marked as seems the character of every man of genius, his very capability of tracking the mazes of human nature makes him the very chameleon and Proteus of his species, and that, after he has assimilated himself, by turns, to every variety of mankind, his masks never fall off without disclosing the very soul and type of the most infantine simplicity. Other men's disguises, too, become a second nature. Those of genius are worn, to their last day, as loosely as the mantles of the gods.

The kind of man called "a penetrating observer," if he had been in the habit of meeting Mr. Clay in London circles, and had afterward seen him rambling through the woods of —— Park with Eve Gore, natural, playful sometimes, and sometimes sad, his manner the reflex of hers, even his voice almost as feminine as hers, in his fine sympathy with her character and attractions—one of these shrewd people, I say, would have shaken his head, and whispered, "Poor girl, how little she understands him!" But, of all the wise and worldly, gentle and simple, who had ever crossed the path of Ernest Clay, this same child-like girl was the only creature to whom he appeared utterly himself, —for whom he wore no disguise—to whose plummet of simple truth he opened the seldom-sounded depths of his prodigal and passionate heart. Lady Mildred knew his weaknesses and his genius. Eve Gore knew his better and brighter nature. And both loved him.

And now, dear reader, having drawn you the portraits of my two heroines, I shall go on, with a disembarrassed narrative, to the end.

CHAPTER II.

Lady Mildred's bays pranced proudly up Bond street, and kept on their way to the publisher's, at whose door they fretted and champed the bit—they and their high-born mistress in attendance upon the poor author, who, in this moment of despondency, complained of the misappreciation of the world! Of the scores of people who knew him and his companion as London celebrities, and who followed the showy equipage with their eyes, how many, think you, looked on Mr. Ernest Clay as a misappreciated man? How many, had they known that the whole errand, of this expensive turn-out, was to call on the publisher for the price of a single magazine paper, would have reckoned those sixteen guineas *with* the chariot of a noble lady to come for the payment? Five hundred pounds for your romance, *and* a welcome to all the best houses and costliest entertainments of England—a hundred pounds for your poem, *and* the attention of a thousand eager admirers—these are some of the "lengthening shadows" to the author's profits, which the author does not reckon, but which the world does. To the rest of mankind these are "chattels," priced and paid for.

Twenty thousand a year would hardly buy, for Mr. Clay, simple and uncelebrated, what Mr. Clay, author, etc., has freely with five hundred. To whose credit shall the remaining nineteen thousand five hundred be set down? Common people who *pay* for these things are not believers in fairy gifts. They see the author in a station of society unattainable except by the wealthiest and best born, with all, that profuse wealth could purchase, as completely at his service, as if the bills of cost were to be brought in to him at Christmas; and besides all this, (once more "into the bargain,") caressed and flattered, as no "golden dulness" ever was or could be. To rate the revenues of such a pampered idol of fortune, what man in his senses would inquire merely into the profits of his book?

And in this lies the whole secret of the envy and malice which is the peculiar inheritance of genius. Generous-minded men, *all* women, the great and rich who are too high themselves to feel envy, and the poor and humble who are too low to feel aught but wonder and grateful admiration—these are the fosterers and flatterers, the paymasters of the real wealth, and the receivers of the choicest fruits, of genius. The aspiring mediocrity, the slighted and eclipsed pretenders to genius, are a large class, to whose eyes all brightness is black, and the great mass of men toil their lives and utmost energies away, for the hundreth part of what the child of genius wins by his unseen pen—by the toil which neither hardens his hands, nor trenches on his hours of pleasure. They see a man no comelier nor better born than they—idle, apparently, as the most spoilt minion of wealth—vying with the best born in the favor of beautiful and proud women, using all the goods of fortune with a profuse carelessness, which the possession of the lamp of Aladdin could not more than inspire—and by bitter criticism, by ingenious slander, by continual depreciation, ridicule, and exaggeration of every petty foible, they attempt to level the inequalities of fortune, and repair the flagrant injustice of the blind goddess to themselves. Upon the class, generally, they are avenged. Their malice poisons the joy and cripples the fine-winged fancy of nineteen in the score. But the twentieth is born proud and elastic, and the shaft his scorn does not fling back, his light-heartedness eludes, and his is the destiny which, more than that of kings or saints, proves the wide inequality in human lot.

I trust, dear reader, that you have been more amused than Lady Mildred, at this half hour's delay at the publisher's. While I have been condensing into a theory my scattered observations of London authors, her ladyship has been musing upon the apparition of the family carriage of the Gores at Mr. Clay's lodgings. Lady Mildred's position in society, though she had the *entrée* to all the best houses in London, precluded an intimate acquaintance with any unmarried girl; but she had seen Eve Gore, and knew and dreaded her loveliness. A match of mere interest would have given her no uneasiness, but she could see far enough into the nature of this beautiful and fresh-hearted girl, to know that hers would be no divided empire. All women are conscious that a single-minded, concentrated, pure affection, melting the whole character into the heart, is omnipotent in perpetuating fidelity.

" Ernest," said Lady Mildred, as the chariot sped from the publisher's door, and took its way to the Park, " you are grown ceremonious. Am I so new a friend, that you cannot open a note in my presence ?"

Clay placed the crushed letter in her hand.

" I will have no secrets from you, dear Lady Mildred. There is probably much in that note that will surprise you. Break the seal, however, and give me your advice. I will not promise to follow it."

The blood flushed to the temples of Lady Mildred as she read, but her lips, though pale and trembling, were compressed, by a strong effort of self-control. She turned back, and read the note again, in a murmuring undertone :—

"Dear Mr. Clay: From causes which you will probably understand, I have been induced to reconsider your proposal of marriage to my niece. Imprudent as I must still consider your union, I find myself in such a situation that, should you persevere, I must decide in its favor, as the least of two evils. You will forgive my anxious care, however, if I exact of you, before taking any decided step, a full and fair statement of your pecuniary embarrassments, (which I understand are considerable,) and your present income and prospects. I think it proper to inform you, that Miss Gore's expectations, beyond an annuity of £300 a year, are very distant, and that all your calculations should be confined to that amount. With this understanding, I should be pleased to see you at Ashurst to-morrow morning. Yours, truly,

"Thomas Gore."

"Hear me, before you condemn, dear Lady Mildred," passionately exclaimed Ernest, as she clasped her hands over the letter, and her tears fell fast upon them : "I was wrong to leave the discovery of this to chance—I should have dealt more frankly with you—indeed, if I had had the opportunity—"

Lady Mildred looked up, as if to reproach him for the evasion half uttered.

"I have seen you daily, it is true, but every hour is not an hour for confession like this, and, besides, my new love was a surprise, and what I have to confess is a change in my feelings still more recent—a constantly brightening vision of a life (pardon me, Lady Mildred!) deeper, a thousand fold, and a thousand times sweeter and more engrossing than ours."

"You are frank," said his pale listener, who had recovered her self-possession, and seemed bent now, as usual, only on listening and entering into his feelings

"I would be so, indeed," he resumed; "but I have not yet come to my confession. Life is too short, Lady Mildred, and youth too vanishing, to waste feeling on delusion."

"Such as your love, do you mean, Ernest?"

"Pardon me! Were you my wife———"

Lady Mildred made a slight motion of impatience with her hand, and unconsciously raised the expressive arching of her lip.

"I must name this forbidden subject to be understood. See what a false position is mine! You are too proud to marry, but have not escaped loving me; and you wish me to be contented with a perfume on the breeze—to feel a property in a bird in the sky. It was very sweet to begin to love you, to win and win, step by step, to have food for hope in what was refused me. But I am checked, and you are still free. I stand at an impassable barrier, and you demand that I should feel united to you."

"You are ungrateful, Ernest!"

"If I were your slave, I am, for you load me with favors—but as your lover, no! It does not fill my heart to open your house to me; to devote to me your dining hours, your horses, and servants; to let the world know that you love me; to make me your romance—yet have all the common interests of life apart, have a station in society apart, an ambition not mine, a name not mine, a hearth not mine. You share my wild passions, and my fashionable negations, not my homely feelings and everyday sorrows. I have a whole existence into which you never enter. I am something besides a fashionable author—but not to you. I have a common human heart—a pillow upon which lies down no fancy—a morning which is not spent in sleep or listlessness, but in the earning of my bread—I have dulness, and taciturnity, and caprice—and in all these you have no share. I am a butterfly and an earth-worm, by turns, and you know me only on the wing. You do not answer me!"

Lady Mildred, as I have said before, was an admirer of genius, and, though Ernest was excusing an infidelity to herself, the novelty of his distinctions opened to her a new chapter in the book of love, and she was interested far beyond resentment. He was talking from his heart, too, and every one who has listened to a murmur of affection, knows what sweetness the breathings of those deeper veins of feeling infuse into the voice. To a palled Sybarite like Lady Mildred, there was a wild-flower freshness in all this that was irresistibly captivating. A smile stole through her lips, instead of the reproach and anger that he expected.

"I do not answer you, my dear Ernest, for the same reason I would not tear a leaf out of one of your books unread. I quite enter into your feelings. I wish I could hear you talk of them, hours longer. Their simplicity and truth enchant me, but I confess I cannot see what you propose to yourself. Do you think to reconcile and blend all these contradictory moods by an imprudent marriage? Or do you mean to vow your butterfly to celibacy, and marry your worm-fly alone, and grovel in sympathy rather than take love with you when you soar, and keep your grovelling to yourself."

"I think Eve Gore would love me, soaring or creeping, Lady

Mildred! She would be happier sitting by my table while I wrote, than driving in this gay crowd with her chariot. She would lose the light of her life in absence from me, like a cloud receding from the moon, whatever stars sparkled around her. She would be with me at all hours of the day and the night, sharing every thought that could spring to my lips, and reflecting my own soul forever. You will forgive me for finding out this want, this void, while you loved me. But I have felt it sickeningly in your bright rooms—with music and perfume, and the touch of your hand all conspiring to enchant me. In the very hours when most men on earth would have envied me, I have felt the humbler chambers of my heart ache with loneliness. I have longed for some still and dark retreat, where the beating of my pulse would be protestation enough, and where she who loved me was blest to overflowing with my presence only. Affection is a glow-worm light, dear Lady Mildred! It pales amid splendor."

"But you should have a glow-worm's habits to relish it, my dear poet. You cannot live on a blade of grass, nor shine brightest out of doors in the rain. Let us look at it without these Claude Lorraine glasses, and see the truth. Mr. Thomas Gore offers you £300 a year with his niece. Your own income, the moment you marry, is converted from pocket-money into subsistence—from the purchase of gloves and Hungary water, into butcher's meat and groceries. You retire to a small house in one of the cheaper streets. You have been accustomed to drive out continually; and, for several years, you have not only been free from the trouble and expence of your own dinner, but you have pampered your taste with the varied *chefs d'œuvre* of all the best cooks of London. You dine at home, now, feeding several mouths beside your own, on what is called a family dinner—say, as a good specimen, a beefsteak and potatoes, with a Yorkshire pudding. Instead of retiring, after your coffee, to a brilliantly, lighted drawing-room, where collision with some portion of the most gifted society of London disciplines your intellect, and polishes your wit and fancy, you sit down by your wife's work-table, and grow sleepy over your plans of economy, sigh for the gay scenes you once moved in, and go to bed to be rid of your regrets."

"But why should I be exiled from society, my dear Lady Mildred? What circle in London would not take a new grace from the presence of such a woman as Eve Gore?"

"Oh, marvellous simplicity! If *men* kept the gates of society, *a la bonne heure!*—for then a party would consist of one man (the host), and a hundred pretty women. But the "free list" of society, you know, as well as I, my love-blind friend, is exclusively masculine. Woman keeps the door, and, easy as turns the hinge to the other sex, it swings reluctant to her own. You may name a hundred men in your circle, whose return for the hospitality of fashionable houses it would be impossible to guess at, but you cannot point me out one married woman, whose price of admission is not as well known, and as rightly exacted, as the cost of an opera-box. Those who do not give sumptuous parties in their turn, (and even these must be well bred and born people,) are, in the first place, very ornamental; but, besides being pretty, they must either sing or flirt. There are but two classes of women in fashionable society—the leaders or party-givers, and the decoys to young men. There is the pretty Mrs. ——, for example, whose habitation nobody knows, but as a card with an address; and why is she everywhere? Simply, because she *draws* four or five fashionable young men, who would find no inducement to come, if she were not there. Then there is Mrs. ——, who sings enchantingly, and Mrs. ——, who is pretty, and a linguist, and entertains stupid foreigners, and Mrs. ——, who is clever at *charades*, and plays quadrilles; and what would Mrs. Clay do? Is she musical?"

"She is beautiful!"

"Well—she must flirt. With three or four fashionable lovers—"

"Lady Mildred!"

"Pardon me, I was thinking aloud. Well—I will suppose you an exception to this Mede-and-Persian law of the *beau monde*, and allow, for a moment, that Mrs. Clay, with an income of five or six hundred a year, with no eyes for anybody but her husband, poor, pretty, and innocent, (what a marvel it would be in May Fair, by-the-way!), becomes as indispensable to a *partie fine* as was Mr. Clay while in unmarried celebrity. Mind, I am not talking of routs and balls, where anybody can go because there must be a crowd, but of *petits soupers*, select dinners, and entertainments where every guest is invited as an ingredient to a well-studied cup of pleasure. I will suppose, for an instant, that a connubial and happy pair could be desirable in such circles. What part of your income, of five or six hundred a year, do you suppose, would dress and jewel your wife, keep carriage and servants, and pay for your concert-tickets and opera-boxes—all absolutely indispensable to people who go out? Why, my dear Ernest, your whole income would not suffice for the half. You must 'live shy,' go about in hackney-coaches, dress economically, (which is execrable in a woman,) and endure the neglects and mortifications which our pampered servants inevitably inflict on shabby people. Your life would be one succession of bitter mortifications, difficulties, and heart-burnings. Believe me, there is no creature on earth so exquisitely wretched, as a man with a fashionable wife and small means."

Lady Mildred had been too much accustomed to the management of men, not to leave Ernest, after this homily, to his own thoughts. A woman of less knowledge and tact would have followed up this argument with an appeal to his feelings. But, beside that she wished the seed she had thus thrown into his mind to germinate with thought, she knew that it was a wise principle in the art of love to be cold by daylight. Ernest sat silent, with his eyes cast musingly down to the corner of the chariot, where the smallest foot and prettiest chaussure conceivable was playing with the tassel of the window-pull; and, reserving her more effective game of feeling for the evening, when they were to meet at Mrs. R——'s, she set him down at his clubhouse with a calm and cold adieu, and drove home to bathe, dine alone, sleep, and refresh body and spirit for the struggle against love and Eve Gore.

CHAPTER III.

Genius is lord of the world. Men labor at the foundation of society, while the lowly lark, unseen and little prized, sits, hard by, in his nest on the earth, gathering strength to bear his song up to the sun. Slowly rise basement and monumental aisle, column and architrave, dome and lofty tower; and when the cloud-piercing spire is burnished with gold, and the fabric stands perfect and wondrous, up springs the forgotten lark, with airy wheel to the pinnacle, and, standing poised and unwondering on his giddy perch, he pours out his celestial music till his bright footing trembles with harmony. And when the song is done, and, mounting thence, he soars away to fill his exhausted heart at the fountains of the sun, the dwellers in the towers below look up to the gilded spire and shout—not to the burnished shaft, but to the lark—lost from it in the sky.

"Mr. Clay!" repeated the last footman on Mrs. R.'s flower-laden staircase.

I have let you down as gently as possible, dear reader; but here we are, in one of the most fashionable houses in May Fair.

Pardon me a moment! Did I say I *had let you down?* What pyramid of the Nile is piled up like the gradations between complete insignificance and the effect of that footman's announcement? On the heels of Ernest, and named with the next breath of the menial's lips, came the bearer of a title laden with the emblazoned honors of descent. Had he entered a hall of statuary, he could not have been less regarded. All eyes were on the pale forehead and calm lips that had entered before him; and the blood of the warrior who made the name, and of the statesmen and nobles who had borne it and the accumulated honors and renown of centuries of unsullied distinction—all these concentrated glories, in the midst of the most polished and discriminating circle on earth, paled before the lamp of yesterday, burning in the eye of genius. Where is distinction felt? In secret, amid splendor? No! In the street and the vulgar gaze? No! In the bosom of love? *She* only remembers it. Where, then, is the intoxicating cup of homage—the delirious draught for which brain, soul, and nerve, are tasked, tortured, and spent—where is it lifted to the lips? The answer brings me back. Eyes shining from amid jewels, voices softened with gentle breeding, smiles awakening beneath costly lamps—an atmosphere of perfume, splendor, and courtesy—these form the poet's Hebe, and the hero's Ganymede. These pour, for Ambition, the draught that slakes his fever—these hold the cup to lips, drinking eagerly, that would turn away, in solitude, from the ambrosia of the gods!

Clay's walk through the sumptuous rooms of Mrs. R—— was like a Roman triumph. He was borne on from lip to lip—those before him anticipating his greeting, and those he left, still sending their bright and kind words after him. He breathed incense.

Suddenly, behind him, he heard the voice of Eve Gore She was making the tour of the rooms on the arm of a friend, and, fol lowing Ernest, had insensibly tried to get nearer to him, and had become flushed and troubled in the effort They had never before met in a large party, and her pride, in the universal attention he attracted, still more flushed her eyelids and injured her beauty. She gave him her hand as he turned; but the greeting that sprang to her lips was checked by a sudden consciousness that many eyes were on her, and she hesitated, murmured some broken words, and was silent. The immediate attention that Clay had given to her, interrupted at the same moment the undertoned murmur around him, and there was a minute's silence, in which the inevitable thought flashed across his mind that he had overrated her loveliness. Still the trembling and clinging clasp of her hand, and the appealing earnestness of her look, told him what was in her heart—and when was ever genius ungrateful for love! He made a strong effort to reason down his disappointment, and, had the embarrassed girl resumed instantly her natural ease and playfulness, his sensitive imagination would have been conquered, and its recoil forgotten. But love, that lends us words, smiles, tears, all we want, in solitude, robs us in the gay crowd of every thing but what we cannot use—tears! As the man she worshipped led her on through those bright rooms, Eve Gore, though she knew not why, felt the large drops ache behind her eyes. She would have sobbed if she had tried to speak. Clay had given her his arm, and resumed his banter of compliment with the crowd, and with it a manner she had never before seen. He had been a boy, fresh, frank, ardent, and unsuspicious, at Annesley Park. She saw him now in the cold and polished armor of a man who has been wounded as well as flattered by the world, and who presents his shield even to a smile. Impossible as it was that he should play the lover now, she felt wronged and hurt by his addressing to her the same tone of elegant trifling and raillery which was the key of the conversation around them. She knew, too, that she herself was appearing to disadvantage; and, before a brief hour had elapsed, she had become a prey to another feeling—that bitter avarice which is the curse of all affection for the gifted or the beautiful—an avarice that makes every smile, given back for admiration, a gem torn from us—every word, even of thanks for courtesy, a life-drop of our hearts drank away.

"The moon looks
On many brooks,
The brook can see no moon but this,"

contains the mordent secret of most hearts vowed to the love of remarkable genius or beauty.

The supper-rooms had been sometime open; from these and the dancing hall, the half-weary guests were coming back to the deep fauteuils, the fresher air, and the graver society of the library, which had served as an apartment of reception. With a clouded brow, thoughtful and silent, Eve Gore sat with her mother in a recess near the entrance, and Clay, who had kept near them, though their conversation had long since languished, stood in the centre of a small group of fashionable men, much more brilliant and far louder in his gaiety than he would have been with a heart at ease. It was one of those nights of declining May, when the new foliage of the season seems to have exhausted the air, and, though it was near morning, there came through the open windows neither coolness nor vitality. Fans, faded wreaths, and flushed faces, were universal.

A footman stood suddenly in the vacant door.

"Lady Mildred —— !"

The announcements had been over for hours, and every eye was turned on the apparition of so late a comer.

Quietly, but with a step as elastic as the nod of a water-lily, Lady Mildred glided into the room, and the high tones and unharmonized voices of the different groups suddenly ceased, and were succeeded by a low and sustained murmur of admiration. A white dress of faultless freshness of fold, a snowy turban, from which hung on either temple a cluster of crimson camelias still wet with the night dew; long raven curls of undisturbed grace falling on shoulders of that undescribable and dewy coolness which follows a morning bath, giving the skin the texture and the opaque whiteness of the lily; lips and skin redolent of repose and purity, and the downcast but wakeful eye so expressive of recent solitude, and so peculiar to one who has not spoken since she slept—these were attractions, which, in contrast with the paled glories around, elevated Lady Mildred at once into the predominant star of the night.

"What news from the bottom of the sea, most adorable Venus?" said a celebrated artist, standing out from the group and drawing a line through the air with his finger as if he were sketching the flowing outline of her form.

Lady Mildred laid her small hand on Clay's, and, with a smile, but no greeting else, passed on. The bantering question of the great painter told her that her spell worked to a miracle, and she was too shrewd an enchantress to dissolve it by the utterance of a word. She glided on like a spirit of coolness, calm, silent, and graceful, and, standing a moment on the threshold of the apartment beyond, disappeared, with every eye fixed on her vanishing form in wondering admiration. *Purity* was the effect she had produced—purity in contrast with the flowers in the room—purity (Ernest Clay felt and wondered at it), even in contrast with Eve Gore! There was silence in the library for an instant, and then, one by one, the gay group around our hero followed in search of the new star of the hour, and he was left standing alone. He turned to speak to his silent friends, but the manner of Mrs. Gore was restrained, and Eve sat pale and tearful within the curtain of the recess, and looked as if her heart were breaking.

"I should like—I should like to go home, mother!" she said presently, with a difficult articulation. "I think I am not well. Mr. Clay—Ernest—will see, perhaps, if our carriage is here."

"You will find us in the shawl-room," said Mrs. Gore, following him to the stair-case, and looking after him with troubled eyes.

The carriage was at the end of the line, and could not come up for an hour. Day was dawning, and Ernest had need of solitude and thought. He crossed to the park, and strode off through the wet grass, bathing his forehead with handfuls of dew. Alas! the fevered eyes and pallid lips he had last seen were less in harmony with the calm stillness of the dawn than the vision his conscience whispered him was charmed for his destruction. As the cool air brought back his reason, he remembered Eve's embarrassed address and his wearisome and vain efforts to amuse her. He remembered her mother's reproving eye, her own colder utterance of his name, and then in powerful relief came up the pictures he had brooded on since his conversation in the chariot with Lady Mildred—visions of self-denial and loss of caste opposed to the enchantments of passion without restraint or calculation—and his head and heart became wild with conflicting emotions. One thing was certain. He must decide *now*. He must speak to Eve Gore before parting, and, in the tone of his voice, if it were but a word, there must be that which her love would interpret as a bright promise or a farewell. He turned back. At the gate of the park stood one of the guilty wanderers of the streets, who seized him by the sleeve and implored charity.

"Who are you?" exclaimed Clay, scarce knowing what he uttered.

"As good as *she* is," screamed the woman, pointing to Lady Mildred's carriage, "only not so rich! Oh, we could change places, if all's true."

Ernest stood still, as if his better angel had spoken through those painted lips. He gasped with the weight that rose slowly from his heart; and, purchasing his release from the unfortunate wretch who had arrested his steps, he crossed slowly to the door crowded with the menials of the gay throng within.

"Lady Mildred's carriage stops the way!" shouted a footman, as he entered. He crossed the hall, and, at the door of the shawl-room he was met by Lady Mildred herself, descending from the hall, surrounded with a troop of admirers. Clay drew back to let her pass; but while he looked into her face, it became radiant with the happiness of meeting him, and the temptation to join her seemed irresistible. She entered the room, followed by her gay suite, and last of all by Ernest, who saw, with the first glance at the Gores, that he was believed to have been with her during the half-hour that had elapsed. He approached Eve; but the sense of an injustice he could not immediately remove, checked the warm impulse with which he was coming to pour out his heart, and against every wish and feeling of his soul, he was constrained and cold.

"No, indeed!" exclaimed Lady Mildred, her voice suddenly becoming audible, "I shall set down Mr. Clay, whose door I pass. Lord George, ask Mr. Clay if he is ready."

Eve Gore suddenly laid her hand on his arm, as if a spirit had whispered that her last chance for happiness was poised on that moment's lapse.

"Ernest," she said, in a voice so unnaturally low that it made his veins creep with the fear that her reason was unseated, "I am lost if you go with her. Stay, dear Ernest! She cannot love you as I do. I implore you, remember that my life—my life——"

"Beg pardon," said Lord George, laying his hand familiarly on Clay's shoulder, and drawing him away, "Lady Mildred waits for you!"

"I will return in an instant, dearest Eve," he said, springing again to her side, "I will apologize and be with you. One instant—only one——"

"Thank God!" said the poor girl, sinking into a chair, and bursting into tears.

Lady Mildred sat in her chariot, but her head drooped on her breast, and her arms hung lifeless at her side.

"She is surely ill," said Lord George; "jump in Clay, my fine fellow. Get her home. Shut the door, Thomas! Go on, coachman!" And away sped the fleet horses of Lady Mildred, but not homeward. Clay lifted her head and spoke to her, but, receiving no answer, he busied himself chafing her hands, and, the carriage blinds being drawn, he thought momently he should be rid of his charge by their arrival in Grosvenor square. But the minutes elapsed, and still the carriage sped on; and surprised at last into suspicion, he raised his hand to the checkstring, but the small fingers he had been chafing so earnestly arrested his arm.

"No, no!" said Lady Mildred, rising from his shoulder, and throwing her arms passionately around his neck, "you must go blindfold, and go with me! Ernest! Ernest!" she continued, as he struggled an instant to reach the string; but he felt her tears on his breast, and his better angel ceased to contend with him. He sunk back in the chariot, with those fragile arms wound around him, and, with fever in his brain, and leaden sadness at his heart, suffered that swift chariot to speed on its guilty way.

In a small *maison de plaisance*, which he well knew, in one of the most romantic dells of Devon, built with exquisite taste by Lady Mildred, and filled with all that art and wealth could minister to luxury, Ernest Clay passed the remainder of the summer, forgetful of everything beyond his prison of pleasure, except a voice full of bitter remorse, which, sometimes, in the midst of his abandonment, whispered the name of Eve Gore.

CHAPTER IV.

THE rain poured in torrents from the broad leads and Gothic battlements of ——— Castle, and the dull and plashing echoes, sent up with steady reverberation from the stone pavement of the terrace and courts, lulled to a late sleep one of the most gay and fashionable parties assembled out of London. It was verging toward noon, and, startled from a dream of music, by the entrance of a servant, Ernest Clay drew back the heavy bed-curtains and looked irresolutely around his luxurious chamber. The coals in the bright fire widened their smoking cracks and parted with an indolent effort, the well-trained menial glided stealthily about, arranging the preparations for the author's toilet, the gray daylight came in grayer and softer through the draped folds which fell over the windows; and, if there was a temptation to get up, it extended no further than to the deeply cushioned and spacious chair, over which was flung a dressing-gown, of the loose and flowing fashion and gorgeous stuff of the Orient.

"Thomas, what stars are visible to the naked eye this morning?" said the couchant poet, with a heavy yawn.

"Sir!"

"I asked if Lady Grace was at breakfast?"

"Her ladyship took breakfast in her own room, I believe, sir!"

"'*Qualis rex, talis grex.*' Bring mine!"

"Beg pardon, sir?"

"I said, I would have an egg and a spatchcock, Thomas! And, Thomas, see if the Duke has done with the Morning Post.

"I could have been unusually agreeable to Lady Grace," soliloquized the author, as he completed his toilet; "I feel both gregarious and brilliant this morning, and should have breakfasted below. Strange that one feels so dexterous-minded sometimes after a hard drink!—Bacchus waking like Aurora! Thomas, you forgot the claret! I could coin this efflux of soul, now, into 'burning words,' and I will. What is the cook's name, Thomas? Gone! So has the builder of this glorious spatchcock narrowly escaped immortality! Fairest Lady Grace, the sonnet shall be yours, at the rebound! A sonnet? N—n—no!

But I could write *such* a love-letter this morning! Morning Post. '*Died, at Brighton, Mr. William Brown.*' Brown—Brown—what was that pretty girl's name that married a Brown—a rich William Brown. Beverly was her name—Julia Beverly—a flower for the garden of Epicurus—a mate for Leontium! I loved her till I was stopped by Mr. Brown—loved her? by Jove, I loved her—as well as I loved anybody that year. Suppose she were now the widow Brown? If I thought so, faith! I would write her such a reminiscent epistle! Why not as it is—on the supposition? Egad, if it is not *her* William Brown, it is no fault of mine. Here goes, at a venture!

"*To her who was* JULIA BEVERLY—

"Your dark eye rests on this once familiar hand-writing. If your pulse could articulate at this moment, it would murmur *he loved me well!* He who writes to you now, after years of silence, parted from you, with your tears upon his lips—parted from you as the last shadow parts from the sun, with a darkness that must deepen till morn again. I begin boldly, but the usage of the world is based upon forgetfulness in absence, and I have not forgotten. Yet, this is not to be a love-letter.

"I am turning back a leaf in my heart. Turn to it in yours! On a night in June, within the shadow of the cypress by the fountain of Ceres, in the ducal gardens of Florence, at the *festa* of the Duke's birthnight, I first whispered to you of love. Is it so writ in your tablet? Or, were those broken words, and those dark tresses drooped on my breast, mockeries of a night—flung from remembrance with the flowers you wore? Flowers, said I? Oh, Heaven! how beautiful you were, with those lotus-stems braided in your hair, and the white chalices gleamimg through your ringlets, as if pouring their perfume over your shoulders! How rosy-pale, like light through alabaster, showed the cheek that shrank from me beneath the betraying brightness of the moon! How musical, above the murmur of the fountain, rose the trembling wonder at my avowal, and the few faint syllables of forgiveness and love, as I strained you wildly to my heart! Oh, can that be forgotten!

"With the news that your husband was dead, rushed back these memories in a whirlwind. For one brief, one delirious moment, I fancied you might yet be mine. I write because the delirium is over. Had it not been, I should be now weeping at your feet—my life upon your lips!

"I will try again to explain to you, calmly, a feeling that I have. We met in the aisle of Santa Croce—strangers. There was a winged lightness in your step, and a lithe wave in the outline of your form, as you moved through the sombre light, which thrilled me like the awakening to life of some piece of ærial sculpture. I watched you to your carriage, and returned, to trace that shadowy aisle for hours, breathing the same air, and trying to conjure up to my imagination the radiant vision lost to me, I feared, for ever. That night your necklace parted and fell at my feet, in the crowd at the Pitti, and, as I returned the warm jewel to your hand, I recognized the haunting features which I seemed to live but to see again. By the first syllable of acknowledgment, I *knew you*—for, in your voice, there was that profound sweetness that comes only from a heart *thought-saddened*, and, therefore, careless of the cold fashion of the world. In the embayed window, looking out on the moonlit terrace of the garden, I joined you, with the confidence of a familiar friend, and, in the low undertone of earnest and sincerity, we talked of the thousand themes with which the walls of that palace of pilgrimage breathe and kindle. Chance-guided, and ignorant even of each other's names, we met on the galleries of art, in the gardens of noble palaces, in the thronged resorts open to all in that land of the sun, and my heart expanded to you like a flower, and love entered it with the fulness of light. Again, I say, we dwelt but upon themes of intellect, and I had not breathed to you of the passion that grew hour by hour.

"We met, for the last time, on the night of the Duke's festa—in that same glorious palace where we had first blended thought and imagination on the wondrous miracles of art. You were sad and lower-voiced than even your wont, and when I drew you from the crowd, and, wandering with you through the flowering alleys of the garden, stood, at last, by that murmuring fountain, and ceased suddenly to speak—*there* was the threshold of love. Did you forbid me to enter? You fell on my bosom and wept!

"Had I brought you to this by love-making? Did I flatter or plead my way into your heart? Were you wooed or importuned? It is true, your presence drew my better angel closer to my side, but I was myself—such as your brother might be to you—such as you would have found me through life; and for this—for being what I was—with no art or effort to win affection, you drew the veil from between us—you tempted from my bosom the bird that comes never back—you suffered me to love you, helplessly and wildly, when you knew that love such as mine impoverishes life for ever. The only illimitable trust, the only boundless belief on earth, is first love! What had I done to be robbed of this irrecoverable gem—to be sent wandering through the world, a hopeless infidel in woman?

"I have become a celebrity since we parted, and perhaps you

have looked into my books, thinking I might have woven, into some one of my many-colored woofs, the bright thread you broke so suddenly. You found no trace of it, and, you thought, perhaps, that all memory of those simpler hours was drowned in the intoxicating cup of fame. I have accounted in this way for your never writing to cheer or congratulate me. But, if this conjecture be true, how little you know the heart you threw away—how little you know of the thrice-locked, light-shunning, care-hidden casket in which is treasured up the refused gold of a first love. What else is there on earth worth hiding and brooding over? Should I wing such treasures with words and lose them?

" And now you ask, why, after years of healing silence, I open this wound afresh, and write to you. Is it to prove to you that I love you?—to prepare the way to see you again, to woo and win you? No—though I was worthy of you once! No—though I feel living in my soul a passion, that, with long silence and imprisonment, has become well-nigh uncontrollable. I am not worthy of you now! My nature is soiled and world-polluted. I am prosperous and famous, and could give you the station you never won, though you trod on my heart to reach it—but the lamp is out, on my altar of truth—I love by my lips—I mock at faith—I marvel at belief in vows or fidelity—I would not trust you—no, if you were mine I would not trust you—though I held every vein of your bosom like a hound's leash. Till you can rebuke whim, till you can chain imagination, till you can fetter blood, I will not believe in woman. *Yet this is your work!*

" Would you know why I write to you? Why has God given us the instinct of outcry in agony, but to inflict on those who wound us a portion of our pain? I would tell you, that the fire you kindled so wantonly burns on—that, after years of distracting ambition, fame, and pleasure, I still taste the bitterness you threw into my cup ; that, in secret, when musing on my triumphs—in the crowd, when sick with adulation—in this lordly castle, when lapt in luxury and regard—in all hours and phases of a life brilliant and exciting above that of most men—I mourn over that betrayed affection, I see that averted face, I worship in bitter despair that surpassing loveliness which should have been mine in its glory and flower.

"I have made my moan. I have given voice to my agony. Farewell!" ERNEST CLAY.

When Mr. Clay had concluded this "airing of his vocabulary," he enclosed it in a hasty note to his friend, the Secretary of legation at the court of Tuscany, requesting him to call on "two abominable old maids, by the name of Buggins or Blidgims," who represented the *scan. mag.* of Florence, and could, doubtless, tell him how to forward his letter to "the Browns;" and the castle-bell sounding as he achieved the superscription, he descended to lunch, very much lightened of his *ennui*, but with no more memory of the "faithless Julia," than of the claret which had supplied some of the "intensity" of his style. The letter—began as a mystification, or, if it had an object beyond the amusement of an idle hour, intended as a whimsical revenge for Miss Beverley's preference of a rich husband to her then undistinguished admirer—had, in the heat of composition, and quite unconsciously to Clay, enlisted real feelings, totally disconnected with the fair Julia, but not the less easily fused into shape and probability by the facile alchymy of genius. The reader will see at once, that the feelings expressed in it could never be the work of imagination. Truth and bitter suffering show through every line, and all its falsehood or fancy lay in its capricious address to a woman who had really not the slightest share in contributing to its material. The irreparable mischief it occasioned will be seen in the sequel.

CHAPTER V.

WHILE the Ambassador's bag is steadily posting over the hills of Burgundy, with Mr. Clay's letter to Julia Beverley, the reader must be content to gain a little upon Her Majesty's courier, and look in upon a family party, in the terraced front of a villa in the neighborhood of Fiesole. The evening was Italian and autumnal, of a ripe golden glory, and the air was tempered to the blood, as daylight is to the eye—so fitly as be a forgotten blessing.

A well-made, well-dressed, robust gentleman, who might be forty-five, or a well-preserved sixty, sat at a stone table, on the westward edge of the terrace. The London Times lay on his lap, and a bottle of sherry and a single glass stood at his right hand, and he was dozing quietly after his dinner. Near a fountain below, two fair English children played with clusters of ripe grapes. An Italian nurse, forgetting her charge, stood, with folded arms, leaning against a rough garden statue, and looked vacantly at the sunset sky, while up and down a level and flowering alley, in the slope of the garden, paced slowly and gracefully Mrs. William Brown, the mother of these children, the wife of the gentleman sleeping over his newspaper, and the heroine of this story.

Julia Beverley had been married five years, and, for three years at least, she had relinquished the habit of dressing her fine person to advantage. Yet, in that untransparent sleeve, was hidden an arm of statuary roundness and polish, and, in those carelessly fitted shoes, were disguised feet of a plump diminutiveness and arched instep worthy to be the theme of a new *Cenerentola*. The voluptuous chisel of the Greek never moulded shoulders and bust of more exquisite beauty, yet, if she had not become unconscious of the possession of these, altogether, she had so far lost the vanity of her girlhood, that the prudery of a quakeress would not have altered a fold of her cashmere. Her bonnet, as she walked, had fallen back, and, holding it by one string, over her shoulder, she put away, from behind her "pearl-round ear," the dark and heavy ringlet it had tangled in its fall, and, with its fellow shading her cheek and shoulder in broken masses of auburn, she presented a picture of luxurious and yet neglected beauty, such as the undress pencil of Greuze would have revelled in portraying. The care of such silent fringes as veiled her indolent eyes, is not left to mortals, and the covert loves, who curve these soft cradles and sleep in them, had kept Julia Beverley's with the fidelity of fairy culture.

The Beverleys had married their daughter to Mr. Brown, with the usual parental care as to his fortune, and the usual parental forgetfulness of everything else. There was a better chance for happiness, it is true, than in most matches of convenience, for the bridegroom, though past his meridian, was a sensible and very presentable sort of man, and the bride was naturally indolent, and therefore likely to travel the road shaped out for her by the very marked hedges of expectation and duty. What she had felt for Mr. Clay, during their casual and brief intimacy, will be seen by-and-by, but it had made no barrier to her union with Mr. Brown. With a luxurious house, fine horses, and her own way, the stream of life, for the first year of marriage, ran smoothly off.

The second year was chequered with misgivings that she had thrown herself away, and nights of bitter weeping over a destiny in which no one of her bright dreams of love seemed possible to be realized; and still, habit riveted its thousand chains, her children grew attractive and attaching, and, by the time at which our story commences, the warm images of a life of passionate devotion had ceased to haunt her dreams, sleeping or waking, and she bade fair to live and die one of the happy many about whom "there is no story to tell."

Mr. Brown, at this period, occupied a villa in the neighborhood of Florence, and, on the arrival of Mr. Clay's letter at the English Embassy, it was at once forwarded to Fiesole, where it intruded, like the serpent of old, on the domestic paradise to which the reader has been introduced.

Weak and ill-regulated as was the mind of Mrs. Brown, her first feeling, after reading the ardent epistle of Mr. Clay, was unmingled resentment at its freedom. Her husband's back was turned to her as he sat on the terrace, and, ascending the garden steps, she threw the letter on the table.

"Here is a letter of condolence on your death," she said, the blood mantling in her cheek, and her lips arched into an expression of wounded pride and indignation.

Alas, for the slight pivot on which turns the balance of destiny —her husband slept!

"William!" she said again, but the tone was fainter, and the hand she raised to touch him, stayed suspended above the fated letter.

Waiting one instant more for an answer, and bendin over her husband to be sure that his sleep was real, she hastily placed the letter in her bosom, and, with pale brow and limbs trembling beneath her, fled to her chamber. Memory had required but an instant to call up the past, and in that instant, too, the honeyed flatteries she had glanced over in such haste, had burnt into her imagination—effacing all else, even the object for which he had written, and the reproaches he had lavished on her unfaithfulness. With locked doors, and curtains dropped between her and the glowing twilight, she reperused the worshipping picture of herself, drawn so covertly under the semblance of complaint, and the feeling of conscious beauty, so long forgotten, stole back into her veins, like the re-incarnation of a departed spirit. With a flashing glance at the tall mirror before her, she stood up, arching her white neck, and threading her fingers through the loosened masses of her hair. She felt that she was beautiful—still superbly beautiful. She advanced to the mirror.

Her bright lips, her pliant motion, the smooth transparence of her skin, the fulness of vein and limb, all mingled in one assurance of youth, in a wild desire for admiration, in a strange, restless, feverish impatience to be away where she could be seen and loved—away to fulfil that destiny of the heart which seemed now the one object of life, though for years so unaccountably forgotten !

" I was born to be loved !" she wildly exclaimed, pacing her chamber, and wondering at her own beauty as the mirror gave back her kindling features, and animated grace of movement. " How could I have forgotten that I was beautiful ?" But at that instant her husband's voice, cold, harsh and unimaginative, forced its way to her ear, and, convulsed with a tumultuous misery she could neither struggle with nor define, she threw herself on her bed, and abandoned herself to an uncontrolled agony of tears.

Let those smile at this paroxysm of feeling, whose " dream has come to pass !" Let those wonder, who have never been startled from their common-place existence with the heart's bitter question —*is this all?*

Reader ! are you loved ?—loved as you dreamed in youth you might and must be—loved by the matchless creature you painted in your imagination, lofty-hearted, confiding, and radiantly fair ? Have you spent your treasure ? Have you lavished the boundless wealth of your affection ? Have you beggared heart and soul by the wild abandonment to love, of which you once felt capable ?

Lady ! of you I ask : Is the golden flow of *your* youth coined as it melts away ? Are your truth and fervor, your delicacy and devotedness, your unutterable depths of tenderness and tears—are they named on another's lips ?—are they made the incense to Heaven of another's nightly prayer ?—Your beauty is in its pride and flower—who lays back, with idolatrous caress, the soft parting of your hair ? Who smiles when your cheek mantles, and shudders when it is pale ?—Who sits with your slender fingers clasped in his —— dumb, because there are bounds to language, and trembling, because death will divide you ? Oh, the ray of light wasted on the ocean, and the ray caught and made priceless in a king's diamond—the wild-flower perishing in the woods, and its sister culled for culture in the garden of a poet—are not wider apart in their destiny than the loved and the neglected !—" Blessed are the beloved," should read a new beatitude—" for theirs is the foretaste of Paradise !"

CHAPTER VI.

THE autumn following, found Mr. Clay a pilgrim for health to the shores of the Mediterranean. Exhausted, body and soul, with the life of alternate gaiety and passion into which his celebrity had drawn him, he had accepted, with a sense of exquisite relief, the offer of a cruise among the Greek Isles in a friend's yacht, and, in the pure stillness of those bright seas, with a single companion and his books, he idled away the summer in a luxury of repose and enjoyment, such as only the pleasure-weary can understand. Recruited in health, and, with a mind beginning to yearn once more for the long foregone stimulus of society, he landed at Naples in the beginning of October.

"We are not very gay just now," said the English Minister, with whom he hastened to renew an acquaintance commenced in his former travels, "but the prettiest woman in the world is 'at home' to-night, and if you are as susceptible as most of the cavaliers of the Chiaja, you will find Naples attractive enough after you have seen her."

"English?"

"Yes—but you cannot have known her, for I think she was never heard of till she came to Naples."

"Her name?"

"Why, you should hear that after seeing her. Call her Queen Giovanna, and she will come nearer your prepossession. By-the-by, what have you to do this morning?"

"I am at your Excellency's disposal."

"Come with me to the *atelier* of a very clever artist, then, and I will show you her picture. It should be the man's *chef-d'œuvre*, for he has lost his wits in painting it."

"Literally, do you mean?"

"It would seem so—for, though the picture was finished some months since, he has never taken it off his easel, and is generally found looking at it. Besides, he has neither cleaned pallet nor brush since the last day she sat to him."

"If he were young and handsome———"

"So he is—and so are scores of the lady's devoted admirers; but she is either prudent or cold, to a degree that effectually repels hope, and the painter pines with the rest."

A few minutes' walk brought them to a large room near the Corso, tenanted by the Venetian artist, Ippolito Incontri. The Minister presented his friend, and Clay forgot their errand in admiration of the magnificent brigand face and figure of the painter, who, after a cold salutation, retreated into the darkest corner of the point of view, and stood gazing past them at his easel, silent and unconscious of observation.

"I have seen your wonder," said Clay, turning to the picture with a smile, and at the first glance only remarking its resemblance to a face that should be familiar to him. "I am surprised that I cannot name her at once, for I am sure I know her well. But, stay!—the light grows on my eye—no!—with that expression, certainly not—I am sure, now, that I have not seen her. Wonderful beauty! Yet there was a superficial likeness! Have you ever remarked, Signor Incontri, that, through very intellectual faces, such as this, you can sometimes see what the countenance would have been in other circumstances—without the advantages of education, I mean?"

No answer. The painter was absorbed in his picture, and Clay turned to the ambassador.

"I have seen somewhere a face, and a very lovely one, too, that was strangely like these features; yet, not only without the soul that is here, but incapable, I should think, of acquiring it by any discipline, either of thought or feeling."

"Perhaps it was the original of this, and the painter has given the soul!"

"He could as soon warm a statue into life, as do it. Invent that look! Oh, he would be a god, not a painter! Raphael copied, and this man copies; but Nature did the original of this, as he did of Raphael's immortal beauties; and the departure of the most vanishing shadow from the truth, would be a blot irremediable."

Clay lost himself in the picture, and was silent. Veil after veil fell away from the expression as he gazed, and the woman seemed melting out from the canvas into life. The *pose* and drapery were nothing. It was the portrait of a female standing still —perhaps looking idly out on the sea—lost in revery perhaps—perhaps just feeling the breath of a coming thought, the stirring of some lost memory that would presently awake. The lips were slightly unclosed. The heavy eyelashes were wakeful, yet couchant in their expression. The large, dark orbs, lustrous and suffused, looked of the depth and intense stillness of the midnight sky close to the silver rim of a moon high in heaven. The coloring was warm and Italian, but every vein of the transparent temple was steeped in calmness; and, even through the bright pomegranate richness of a mouth full of the capability of passion, there seemed to breathe the slumberous fragrance of a flower motionless under its night-burthen of dew. It portrayed no rank in life. The drapery might have been a queen's or a contadina's. It was a woman stolen to the canvas from her inmost cell of privacy, with her soul unstartled by a human look, and mere life and freedom from pain or care expressed in her form and countenance—yet, with all this, a radiance of beauty, and a sustained loftiness of feeling, as apparent as the altitude of the stars. It was a matchless woman incomparably painted; and, though not a man to fall in love with a semblance, Clay felt, and struggled in vain against the feeling, that the creature drawn in that portrait controlled the next, and perhaps the most eventful, revolution of his many-sphered existence.

The next five hours have (for this tale) no history.

" I have perplexed myself in vain, since I left you," Clay said to the Ambassador, as they rolled on their way to the palace of the fair Englishwoman, " but when I yield to the secret conviction that I have seen the adorable original of the picture, I am lost in a greater mystery—how I ever could have forgotten her. The coming five minutes will undo the Sphinx's riddle for me."

" My life on it, you have never seen her," said his friend, as the carriage turned through a reverberating archway, and, rapidly making the circuit of a large court, stopped at the door of a palace blazing with light.

An opening was made through the crowd, as the Ambassador's name was announced, and Clay followed him through the brilliant rooms with an agitation to which he had long been a stranger. Taste, as well as sumptuous expensiveness, was stamped on everything around, and there was that indefinable expression in the assembly, which no one could detect or appreciate better than Clay, and which is composed, among other things, of a perfect conviction, on the part of the guests, that their time, presence, and approbation, are well bestowed where they are.

At the curtained door of a small boudoir, draped like a tent, a Neapolitan noble, of high rank, turned smiling to the Ambassador, and placed his finger on his lip. The silken pavilion was crowded, and only uniforms and heads, fixed in attention, could be seen by those without; but, from the arching folds of the curtain, came a female voice of the deepest and sweetest melodiousness, reading, in low and finely-measured cadence, from an English poem.

"Do you know the voice?" asked the Ambassador, as Clay stood like a man fixed to marble, eagerly listening.

"Perfectly! I implore you tell me who reads!"

"No!—though your twofold recognizance is singular. You shall see her before you hear her name. What is she reading?"

"My own poetry, by Heaven! and yet I cannot name her! This passes belief. I have heard that voice sob—sob convulsively, and with accents of love—I have heard it whisper and entreat—you look incredulous, but it is true. If she do not know me—nay, if she has not——" he would have said "loved me"—but the look of scrutiny and surprise on the countenance of the Ambassador checked the imprudent avowal, and he became aware that he was on dangerous ground. He relapsed into silence, and, crowding close to the tent, heard the numbers he had long ago linked and forgotten, breathing in music from those mysterious lips, and, possessed as he was by suspense and curiosity, he could have wished that sweet moment to have lasted for ever. I call upon the poet, if there be one who reads this idle tale, to tell me if there be a flattery more exquisite on earth, if there be a deeper-sinking plummet of pride, ever dropped into the profound bosom of the bard, than the listening to thoughts born in pain and silence, articulate in the honeyed accents of woman? Answer me, poet! Answer me, women, beloved of poets, who have breathed their worshipping incense, and know by what its bright censer was kindled!

The voice ceased, and there was one moment of stillness, and then the rooms echoed with acclamation. "Crown her!" cried a tall old man, who stood near the entrance covered with military orders. "Crown her!" repeated every tongue; and, from a vase that hung suspended in the centre of the pavilion, the fresh flowers were snatched by eager hands and wreathed into a chaplet. But those without became clamorous to see the imposition of the crown; and, clearing a way through the entrance, the old man took the chaplet from the busy hands that had entwined it, and crying out with Italian enthusiasm, "A triumph! a triumph!" led forth the majestic Corinna to the crowd.

The Ambassador looked for Clay. He had shrunk behind the statue of a winged Cupid, and, though his eyes were fixed with a gaze of stone on the magnificent creature who was the centre of all regards, he seemed, by his open lips and heaving chest, to be gasping with some powerful emotion.

"Give me the chaplet!" suddenly exclaimed the magnificent idol of the crowd. And, with no apparent emotion, except a glowing spot in her temples, and a quicker throb in the snowy curve of her neck and bosom, she waved back the throng upon her right, and advanced with majestic steps to the statue of Love.

"Welcome, Ernest!" she said in a low voice, taking him by the hand, and losing, for a scarce perceptible moment, the smile from her lips. "Here, my friends! she exclaimed, turning again, and leading him from his concealment, "honor to whom honor is due! A crown for the poet of my country, Ernest Clay!"

"Clay, the poet!" "The English poet!" "The author of the poem!" were explanations that ran quickly through the room, and, as the crowd pressed closer around, murmuring the enthusiasm native to that southern clime, Julia Beverley sprang upon an ottoman, and standing, in her magnificent beauty, conspicuous above all, she placed the crown above Clay's head, and bending gracefully and smilingly over him, impressed a kiss on his forehead, and said, "*This for the poet!*"

And, of the many lovers of this superb woman who saw that kiss, not one showed a frown or turned away—so natural to the warm impulse of the hour did it seem—so pure an expression of admiration of genius—so mere a tribute of welcome from Italy to the bard, by an inspiration born of its sunny air. Surrounded with eager claimants for his acquaintance, intoxicated with flattery, giddy with indefinable emotions of love and pleasure, Ernest Clay lost sight for a moment of the face that beamed on him, and in that moment she had made an apology of fatigue, and retired, leaving her guests to their pleasures.

CHAPTER VII.

"*Un amour rechauffé ne vaut jamais rien,*" is one of those common-places in the book of love, which are true only of the common-place and unimaginative. The rich gifts of affection, which surfeit the cold bosom of the dull, fall upon the fiery heart of genius like spice-wood and incense, and, long after the giver's prodigality has ceased, the mouldering embers lie warm beneath the ashes of silence, and a breath will uncover and rekindle them. The love of common men is a world without moon or stars. When the meridian is passed, the shadows lengthen, and the light departs, and the night that follows is dark indeed. But, as the twilight closes on the bright and warm passion of the poet, memory lights her pale lamp, like the moon, and brightens as the darkness deepens ; and the warm sacrifices made in love's noon and eve, go up to their places like stars, and, with the light treasured from that fervid day, shine in the still heaven of the past, steadfast though silent. If there be a feature of the human soul in which, more than in all others, the fiend is manifest, it is the masculine *ingratitude for love.* What wrongs, what agonies, what unutterable sorrows are the reward of lavished affection, of generous self-abandonment, of unhesitating and idolatrous trust! Yet who are the ungrateful? Men lacking the imagination which can reclothe the faded form in its youthful beauty—men dead to the past—with no perception but sight and touch—to whom woman is a flower and no more—fair to look on, and sweet to pluck in her pride and perfume, but scarce possessed ere trampled on and forgotten! Genius alone treasures the perishing flower and remembers its dew and fragrance, and so, immemorially and well, poets have been beloved of women.

I am recording the passions of genius. Let me say to *you*, lady! (reading this tale understandingly, for you have been beloved by a poet), trust neither absence, nor silence, nor untoward circumstances! He has loved you once. Let not your eye rest on him when you meet—and, if you speak, speak coldly!—for, with a passion strengthened and embellished tenfold by a memory all imagination, he will love you again! The hours you passed with him, the caresses you gave him, the tears you shed, and the beauty with which you bewildered him, have been hallowed in poetry, and glorified in revery and dream, and he will come back to you, as he would spring into paradise were it so lost and recovered!

But to my story!

Clay's memory had now become the home of an all-absorbing passion. By a succession of mischances, or by management so adroit as never to alarm his pride, a week passed over, and he had found no opportunity of speaking alone to the object of his adoration. She favored him in public, talked to him at the opera, leaned on his arm in the crowd, caressed his genius with exquisite flattery, and seemed at moments to escape narrowly from a phrase too tender or a subject that would lead to the past—yet, without a violation of the most palpable tact, love was still an impossible topic. That he could have held her hand in his, unforbidden—that he could have pressed her to his bosom while she wept—that she could have loved him ever, though but for an hour—seemed to him sometimes an incredible dream, sometimes a most passionate happiness only to believe. He left her at night to pace the sands of the bay till morning, remembering—forever remembering—the scene by the fountain at Florence ; and he passed his day between her palace and the picture of poor Incontri, who loved her more helplessly than himself, but found a sympathy in the growing melancholy of the poet.

" She has no heart," said the painter ; but Clay had felt it bear against his own, and he fed his love in silence on that remembrance.

They sat upon the rocks by the gate of the Villa Real. The sun was just setting, and, as the waves formed near the shore and rode in upon the glassy swell of the bay, there seemed to writhe, on each wavy back, a golden serpent, who broke on the sands at their feet in sparkles of fire. At a little distance lay the swallow-like yacht, in which Clay had threaded the Archipelago, and, as the wish to feel the little craft bounding once more beneath him was checked by the anchor-like heaviness of his heart, an equestrian party stopped suddenly on the Chiaja.

" There is Mr. Clay !" said the thrilling voice of Julia Beverley, " perhaps he will take us over in the yacht. Sorrento looks so blue and tempting in the distance."

Without waiting for a repetition of the wish he had overheard,

Clay sprang upon a rock, and made signal for the boat, and, before the crimson of the departing day had faded from the sky, the fair Julia and her party of cavaliers were standing on the deck of the swift vessel, bound on a moonlight voyage to Sorrento, and watching on their lee the reddening ribs and lurid eruption of the volcano. The night was Neapolitan, and the air was the food of love.

It was a voyage of silence, for the sweetness of life, in such an atmosphere and in the midst of that matchless bay, lay like a voluptuous burthen in the heart, and the ripple under the clearing prow was language enough for all. Incontri leaned against the mast, watching the moonlit features of the signora with his melancholy but idolizing gaze, and Clay lay on the deck at her feet, trying, with pressed-down lids, to recall the tearful eyes of the Julia Beverley he had loved at the fountain.

It was midnight when the breath of the orange groves of Sorrento, stealing seaward, slackened the way of the little craft, and, running in close under the rocky foundations of the house of Tasso, Clay dropped his anchor, and landed his silent party at their haven. Incontri was sent forward to the inn to prepare their apartments, and, leaning on Clay's arm and her husband's, the superb Englishwoman ascended to the overhanging balcony of the dwelling of the Italian bard, and, in a few words of eloquent sympathy in the homage paid by the world to these shrines of genius, added to the overflowing heart of her gifted lover one more intoxicating drop of flattery and fascination. They strolled onward to the inn, and he bade her good night at the gate, for he could no longer endure the fetter of another's presence, and the emotion stifled in his heart and lips.

I have forgotten the name of that pleasant inn at Sorrento,

built against the side of its mountain shore, with terraced orange-groves piled above its roof, and the golden fruit nodding in at its windows. From the principal floor, you will remember, projects a broad verandah, jutting upon one of these fruit-darkened alleys. If you have ever slept there, after a scramble over Scaricatoja, you have risen, even from your fatigued slumber, to go out and pace awhile that overhanging garden, oppressed with the heavy perfume of the orange flowers. Strange that I should forget the name of that inn! I thought, when the busy part of my life should be well over, I should go back and die there.

The sea had long closed over the orbed forehead of the moon, and still Clay restlessly hovered around the garden of the inn. Mounting at last to the alley on a level with the principal chambers of the house, he saw, outlined in shadow upon the curtain of a long window, a female figure holding a book, with her cheek resting on her hand. He threw himself on the grass and gazed steadily. The hand moved from the cheek, and raised a pencil from the table, and wrote upon the margin of the volume, and then the pencil was laid down, and the slender fingers raised the masses of fallen hair from the shoulder, and threaded the wavy ringlets indolently as she read. From the slightest motion of that statuary hand, from the most fragmented outline of that bird-like neck, Clay would have known Julia Beverley; and, as he watched her graceful shadow, the repressed and pent-up feelings of that evening of restraint, fed as they had been by every voluptuous influence known beneath the moon, rose to a height that absorbed brain and soul in one wild tumult of emotion. He sprang to his feet to rush into her presence, but at that instant a footstep started from the darkness of a tree, at the extremity of the alley. He paused, and the shadow arose, and, laying aside the book, leaned

12*

back, and lifted the tapering arms, and wound up the long masses of fallen hair, and then, kneeling, remained a few minutes motionless, with the face buried in the hands.

Clay trembled and felt rebuked.

Once more the flowing drapery swept across the curtain, the light was extinguished, and the window thrown open to the night air; and then all was still.

Clay walked to and fro in an agitation bordering on delirium. "I must speak to her!" he said, murmuring audibly, and advancing toward the window. But hurried footsteps started again from the shadow of the pine, and he stopped to listen. All was silent, and he stood a moment pressing his hands on his brow, and trying to struggle with the wild impulse in his brain. His closed eyes brought back instantly the unfading picture of Julia Beverley, weeping on his breast at the fountain; and, with one rapid movement, he divided the curtains and stood breathless in her chamber.

The heavy breathing of the unconscious husband fell like music on his ear.

"Julia!" he exclaimed in a hoarse whisper, "I am here—Ernest Clay!"

"You are frantic, Ernest!" said a voice so calm that it fell on his ear like an assurance of despair. "I have no feeling for you that answers to this freedom. Leave my chamber!"

"No!" said Clay, dropping the curtain behind him, and advancing into the room, "wake your husband if you will—this is the only spot on earth where I can breathe, and if you are relentless, here will I die! Was it false when you said you loved me? Speak, Julia!"

"Ernest!" she said, in a less assured tone, "I have done wrong not to check this wild passion earlier, and I have that to say to you which, perhaps, had better be said now. I will come to you in the garden."

"My vessel waits, and in an hour——"

"Nay, nay, you mistake me. But go! I will follow instantly!"

Vesuvius was burning with an almost smokeless flame when Clay stood again in the night air, and every object was illuminated with the clearness of a conflagration. At the first glance around, he fancied he saw figures gliding behind the lurid body of a pine opposite the window, but, in the next moment, the curtain again parted, and Julia Beverley, wrapped in a cloak, stood beside him on the verandah.

"Stand back!" she said, as he endeavored to put his arm around her, "I have more than one defender within call, and I must speak to you where I am. Will you listen to me, Ernest?"

Clay's breast heaved; but he folded his arms and leaned against the slender column of the verandah in silence.

"Were it any other person who had so far forgotten himself," she continued, "it would be sufficient to say, 'I can never love you," and leave my privacy to be defended by my natural protector. But I wish to show you, Ernest, not only that you can have no hope in loving me, but that you have made me the mischievous woman I have become. From an humble wife to a dangerous coquette, the change may well seem startling—but it is of your working."

"Mine, madam!" said Clay, whose pride was aroused with the calm self-possession and repulse of her tone and manner.

"I have never answered the letter you wrote me."

"Pardon, and spare me!" said Clay, who remembered, at the instant only, the whim under which it was written.

"It awoke me to a new existence," she continued, without heeding his confusion, "for it first made me aware that I could ever be the theme of eloquent admiration. I had never been praised but in idle compliment, and by those whose intellect I despised; and though, as a girl, I had a vague feeling that I was slighted and unappreciated, I yielded, gradually, to the conviction that the world was right, and that women sung by poets, and described in the glowing language of romance, were of another mould. I scarce reasoned upon it. I remember, on first arriving in Italy, drawing a comparison favorable to myself, between my own beauty and the Fornarina's, and the portraits of Laura and Leonora D'Este; but, as I was loved by neither painters nor poets, I accused myself of presumption, and, with a sigh, returned to my humility. My life seemed more vacant than it should be, and I sometimes wept from an unhappiness I could not define; and I once or twice met persons who seemed to have begun to love me, and appreciate my beauty as I wished; and, in this lies the history of my heart up to the time of your writing to me. That letter, Ernest—"

"You believed that I loved you, then!" passionately interrupted her listener—"you know, now, that I loved you! Tell me so, I implore you!"

"My dear poet," said the self-possessed beauty, with a smile, expressive of as much mischief as frankness, "let us be honest! You never loved me! I never believed it, but for one silly hour. Stay!—stay!—you shall not answer me! I have not left my bed at this unseasonable hour, to listen to protestations. At least, let me first conclude the history of my metempsychosis! I can tell it to nobody else; and, like the Ancient Mariner's, it is a tale that must be told. *Revenons!* Your very brilliant letter awoke me from the most profound lethargy by which beauty such as mine was ever overtaken. A moment's inventory of my attractions, satisfied me that your exquisite description (written, I have since suspected, to amuse an idle hour, but done, nevertheless, with the fine memory and graphic power of genius) was neither fanciful nor over-colored; and, for the first time in my life, I *felt beautiful.* You are an anatomist of the heart; and, I may say to you, that I looked at my own dark eyes, and fine features and person, with the admiration and wonder of a blind beauty restored to sight, and beholding herself in a mirror. You will think, perhaps, that love for the writer of this magic letter should have been the inevitable sequel. But I am here to avert the consequences of my coquetry, and I will be frank with you. *I forgot you in a day!* In the almost insane desire to be seen and appreciated, painted, sung, and loved, which took possession of me when the tumult of my first feeling had passed away, your self-controlled and manageable passion seemed to me frivolous and shallow."

"Have you been better loved?" coldly asked Clay.

"I will answer that question before we part. I did not suffer myself to think of a love that could be returned—for I had husband and children; and, though I felt that a mutual passion, such as I could imagine, would have absorbed, under happier circumstances, every energy of my soul, I had no disposition to make wreck of another's happiness and honor, whatever the temptation. Still, I must be loved—I must come out from my obscurity and shine—I must control the painter's pencil, and the poet's pen, and the statesman's scheme—I must sun my beauty in men's eyes, and be caressed and conspicuous—I must use my gift, and fulfil my destiny! I told my husband this. He secured my devotion to his peace and honor forever, by giving me unlimited control over his fortune and himself. We came to Naples, and my star, hitherto clouded in its own humility, sprang at once to the ascendant. The "attraction of unconscious beauty," is a poet's fiction, believe me! Set it down in your books, Ernest—we are our own nomenclators—the belle as well as the hero! I claimed to be beautiful, and queened it to the top of my bent—and all Naples is at my feet! Oh, Ernest! it is a delicious power to hold human happiness in your control—to be the loadstar of eminent men and bright intellects! Perhaps a woman who is absorbed in one passion, finds, in her lover's character and fame, room enough for her pride and her thirst for influence; but, to me, giving nothing in return but the light of my eyes, there seems, scarce in the world, celebrity, rank, genius enough, to limit my ambition. I would be Helen! I would be Mary of Scots! I would have my beauty as undisputed and renowned as the Apollo's! Am I insane or heartless?"

Clay smiled at the abrupt *naiveté* of the question, but his eyes were full of visible admiration of the glowing pictures before him.

"You are beautiful!" was his answer.

"Am I not! Shall I be celebrated hereafter, Ernest? I should be willing to grow old, if my beauty were 'in amber'—if, by some burning line in your book, some wondrous touch of the pencil, some bold novelty in sculpture, my beauty would live on men's lips forever! Incontri's picture is beautiful, and like; but it is not, if you understand, a conception—it is not a memoir of the woman, as the Cenci's is—it does not embody a complete fame in itself, like the 'Bella' of Titian, or the 'Wife of Giorgione.' If *you* loved me Ernest—"

"If you loved *me*, Julia!" echoed Clay, with a tone rather of mockery than sincerity.

"Ah, but you threw me away; and, even with my own consent, I could never be recovered! Believe me, Ernest, there never was a coquette, who, in some one of her early preferences, had not made a desperate and single venture of her whole heart's devotion. That wrecked—she was lost to love! I embarked with you, soul and heart; and you left to the mercy of the chance of wind, a freight that no tide could bring to port again!"

"You forget the obstacles."

"A poet! and talk of obstacles in love! Did you even ask me to run away with you, Ernest! I would have gone! Ay—coldly as I talk to you now, I would have followed you to a hovel—for it was first love to me. Had it been first love to both of us, I should now be your wife—sharer of your fame! And, oh! how jealous!"

"With your beauty, jealous?"

"Not of flesh-and-blood women, Ernest! With a wife's opportunities, I could outcharm, with half my beauty, the whole troop of Circe. I was thinking of the favors of your pen! Whom would I let you describe! What eyes, what hair, what form but mine—what character, what name, would I ever suffer you to make immortal! Paul Veronese had a wife with my avarice. In his hundred pictures, there is the same blue-eyed, golden-haired woman, as much linked to his fame as Laura to Petrarch's. If he had drawn her but once, she would have been known as the woman Paul Veronese *painted!* She is known now as the woman he *loved*. Delicious immortality!"

"Yet, she could not have exacted it. That would have required an intellect which looked abroad; and poets love no women who are not like birds—content with the summer around them, but with every thought in their nest. Paul Veronese's *Bionda*, with her soft, mild eyes, and fair hair, is the very type of such a woman; and she would not have foregone a caress for twenty immortalities."

"May I ask, what was my attraction then?" said the proud beauty, with a tone of pique.

"Julia Beverley, unconscious and unintellectual!" answered Clay, drawing on his gloves with the air of a man who has got through with an interview. "You have explained your 'metempsychosis,' but I was in love with the form you have cast off. The night grows chill. Sweet dreams to you!"

"Stay, Mr. Clay! You asked me if I had ever been 'better loved,' and I promised you an answer. What think you of a lover who has forgotten the occupation that gave him bread, abandoned his ambition, and, at all hours of the night, is an unrewarded and hopeless watcher beneath my window?"

"To-night excepted," said Clay, looking around.

"Incontri!" called Mrs. Brown, without raising her voice.

Clay started and frowned, as the painter sprang from the shadow of the pine-tree which had before attracted his attention. Falling on his knee, the unhappy lover kissed the jewelled fingers extended to him; and, giving Clay his hand in rising, the poet sprang back, for he had clasped the handle of a stiletto!

"Fear not—she does not love you!" said Incontri, remarking his surprise, and concealing the weapon in his sleeve.

"I was destined to get cured of my love either way," said Clay, bowing himself off the verandah with a shudder and half a smile.

The curtain closed, at the same moment, over the retreating

form of Julia Beverley; and so turned another leaf of Clay's voluminous book of love.

CHAPTER VIII.

Clay threw the volume aside, in which he had been reading, and taking up "the red book," looked out for the county address of Sir Harry Freer, the exponent (only) of Lady Fanny Freer, who, though the "nicest possible creature," is *not* the heroine of this story. Sir Harry's ancestral domain turned out to be a portion of the earth's surface, in that county of England where the old gentry look down upon very famous lords as *too new*, and proportionately upon all other families that have not degenerated since William the Conqueror.

Sir Harry had married an Earl's daughter; but, as the earldom was only the fruit of two generations of public and political eminence, Sir Harry was not considered in Cheshire as having made more than a tolerable match; and, if *she* passed for a "Cheshire cheese" in London, he passed for but the *rind* in the county. In the county, therefore, there was a lord paramount of Freer Hall, and in town, a lady paramount of Brook-street; and it was under the town dynasty, that Miss Blanche Beaufin was invited up from Cheshire to pass a first winter in London—Miss Beaufin being the daughter of a descendant of a Norman retainer of the first Sir Harry, and the relative position of the families having been rigidly kept up to the existing epoch.

The address found in the red book was described in the following letter:

"Dear Lady Fanny—If you have anything beside the ghost room vacant at Freer Hall, I will run down to you. Should you, by chance, be alone, ask up the curate for a week, to keep Sir Harry off my hands; and, as you don't flirt, provide me with somebody more pretty than yourself, for our mutual security. As my autograph sells for eighteen pence, you will excuse the brevity of "Yours, truly,

"Ernest Clay.

"N.B.—Tell me, in your answer, if Blanche Beaufin is within a morning's ride."

Lady Fanny was a warm-hearted, extravagant, beautiful creature of impulse—a passionate friend of Clay's, (for such women there are,) without a spice of flirtation. She was a perennial belle in London; and he had begun his acquaintance with her, by throwing himself at her head, in the approved fashion—in love to the degree of rose-asking and sonnet-writing. As she did not laugh when he sighed, however, but only told him very seriously, that she was not a bit in love with him, and thought he was thowing away his time, he easily forgave her insensibility, and they became very warm allies. Spoiled favorite, as he was, of London society, Clay had qualities for a very sincere friendship; and Lady Fanny, full of irregular talent, had also a strong vein of common sense, and perfectly understood him. This explanation to the reader. It would have saved some trouble and pain, if it had been made by some good angel to Sir Harry Freer.

As the London coach rattled under the bridged gate of the gloomy old town of Chester, Lady Fanny's dashing ponies were almost on their haunches, with her impetuous pull-up at the hotel; and, returning with a nod the coachman's respectful bow, she put her long whip in, at the coach-window, to shake hands with Clay, and, in a few minutes, they were again off the pavements, and taking the road at her ladyship's usual speed.

"Steady, Flash! steady!" (she ran on, talking to Clay, and her ponies, in the same breath;) "doleful ride down, isn't it?—(keep up, Tom, you villain!)—very good of you to come, I'm sure, dear Ernest, and you'll stay—how long will you stay?—(down, Flash)—oh, Miss Beaufin! I've something to say to you about Blanche Beaufin! I didn't answer your *nota bene*—(go along, Tom! that pony wants blooding)—because, to tell you the truth, it's a delicate subject at Freer Hall, and I would rather talk than write about it. You see—(will you be done, Flash!)—the Beaufins, though very nice people, and Blanche quite a love—(go along, lazy Tom!)—the Beaufins, I say, are rated rather crockery in Cheshire. And I am ashamed to own, really quite ashamed, I have not been near them in a month. Shameful, isn't it? There's good action, Ernest! Look at that nigh pony; not a blemish in him; and such a goer in single harness! Well, I'll go around by the Beaufins now."

"Pray, consider, Lady Fanny!" interrupted Clay, deprecatingly, "eighteen hours in a coach."

"Not to go in! oh, not to go in! Blanche is very ill, and sees nobody; and—(come, Tom! come!)—I only heard of it this morning—(there's for your laziness, you stupid horse!)—We'll just call and ask how she is, though Sir Harry—"

"Is she very ill, then?" asked Clay, with a concern which made Lady Fanny turn her eyes from her ponies' ears to look at him.

"They say, very! Of course, Sir Harry can't forbid a visit to the sick."

"Surely he does not forbid you to call on Blanche Beaufin!"

"Not 'forbid' precisely; that wouldn't do—(gently, sweet Flash! now, Tom! now, lazy! trot fair through the hollow!)—but, I invited her to pass the winter with me, without consulting him, and he liked it well enough, till he got back among his stupid neighbors—(well done, Flash!—plague take that bothering whipple-tree!)—and they, and their awkward daughters, whom I might have invited—(whoa! Flash!)—if I had wanted a menagerie, set him to looking into her pedigree. There's the house; the old house, with the vines over it, yonder! So then, Sir Harry—such a sweet girl, too—set his face against the acquaintance. Here we are!—(Whoa, boys! whoa!) Hold the reins a moment, while I run in!"

More to quell a vague and apprehensive feeling of remorse, than to while away idle time, Clay passed the reins back to the stripling in grey livery behind, and walked round Lady Fanny's ponies, expressing his admiration of them, and the turn-out altogether.

"Yes, sir," said the lad, who seemed to have caught some of the cleverness of his mistress, for he scarce looked fourteen, "they're a touch above anything in Cheshire! Look at the forehand of that nigh 'un, sir!—arm and withers like a greyhound, and yet, what a quarter for trotting, sir! Quite the right thing, all over! Carries his flag that way quite nat'ral; never was nick'd, sir! Did you take notice, begging your pardon, sir, how milady put through that hollow? Wasn't it fine, sir? T'other's a goodish nag, too, but nothing to Flash; can't spread, somehow; that's Sir Harry's picking up, and never was a match; no blood in Tom, sir! Look at his fetlock; underbred, but a jimpy nag for a roadster, if a man wanted work out on him. See how he blows, sir, and Flash as still as a stopped wheel!"

Lady Fanny's reappearance at the door of the house, interrupted her page's eulogy on the bays; and, with a very altered expression of countenance, she resumed the reins, and drove slowly homeward.

"She is very ill—very ill! but, she wishes to see you, and you must go there; but not to-morrow. She is passing a crisis now, and, her physician says, will be easier, if not better, after to-morrow. Poor girl! Dear Blanche! Ah, Clay! but no—no matter; I shall talk about it with more composure, by-and-bye—poor Blanche!"

Lady Fanny's tears rained upon her two hands, as she let out her impatient horses, to be sooner at home; and, in half an hour, Clay was alone in his luxurious quarters, under Sir Harry's roof, with two hours to dinner, and more than thoughts enough, and very sad ones, to make him glad of time and solitude.

Freer Hall was full of company—Sir Harry's company; and Clay, with the quiet assurance of a London star, used to the dominant, took his station by Lady Fanny, on entering the drawing-room, and, when dinner was announced, gave her his arm, without troubling himself to remember that there was a baronet who had claim to the honor, and of whom he must simply make a mortal enemy. At table, the conversation ran mainly in Sir Harry's vein—hunting; and Clay did not even take a listener's part; but, in a low tone, talked of London to Lady Fanny—her ladyship (unaccountably to her husband and his friends, who were used to furnish her more merriment than revery) pensive, and out of spirits. With the announcement of coffee in the drawing-room, Clay disappeared with her, and their evening was *tête-*

a-tête; for Sir Harry and his friends were three-bottle men, and commonly bade good-night to ladies when the ladies left the table. If there had been a second thought in the convivial squirearchy, they would have troubled their heads less about a man who did not exhibit the first symptom of love for the wife—civility to the husband. But, this is a hand-to-mouth world, in the way of knowledge; and nothing is stored but experiences, lifetime by lifetime.

Another day passed, and another, and mystery seemed the ruling spirit of the hour, for there were enigmas for all. Regularly, morning and afternoon, the high-stepping ponies were ordered round, and Lady Fanny (with Mr. Clay for company to the gate) visited the Beaufins, now against positive orders from the irate Sir Harry; and daily, Clay's reserve with his beautiful hostess increased, and his distress of mind with it; for both he and she were alarmed with the one piece of unexplained intelligence between them—Miss Beaufin would see Mr. Clay when she would be dying! Not before—for worlds, not before—and, of the physician constantly in attendance, (Lady Fanny often present,) Clay knew that the poor girl besought, with an eagerness to the last degree touching and earnest, to know when hope could be given over. She was indulged, unquestioned, as a dying daughter; and, whatever might be her secret, Lady Fanny promised, that, at the turning hour, come what would of distressing and painful, she would herself come with Mr. Clay to her death-bed.

Sir Harry and his friends were in the billiard-room, and Lady Fanny and Clay breakfasting together, when a note was brought in by one of the footmen, who waited for an answer.

"Say that I will come," said Lady Fanny; and—stay, George! See that my ponies are harnessed immediately; put the head of the phaeton up, and let it stand in the coach-house. And, Timson!" she added, to the butler, who stood at the side-table, "if Sir Harry inquires for me, say that I am gone to visit a sick friend."

Lady Fanny walked to the window. It rained in torrents. There was no need of explanation to Clay; he understood the note, and its meaning.

"The offices connect with the stables, by a covered way," she said, "and we will get in there. Shall you be ready in a few minutes?"

"Quite, dear Lady Fanny! I am ready now."

"The rain is rather fortunate than otherwise," she added, in going out, "for Sir Harry will not see us go; and he might throw an obstacle in the way, and make it difficult to manage. Wrap well up, Ernest!"

The butler looked inquisitively at Clay and his mistress; but, both were pre-occupied, and, in ten minutes, the rapid phaeton was on its way, the ponies pressing on the bit, as if the eagerness of the two hearts beating behind them, was communicated through the reins; and Lady Fanny, contrary to her wont, driving in unencouraging silence. The three or four miles between Freer Hall and their destination, were soon traversed; and under the small *porte-cochère* of the ancient mansion, the ponies stood panting and sheltered.

"Kind Lady Fanny! God bless you!" said a tall, dark man, of a very striking exterior, coming out to the phaeton. "And you, sir, are welcome!"

They followed him into the little parlor, where Clay was presented by Lady Fanny to the mother of Miss Beaufin—a singularly, yet sadly sweet woman, in voice, person, and address;

to the old, white-haired vicar, and to the physician, who returned his bow with a cold and very formal salute.

"There is no time to be lost," said he, "and, at the request of Miss Beaufin, Lady Fanny and this gentleman will please go to her chamber without us. I can trust your Ladyship to see that the remainder of life is not shortened nor harrassed by needless agitation."

Clay's heart beat violently. At the extremity of the long and dimly-lighted passage, thrown open by the father to Lady Fanny, he saw a white-curtained bed—the death-bed, he knew, of the gay and fair flower of a London season, the wonder and idol of difficult fashion, and unadmiring rank. Blanche Beaufin had appeared, like a marvel, in the brilliant circles of Lady Fanny's acquaintance—a distinguished, unconscious, dazzling girl, of whom her fair introductress (either in mischief or good nature) would say nothing, but that she was her neighbor in Cheshire; though all that nature could lavish, on one human creature, seemed hers, with all that high birth could stamp on mien, countenance, and manners. Clay paid her his tribute with the rest—the hundred who flattered and followed her—but, she was a proud girl, and, though he seized every opportunity of being near her, nothing in her manner betrayed to him that he was not counted among the hundred. A London season fleets fast, and, taken by surprise with Lady Fanny's early departure for the country, her farewells were written on the corners of cards; and, with a secret deep buried in the heart, she was brought back to the retirement of home.

Brief history of the breaking of a heart!

Lady Fanny started slightly on entering the chamber. The sick girl sat propped in an arm-chair, dressed in snowy white;

even her slight foot appearing beneath the edge of her dress, in a slipper of white satin. Her brown hair fell in profuse ringlets over her shoulders; but it was gathered behind into a knot, and from it depended a white veil, the diamonds which fastened it pressing, to the glossy curve of her head, a slender stem of orange flowers. Her features were of that slight mould which shows sickness by little except higher transparency of the blue veins, and brighter redness in the lips; and, as she smiled with suffused cheek, and held out her gloved hand to Clay, with a vain effort to articulate, he passed his hands across his eyes, and looked inquiringly at his friend. He had expected, though he had never realized, that she would be altered. She looked almost as he had left her. He remembered her only as he had oftenest seen her—dressed for ball or party; and, but for the solemnity of the preparation he had gone through, he might have thought his feelings had been played upon, only; that Blanche Beaufin was well—still beautiful and well; that he should again see her in the brilliant circles of London; still love her as he secretly did, and receive what he now felt would be, under any circumstances, a gift of heaven—the assurance of a return. This, and a world of confused emotion, tumultuously, and in an instant, rushed through his heart; for there are moments in which we live lives of feeling and thought—moments, glances, which supply years of secret or bitter memory.

This is but a sketch—but an outline of a tale over true. Were there space—were there time, to follow out the traverse thread of its mere mournful incidents, we might write the reverse side of a leaf of life ever read partially and wrong—the life of the gay and unlamenting. Sickness and death had here broken down a wall of adamant, between two creatures every way formed for each other. In health, and ordinary regularity of circumstances, they would have loved as truly and deeply as those in humbler, or in more fortunate relative positions; but they, probably, would never have been united. It is the system—the necessary system, of the class to which Clay belonged, to turn adroitly and gayly off every shaft to the heart; to take advantage of no opening to affection; to smother all preference that would lead to an interchange of hallowed vows; to profess insensibility equally polished and hardened, on the subject of pure love; to forswear marriage, and make of it a mock and an impossibility. And whose handiwork is this unnatural order of society? Was it established by the fortunate and joyous—by the wealthy and untrammelled, at liberty to range the world if they liked, and marry where they chose, but, preferring gaiety to happiness, and lawless liberty to virtuous love? No, indeed! not by these! Show me one such man, and I will show you a rare perversion of common feeling—a man, who, under any circumstances, would have been cold and eccentric. It is not to those able to marry where they will, that the class of London gay men owe their system of mocking opinions. But it is to the *companions* of fortunate men—gifted, like them, in all but fortune, and holding their caste by the tenure of forsworn ties—abiding in the paradise of aristocracy, with pure love for the forbidden fruit! Are such men insensible to love? Has this forbidden joy—this one thing hallowed in a bad world—has it no temptation for the gay man? Is his better nature quite dead within him? Is he never ill and sad, where gaiety cannot reach him? Does he envy the rich young lord (his friend) everything but his blushing and pure bride? Is he poet or wit, or the mirror of taste and elegance, yet incapable of discerning the qualities of a true love—the celestial refinement of a maiden passion, lawful and fearless, devoted because spotless, and enduring because made up half of prayer and gratitude to her Maker? Does he not know distinctions of feeling, as he knows character in a play? Does he not discriminate between purity and guilt in love, as he does in his nice judgment of honor and taste? Is he gayly dead to the deepest and most elevated cravings of nature—*love*, passionate, single-hearted, and holy Trust me, there is a bitterness whose depths we can only fathom by refinement! To move among creatures embellished and elevated to the last point of human attainment, lovely and unsullied, and know yourself, (as to all but gazing on, and appreciating them,) a pariah and an outcast—to breathe their air, and be the companion and apparent equal of those for whose bliss they were created, and to whom they are offered for choice, with the profusion of flowers in a garden, (the chooser and possessor of the brightest, your inferior in all else,)—to live thus, to suffer thus, and still smile and call it choice, and your own way of happiness—this is mockery, indeed! He who now stood in the death-room of Blanche Beaufin, had felt it, in its bitterest intensity!

"Mr. Clay!—Ernest!" said the now pale creature, breaking the silence, with a strong effort, for he had dropped on his knee at her side, in ungovernable emotion, and, as yet, had but articulated her name—"Ernest! I have but little time for anything—least of all, for disguise or ceremony. I am assured that I am dying. I am convinced," she added, firmly, taking up the watch that lay beside her, "that I have been told the truth, and that, when this hour-hand comes round again, I shall be dead. I will conceal nothing. They have given me cordials that will support me one hour, and, for that hour—and for eternity—I wish—if I may be so blest—if God will permit—to be your wife!"

Lady Fanny Freer rose, and came to her with rapid steps; and Clay sprang to his feet, and in a passion of tears exclaimed, "Oh, God! can this be true!"

"Answer me, quickly!" she continued, in a voice raised, but breaking through sobs—"an hour is short; oh, *how* short, when it is the last! I cannot stay with you long, were you a thousand times mine. Tell me, Ernest!—shall it be?—shall I be wedded ere I die?—wedded now?"

A passionate gesture to Lady Fanny, was all the answer Clay could make; and, in another moment, the aged vicar was in the chamber, with her parents and the physician—to all of whom a few words explained a mystery which her bridal attire had already half unravelled.

Blanche spoke quickly, "Shall he proceed, Ernest?"

Her prayer-book was open on her knee, and Clay gave it to the vicar, who, with a quick sense of sympathy, and with but a glance at the weeping and silent parents, read, without delay, the hallowed ceremonial.

Clay's countenance elevated and cleared as he proceeded, and Blanche, with her large suffused eyes fixed on his, listened with a smile, serene, but expressive of unspeakable rapture. Her beauty had never been so radiant, so angelic. In heaven, on her bridal night, beatified spirit as she was, she could not have been more beautiful!

One instant of embarrassment occurred, unobserved by the dying bride, but, with the thoughtfulness of womanly generosity, Lady Fanny had foreseen it, and, drawing off her own wedding-ring, she passed it into Ernest's hand ere the interruption became apparent. Alas! the emaciated hand ungloved to receive it! The wasted finger pointed, indeed, to heaven! Till then, Clay had felt almost in a dream. But here was suffering—sickness—death! This told what the hectic brightness, and the faultless features, would fain deny—what the fragrant and still unwithering flowers upon her temples would seem to mock! But the hectic was already fading, and the flowers outlived the light in the dark eyes they shaded!

The vicar joined their hands with the solemn adjuration, "Those whom God hath joined together let no man put asunder;" and Clay rose from his knees, and pressing his first kiss upon her lips, strained her passionately to his heart.

"Mine in heaven!" she cried, giving way at last to her tears, as she closed her slight arms over his neck; "mine in heaven! Is it not so, mother! father! is he not mine now? There is no giving in marriage in heaven, but the ties, hallowed here, are not forgotten there! Tell me they are not! Speak to me, my husband! Press me to your heart, Ernest! Your wife—oh, I thank God!"

The physician sprang forward and laid his hand upon her pulse. She fell back upon her pillows, and, with a smile upon her lips, and the tears still wet upon her long and drooping lashes, lay dead.

Lady Fanny took the mother by the arm, and, with a gesture to the father and the physician to follow, they retired and left the bridegroom alone.

* * * * * *

Life is full of sudden transitions; and the next event in that of Ernest Clay, was a duel with Sir Harry Freer—if the Morning Post was to be believed—"occasioned by the indiscretion of Lady

Fanny, who, in a giddy moment, *it appears*, had given to her ad mirer, Sir Harry's opponent, her wedding-ring!"

CHAPTER IX.

Late one night in June two gentlemen arrived at the Villa Hotel of the Baths of Lucca. They stopped the low britzka in which they travelled, and, leaving a servant to make arrangements for their lodging, linked arms and strolled up the road toward the banks of the Lima. The moon was chequered at the moment with the poised leaf of a tree-top, and, as it passed from her face, she arose and stood alone in the steel-blue of the unclouded heavens—a luminous and tremulous plate of gold. And you know how beautiful must have been the night, a June night in Italy, with a moon at the full!

A lady, with a servant following her at a little distance, passed the travellers on the bridge of the Lima. She dropped her veil and went by in silence. But the Freyherr felt the arm of his friend tremble within his own.

"Do you know her, then?" asked Von Leisten.

"By the thrill in my veins we have met before," said Clay; "but whether this involuntary sensation was pleasurable or painful, I have not yet decided. There are none I care to meet—none who can be here." He added the last few words after a moment's pause, and sadly.

They walked on in silence to the base of the mountain, busy, each, with such coloring as the moonlight threw on their thoughts, but neither of them was happy.

Clay was humane, and a lover of nature—a poet, that is to say—and, in a world so beautiful, could never be a prey to disgust;

but he was satiated with the common emotions of life. His heart, for ever overflowing, had filled many a cup with love, but with strange tenacity he turned back for ever to the first. He was weary of the beginnings of love—weary of its probations and changes. He had passed the period of life when inconstancy was tempting. He longed now for an affection that would continue into another world—holy and pure enough to pass a gate guarded by angels. And his first love—recklessly as he had thrown it away—was now the thirst of his existence.

It was two o'clock at night. The moon lay broad upon the southern balconies of the hotel, and every casement was open to its luminous and fragrant stillness. Clay and the Freyherr Von Leisten, each in his apartment, were awake, unwilling to lose the luxury of the night. And there was one other, under that roof, waking, with her eyes fixed on the moon.

As Clay leaned his head on his hand, and looked outward to the sky, his heart began to be troubled. There was a point in the path of the moon's rays where his spirit turned back. There was an influence, abroad in the dissolving moonlight around him, which resistlessly awakened the past—the sealed but unforgotten past. He could not single out the emotion. He knew not whether it was fear or hope—pain or pleasure. He called, through the open window, to Von Leisten.

The Freyherr, like himself, and like all who have outlived the effervescence of life, was enamored of the night. A moment of unfathomable moonlight was dearer to him than hours disenchanted with the sun. He, too, had been looking outward and upward—but with no trouble at his heart.

"The night is inconceivably sweet," he said, as he entered,

"and your voice called in my thought and sense from the intoxication of a revel. What would you, my friend?"

"I am restless, Von Leisten! There is some one near us whose glances cross mine on the moonlight, and agitate and perplex me. Yet there was but one, on earth, deep enough in the life-blood of my being to move me thus—even were she here! And she is not here!"

His voice trembled and softened, and the last word was scarce audible on his closing lips, for the Freyherr had passed his hands over him while he spoke, and he had fallen into the trance of the spirit-world.

Clay and Von Leisten had retired from the active passions of life together, and had met and mingled at that moment of void and thirst when each supplied the want of the other. The Freyherr was a German noble, of a character passionately poetic, and of singular acquirement in the mystic fields of knowledge. Too wealthy to need labor, and too proud to submit his thoughts or his attainments to the criticism or judgment of the world, he lavished on his own life, and on those linked to him in friendship, the strange powers he had acquired, and the prodigal overthrow of his daily thought and feeling. Clay was his superior, perhaps, in genius, and necessity had driven him to develop the type of his inner soul, and leave its impress on the time. But he was inferior to Von Leisten in the power of will, and he lay in his control like a child in its mother's. Four years they had passed together, much of it in the secluded castle of Von Leisten, busied with the occult studies to which the Freyherr was secretly devoted; but they were now travelling down to Italy to meet the luxurious summer, and dividing their lives between the enjoyment of nature and the ideal world they had unlocked. Von Leisten had lost, by death, the human altar on which his heart could alone burn the incense of love; and Clay had flung aside in an hour of intoxicating passion the one pure affection in which his happiness was sealed—and both were desolate. But in the world of the past, Von Leisten, though more irrevocably lonely, was more tranquilly blest.

The Freyherr released the entranced spirit of his friend, and bade him follow back the rays of the moon to the source of his agitation.

A smile crept slowly over the speaker's lips.

In an apartment flooded with the silver lustre of the night, reclined, in an invalid's chair, propped with pillows, a woman of singular, though most fragile beauty. Books and music lay strewn around, and a lamp, subdued to the tone of the moonlight by an orb of alabaster, burned beside her. She lay bathing her blue eyes in the round chalice of the moon. A profusion of brown ringlets fell over the white dress that enveloped her, and her oval cheek lay supported on the palm of her hand, and her bright red lips were parted. The pure, yet passionate spell of that soft night possessed her.

Over her leaned the disembodied spirit of him who had once loved her—praying to God that his soul might be so purified as to mingle unstartlingly, unrepulsively, in hallowed harmony with hers. And presently he felt the coming of angels toward him, breathing into the deepest abysses of his existence a tearful and purifying sadness. And, with a trembling aspiration of grateful humility to his Maker, he stooped to her forehead, and, with his impalpable lips, impressed upon its snowy tablet a kiss.

It seemed to Eve Gore a thought of the past that brought the blood suddenly to her cheek. She started from her reclining position, and, removing the obscuring shade from her lamp, arose and crossed her hands upon her wrists, and paced thoughtfully to and fro. Her lips murmured inarticulately. But the thought, painfully though it came, changed unaccountably to melancholy sweetness; and, subduing her lamp again, she resumed her steadfast gaze upon the moon.

Ernest knelt beside her, and, with his invisible brow bowed upon her hand, poured forth, in the voiceless language of the soul, his memories of the past, his hope, his repentance, his pure and passionate adoration at the present hour.

And thinking she had been in a sweet dream, yet wondering at its truthfulness and power, Eve wept, silently and long. As the morning touched the east, slumber weighed upon her moistened eyelids, and, kneeling by her bedside, she murmured her gratitude to God for a heart relieved of a burden long borne, and so went peacefully to her sleep. * * * * * *

It was in the following year, and in the beginning of May. The gay world of England was concentrated in London, and at the entertainments of noble houses there were many beautiful women and many marked men. The Freyherr Von Leisten, after years of absence, had appeared again, his mysterious and undeniable superiority of mien and influence again yielded to, as before, and again bringing to his feet the homage and deference of the crowd he moved among. To his inscrutable power the game of society was easy, and he walked where he would, through its barriers of form.

He stood one night looking on at a dance. A lady of a noble air was near him, and both were watching the movements of the loveliest woman present, a creature in radiant health, apparently about twenty-three, and of matchless fascination of person and manner. Von Leisten turned to the lady near him to inquire her name, but his attention was arrested by the resemblance between her and the object of his admiring curiosity, and he was silent.

The lady had bowed before he withdrew his gaze, however.

"I think we have met before!" she said; but at the next instant a slight flush of displeasure came to her cheek, and she seemed regretting that she had spoken.

"Pardon me!" said Von Leisten, "but—if the question be not rude—do you remember where?"

She hesitated a moment.

"I have recalled it since I have spoken," she continued; "but as the remembrance of the person who accompanied you always gives me pain, I would willingly have unsaid it. One evening of last year, crossing the bridge of the Lima, you were walking with Mr. Clay. Pardon me—but, though I left Lucca with my daughter on the following morning, and saw you no more, the association, or your appearance, had imprinted the circumstance on my mind."

"And is that Eve Gore!" said Von Leisten, musingly, gazing on the beautiful creature now gliding with light step to her mother's side.

But the Freyherr's heart was gone to his friend.

As the burst of the waltz broke in upon the closing of the quadrille, he offered his hand to the fair girl, and, as they moved round to the entrancing music, he murmured in her ear, "He who came to you in the moonlight of Italy will be with you again, if you are alone, at the rising of to-night's late moon. Believe the voice that then speaks to you!" * * * *

It was with implacable determination that Mrs. Gore refused, to the entreaties of Von Leisten, a renewal of Clay's acquaintance with her daughter. Resentment for the apparent recklessness with which he had once sacrificed her maiden love for an unlawful passion—scornful unbelief of any change in his character—distrust of the future tendency of the powers of his genius—all mingled together, in a hostility proof against persuasion. She had expressed this with all the positiveness of language, when her daughter suddenly entered the room. It was the morning after the ball, and she had risen late. But, though subdued and pensive in her air, Von Leisten saw at a glance that she was happy.

"Can you bring him to me?" said Eve, letting her hand remain in Von Leisten's, and bending her deep blue eyes inquiringly on his.

And, with no argument but tears and caresses, and an unexplained assurance of her conviction of the repentant purity and love of him to whom her heart was once given, the confiding and strong-hearted girl bent, at last, the stern will that forbade her happiness. Her mother unclasped the slight arms from her neck, and gave her hand in silent consent to Von Leisten.

The Freyherr stood a moment with his eyes fixed on the ground. The color fled from his cheeks, and his brow moistened.

"I have called him," he said—"he will be here!"

"An hour elapsed, and Clay entered the house. He had risen from a bed of sickness, and came, pale and in terror—for the spirit-summons was powerful. But Von Leisten welcomed him at the door with a smile, and withdrew the mother from the room, and left Ernest alone with his future bride—the first union, save in spirit, after years of separation.

"BEAUTY AND THE BEAST;"

OR,

HANDSOME MRS. TITTON AND HER PLAIN HUSBAND.

> "That man i' the world who shall report he has
> A better wife, let him in naught be trusted
> For speaking false in that."—HENRY VIII.

I HAVE always been very fond of the society of portrait-painters. Whether it is, that the pursuit of a beautiful and liberal art softens their natural qualities, or that, from the habit of conversing while engrossed with the pencil, they like best that touch-and-go talk which takes care of itself; or, more probably still, whether the freedom with which they are admitted behind the curtains of vanity and affection, gives a certain freshness and truth to their views of things around them—certain it is, that, in all countries, their rooms are the most agreeable of haunts, and they themselves the most enjoyable of cronies.

I had chanced, in Italy, to make the acquaintance of S——, an English artist of considerable cleverness in his profession, but more remarkable for his frank good breeding, and his abundant good nature. Four years after, I had the pleasure of renewing my intercourse with him in London, where he was flourishing, quite up to his deserving, as a portrait-painter. His rooms were hard-by one of the principal thoroughfares, and, from making an occasional visit, I grew to frequenting them daily, often joining him at his early breakfast, and often taking him out with me to drive whenever we chanced to tire of our twilight stroll. While rambling in Hyde Park, one evening, I mentioned, for the twentieth time, a singularly ill-assorted couple I had once or twice met at his room—a woman of superb beauty, attended by a very inferior-looking and ill-dressed man. S—— had, previously, with a smile at my speculations, dismissed the subject rather crisply; but, on this occasion, I went into some surmises as to the probable results of such "pairing and matching," and he either felt called upon to defend the lady, or made my misapprehension of her character an excuse for telling me what he knew about her. He began the story in the Park, and ended it over a bottle of wine in the Haymarket—of course, with many interruptions and digressions. Let me see if I can tie his broken threads together.

"That lady is Mrs. Fortescue Titton, and the gentleman you so much disparage, is, if you please, the incumbrance to ten thousand a year—the money as much at her service as the husband by whom she gets it. Whether he could have won her, had he been

"Bereft and gelded of his patrimony,"

I will not assert, especially to one who looks on them as 'Beauty and the Beast;' but, that she loves him, or, at least, prefers to him no handsomer man, I may say I have been brought to believe, in the way of my profession."

"You have painted her, then?" I asked rather eagerly, thinking I might get a sketch of her face to take with me to another country.

"No, but I have painted *him*—and for her—and it is not a case of Titania and Bottom, either. She is quite aware he is a monster; and wanted his picture for a reason you would never divine. But I must begin at the beginning.

"After you left me in Italy, I was employed, by the Earl of ——, to copy one or two of his favorite pictures in the Vatican, and that brought me rather well acquainted with his son. Lord George was a gay youth, and a very 'look-and-die' style of fellow; and, as much from admiration of his beauty as anything else, I asked him to sit to me, on our return to London. I painted him very fantastically in an Albanian cap and Oriental morning-gown and slippers, smoking a narghile—the room in which he sat, by the way, being a correct portrait of his own den—a perfect museum of costly luxury. It was a pretty gorgeous turn out, in the way of color, and was severely criticised, but still a good deal noticed—for I sent it to the exhibition.

"I was one day going into Somerset House, when Lord George hailed me, from his cab. He wished to suggest some alteration in his picture, or, to tell me of some criticism upon it—I forget exactly what; but we went up together. Directly before the portrait, gazing at it with marked abstraction, stood a beautiful woman, quite alone; and, as she occupied the only point where the light was favorable, we waited a moment, till she should pass on—Lord George, of course, rather disposed to shrink from being recognized as the original. The woman's interest in the picture seemed rather to increase, however; and, what with variations of the posture of her head, and pulling at her glove-fingers, and other female indications of restlessness and enthusiasm, I thought I was doing her no injustice by turning to my companion with a congratulatory smile.

"'It *seems* a case, by Jove!' said Lord George, trying to look as if it were a matter of very simple occurrence; 'and she's as fine a creature as I've seen this season! Eh, old boy? We must run her down, and see where she burrows—and there's nobody with her, by good luck!'

"A party entered just then, and passed between her and the picture. She looked annoyed, I thought, but started forward, and borrowed a catalogue of a little girl; and, we could see that she turned to the last page, on which the portrait was numbered, with, of course, the name and address of the painter. She made a memorandum on one of her cards, and left the house. Lord George followed, and I, too, as far as the door, where I saw her get into a very stylishly-appointed carriage and drive away, followed closely by the cab of my friend, whom I had declined to accompany.

"You wouldn't have given very heavy odds against his chance, would you?" said S——, after a moment's pause.

"No, indeed!" I answered, quite sincerely.

"Well, I was at work, the next morning, glazing a picture I had just finished, when the servant brought up the card of Mrs. Fortescue Titton. I chanced to be alone, so the lady was shown at once into my painting room; and lo! the *incognita* of Somerset House. The plot thickens, thought I! She sat down in my 'subject' chair; and, faith! her beauty quite dazzled me! Her first smile—but, you have seen her; so I'll not bore you with a description.

"Mrs. Titton blushed on opening her errand to me—first, inquiring if I was the painter of 'No. 403,' in the exhibition, and saying some very civil things about the picture. I mentioned that it was a portrait of Lord George ——, (for his name was not in the catalogue,) and I thought she blushed still more confusedly; but, that, I think now, was fancy, or, at any rate, had nothing to do with feeling for his lordship. It was natural enough for me to be mistaken; for she was very particular in her inquiries as to the costume, furniture, and little belongings of the picture, and asked me, among other things, whether it was a flattered likeness?—this last question very pointedly, too!

"She arose to go. Was I at leisure—and could I sketch a head for her—and when?

"I appointed the next day, expecting, of course, that the subject was the lady herself, and scarcely slept with thinking of it, and starved myself at breakfast to have a clear eye, and a hand wide awake. And, at ten she came, with her Mr. Fortescue Titton! I was sorry to see that she had a husband; for I had indulged myself with a vague presentiment that she was a widow; but I begged him to take a chair, and prepared the platform for my beautiful subject.

"'Will you take your seat?' I asked, with all my suavity, when my palette was ready.

"'My dear,' said she, turning to her husband, and pointing to the chair, 'Mr. S—— is ready for you.'

"I begged pardon for a moment, crossed over to Verey's, and bolted a beefsteak! A cup of coffee, and a glass of Curaçoa, and a little walk round Hanover square, and I recovered from the shock a little. It went very hard, I give you my word.

"I returned, and took a look, for the first time, at Mr. Titton. You have seen him, and have some idea of what his portrait might be, considered as a pleasure to the artist—what it might promise, I should rather say; for, after all, I ultimately enjoyed working at it, quite aside from the presence of Mrs. Titton. It was the ugliest face in the world, but full of good-nature; and, as I looked closer into it, I saw, among its coarse features, lines of almost feminine delicacy, and capabilities of enthusiasm, of which the man himself was probably unconscious. Then a certain helpless style of dress was a wet blanket to him. Rich from his cradle, I suppose his qualities had never been needed on the surface. His wife knew them.

"From time to time, as I worked, Mrs. Titton came and looked over my shoulder. With a natural desire to please her, I, here and there, softened a harsh line, and was going on to flatter the likeness—not as successfully as I could wish, however; for it is much easier to get a faithful likeness, than to flatter without destroying it.

"'Mr. S——,' said she, laying her hand on my arm, as I thinned away the lumpy rim of his nostril, 'I want, first, a literal copy of my husband's features. Suppose, with this idea, you take a fresh canvas?'

"Thoroughly mystified by the whole business, I did as she requested; and, in two sittings, made a likeness of Titton, which would have given you a face-ache. He shrugged his shoulders at it, and seemed very glad when the bore of sitting was over; but, they seemed to understand each other very well, or, if not, he reserved his questions till there could be no restraint upon the answer. He seemed a capital fellow, and I liked him exceedingly.

"I asked if I should frame the picture, and send it home? No! I was to do neither. If I would be kind enough not to show it, nor to mention it, to any one, and come next day and dine with them, *en famille*, Mrs. Titton would feel very much obliged to me. And this dinner was followed up by breakfasts and lunches and suppers; and, for a fortnight, I really lived with the Tittons—and, pleasanter people to live with, by Jove, you haven't seen in your travels, though you *are* 'a picked man of countries!'

"I should mention, by-the-way, that I was always placed opposite Titton at table, and that he was a good deal with me, one way and another, taking me out, as you do, for a stroll, calling and sitting with me when I was at work, etc. And, as to Mrs. Titton—if I did not mistrust your *arriere penseé*, I would enlarge a little on my intimacy with Mrs. Titton! But, believe me when I tell you, that, without a ray of flirtation, we became as cosily intimate as brother and sister."

"And what of Lord George, all this time?" I asked.

"Oh, Lord George!—Well, Lord George, of course, had no difficulty in making Mrs. Titton's acquaintance, though they were not quite in the same circle; and he had been presented to her, and had seen her at a party or two, where he managed to be invited on purpose; but of this, for a while, I heard nothing. She had not yet seen him at her own house, and I had not chanced to encounter him. But, let me go on with my story.

"Mrs. Titton sent for me to come to her, one morning rather early. I found her in her boudoir, in a *negligé* morning-dress, and looking adorably beautiful, and as pure as beautiful, you smiling villain! She seemed to have something on her mind, about which she was a little embarrassed; but, I knew her too well, to lay any unction to my soul. We chatted about the weather a few moments, and she came to the point. You will see that she was a woman of some talent, *mon ami!*

"'Have you looked at my husband's portrait since you finished it?" she asked.

"'No, indeed!' I replied, rather hastily—but immediately apologized.

"'Oh, if I had not been certain you would not,' she said, with a smile, 'I should have requested it, for I wished you to forget it, as far as possible. And now, let me tell you what I want of you! You have got, on canvas, a likeness of Fortescue, as the world sees him. Since taking it, however, you have seen him more intimately, and—and—like his face better—do you not?'

"'Certainly! certainly!'" I exclaimed, in all sincerity.

"'Thank you! If I mistake not, then, you do not, when thinking of him, call up to your mind the features in your portrait, but a face formed rather of his good qualities, as you have learned to trace them in his expression.'

"'True,' I said, 'very true!'

"'Now, then,' she continued, leaning over to me very earnestly, 'I want you to paint a new picture, and, without departing from the real likeness, which you will have to guide you—breathe into it the expression you have in your ideal likeness. Add—to what the world sees—what I see, what you see, what all who love him see, in his plain features. Idealize it—spiritualize it, and, without lessening the resemblance. Can this be done?'

"I thought it could. I promised to do my utmost.

"'I shall call and see you as you progress in it,' she said, 'and now, if you have nothing better to do, stay to lunch, and come out with me in the carriage. I want a little of your foreign taste in the selection of some pretty nothings for a gentleman's toilet.'

"We passed the morning in making what I should consider very extravagant purchases for anybody but a prince-royal, winding up with some delicious cabinet pictures, and some gems of statuary—all suited only, I should say, to the apartments of a fastidious luxuriast. I was not yet at the bottom of her secret.

"I went to work upon the new picture, with the zeal always given to an artist by an appreciative and confiding employer. She called every day, and made important suggestions, and, at last, I finished it to her satisfaction and mine; and, without speaking of it as a work of art, I may give you my opinion, that Titton will scarcely be more embellished in the other world—that is, if it be true, as the divines tell us, that our mortal likeness will be so far preserved, though improved upon, that we shall be recognizable by our friends. Still, I was to paint a third picture—a cabinet full length; and, for this, the other two were but studies, and so intended by Mrs. Fortescue Titton. It was to be an improvement upon Lord George's portrait, (which, of course, had given her the idea,) and was to represent her husband in a very costly, and an exceedingly *recherché* morning costume—dressing-gown, slippers, waistcoat, and neckcloth worn with perfect elegance, and representing a Titton with a faultless attitude, (in a *fauteuil*, reading,) a faultless exterior, and around him the most sumptuous appliances of dressing-room luxury. This picture cost me a great deal of vexation and labor; for it was, emphatically, a *fancy* picture—poor Titton never having appeared in that character, even 'by particular desire.' I finished it, however, and again to her satisfaction. I afterward added some finishing touches to the other two, and sent them home, appropriately framed, according to very minute instructions."

"How long ago was this?" I asked.

"Three years," replied S——, musing over his wine.

"Well—the sequel?" said I, a little impatient.

"I was thinking how I should let it break upon you, as it took effect upon her acquaintances; for, understand, Mrs. Titton is too much of a diplomatist to do anything obviously dramatic in this age of ridicule. She knows very well that any sudden 'flare-up' of her husband's consequence—any new light on his character obviously calling for attention—would awaken speculation, and set to work the watchful anatomizers of the body fashionable. Let me see! I will tell you what I should have known about it, had I been only an ordinary acquaintance—not in the secret, and not the painter of the pictures.

"Some six months after the finishing of the last portrait, I was at a large ball at their house. Mrs. Titton's beauty, I should have told you, and the style in which they lived, and, very possibly, a little of Lord George's good will, had elevated them, from the wealthy and respectable level of society, to the fashionable and exclusive. All the best people went there. As I was going in, I overtook, at the head of the stairs, a very clever little widow, an acquaintance of mine, and she honored me by taking my arm, and keeping it for a promenade through the rooms. We made our bow to Mrs. Titton, and strolled across the reception-room, where the most conspicuous object, dead facing us, with a flood of light upon it, was my first veracious portrait of Titton! As I was not known as the artist, I indulged myself in some commonplace exclamations of horror.

"'Do not look at that,' said the widow, 'you will distress poor Mrs. Titton. What a quiz that clever husband of hers must be, to insist on exposing such a caricature!'

"'How insist upon it?' I asked.

"'Why, have you never seen the one in her boudoir? Come with me?'

"We made our way through the apartments, to the little retreat lined with silk, which was the morning lounge of the fair mistress of the house. There was but one picture, with a curtain drawn carefully across it—my second portrait! We sat down on the luxurious cushions, and the widow went off into a discussion of it and the original, pronouncing it a perfect likeness, not at all flattered, and very soon begging me to re-draw the curtain, lest we should be surprised by Mr. Titton himself.

"'And suppose we were?' said I.

"'Why, he is such an oddity!' replied the widow, lowering her tone. 'They say, that in this very house, he has a suite of apartments entirely to himself, furnished with a taste and luxury really wonderful! There are *two* Mr. Tittons, my dear friend!—one a perfect Sybarite, very elegant in his dress, when he chooses to be, excessively accomplished and fastidious, and brilliant and fascinating to a degree! (and, in this character, they say he won that superb creature for a wife;) and the other Mr. Titton is just the slovenly monster that everybody sees! Isn't it odd?'

"'Queer enough!' said I, affecting great astonishment; 'pray, have you ever been into these mysterious apartments?'

"'No! They say only his wife and himself, and one confidential servant, ever pass the threshold. Mrs. Titton don't like to talk about it, though one would think she could scarcely object to her husband's being thought better of. It's pride on his part —sheer pride, and I can understand the feeling very well! He's a very superior man, and he has made up his mind that the world thinks him very awkward and ugly; and he takes a pleasure in showing the world that he don't care a rush for its opinion, and has resources quite sufficient within himself. That's the reason that atrocious portrait is hung up in the best room, and this good-looking one covered up with a curtain! I suppose *this* wouldn't be here, if he could have his own way, and if his wife weren't so much in love with him!'

"This, I assure you," said S——, "is the impression throughout their circle of acquaintances. The Tittons, themselves, maintain a complete silence on the subject. Mr. Fortescue Titton is considered a very accomplished man, with a very proud and very secret contempt for the opinions of the world—dressing badly on purpose, silent and simple by design, and only caring to show himself in his real character to his beautiful wife, who is thought to be completely in love with him, and quite excusable for it! What do you think of the woman's diplomatic talents?"

"I think I should like to know her," said I; "but what says Lord George to all this?"

"I had a call from Lord George, not long ago," replied S——, "and, for the first time since our chat at Somerset House, the conversation turned upon the Tittons.

"'Devilish sly of you!' said his Lordship, turning to me half angry, 'why did you pretend not to know the woman at Somerset House? You might have saved me lots of trouble and money, for I was a month or two finding out what sort of people they were—feeing the servants and getting them called on and invited here and there—all with the idea that it was a rich donkey with a fine toy that didn't belong to him!"

"'Well!' exclaimed I—

"'*Well!*—not at all well! I made a great ninny of myself, with that satirical slyboots, old Titton, laughing at me all the time, when you, that had painted him in his proper character, and knew what a deep devil he was, might have saved me with but half a hint!'

"'You have been in the lady's boudoir, then!'

"'Yes, and in the gentleman's *sanctum sanctorum*! Mrs. Titton sent for me about some trumpery thing or other, and when I called, the servant showed me in there by mistake. There was a great row in the house about it, but I was there long enough to see what a monstrous nice time the fellow has of it, all to himself, and to see your picture of him in his private character. The picture you made of *me*, was only a copy of that, you sly traitor! And, I suppose, Mrs. Titton didn't like your stealing from hers, did she?—for, I take it, that was what ailed her at the exhibition, when you allowed me to be so humbugged!'

"I had a good laugh; but it was as much at the quiet success of Mrs. Titton's tactics, as at Lord George's discomfiture. Of course, I could not undeceive him. And now," continued S——, very good-naturedly, "just ring for a pen and ink, and I'll write a note to Mrs. Titton, asking leave to bring you there this evening, for it's her 'night at home,' and *she's* worth seeing, if my pictures, which you will see there, are not."

MISS JONES'S SON

One night, toward the close of the London season—the last week in August, or thereabouts—the Deptford omnibus set down a gentleman at one of the small brick-block cottages on the Kent road. He was a very quietly disposed person, with a face rather inscrutable to a common eye, and might, or might not, pass for what he was—a man of mark. His age was perhaps thirty, and his manners and movements had that cool security which can come only from conversance with a class of society that is beyond being laughed at. He was handsome—but, when the style of a man is well pronounced, that is an unobserved trifle.

Perhaps the reader will step in to No. 10, Verandah Row, without further ceremony.

The room—scarce more than a squirrel-box from back to front—was divided by folding doors, and the furniture was fanciful and neatly kept. The canary-bird, in a very small cage, in the corner, seemed rather an intruder on such small quarters. You could scarce give a guess what style of lady was the tenant of such miniature gentility.

The omnibus passenger sat down in one of the little cane bottomed and straight-backed chairs, and presently the door opened, and a stout elderly woman, whose skirts really filled up the remaining void of the little parlor, entered with a cordial exclamation, and an affectionate embrace was exchanged between them.

"Well, my dear mother!" said the visitor, "I am off to-morrow to Warwickshire to pass the shooting season, and I came to wind up your household clockwork, to go for a month—(*ticking*, I am sorry to say!) What do you want? How is the tea-caddy?"

"Out of green, James, but the black will do till you come back. La! don't talk of such matters when you are just going to leave me. I'll step up stairs and make you out a list of my wants presently. Tell me—where are you going in Warwickshire? I went to school in Warwickshire. Dear me! the lovers I had there! Well, well! Where did you say you were going?"

"To the Marquis of Headfort—Headfort Court, I think his place is called—a post and a half from Stratford. Were you ever there, mother?"

"*I* there, indeed! no, my son! But I had a lover near Stratford—young Sir Humphrey Fencher, he was then—old Sir Humphrey now! I'm sure he remembers me, long as it is since I saw him—and, James, I'll give you a letter to him. Yes—I should like to know how he looks, and what he will say to my grown-up boy. I'll go and write it now, and I'll look over the groceries at the same time. If you move your chair, James, don't crush the canary-bird!"

The mention of the letter of introduction lingered in the ear of the gentleman left in the parlor, and, smiling to himself with a look of covert humor, he drew from his pocket a letter of which it reminded him—the letter of introduction, on the strength of which he was going to Warwickshire. As this and the one which was being written up stairs, were the two pieces of ordnance destined to propel the incidents of our story, the reader will excuse us for presenting them as a " make ready."

" *Crockford's, Monday*

" Dear Fred : Nothing going on in town, except a little affair of my own, which I can't leave to go down to you. Dull even at Crocky's—nobody plays, this hot weather. And now, as to your commissions. You will receive Duprez, the cook, by to-night's mail. Grisi won't come to you without her man—' 'twasn't thus when we were boys !'—so I send you a figurante, and you must do tableaux. I was luckier in finding you a wit. S—— will be with you to-morrow, though, by the way, it is only on condition of meeting Lady Midge Bellasys, for whom, if she is not with you, you must exert your inveiglements. This, by way only of shuttlecock and battledore, however, for they play at wit together—nothing more, on *her* part at least. Look out for this devilish fellow, my lord Fred !—and live thin till you see the last of him —for he'll laugh you into your second apoplexy with the dangerous ease of a hair-trigger. I could amuse you with a turn or two in my late adventures, but Black and White are bad confidants, though very well as a business firm. And, mentioning them, I have drawn on you for a temporary £500, which please lump with my other loan, and oblige

" Yours, faithfully,

" Vaurien."

And here follows the letter of Mrs. S—— to her ancient lover, the baronet of Warwickshire :—

" *No.* 10 *Verandah Row, Kent Road.*

" Dear Sir Humphrey : Perhaps you will scarce remember Jane Jones, to whom you presented the brush of your first fox.

This was thirty years ago. I was then at school in the little village near Tally-ho hall. Dear me! how well I remember it! On hearing of your marriage, I accepted an offer from my late husband, Mr. S——, and our union was blessed with one boy, who, I must say, is an angel of goodness. Out of his small income, my dear James furnished and rented this very genteel house, and he tells me I shall have it for life, and provides me one servant, and everything I could possibly want. Thrice a week he comes out to spend the day and dine with me, and, in short, he is the pattern of good sons. As this dear boy is going down to Warwickshire, I cannot resist the desire I have that you should know him, and that he should bring me back an account of my lover in days gone by. Any attention to him, dear Sir Humphrey, will very much oblige one whom you once was happy to oblige, and still Your sincere friend, JANE S——,

"Formerly JONES."

It was a morning astray from Paradise when S——— awoke at Stratford. Ringing for his breakfast, he requested that the famous hostess of the Red Horse would grace him so far, as to join him over a muffin and a cup of coffee, and, between the pauses of his toilet, he indited a note, enclosing his mother's letter of introduction to Sir Humphrey.

Enter dame hostess, prim and respectful, and, as breakfast proceeded, S——— easily informed himself of the geography of Tally-ho hall, and the existing branch and foliage of the family tree. Sir Humphrey's domestic circle consisted of a daughter and a niece, (his only son having gone with his regiment to the Canada wars,) and the hall lay half way to Headfort Court—the Fenchers his lordship's nearest neighbors, Mrs. Boniface was inclined to think

S——— divided his morning very delightfully between the banks of the Avon, and the be-scribbled localities of Shakspere's birth and residence, and, by two o'clock, the messenger had returned with this note from Sir Humphrey :—

" DEAR SIR : I remember Miss Jones very well. God bless me, I thought she had been dead many years. I am sure I shall be very happy to see her son. Will you come out and dine with us ?—dinner at seven. Your ob't servant

" HUMPHREY FENCHER.

" James S———, Esq."

As the crack wit and diner-out of his time, S——— was as well known to the brilliant society of London as the face of the " gold stick in waiting" at St. James's, and, with his very common name, he was as little likely to be recognized, out of his peculiar sphere, as the noble lord, when walking in Cheapside, to be recognized as *the* " stick," so often mentioned in the Court Journal. He had delayed his visit to Headfort Court for a day, and undertaken to deliver his mother's letter, and look up her langsyne lover, very much as he would stop in the Strand to purchase her a parcel of snuff—purely from the filial habit of always doing her bidding, even in whims. He had very little curiosity to see a Warwickshire Nimrod, and, till his post-chaise stopped at the lodge-gate of Tally-ho hall, it had never entered his head to speculate upon the ground of his introduction to Sir Humphrey, nor to anticipate the nature of his reception. His name had been so long to him an " open sesame," that he had no doubt of its potency, and least of all when he pronounced it at an inferior gate in the barriers of society.

The dressing-bell had rang, and S——— was shown into the

vacant drawing-room, where he buried himself in the deepest chair he could find, and sat looking at the wall with the composure of a barber's customer waiting to be shaved. There presently entered two young ladies, very showily dressed, who called him Mr. "Jones," in replying to his salutation, and immediately fell to promenading between the two old mirrors at the extremities of the room, discoursing upon topics evidently chosen to exclude the new-comer from the conversation. With *rather* a feeling that it was their loss, not his, S——— recomposed himself in the leathern chair, and resumed the perusal of the oaken ceiling. The neglect sat upon him a little uncomfortably withal.

"How d'ye do, young man! What! are you Miss Jones's son, eh?" was the salutation of a burly old gentleman, who now entered and shook hands with the great incognito. "Here, 'Bel! Fan! Mr. Jones. My daughter and my niece, Mr. Jones!"

S——— was too indignant, for a moment, to explain that Miss Jones had changed her name before his birth, and, on second thought, finding that his real character was not suspected, and that he represented to Sir Humphrey simply the obscure son of an obscure girl, pretty, thirty years ago, he fell quietly into the *role* expected of him, and walked patiently into dinner with Miss Fencher, who accepted his arm for that purpose, but forgot to take it!

It was hard to be witty as *a* Mr. Jones, but the habit was strong and the opportunities were good, and S———, warming with his first glass of sherry, struck out some sparks that would have passed for gems of the first water, with choicer listeners; but wit is slowly recognized when not expected, and, though now and then the young ladies stared, and now and then the old baronet chuckled, and said, "egad! very well!" there was evidently no material rise in the value of Mr. Jones, and he at last confined his social talents exclusively to his wine-glass and nut-picker, feeling, spite of himself, as stupid as he seemed.

Relieved of the burden of replying to their guest, the young ladies now took up a subject which evidently lay nearest their hearts—a series of *dejeuners*, the first of which was to come off the following morning at Headfort Court. As if by way of *caveat*, in case Mr. Jones should fancy that he could be invited to accompany Sir Humphrey, Miss Fencher took the trouble to explain that these were, by no means, common country entertainments, but exclusive and select parties, under the patronage of the beautiful and witty Lady Imogen Bellasys, now a guest at Headfort. Her ladyship had not only stipulated for *societé choisie*, but had invited down a celebrated London wit, a great friend of her own, to do the mottoes and keep up the spirit of the masques and tableaux. Indeed, Miss Fencher considered herself as more particularly the guest and ally of Lady Imogen, never having been permitted, during her mother's life, to visit Headfort (though she did not see what the marquis's private character had to do with his visiting list), and she expected to be called upon to serve as a sort of maid of honor, or in some way to assist Lady Imogen, who had invited her, very affectionately, after church, on Sunday. She thought, perhaps, she had better wake up Sir Humphrey, while she thought of it, (and while papa was good-natured, as he always was after dinner), and exact of him a promise that the great London Mr. What d'ye call 'im, should be invited to pass a week at Tally-ho hall—for, of course, as mutual allies of Lady Imogen, Miss Fencher and he would become rather well acquainted.

To this enlightenment, of which we have given only a brief *resumér*, Mr. Jones listened attentively, as he was expected to do, and was very graciously answered, when, by way of feeling one of the remote pulses of his celebrity, he ventured to ask for some further particulars about the London wit aforementioned. He learned, somewhat to his disgust, that his name was either Brown or Simpson—some very common name, however—but that he had a wonderful talent for writing impromptu epigrams on people, and singing them afterward to impromptu music on the piano, and that he was supposed to be a natural son of Talleyrand or Lord Byron, Miss Fencher had forgotten which. He had written something, but Miss Fencher had forgotten what. He was very handsome—no, very plain—indeed, Miss Fencher had forgotten which—but it was one or the other.

At this crisis of the conversation Sir Humphrey roused from his post-prandial snooze, and begged Mr. Jones to pass the port, and open the door for the ladies. By the time the gloves were rescued from under the table, the worthy Baronet had drained a bumper, and, with his descending glass, dropped his eyes to the level of his daughter's face, where they rested with paternal admiration. Miss Fencher was far from ill-looking, and she well knew that her father waxed affectionate over his wine.

"Papa!" said she, coming behind him, and looking down his throat, as he strained his head backward, leaving his reluctant double chin resting on his cravat. "I have a favor to ask, my dear papa!"

"He shall go, my dear! he shall go! I have been thinking of it—I'll arrange it, Bel, I'll arrange it! Go your ways, chick, and send me my slippers!" gurgled the baronet, with his usual rapid brevity, when slightly elevated.

Miss Fencher turned quite pale.

"Pa—pa!" she exclaimed, with horror in her voice, coming

round front, "pa—pa!—good gracious! Do you know it is the most exclusive—however, papa! let us talk that over in the other room. What I wish to ask is quite another matter. You know that Mr.— Mr.—"

"The gentleman you mean is probably James S———," interrupted Mr. Jones.

"Thank you, sir, so it is?" continued Miss Fencher, putting her hand upon the Baronet's mouth, who was about to speak—"It is Mr. James S———; and what I wish, papa, is, to have Mr. James S——— invited to pass a week with us. You know, papa, we shall be very intimate—James S——— and I—both of us assisting Lady Imogen, you know, papa! and—and—stay till I get some note-paper—will you, dear papa?"

"You *will* have your way, chick, you *will* have your way," sighed Sir Humphrey, getting his spectacles out of a very tight pocket on his hip. "But, bless me, I can't write in the evening. Mr. Jones—perhaps Mr. Jones will write the note for me—just present my compliments to Mr. S———, and request the honor, and all that—can you do it, Mr. Jones?"

S——— rapidly indited a polite note to himself, which he handed to Miss Fencher for her approbation, and, meantime, entered the butler with the coffee.

"Stuggins!" cried Sir Humphrey—"I wish Mr. Jones—"

"Good Heavens! papa!" exclaimed Miss Fencher, ending the remainder of her objurgation in a whisper in her father's ear. But the Baronet was not in a mood to be controlled.

"My love!—Bel, I say—he *shall* go. You d-d-d-diddedent see Miss Jones's letter. He's a p-p-p-pattern of filial duty!—he gives his mother a house, and all she wants!—he's a good son, I tell you! St-Stuggins, come here! Pass the port, Jones, my good fellow!"

Stuggins stepped forward a pace, and presented his white waistcoat, and Miss Fencher flounced out of the room in a passion.

"Stuggins!" said the old man, a little more tranquilly, since he had no fear now of being interrupted, "I wish my friend, Mr. Jones, here, to see this cock-a-hoop business to-morrow. It'll be a fine sight, they tell me. I want him to see it, Stuggins! You understand me. His mother, Miss Jones, was a pretty girl, Stuggins! And she'll be very glad to hear that her boy has seen such a fine show—eh, Jones? eh, Stuggins? Well, you know what I want. The Headfort tenants will have a place provided for them, of course,—some shrubbery, eh?—some gallery—some place behind the musicians, where they are out of the way, but can see—is'nt it so? eh? eh?"

"Yes, Sir Humphrey—no doubt, Sir Humphrey!" acceded Stuggins, with his ears still open to know how the details were to be managed.

"Well—very well—and you'll take Jones with you in the dickey, eh?—Thomas will go on the box—eh? Will that do?—and Mr. Jones will stay with us to-night, and perhaps you'll show him his room, now, and talk it over, eh, Stuggins?—good night, Mr. Jones!—good night, Jones, my good fellow!"

And Sir Humphrey, having done this act of grateful reminiscence for his old sweetheart, managed to find his way into the next room unaided.

S——— had begun, by this time, to see "straw for his bricks," in the course matters were taking; and, instead of throwing a decanter after Sir Humphrey, and knocking down the butler for calling him Mr. Jones, he accepted Stuggins's convoy to the housekeeper's room, and, with his droll stories and funny ways, kept the maids and footmen in convulsions of laughter till break of day. Such a merry time had not come off in servants' hall for many a day, and, of many a precious morsel of the high life below stairs of Tally-ho hall, did he pick the brains of the delighted Abigails.

The ladies, busied with their toilets, had their breakfasts in their own rooms, and Mr. Jones did not make his appearance till after the Baronet had achieved his red herring and seltzer. The carriage came round at twelve, and the ladies stepped in, dressed for triumph, tumbled after by burly Sir Humphrey, who required one side of the vehicle to himself—Mr. Jones outside, on the dickey with Stuggins, as previously arranged.

Half way up the long avenue of Headfort Court, Stuggins relinquished the dickey to its rightful occupant, Thomas, and, with Mr. Jones, turned off by a side-path that led to the dairy and offices—the latter barely saving his legs, however, for the manœuvre was performed servant fashion, while the carriage kept its way.

Lord Headfort was a widower, and his niece, Lady Imogen Bellasys, the wittiest and loveliest girl in England, stood upon the lawn for the mistress of the festivities. She had occasion for a petticoat *aid-de-camp*, and she knew that Lord Headfort wished to propitiate his Warwickshire neighbors ; and, as Miss Fencher was a fine grenadier-looking girl, she promoted her to that office immediately on her arrival, decking her for the nonce with a broad blue riband of authority. Miss Fencher made the best use of her powers of self-congratulation, and thanked God privately, besides, that Sir Humphrey had provided an eclipse for Mr. Jones ; for, with the drawback of presenting such a superfluous acquaintance of their own to the fastidious eyes of Lady Imogen, she felt assured that her new honors would never have arrived to her. She had had a hint, moreover, from her dressing-maid, of Mr. Jones's comicalities below stairs ; and the fact that he was a person who could be funny in a kitchen, was quite enough to confirm the aristocratic instinct by which she had at once pronounced upon his condition. If her papa *had* been gay in his youth, there was no reason why every Miss Jones should send her child to him to be made a gentleman of ! "Filial pattern," indeed !

The gayeties began. The French figurante, despatched by Lord Vaurien from the opera, made up her tableaux from the beauties, and those who had ugly faces but good figures, tried their attitudes on the archery lawn, and those whose complexions would stand the aggravation, tripped to the dancing-tents, and the falcon was flown, and the grey-hounds were coursed, and a few couple of Warwickshire lads tried their backs at a wrestling fall, and the time wore on. But, to Lady Imogen's shrewd apprehension, it wore on very heavily. There was no wit afloat. Nobody seemed gayer than he meant to be. The bubble was wanting to their champagne of enjoyment. Miss Fencher's blue riband went to and fro like a pendulum, perpetually crossing the lawn between Lady Imogen and the footman in waiting, to inquire if a post-chaise had arrived from London.

"I will never forgive that James S——, never!" pettishly vowed her ladyship, as Miss Fencher came back for the fiftieth time with no news of his arrival.

"Better feed your menagerie at once!" whispered Lord Headfort to his niece, as he caught a glance at her vexed face in passing.

The decision with which the order was given to serve breakfast, seemed to hurry the very heat of the kitchen fires, for, in an incredibly short time, the hot soups and delicate *entremets* of Monsieur Duprez were on the tables, and breakfast was announced. The band played a march, the games were abandoned, Miss Fencher followed close upon the heel of her *chef*, to secure a seat in her neighborhood, and, in ten minutes, a hundred questions of precedence were settled, and Sir Humphrey, somewhat to his surprise, and as much to his delight, was called to the left hand of the Marquis. Tally-ho hall was in the ascendant.

During the first assault upon the soups, the band played a delicious set of waltzes, terminating with the clatter of changing plates. But, at the same moment, above all the ring of impinging china, arose a shout of laughter from a party somewhere without the pavilion, and so sustained and hearty was the peal, that the servants stood petrified with their dishes, and the guests sat in wondering silence. The steward was instantly despatched to enforce order, and Lord Headfort explained, that the tenants were feasted on beef and ale, in the thicket beyond, though he could scarce imagine what should amuse them so uncommonly.

"They have promised to maintain order, my lord!" said the steward, returning, and stooping to his master's ear, "but there is a droll gentleman among them, my lord!"

"Then I dare swear it's better fun than this!" mumbled his lordship for the steward's hearing, as he looked round upon the unamused faces in his neighborhood.

"Headfort," cried Lady Imogen, presently, from the other end of the table, "did you send to Stratford for S——, or did you not? Let us know whether there is a chance of his coming!"

"Upon my honor, Lady Imogen, my own chariot has been at the Stratford inn, waiting for him since morning," was the Marquis's answer. "Vaurien wrote that he had booked him by the mail of the night before! I'd give a thousand pounds if he were here!"

Bursts of laughter, breaking through all efforts to suppress them, again rose from the offending quarter.

"It's a Mr. Jones, my lord," said the steward, speaking between the Marquis and Sir Humphrey; "he's a friend of Sir Humphrey's butler—and—if you will excuse me, my lord—Stuggins says he is the son of a Miss Jones, formerly an acquaintance of Sir Humphrey's!"

Red as a turkey-cock grew the old baronet in a moment. "I beg ten thousand pardons for having intruded him here, my lord!" said Sir Humphrey; "it's a poor lad that brought me a letter from his mother, and I told Stuggins—"

But here Stuggins approached with a couple of notes for his master, and, begging permission of the Marquis, Sir Humphrey put on his spectacles to read. The guests at the table, meantime, were passing the wine very slowly, and conversation more slowly still, and, with the tranquillity that reigned in the pavilion, the continued though half-smothered merriment of the other party was provokingly audible.

"Can't we borrow a little fun from those merry people!" cried Lady Imogen, throwing up her eyes despairingly as the Marquis exchanged looks with her.

"If we could persuade Sir Humphrey to introduce his friend, Jones, to us—"

"*I* introduce him!" exclaimed the fuming Baronet, tearing off his spectacles in a rage, "read that before you condescend to talk of noticing such a varlet! Faith! I think he's the clown from a theatre, or the waiter from a pot-house!"

The Marquis read:-

"DEAR NUNCLE: It's hard on to six o'clock, and I'm engaged at seven to a junketing at the 'Hen and Chickens,' with Stuggins and the maids. If you intend to make me acquainted with your great lord, now is the time. If you don't, I shall walk in presently, and introduce myself; for I know how to make my own way, nuncle—ask Miss Bel's maid, and the other girls you introduced me to, at Tally-ho hall! Be in a hurry. I'm just outside.

"Yours, JONES.

"Sir Humphrey Fencher."

The excitement of Sir Humphrey, and the amused face of the Marquis as he read, had drawn Lady Imogen from her seat, and as he read aloud, at her request, the urgent epistle of Mr. Jones, she clapped her hands with delight, and insisted on having him in. Sir Humphrey declared he should take it as an affront if the thing was insisted on, and Miss Fencher, who had followed to her father's chair, and heard the reading of the note, looked the picture of surprised indignation. "Insolent! vulgar! abominable!' was all the compliment she ventured upon, however.

"Will you let me look at Mr. Jones's note?" said Lady Imogen.

"Good Heavens!" she exclaimed, after glancing at it an instant, "I was sure it must be he!"

And out ran the beautiful queen of the festivities, and the next moment, to Sir Humphrey's amazement, and Miss Fencher's utter dismay, she returned, dragging in, with her own scarf around his body, and her own wreath of roses around his head, the friend of Stuggins—the abominable Jones! Up jumped the Marquis, and called him by name (not Jones), and seized him by both hands, and up jumped with delighted acclamation half a dozen other of the more distinguished guests at table, and the merriment was now on the other side of the thicket.

It was five or ten minutes before they were again seated at table, S—— on Lady Imogen's right hand, but there were two vacant chairs, for Sir Humphrey and his daughter had taken advantage of the confusion to disappear, and the field was open, therefore, for a full account of Mr. Jones's adventures above and below stairs at Tally-ho hall. A better subject never fell into the hand of that inimitable humorist, and gloriously he made use of it.

As he concluded, amid convulsions of laughter, the butler brought, in a note addressed to James S——, Esq., which had been given him by Stuggins early in the day—his own autograph invitation to the hospitalities of Tally-ho hall!

LADY RACHEL.

' Beauty, alone, is ost, too warily kept."

I ONCE had a long conversation with a fellow-traveller in the *coupè* of a French diligence. It was a bright moonlight night, early in June—not at all the scene or season for talking long on very dry topics—and, with a mutual *abandon* which must be explained by some theory of the silent sympathies, we fell to chatting rather confidentially on the subject of love. He gave me some hints as to a passage in his life which seemed to me, when he told it, a definite and interesting story; but, in recalling it to mind afterwards, I was surprised to find how little he really said, and how much, from seeing the man and hearing his voice, I was enabled without effort to supply. To save roundabout, I'll tell the story in the first person, as it was told to me, begging the reader to take my place in the *coupè* and listen to a very gentlemanly man, of very loveable voice and manners; supplying, also, as I did, by the imagination, much more than is told in the narration.

"I am inclined to think that we are sometimes best loved by those whom we least suspect of being interested in us; and, while a sudden laying open of hearts would give the lie to many a love professed, it would, here and there, disclose a passion which, in the ordinary course of things, would never have been betrayed. I was once a little surprised with a circumstance of the kind I allude to.

"I had become completely domesticated in a family living in the neighborhood of London—I can scarce tell you how, even if it were worth while. A chance introduction, as a stranger in the country, first made me acquainted with them, and we had gone on, from one degree of friendship to another, till I was as much at home at Lilybank as any one of the children. It was one of those little English paradises, rural and luxurious, where love, confidence, simplicity, and refinement, seem natural to the atmosphere, and I thought, when I was there, that I was probably as near to perfect happiness as I was likely to be in the course of my life. But I had my annoyance even there.

"Mr. Fleming (the name is fictitious, of course) was a man of sufficient fortune, living, without a profession, on his means. He was avowedly of the middle class, but his wife, a very beautiful specimen of the young English mother, was very highly connected, and might have moved in what society she pleased. She chose to find her happiness at home, and leave society to come to her by its own natural impulse and affinity—a sensible choice, which shows you at once the simple and rational character of the woman. Fleming and his wife were very fond of each other, but, at the same time, very fond of the companionship of those who were under their roof; and, between them and their three or four lovely children, I could have been almost contented to have been a prisoner at Lilybank, and to have seen nobody but its charming inmates for years together.

"I had become acquainted with the Flemings, however, during the absence of one of the members of the family. Without being at all aware of any new arrival in the course of the morning, I went late to dinner after a long and solitary ride on horseback, and was presented to Lady Rachel ——, a tall and reserved-looking person, sitting on Fleming's right hand. Seeing no reason to abate any of my outward show of happiness, or to put any restraint on the natural impulse of my attentions, I took my accustomed seat by the sweet mistress of the house, wrapped up my entire heart, as usual, in every word and look that I sent toward her, and played the schoolboy that I felt myself, uncloudedly frank and happy. Fleming laughed and mingled in our chat occasionally, as he was wont to do, but a glance now and then at his stately right-hand neighbor made me aware that I was looked upon with some coolness, if not with a marked disapproval. I tried the usual peace-offerings of deference and marked courtesy, and lessened somewhat the outward show of my happiness, but Lady Rachel was apparently not propitiated. You know what it is to have one link cold in the chain of sympathy around a table.

"The next morning I announced my intention of returning to town. I had hitherto come and gone at my pleasure. This time the Flemings showed a determined opposition to my departure. They seemed aware that my enjoyment under their roof had been, for the first time, clouded over, and they were not willing I should leave till the accustomed sunshine was restored. I felt that I owed them too much to resist any persuasion of theirs against my own feelings merely, and I remained.

"But I determined to overcome Lady Rachel's aversion—a little from pique, I may as well confess, but mostly for the gratification I knew it would give to my sweet friends and entertainers. The saddle is my favorite thinking-place. I mounted a beautiful hunter which Fleming always put at my disposal while I stayed with them, and went off for a long gallop. I dismounted at an inn, some miles off, called for black-wax, and writing myself a letter, despatched it to Lilybank. To play my part well, you will easily conceive, it was necessary that my kind friends should not be in the secret.

" The short road to the heart of a proud woman, I well knew, was pity. I came to dinner, that day, a changed man. It was known through the family, of course, that a letter sealed with black had arrived for me, during my ride, and it gave me the apology I needed for a sudden alteration of manner. Delicacy would prevent any one, except Mrs. Fleming, from alluding to it, and she would reserve the inquiry till we were alone. I had the evening before me, of course.

" Lady Rachel, I had remarked, showed her superiority by habitually pitching her voice a note or two below that of the persons around her—as if the repose of her calm mind was beyond the plummet of their superficial gaiety. I had also observed, however, that if she succeeded in rebuking now and then the high spirits of her friends, and lowered the general diapason till it harmonized with her own voice, she was more gratified than by any direct compliment or attention. I ate my soup in silence, and while the children, and a chance guest or two, were carrying on some agreeable banter in a merry key, I waited for the first opening of Lady Rachel's lips, and, when she spoke, took her tone like an echo. Without looking at her, I commenced a subdued and pensive description of my morning's ride, like a man unconsciously awakened from his revery by a sympathetic voice, and betraying, by the tone in which he spoke, the chord to which he responded. A newer guest had taken my place, next to Mrs. Fleming, and I was opposite Lady Rachel. I could feel her eyes suddenly fixed on me as I spoke. For the first time, she addressed a remark to me, in a pause of my description. I raised my eyes to her with as much earnestness and deference as I could summon into them, and, when I had listened to her and answered her observation, kept them fastened on her lips, as if I hoped she would speak to me again—yet without a smile, and with an expression that I meant should be that of sadness, forgetful of usages, and intent only on an eager longing for sympathy. Lady Rachel showed her woman's heart, by an almost immediate change of countenance and manner. She leaned slightly over the table toward me, with her brows lifted from her large dark eyes, and the conversation between us became continuous and exclusive. After a little while, my kind host, finding that he was cut off from his other guests by the fear of interrupting us, proposed to give me the head of the table, and I took his place at the left hand of Lady Rachel. Her dinner was forgotten. She introduced topics of conversation such as she thought harmonized with my feelings, and, while I listened, with my eyes alternately cast down or raised timidly to hers, she opened her heart to me on the subject of death, the loss of friends, the vanity of the world, and the charm, to herself, of sadness and melancholy. She seemed unconscious of the presence of others as she talked. The tears suffused her fine eyes, and her lips quivered, and I found, to my surprise, that she was a woman, under that mask of haughtiness, of the keenest sensibility and feeling. When Mrs. Fleming left the table, Lady Rachel pressed my hand, and, instead of following into the drawing-room, went out by the low window upon the lawn. I had laid up some little food for reflection as you may conceive, and I sat the next hour looking into my wine glass, wondering at the success of my manœuvre, but a little out of humor with my own hypocrisy, notwithstanding.

"Mrs. Fleming's tender kindness to me when I joined her at the tea-table, made me again regret the sacred feelings upon which I had drawn for my experiment. But there was no retreat. I excused myself hastily, and went out in search of Lady Rachel, meeting her ladyship, as I expected, slowly pacing the dark avenues of the garden. The dimness of the starlight relieved me from the effort of keeping sadness in my countenance, and I easily played out my part till midnight, listening to an outpouring of mingled kindness and melancholy, for the waste of which I felt some need to be forgiven.

"Another day of this, however, was all that I could bring my mind to support. Fleming and his wife had entirely lost sight—in sympathy with my presumed affliction—of the object of detaining me at Lilybank, and I took my leave, hating myself for the tender pressure of the hand, and the sad and sympathizing farewells which I was obliged to received from them. I did not dare to tell them of my unworthy *ruse*. Lady Rachel parted from me as kindly as the rest, and I had gained my point with the loss of my self-esteem. With a prayer that, notwithstanding this deceit and misuse, I might find pity when I should indeed stand in need of it, I drove from the door.

"A month passed away, and I wrote, once more, to my friends at Lilybank, that I would pass a week with them. An occurrence, in the course of that month, however, had thrown another mask over my face, and I went there again with a part to play—and, as if by a retributive Providence, it was now my need of sympathy that I was most forced to conceal. An affair which I saw no possibility of compromising, had compelled me to call out a man who was well known as a practised duellist. The particulars would not interest you. In accepting the challenge, my antagonist asked a week's delay, to complete some important business from which he could not withdraw his attention. And that week I passed with the Flemings.

"The gaiety of Lilybank was resumed with the smile I brought back, and chat and occupation took their course. Lady Rachel, though kind and courteous, seemed to have relapsed into her reserve, and, finding society an effort, I rode out daily alone, seeing my friends only at dinner and in the evening. They took it to be an indulgence of some remainder of my former grief, and left me consequently to the disposition of my own time.

"The last evening before the duel arrived, and I bade my friends good-night as usual, though with some suppressed emotion. My second, who was to come from town and take me up at Lilybank on his way to the ground, had written to me that, from what he could gather, my best way was to be prepared for the worst, and, looking upon it as very probably the last night of my life, I determined to pass it waking, and writing to my friends at a distance. I sat down to it, accordingly, without undressing.

"It was toward three in the morning that I sealed up my last letter. My bedroom was on the ground-floor, with a long window opening into the garden; and, as I lifted my head up from leaning over the seal, I saw a white object standing just before the casement, but at some little distance, and half buried in the darkness. My mind was in a fit mood for a superstitious feeling, and my blood crept cold for a moment; I passed my hand across my eyes —looked again. The figure moved slowly away.

"To direct my thoughts, I took up a book and read. But, on looking up, the figure was there again, and, with an irresistible impulse, I rushed out to the garden. The figure came toward me, but, with its first movement, I recognised the stately step of Lady Rachel.

"Confused at having intruded on her privacy—for I presumed that she was abroad for solitude, and with no thought of being disturbed—I turned to retire. She called to me, however, and, sinking upon a garden-seat, covered her face with her hands. I stood before her, for a moment, in embarrassed silence.

"'You keep late hours,' she said, at last, with a tremulous voice, but rising at the same time, and, with her arm put through mine, leading me to the thickly-shaded walk.

"'To-night I do,' I replied; 'letters I could not well defer—'

"'Listen to me!' interrupted Lady Rachel. 'I know your business for the morning—'

"I involuntary released my arm and started back. The chance of an interruption that would seem dishonorable flashed across my mind.

"'Stay!' she continued; 'I am the only one in the family who knows of it, and my errand with you is not to hinder this dreadful meeting. The circumstances are such, that, with society as it is, you could not avoid it with honor.'

"I pressed her arm with a feeling of gratified justification, which quite overcame, for the moment, my curiosity as to the source of her knowledge of the affair.

"'You must forgive me,' she said, 'that I come to you like a bird of ill omen. I cannot spare the precious moments, to tell you how I came by my information as to your design. I have walked the night away, before your window, not daring to interrupt you in what was, probably, the performance of sacred duties. But I know your antagonist—I know his demoniac nature, and—pardon me!—I dread the worst!'

"I still walked by her side in silence. She resumed, though strongly agitated.

"'I have said that I justify you in an intention which will, probably, cost you your life. Yet, but for a feeling which I am about to disclose to you, I should lose no time, and spare no pains, in preventing this meeting. Under such circumstances, your honor would be less dear to me than now, and I should be acting as one of my sex who had but a share of interest in resisting and striving to correct this murderous exaction of public opinion. I would condemn duelling in argument—avoid the duellist in society—make any sacrifice with others to suppress it in the abstract; but, till the feeling changes in reference to it, I could not bring myself to sacrifice, in the honor of the man I loved, my world of happiness for my share only.'

"'And mean you to say—' I began, but, as the light broke in upon my mind, amazement stopped my utterance.

"'Yes—that I love you!—that I love you!' murmured Lady Rachel, throwing herself into my arms, and fastening her lips to mine in a long and passionate kiss—'that I love you, and, in this last hour of your life, must breathe to you what I never before breathed to mortal!'

"She sank to the ground; and, with handfuls of dew, swept from the grass of the lawn, I bathed her temples, as she leaned senseless against my knee. The moon had risen above the trees, and poured its full radiance on her pale face and closed eyes. Her hair loosened, and fell in heavy masses over her shoulders and bosom; and, for the first time, I realized Lady Rachel's extraordinary beauty. Her features were without a fault, her skin was of marble fairness and paleness, and her abandonment to passionate feeling, had removed, for the instant, a hateful cloud of pride and superciliousness, that, at all other times, had obscured her loveliness. With a new-born emotion in my heart, I seized the first instant of returning consciousness, and pressed her, with a convulsive eagerness, to my bosom.

"The sound of wheels aroused me from this delirious dream, and, looking up, I saw the grey of the dawn struggling with the moonlight. I tore myself from her arms, and, the moment after, was whirling away to the appointed place of meeting.

"I was in my room, at Lilybank, dressing, at eleven of that same day. My honor was safe, and the affair was over, and now my whole soul was bent on this new and unexpected vision of love. True—I was but twenty-five, and Lady Rachel, probably, twenty years older; but, she loved me—she was high-born and beautiful—and love is not so often brought to the lip in this world, that we can cavil at the cup which holds it. With these thoughts and feelings wrangling tumultuously in my heated blood, I took the following note from a servant at my door.

"'Lady Rachel —— buries, in entire oblivion, the last night past. Feelings over which she has full control, in ordinary circumstances, have found utterance under the conviction that they were words to the dying. They would never have been betrayed without impending death; and they will never, till death be near to one of us, find voice, or give token of existence again. Delicacy and honor will prompt you to visit Lilybank no more.'

"Lady Rachel kept her room till I left, and I have never visited Lilybank, nor seen her since."

WIGWAM versus ALMACK'S.

CHAPTER I.

In one of the years not long since passed to your account and mine, by the recording angel, gentle reader, I was taking my fill of a delicious American June, as Ducrow takes his bottle of wine, on the back of a beloved horse. In the expressive language of the raftsmen on the streams of the West, I was "following" the Chemung—a river whose wild and peculiar loveliness is destined to be told in undying song, whenever America can find leisure to look up her poets. Such bathing of the feet of precipices—such kissing of flowery slopes—such winding in and out of the bosom of round meadows—such frowning amid broken rocks, and smiling through smooth valleys, you would never believe could go on, in this out-of-doors world, unvisited and uncelebrated.

Not far from the ruins of a fortification, said to have been built by the Spaniards before the settlement of New England by the English, the road along the Chemung dwindles into a mere ledge at the foot of a precipice, the river wearing into the rock at this spot by a black and deep eddy. At the height of your lip above the carriage-track, there gushes from the rock a stream of the size and steady clearness of a glass rod; and all around it, in the small rocky lap which it has worn away, there grows a bed of fragrant mint, kept, by the shade and moisture, of a perpetual green, bright as emerald. Here stops every traveller, who is not upon an errand of life and death; and, while his horse stands up to his fetlocks in the river, he parts the dewy stems of the mint, and drinks, for once in his life, like a fay or a poet. It is one of those exquisite spots which paint their own picture insensibly in the memory, even while you look on them—natural "Daguerreotypes," as it were; and you are surprised, years afterward, to find yourself remembering every leaf and stone, and the song of every bird that sung in the pine-trees overhead, while you were watching the curve of the spring-leap. As I said before, it will be sung and celebrated, when America sits down weary with her first century of toil, and calls for her minstrels, now toiling with her in the fields.

Within a mile of this spot, to which I had been looking forward with delight for some hours, I overtook a horseman. Before coming up with him, I had at once decided he was an Indian. His relaxed limbs, swaying to every motion of his horse with the grace and ease of a wreath of smoke, his neck and shoulders so cleanly shaped, and a certain watchful look about his ears which I cannot define, but which you see in a spirited horse, were infallible marks of the race whom we have driven from the fair land of our independence. He was mounted upon a small, black horse—of the breed commonly called Indian ponies, now not very common so near the Atlantic—and rode with a slack rein, and an air, I thought, rather more dispirited than indolent.

The kind of morning I have described, is, as every one must

remember, of a sweetness so communicative, that one would think two birds could scarce meet on the wing without exchanging a carol; and I involuntarily raised my bridle, after a minute's study of the traveller before me, and, in a brief gallop, was at his side. With the sound of my horse's feet, however, he changed in all his characteristics to another man—sat erect in his saddle, and assumed the earnest air of an American, who never rides but upon some errand; and, on his giving me back my "good morning," in the unexceptionable accent of the country, I presumed I had mistaken my man. He was dark, but, not darker than a Spaniard, of features singularly handsome and regular, dressed with no peculiarity except an otter-skin cap, of a silky and golden-colored fur too expensive and rare for any but a fanciful as well as a luxurious purchaser. A slight wave in the black hair which escaped from it and fell back from his temples, confirmed me in the conviction that his blood was of European origin.

We rode on together with some indifferent conversation, till we arrived at the spring-leap I have described; and here my companion, throwing his right leg over the neck of his pony, jumped to the ground very actively, and, applying his lips to the spring, drank a free draught. His horse seemed to know the spot, and, with the reins on his neck, trotted on to a shallower ledge in the river, and stood with the water to his knees, and his quick eye turned on his master with an expressive look of satisfaction.

"You have been here before," I said, tying my less-disciplined horse to the branch of an overhanging shrub.

"Yes—often!" was his reply, with a tone so quick and rude, however, that, but for the softening quality of the day, I should have abandoned there all thought of further acquaintance.

I took a small valise from the pommel of my saddle, and, while my fellow-traveller sat on the rock-side, looking moodily into the river, I drew forth a flask of wine and a leathern cup, a cold pigeon wrapped in a cool cabbage leaf, the bigger end of a large loaf, and as much salt as could be tied up in the cup of a large water-lily—a set-out of provender which owed its dantiness to the fair hands of my hostess of the night before.

The stranger's first resemblance to an Indian had probably given a color to my thoughts; for, as I handed him a cup of wine, I said, "I wish the Shawanee Chief, to whose tribe this valley belongs, were here to get a cup of my wine."

The young man sprang to his feet with a sudden flash through his eyes, and, while he looked at me, he seemed to stand taller than, from my previous impression of his height, I should have thought possible. Surprised, as I was, at the effect of my remark, I did not withdraw the cup, and, with a moment's searching look into my face, he changed his attitude, begged pardon rather confusedly, and, draining the cup, said, with a faint smile, "The Shawanee Chief thanks you!"

"Do you know the price of land in the valley?" I asked, handing him a slice of bread, with the half pigeon upon it, and beginning to think it was best to stick to commonplace subjects with a stranger.

"Yes!" he said, his brow clouding over again. "It was bought from the Shawanee Chief you speak of, for a string of beads the acre. The tribe had their burial-place on the Susquehannah, some twenty miles from this; and they cared little about a strip of a valley which, now, I would rather have for my inheritance than the fortune of any white man in the land."

"Throw in the landlord's daughter at the village below," said

I, "and I would take it before any half-dozen of the German principalities. Have you heard the news of *her* inheritance?"

Another moody look, and a very crisp "Yes," put a stop to all desire on my part to make further advances in my companion's acquaintance. Gathering my pigeon bones together, therefore, and putting them on the top of a stone, where they would be seen by the first "lucky dog" that passed, flinging my emptied water-lily on the river, and strapping up cup and flask once more in my valise, I mounted, and, with a crusty good morning, set off at a hand-gallop down the river.

My last unsuccessful topic was, at the time I write of, the subject of conversation all through the neighborhood of the village toward which I was travelling. The most old-fashioned and comfortable inn on the Susquehannah, or Chemung, was kept at the junction of these two noble rivers, by a certain Robert Plymton, who had "one fair daughter, and no more." He was a plain farmer of Connecticut, who had married the grand-daughter of an English emigrant, and got, with his wife, a chest of old papers, which, he thought, had better be used to mend a broken pane, or wrap up groceries, but which his wife, on her death-bed, told him "might turn out worth something." With this slender thread of expectation, he had kept the little chest under his bed, thinking of it, perhaps, once a year, and satisfying his daughter's inquisitive queries with a shake of the head, and something about "her poor mother's tantrums," concluding, usually, with some reminder to keep the parlor in order, or mind her housekeeping. Ruth Plymton had had some sixteen "winters' schooling," and was known to be much "smarter," (*Anglicé*, cleverer,) than was quite necessary for the fulfilment of her manifold duties. Since twelve years of age, (the period of her mother's death,) she had officiated with more and more success as bar-maid and host's daughter to the most frequented inn of the village, till, now, at eighteen, she was the only ostensible keeper of the inn, the old man usually being absent in the fields with his men, or embarking his grain in an " ark," to take advantage of the first freshet. She was civil to all comers; but her manner was such as to make it perfectly plain, even to the rudest raftsman and hunter, that the highest respect they knew how to render to a woman, was her due. She was rather unpopular with the girls of the village, from what they called her pride, and " keeping to herself;" but, the truth was, that the cheap editions of romances which Ruth took instead of money, for the lodging of the itinerant book-pedlars, were more agreeable companions to her, than the girls of the village; and the long summer forenoons, and half the long winter nights, were little enough for the busy young hostess, who, seated on her bed, devoured tales of high-life, which harmonized with some secret longing in her breast—she knew not, and scarce thought of asking herself, why.

I had been twice at Athens, (by this classical name is known the village I speak of,) and each time had prolonged my stay at Plymton's inn for a day longer than my horse or my repose strictly exacted. The scenery at the junction is magnificent, but it was scarce that. And I cannot say that it was altogether admiration of the host's daughter; for, though I breakfasted late, for the sake of having a clean parlor while I ate my broiled chicken, (and, having been once to Italy, Miss Plymton liked to pour out my tea, and hear me talk of St. Peter's and the Carnival,) yet, there was that marked *retenu* and decision in her manner, that made me feel quite too much like a culprit at school; and, large and black as her eyes were, and light and airy as were all her motions, I mixed up, with my propensity for her society, a sort of dislike. In short, I never felt a tenderness for a woman who could "queen it" so easily, and I went heart-whole on my journey, though always with a high respect for Ruth Plymton, and a pleasant remembrance of her conversation.

The story which I had heard farther up the river, was, briefly, that there had arrived at Athens an Englishman, who had found, in Miss Ruth Plymton, the last surviving descendant of the family of her mother—that she was the heiress of a large fortune, if the proof of her descent were complete, and that the contents of the little chest had been the subject of a week's hard study by the stranger, who had departed, after a vain attempt to persuade old Plymton to accompany him to England with his daughter. This was the rumor, the allusion to which had been received with such repulsive coldness by my dark companion at the spring-leap.

America is so much of an asylum for despairing younger sons, and the proud and starving branches of great families, that a discovery of heirs to property, among people of very inferior condition, is by no means uncommon. It is a species of romance in real life, however, which we never believe upon hearsay, and I rode on to the village, expecting my usual reception by the fair damsel of the inn. The old sign still hung askew as I approached, and the pillars of the old wooden "stoop" or portico, were as much off their perpendicular as before, and, true to my augury, out-stepped my fair acquaintance at the sound of my horse's feet, and called to Reuben the ostler, and gave me an unchanged welcome. The old man was down at the river's side, and the key of the grated bar hung at the hostess's girdle, and with these signs of times as they were, my belief in the marvellous tale vanished into thin air.

"So you are not gone to England to take possession?" I said.

Her serious "No!" unsoftened by any other remark, put a stop to the subject again, and taking myself to task for having been all day stumbling on *mal-apropos* subjects, I asked to be shown to my room, and spent the hour or two before dinner in watching the chickens from the window, and wondering a great deal as to the "whereabouts" of my friend in the otter-skin cap.

The evening of that day was unusually warm, and I strolled down to the bank of the Susquehannah, to bathe. The moon was nearly full and half way to the zenith; and, between the lingering sunset and the clear splendor of the moonlight, the dusk of the "folding hour" was forgotten, and the night went on almost as radiant as day. I swam across the river, delighting myself with the gold rims of the ripples before my breast, and was within a yard or two of the shore on my return, when I heard a woman's voice approaching in earnest conversation. I shot forward, and drew myself in beneath a large clump of alders, and, with only my head out of water, lay in perfect concealment.

"You are not just, Shahatan!" were the first words I distinguished, in a voice I immediately recognised as that of my fair hostess. "You are not just. As far as I know myself, I love you better than any one I ever saw—but—"

As she hesitated, the deep, low voice of my companion at the spring-leap, uttered, in a suppressed and impatient guttural, "But what?" He stood still, with his back to the moon, and, while the light fell full on her face, she withdrew her arm from his, and went on.

"I was going to say, that I do not yet know myself, or the world, sufficiently, to decide that I shall always love you. I would not be too hasty in so important a thing, Shahatan! We have talked of it before, and, therefore, I may say to you, now, that the prejudices of my father, and all my friends, are against it.

"My blood," interrupted the young man, with a movement of impatience.

She laid her hand on his arm. "Stay! the objection is not mine. Your Spanish mother, besides, shows more in your look and features than the blood of your father. But it would still be said I married an Indian, and, though I care little for what the village would say, yet must I be certain that I shall love you with all my heart and till death, before I set my face, with yours, against the prejudices of every white man and woman in my native land! You have urged me for my secret, and there it is I feel relieved to have unburthened my heart of it."

"That secret is but a summer old!" said he, half turning on his heel, and looking from her upon the moon's path across the river.

"Shame!" she replied; "you know that long before this news came, I talked with you constantly of other lands, and of my irresistible desire to see the people of great cities, and satisfy myself whether I was like them. That curiosity, Shahatan, is, I fear, even stronger than my love, or, at least, it.is more impatient; and, now that I have the opportunity fallen to me like a star out of the sky, shall I not go? I must Indeed I must."

The lover felt that all had been said, or was too proud to answer, for they fell into the path again, side by side, in silence, and, at a slow step, were soon out of my sight and hearing. I emerged from my compulsory hiding-place, wiser than I went in, dressed, and strolled back to the village, and, finding the old landlord smoking his pipe alone, under the portico, I lighted a cigar, and sat down to pick his brains of the little information I wanted to fill out the story.

I took my leave of Athens on the following morning, paying my bill duly to Miss Plymton, from whom I requested a receipt in writing, for I foresaw, without any very sagacious augury beside what the old man told me, that it might be an amusing document by-and-by. You shall judge, by the sequel of the story, dear reader, whether you would like it in your book of autographs.

Not long after the adventure described in the preceding chapter, I embarked for a ramble in Europe. Among the newspapers which were lying about in the cabin of the packet, was one which contained this paragraph, extracted from a New Orleans Gazette. The American reader will at once remember it:—

"*Extraordinary attachment to savage life.*—The officers at Fort —— (one of the most distant outposts of human habitation in the West,) extended their hospitality lately to one of the young *protegés* of government, a young Shawanee Chief, who has been educated at public expense for the purpose of aiding in the civilization of his tribe. This youth, the son of a Shawanee chief by a Spanish mother, was put to a preparatory school, in a small village on the Susquehannah, and, subsequently, was graduated at ——— College, with the first honors of his class. He had become a most accomplished gentleman, was apparently fond of society, and, except in a scarce distinguishable tinge of copper color in his skin, retained no trace of his savage origin. Singular to relate, however, he disappeared suddenly from the Fort, leaving behind him the clothes in which he had arrived, and several articles of a gentleman's toilet; and, as the sentry on duty was passed at dawn of the same day by a mounted Indian, in the usual savage dress, who gave the pass-word in issuing from the gate, it is presumed it was no other than the young Shahatan, and that he has joined his tribe, who, were removed, some years since, beyond the Mississippi."

The reader will agree with me, that I possessed the key to the mystery.

As no one thinks of the thread that disappears in an intricate embroidery, till it comes out again on the surface, I was too busy in weaving my own less interesting woof of adventure for the two years following, to give Shahatan and his love even a passing thought. On a summer's night, in 18—, however, I found myself on a banquette at an Almack's ball, seated beside a friend, who, since we had met last at Almack's, had given up the white rose of girlhood for the diamonds of the dame, timidity and blushes for self-possession and serene sweetness, dancing for conversation, and the promise of beautiful and admired seventeen for the perfection of more lovely and adorable twenty-two. She was there as chaperon to a younger sister, and it was delightful, in that whirl of giddy motion and more giddy thought, to sit beside a tranquil and unfevered mind, and talk with her of what was passing, without either bewilderment or effort.

"What is it," she said, "that constitutes aristocratic beauty?—for it is often remarked that it is seen no where in such perfection as at Almack's; yet, I have, for a half-hour looked in vain among these handsome faces for a regular profile, or even a perfect figure. It is not symmetry, surely, that gives a look of high breeding—nor regularity of feature."

"If you will take a leaf out of a traveller's book," I replied, "we may, at least, have the advantage of a comparison. I remember recording, when travelling in the East, that for months I had not seen an irregular nose or forehead in a female face; and, almost universally, the mouth and chin of the Orientals, are, as well as the upper features, of the most classic correctness. Yet where, in civilized countries, do women look lower-born, or more degraded?"

"Then it is not in the features," said my friend.

"No, nor in the figure, strictly, " I went on to say, "for the French and Italian women (*vide* the same book of *mems.*) are generally remarkable for shape and fine contour of limb, and the French are, we all know, (begging your pardon,) much better dancers, and more graceful in their movements, than all other nations. Yet what is more rare than a 'thorough-bred' looking Frenchwoman?"

"We are coming to a conclusion very fast," she said, smiling. "Perhaps we shall find the great secret in delicacy of skin after all."

"Not unless you will agree that Broadway, in New York, is the '*prato fiorito*' of aristocratic beauty—for, no where, on the face of the earth, do you see such complexions. Yet, my fair countrywomen stoop too much, and, are rather too dressy in their tastes, to convey, very generally, the impression of high birth."

"Stay!" interrupted my companion, laying her hand on my arm, with a look of more meaning than I quite understood; "before you commit yourself farther on that point, look at this tall girl coming up the floor, and tell me what you think of her, *apropos* to the subject."

"Why, that she is the very forth-shadowing of noble parentage," I replied, "in step, air, form,—everything. But surely the face is familiar to me."

"It is the Miss Trevanion whom you said you had never met. Yet, she is an American, and, with such a fortune as hers, I wonder you should not have heard of her at least.'

"Miss Trevanion! I never knew anybody of the name, I am perfectly sure—yet that face I have seen before, and I would stake my life I have known the lady, and not casually either.

My eyes were rivetted to the beautiful woman who now sailed past with a grace and stateliness that were the subject of universal admiration, and I eagerly attempted to catch her eye; but on the other side of her walked one of the most agreeable flatterers of the hour, and the crowd prevented my approaching her, even if I had solved the mystery so far as to know in what terms to address her. Yet, it was marvellous that I could ever have seen such beauty, and forgotten the when and where; or, that such fine and unusually lustrous eyes could ever have shone on me, without inscribing well on my memory their "whereabout" and history.

"Well!" said my friend, "are you making out your theory, or, are you 'struck home' with the first impression, like many another dancer here to-night?"

"Pardon me! I shall find out, presently, who Miss Trevanion is—but, meantime, *revenons*. I will tell you where I think lies the secret of the aristocratic beauty of England. It is in the lofty *maintien* of the head and bust—the proud carriage, if you remark, in all these women—the head set back, the chest elevated and expanded, and the whole port and expression that of pride and conscious superiority. This, mind you, though the result of qualities in the character, is not the work of a day, nor, perhaps, of a single generation. The effect of expanding the breast, and preserving the back straight, and the posture generally erect, is the high health and consequent beauty of those portions of the frame; and, the physical advantage, handed down with the pride which produced it from mother to child, the race gradually has become perfect in those points, and the look of pride and high-bearing is now easy, natural, and unconscious. Glance your eye around, and you will see that there is not a defective bust, and hardly a head ill set on, in the room. In an assembly in any other part of the world, *to find* a perfect bust, with a gracefully carried head, is as difficult as here to find the exception."

"What a proud race you make us out, to be sure," said my companion rather dissentingly.

"And so you are, eminently and emphatically proud," I replied. "What English family does not revolt from any proposition of marriage with a foreigner? For an English girl to marry a Frenchman or an Italian, a German or a Russian, Greek, Turk, or Spaniard, is to forfeit a certain degree of respectability, let the match be as brilliant as it may. The first feeling on hearing of it, is against the girl's sense of delicacy. It extends to everything else. Your soldiers, your sailors, your tradesmen, your gentlemen, your common people, and your nobles, are all (who ever doubted it you are mentally asking,) out of all comparison, better than the same ranks and professions in any other country. John Bull is literally surprised if any one doubts this —nay, he does not believe that any one *does* doubt it. Yet you call the Americans ridiculously vain, because they believe their institutions better than yours, that their ships fight as well, their women are as fair, and their men as gentlemanly, as any in the world. The 'vanity' of the French, who believe in themselves, just as the English do, only in a less blind *entireness* of self-glorification, is a common theme of ridicule in English newspapers; and the French and the Americans, for a twentieth part of English intolerance and self-exaggeration, are written down daily, by the English, as the two vainest nations on earth."

"Stop!" said my fair listener, who was beginning to smile at my digression from female beauty to national pride, "let me make a distinction there. As the English and French are quite indifferent to the opinion of other nations on these points, and not at all shaken in their self-admiration by foreign incredulity, theirs may fairly be dignified by the name of *pride*. But what shall I say of the Americans, who are in a perpetual fever at the ridicule of English newspapers, and who receive, I understand, with a general convulsion throughout the States, the least slur in a review, or the smallest expression of disparagement in a tory newspaper. This is not pride, but vanity.

"I am hit, I grant you. A home thrust that I wish I could foil. But here comes Miss Trevanion, again, and I must make her out, or smother of curiosity. I leave you a victor."

The drawing of the cord which encloses the dancers, narrowed the path of the promenaders so effectually, that I could easily take my stand in such a position that Miss Trevanion could not pass without seeing me. With my back to one of the slight pillars of the orchestra, I stood facing her as she came down the room; and, within a foot or two of my position, yet, with several persons between us, her eye, for the first time, rested on me. There was a sudden flush, a look of embarrassed, but momentary curiosity, and the beautiful features cleared up, and I saw, with vexatious mortification, that she had the advantage of me, and was even pleased to remember where we had met. She held out her hand the next moment, but evidently understood my reserve, for, with a mischievous compression of the lips, she leaned over, and said, in a voice intended only for my ear, "Reuben! take the gentleman's horse!"

My sensations were very much those of the Irishman who fell into a pit in a dark night, and, catching a straggling root in his descent, hung suspended by incredible exertion and strength of arm till morning, when daylight disclosed the bottom, at just one inch below the points of his toes. So easy seemed the solution—after it was discovered.

Miss Trevanion (ci-devant Plymton) took my arm. Her companion was engaged to dance. Our meeting at Almack's was certainly one of the last events either could have expected when we parted—but Almack's is not the place to express strong emotions. We walked leisurely down the sides of the quadrilles to the tea-room, and, between her bows and greetings to her acquaintances, she put me *au courant* of her movements for the last two years—Miss Trevanion being the name she had inherited with the fortune from her mother's family, and her mother's high but distant connection having recognized and taken her by the hand in England. She had come abroad with the representative of her country, who had been at the trouble to see her installed in her rights, and had but lately left her, on his return to America. A house in May Fair, and a chaperon in the shape of a card-playing and aristocratic aunt, were the other principal points in her parenthetical narration. Her communicativeness, of course, was very gracious, and, indeed, her whole manner was softened and mellowed down, from the sharpness and hauteur of Miss Plymton. Prosperity had improved even her voice.

As she bent over her tea, in the ante-room, I could not but remark how beautiful she was, by the change usually wrought by the soft moisture of the English air, on persons from dry climates —Americans particularly. That filling out and rounding of the features, and renewing and freshening of the skin, becoming and improving to all, had, to her, been like Juno's bath. Then who does not know the miracles of dress! A circlet of diamonds, whose "water" was light itself, followed the fine bend on either side backward from her brows, supporting, at the parting of her hair, one large emerald. And, on what neck (ay—even of age) is not a diamond necklace beautiful? Miss Trevanion was superb.

The house in Grosvenor-place, at which I knocked the next morning, I well remembered as one of the most elegant and sumptuous in London. Lady L—— had ruined herself in completing and furnishing it, and her parties "in my time" were called, by the most apathetic *blasé*, truly delightful.

"I bought this house of Lady L——," said Miss Trevanion, as we sat down to breakfast, "with all its furniture, pictures, books, incumbrances and trifles, even to the horses in the stables, and the coachman in his wig; for I had too many things to learn, to study furniture and appointments, and, in this very short life, time is sadly wasted in beginnings. People are for ever *getting ready* to live. What think you? Is not this true in everything?"

"Not in love, certainly."

Ah ! very true !" And she became suddenly thoughtful, and, for some minutes, sipped her coffee in silence. I did not interrupt it, for I was thinking of Shahatan, and our thoughts, very possibly, were on the same long journey.

" You are quite right," said I, looking round at the exquisitely-furnished room in which we were breakfasting, " you have bought these things at their intrinsic value, and you have all Lady L——'s taste, trouble, and vexation for twenty years, thrown into the bargain. It is a matter of a lifetime to complete a house like this, and, just as it is all done, Lady L—— retires, an old woman, and you come all the way from a country inn on the Susquehannah to enjoy it. What a whimsical world we live in !"

" Yes," she said, in a sort of soliloquizing tone, " I do enjoy it. It is a delightful sensation to take a long stride at once in the art of life—to have lived for years believing that the wants you felt could only be supplied in fairy-land ; and suddenly to change your sphere, and discover that not only these wants, but a thousand others, more unreasonable, and more imaginary, had been the subject of human ingenuity and talent, till those who live in luxury *have no wants*—that science, and chemistry, and mechanics have left no nerve in the human system, no recess in human sense, unquestioned of its desire ; and that every desire is supplied ! What mistaken ideas most people have of luxury ! They fancy the senses of the rich are over-pampered, that their zest of pleasure is always dull with too much gratification, that their health is ruined with excess, and their tempers spoiled with ease and subserviency. It is a picture drawn by the poets in times when money could buy nothing but excess, and when those who were prodigal, could only be gaudy and intemperate. It was necessary to practise upon the reverse, too; and, hence all the world is convinced of the superior happiness of the ploughman, the absolute necessity of early rising and coarse food to health, and the pride that *must* come with the flaunting of silk and satin."

I could not but smile at this cool upset of all the received phi losophy of the poets.

"You laugh," she continued, "but is it not true, that, in England, at this moment, luxury is the science of keeping up the zest of the senses rather than of pampering them—that the children of the wealthy are the healthiest and fairest, and the sons of the aristocracy are the most athletic and rational, as well as the most carefully nurtured and expensive of all classes—that the most costly dinners are the most digestible, the most expensive wines the least injurious, the most sumptuous houses the best ventilated and wholesome, and the most aristocratic habits of life the most conducive to the preservation of the constitution and consequent long life. There will be excesses, of course, in all spheres, but is not this true?"

"I am wondering how so gay a life as yours could furnish such very grave reflections."

"Pshaw! I am the very person to make them. My aunt (who, by-the-way, never rises till four in the afternoon) has always lived in this sublimated sphere, and takes all these luxuries to be matters of course, as much as I take them to be miracles. She thinks a good cook as natural a circumstance as a fine tree, and would be as much surprised and shocked at the absence of wax candles, as she would at the going out of the stars. She talks as if good dentists, good milliners, opera-singers, perfumers, &c., were the common supply of nature, like dew and sunshine to the flowers. My surprise and delight amuse her, as the child's wonder at the moon amuses the nurse."

"Yet you call this dull unconsciousness the perfection of civilized life."

"I think my aunt, altogether, is not a bad specimen of it, certainly. You have seen her, I think."

"Frequently."

"Well, you will allow that she is still a very handsome woman. She is past fifty, and has every faculty in perfect preservation—an erect figure, undiminished delicacy and quickness in all her senses and tastes—and is still an ornament to society, and an attractive person in appearance and conversation. Contrast her (and she is but one of a class) with the women past fifty in the middle and lower walks of life in America. At that age, with us, they are old women in the commonest acceptation of the term. Their teeth are gone, or defective from neglect, their faces are wrinkled, their backs bent, their feet enlarged, their voices cracked, their senses impaired, their relish in the joys of the young entirely gone by. What makes the difference? *Costly care.* The physician has watched over her health at a guinea a visit. The dentist has examined her teeth at twenty guineas a year. Expensive annual visits to the sea-side have renewed her skin. The friction of the weary hands of her maid has kept down the swelling of her feet and preserved their delicacy of shape. Close and open carriages, at will, have given her daily exercise, either protected from the damp, or refreshed with the fine air of the country. A good cook has kept her digestion untaxed, and good wines have invigorated without poisoning her constitution."

"This is taking very unusual care of oneself, however."

"Not at all. My aunt gives it no more thought than the drawing on of her glove. It is another advantage of wealth, too, that your physician and dentist are distinguished persons who meet you in society, and call on you unprofessionally, see when they are needed, and detect the approach of disease before you are aware of it yourself. My aunt, though naturally delicate, has never been ill. She was watched in childhood with great cost and pains, and, with the habit of common caution herself, she is taken such care of, by her physician and servants, that nothing but some extraordinary fatality could bring disease near her."

"Blessed are the rich, by your showing."

"Why, the beatitudes were not written in our times. If long life, prolonged youth and beauty, and almost perennial health, are blessings, certainly, now-a-days, blessed are the rich."

"But is there no drawback to all this? Where people have surrounded themselves with such costly and indispensable luxuries, are they not made selfish by the necessity of preserving them? Would any *exigeance* of hospitality for instance, induce your aunt to give up her bed, and the comforts of her own room, to a stranger?"

"Oh dear, no!"

"Would she eat her dinner cold for the sake of listening to an appeal to her charity?"

"How can you fancy such a thing?"

"Would she take a wet and dirty, but perishing beggar-woman, into her chariot, on her way to a dinner-party, to save her from dying by the roadside?"

"Um—why, I fear she would be very near-sighted till she got fairly by."

"Yet these are charities that require no great effort in those whose chambers are less costly, whose stomachs are less carefully watched, and whose carriages and dresses are of a plainer fashion."

"Very true!

"So far, then, 'blessed are the poor!' But is not the heart slower in all its sympathies, among the rich? Are not friends chosen and discarded, because their friendship is convenient or the contrary? Are not many worthy people 'ineligible' acquaintances, many near relations unwelcome visitors, because they are out of keeping with these costly circumstances, or involve some sacrifice of personal luxury? Are not people, who would preserve their circle choice and aristocratic, obliged to inflict cruel insults on sensitive minds, to slight, to repulse, to neglect, to equivocate, and play the unfeeling and ungrateful, at the same time that to their superiors they must often sacrifice dignity, and contrive and flatter, and deceive—all to preserve the magic charm of the life you have painted so attractive and enviable?"

"Heigho! it's a bad world, I believe!" said Miss Trevanion, betraying, by that ready sigh, that, even while drawing the attractions of high life, she had not been blind to this more unfavorable side of the picture.

"And, rather more important query still, for an heiress," I said, "does not an intimate acquaintance with these luxurious necessities, and the habit of thinking them indispensable, make all lovers in this class mercenary, and their admiration, where there is wealth, subject, at least, to scrutiny and suspicion?"

A quick flush almost crimsoned Miss Trevanion's face, and she fixed her eyes upon me so inquisitively, as to leave me in no doubt that I had, inadvertently, touched upon a delicate subject.

Embarrassed by a searching look, and not seeing how I could explain that I meant no allusion, I said hastily, "I was thinking of swimming across the Susquehannah by moonlight."

"Puck is at the door, if you please, miss!" said the butler, entering at the moment.

"Perhaps, while I am putting on my riding hat," said Miss Trevanion, with a laugh, "I may discover the connection between your two last observations. It certainly is not very clear at present."

I took up my hat.

"Stay—you must ride with me. You shall have the groom's horse and we shall go without him. I hate to be chased through the park by a flying servant—one English fashion, at least, that I think uncomfortable. They manage it better where I learned to ride," she added with a laugh.

"Yes, indeed! I do not know which they would first starve to death in the backwoods—the master for his insolence in requiring the servant to follow him, or the servant for being such a slave as to obey."

I never remember to have seen a more beautiful animal than the high-bred bloodmare on which my *ci-devant* hostess of the Plymton inn rode through the park gates, and took the serpentine path at a free gallop. I was as well mounted myself as ever I had been in my life, and delighted, for once, not to fret a hundred yards behind; the ambitious animal seemed to have wings to his feet.

"Who ever rode such a horse as this," said my companion, "without confessing the happiness of riches! It is the one luxury of this new life that I should find it misery to forego. Look at the eagerness of his ears! See his fine limbs as he strikes forward! What nostrils! What glossy shoulders! What bounding lightness of action! Beautiful Puck! I could never live without you! What a shame to nature that there are no such horses in the wilderness!"

"I remember seeing an Indian pony," said I, watching her face for the effect of my observation, "which had as many fine qualities, though of a different kind—at least when his master was on him."

She looked at me inquiringly.

"By-the-way, too, it was at your house on the Susquehannah," I added, "you must remember the horse—a black, double-jointed——

"Yes, yes, I know. I remember. Shall we quicken our pace? I hear some one overtaking us, and, to be passed with such horses as ours were a shame indeed."

We loosed our bridles and flew away like the wind; but a bright tear was presently tossed from her dark eyelash, and fell glittering on the dappled shoulder of her horse. "Her heart is Shahatan's," thought I, "whatever chance there may be that the gay Honorable who is at our heels may dazzle her into throwing away her hand.

Mounted on a magnificent hunter, whose powerful and straightforward leaps, soon told against the lavish and high action of our more showy horses, the Hon. Charles ——— (the gentleman who had engrossed the attention of Miss Trevanion the night before at Almack's) was soon beside my companion, and, leaning from his saddle, was taking pains to address conversation to her in a tone not meant for my ear. As the lady picked out her path with a marked preference for his side of the road, I, of course, rode with a free rein on the other, rather discontented, however,

I must own, to be playing Monsieur de Trop. The Hon. Charles, I very well knew, was enjoying a temporary relief from the most *pressing* of his acquaintances, by the prospect 'of his marrying an heiress,' and, in a two years' gay life in London I had traversed his threads too often to believe that he had a heart to be redeemed from dissipation, or a soul to appreciate the virtues of a high-minded woman. I found myself, besides, without wishing it, attorney for Shahatan in the case.

Observing that I "sulked," Miss Trevanion, in the next round, turned her horse's head toward the Serpentine Bridge, and we entered into Kensington Gardens. The band was playing on the other side of the ha-ha, and fashionable London was divided between the equestrians on the road, and the promenaders on the greensward. We drew up in the thickest of the crowd, and, presuming that, by Miss Trevanion's tactics, I was to find some other acquaintance to chat with, while our horses drew breath, I spurred to a little distance, and sat mum in my saddle, with forty or fifty horsemen between me and herself. Her other companion had put his horse as close by the side of Puck as possible; but there were other dancers at Almack's who had an eye upon the heiress, and their *téte-à-téte* was interrupted presently by the how-d ye-do's and attention of half a dozen of the gayest men about town. After looking black at them for a moment, Charles ——— drew bridle, and, backing out of the press rather unceremoniously, rode to the side of a lady who sat in her saddle with a mounted servant behind her, separated from me by only the trunk of a superb lime-tree. I was fated to see all the workings of Miss Trevanion's destiny.

"You see what I endure for you," he said, as a flush came and went upon his pale face.

"You are false!" was the answer. "I saw you ride in—your eyes fastened to hers—your lips open with watching for her words—your horse in a foam, with your agitated and nervous riding. Never call her a giraffe, or laugh at her again, Charles! She is handsome enough to be loved for herself, and you love her."

"No, by heaven!"

The lady made a gesture of impatience, and whipped her stirrup, through the folds of her riding-dress, till it was heard even above the tinkling triangle of the band.

"No," he continued, "and you are less clever than you think, if you interpret my excitement into love. I am excited, most eager in my chase after this woman. *You shall know why.* But for herself—good heaven!—why, you have never heard her speak! She is never done wondering at silver forks, never done with ecstatics about finger-glasses and pastilles. She is a boor—and you are silly enough to put her beside yourself!"

The lady's frown softened, and she gave him her whip to hold, while she re-imprisoned a stray ringlet.

"Keep an eye on her, while I am talking to you," he continued, "for I must stick to her, like her shadow. She is full of mistrust, and, if I lose her by the want of attention for a single hour, that hour will cost me yourself, dearest, first and most important of all, and it will cost me England or my liberty—for failing this, I have not a chance."

"Go, go," said the lady, in a new and now anxious tone, touching his horse at the same time with the whip he had just restored to her, "she is off! Adieu!"

And, with half a dozen attendants, Miss Trevanion took the road at a gallop, while her contented rival followed at a pensive amble, apparently quite content to waste the time as she best might till dinner. The handsome fortune-hunter watched his opportunity and regained his place at Miss Trevanion's side, and, with an acquaintance, who was one of her self-elected troop, I kept in the rear, chatting of the opera, and enjoying the movement of a horse, of as free and admirable action as I had ever felt communicated like inspiration through my blood.

I was resumed as sole cavalier and attendant at Hyde Park gate.

"Do you know the Baroness ——?" I asked, as we walked our horses slowly down Grosvenor Place.

"Not personally," she replied; "but I have heard my aunt speak of her, and I know she is a woman of most seductive manners, though said to be one of very bad morals. But from what Mr. Charles —— tells me, I fancy high play is her only vice. And, meantime, she is received every where.

"I fancy," said I, "that the Hon. Charles —— is good authority for the number of her vices, and, begging you, as a parting request, to make this remark the key to your next month's observation, I have the honor to return this fine horse to you, and make my adieux."

"But you will come to dinner! And, by-the-by, you have not explained to me what you meant by 'swimming across the Susquehannah,' in the middle of your breakfast, this morning."

While Miss Trevanion gathered up her dress to mount the steps, I told her the story which I have already told the reader, of my involuntary discovery, while lying in that moonlit river, of Shahatan's unfortunate passion Violently agitated by the few words in which I conveyed it, she insisted on my entering the house and waiting while she recovered herself sufficiently to talk to me on the subject. But I had no fancy for match making or breaking. I reiterated my caution touching the intimacy of her fashionable admirer with the baroness, and said a word of praise of the noble savage who loved her.

CHAPTER II.

In the autumn of the year after the events outlined in the previous chapter, I received a visit, at my residence on the Susquehannah, from a friend I had never before seen a mile from St. James's street—a May-fair man of fashion, who took me on his way back from Santa Fé. He staid a few days to brush the cobwebs from a fishing-rod and gun which he found in inglorious retirement in the lumber-room of my cottage, and, over our dinners, embellished with his trout and woodcock, the relations of his adventures (compared, as everything was, with London experience exclusively,) were as delightful to me as the tales of Scheherezade to the calif.

"I have saved to the last," he said, pushing me the bottle, the evening before his departure, "a bit of romance which I stumbled over in the prairie, and, I dare say, it will surprise you as much as it did me, for I think you well remember having seen the heroine at Almack's."

"At Almack's?"

"You may well stare. I have been afraid to tell you the story, lest you might think I drew too long a bow. I certainly should never have been believed in London."

"Well—the story?"

"I told you of my leaving St. Louis with a trading party for Sante Fé. Our leader was a rough chap, big-boned, and ill put together, but honestly fond of fight, and never content with a stranger till he had settled the question of which was the better man. He refused, at first, to take me into his party, assuring me that his exclusive services and those of his company had been engaged at a high price, by another gentleman. By dint of drinking 'juleps,' with him, however, and giving him a thorough 'mill' (for, though strong as a rhinoceros, he knew nothing of 'the science') he at last elected me to the honor of his friendship, and took me into the party as one of his own men.

"I bought a strong horse, and, on a bright May morning, the party set forward, bag and baggage, the leader having stolen a march upon us, however, and gone a-head with the person who hired his guidance. It was fine fun at first, as I have told you, to gallop away over the prairie, without fence or ditch, but I soon tired of the slow pace and the monotony of the scenery, and began to wonder why the dence our leader kept himself so carefully out of sight—for, in three days' travel, I had seen him but once, and then at our bivouac fire on the second evening. The men knew or would tell nothing, except that he had one man and a packhorse with him, and that the 'gentleman' and he encamped farther on. I was under promise to perform only the part of one of the hired carriers of the party, or I should soon have made a push to penetrate the 'gentleman's' mystery.

"I think it was on the tenth day of our travel, that the men began to talk of falling in with a tribe of Indians, whose hunting grounds we were close upon, and at whose village, upon the bank of a river, they usually got fish and buffalo-hump, and other luxuries not picked up on the wing. We encamped about sunset that night, as usual, and after picketing my horse, I strolled off to a round mound not far from the fire, and sat down upon the top to see the moon rise. The east was brightening, and the evening was delicious.

"Up came the moon, looking like one of the Duke of Devonshire's gold plates, (excuse the poetry of the comparison,) and still the rosy color hung on in the west, and, turning my eyes from one to the other, I at last perceived, over the southwestern horizon, a mist slowly coming up, which indicated the course of a river. It was just in our track, and the whim struck me to saddle my horse and ride on in search of the Indian village, which, by their description, must be on its banks.

"The men were singing songs over their supper, and, with a flask of brandy in my pocket, I got off unobserved, and was soon in a flourishing gallop over the wild prairie, without guide or compass. It was a silly freak, and might have ended in an unpleasant adventure. Pass the bottle and have no apprehensions, however.

"For an hour or so, I was very much elated with my independence, and my horse, too, seemed delighted to get out of the slow pace of the caravan. It was as light as day, with the wonderful clearness of the atmosphere, and the full moon and the coolness of the evening air made exercise very exhilarating. I rode on, looking up occasionally to the mist, which retreated, long after I thought I should have reached the river, till I began to feel uneasy at last, and wondered whether I had not embarked in a very mad adventure. As I had lost sight of our own fires, and might miss my way in trying to retrace my steps, I determined to push on.

"My horse was in a walk, and I was beginning to feel very grave, when, suddenly, the beast pricked up his ears and gave a loud neigh. I rose in my stirrups, and looked round in vain for the secret of his improved spirits, till, with a second glance forward, I discovered what seemed the faint light reflected upon the smoke of a concealed fire. The horse took his own counsel, and set up a sharp gallop for the spot, and, a few minutes brought me in sight of a fire half concealed by a clump of shrubs, and a white object near it, which, to my surprise, developed to a tent. Two horses picketed near, and a man sitting by the fire with his hands crossed before his shins, and his chin on his knees, completed the very agreeable picture.

"Who goes there ?" shouted this chap, springing to his rifle, as he heard my horse's feet sliding through the grass.

"I gave the name of the leader, comprehending at once that this was the advanced guard of our party ; but, though the fellow lowered his rifle, he gave me a very scant welcome, and motioned me away from the tent-side of the fire. There was no turning a man out of doors in the midst of a prairie ; so, without ceremony, I tethered my horse to his stake, and getting out my dried beef and brandy, made a second supper with quite as good an appetite as had done honor to the first.

"My brandy-flask opened the lips of my sulky friend after a while, though he kept his carcass very obstinately between me and the tent, and I learned that the leader, (his name was Rolfe, by-the-by,) had gone on to the Indian village, and, that the 'gentleman' had dropped the curtain of his tent at my approach, and was, probably, asleep. My word of honor to Rolfe, that I would 'cut no capers,' (his own phrase in administering the obligation,) kept down my excited curiosity, and prevented me, of course, from even pumping the man beside me, though I might have done so with a little more of the contents of my flask.

"The moon was pretty well over head when Rolfe returned,

and found me fast asleep by the fire. I awoke with the trampling and neighing of horses, and, springing to my feet, I saw an Indian dismounting, and Rolfe and the fire-tender conversing together while picketing their horses. The Indian had a tall feather in his cap, and trinkets on his breast, which glittered in the moonlight; but he was dressed otherwise like a white man, with a hunting-frock and very loose large trowsers. By thy way, he had moccasins, too, and a wampum belt; but he was a clean-limbed, lithe, agile-looking devil, with an eye like a coal of fire.

"'You've broke your contract, mister!" said Rolfe, coming up to me; 'but stand by and say nothing.'

"He then went to the tent, gave an 'ehem!' by way of a knock, and entered.

"It's a fine night," said the Indian, coming up to the fire and touching a brand with the toe of his moccasin.

"I was so surprised at the honest English in which he delivered himself, that I stared at him without answer.

"'Do you speak English?' he said.

"'Tolerably well,' said I, 'but I beg your pardon for being so surprised at your own accent that I forgot to reply to you. And, now I look at you more closely, I see that you are rather Spanish than Indian.'

"'My mother's blood," he answered rather coldly, 'but my father was an Indian, and I am a chief.'

"'Well, Rolfe,' he continued, turning the next instant to the trader, who came towards us, 'who is this that would see Shahatan?'

"The trader pointed to the tent. The curtain was put aside, and a smart-looking youth, in a blue cap and cloak, stepped out and took his way off into the prairie, motioning to the chief to follow.

"'Go along! he won't eat you!' said Rolfe, as the Indian hesitated, from pride or distrust, and laid his hand on his tomahawk.

"I wish I could tell you what was said at that interview, for my curiosity was never so strongly excited. Rolfe seemed bent on preventing both interference and observation, however, and, in his loud and coarse voice, commenced singing and making preparations for his supper; and, persuading me into the drinking part of it, I listened to his stories and toasted my shins till I was too sleepy to feel either romance or curiosity; and, leaving the moon to waste its silver on the wilderness, and the mysterious colloquists to ramble and finish their conference as they liked, I rolled over on my buffalo-skin and dropped off to sleep.

"The next morning I rubbed my eyes to discover whether all I have been telling you was not a dream, for tent and demoiselle had evaporated, and I lay with my feet to the smouldering fire, and all the trading party preparing for breakfast around me. Alarmed at my absence, they had made a start before sunrise to overtake Rolfe, and had come up while I slept. The leader, after a while, gave me a slip of paper from the chief, saying that he should be happy to give me a specimen of Indian hospitality at the Shawanee village, on my return from Santa Fé—a neat hint that I was not to intrude upon him at present."

"Which you took?"

"Rolfe seemed to have had a hint which was probably in some more decided shape, since he took it, for us all. The men grumbled at passing the village without calling for fish, but the leader was inexorable. and we left it to the right, and 'made tracks,' as the hunters say, for our destination. Two days from there we saw a buffalo——"

"Which you demolished. You told me that story last night. Come, get back to the Shawanees! You called on the village at your return?"

"Yes, and an odd place it was. We came upon it from the west, Rolfe having made a bend to the westward on his return back. We had been travelling all day over a long plain, wooded in clumps, looking very much like an immense park, and I began to think that the trader intended to cheat me out of my visit—for he said we should sup with the Shawanees that night, and I did not in the least recognize the outline of the country. We struck the bed of a small and very beautiful river, presently however, and, after following it through a wood for a while, came to a sharp brow where the river suddenly descended to a plain at least two hundred feet lower than the table land on which we had been travelling. The country below looked as if it might have been the bed of an immense lake, and we stood on the shore of it.

"I sat on my horse, geologizing in fancy about this singular formation of land, till, hearing a shout, I found the party had gone on, and Rolfe was hallooing to me to follow. As I was trying to get a glimpse of him through the trees, up rode my old acquaintance Shahatan, with his rifle across his thigh, and gave me a very cordial welcome. He then rode on to show me the the way. We left the river, which was foaming among some fine rapids, and, by a zig-zag side-path through the woods, descended about half-way to the plain, where we rounded a huge rock, and stood suddenly in the village of the Shawanees. You cannot fancy anything so picturesque. On the left, for a quarter of a mile, extended a natural *steppe*, or terrace, a hundred yards wide, and rounding in a crescent to the south. The river came in toward it, on the right, in a superb cascade, visible from the whole of the platform, and, against the rocky wall at the back, and around on the edge overlooking the plain, were built the wigwams and log-huts of the tribe; in front of which lounged men, women, and children, enjoying the cool of the summer evening. Not far from the base of the hill, the river reappeared from the woods, and I distinguished some fields planted with corn along its banks, and horses and cattle grazing. What with the pleasant sound of the falls, and the beauty of the scene altogether, it was to me more like the primitive Arcadia we dream about, than anything I ever saw.

"Well, Rolfe and his party reached the village presently, for the chief had brought me by a shorter cut, and, in a moment, the whole tribe was about us, and the trader found himself apparently among old acquaintances. The chief sent a lad with my horse down into the plain to be picketed where the grass was better, and took me into a small hut, where I treated myself to a little more of a toilet than I had been accustomed to, of late, in compliment to the unusual prospect of supping with a lady. The hut was lined with bark, and seemed used by the chief for the same purpose, as there were sundry articles of dress and other civilized refinements hanging to the bracing-poles, and covering a rude table in the corner.

"Fancy my surprise, on coming out, to meet the chief strolling up and down his prairie shelf with, not one lady, but half a dozen —a respectable-looking gentleman in black, (I speak of his coat,) and a bevy of nice-looking girls, with our Almack's acquaintance in the centre—the whole party, except the chief, dressed in a way that would pass muster in any village in England. Shahatan wore the Indian's blanket, modified with a large mantle of fine blue cloth, and crossed over his handsome bare chest, something after the style of a Hieland tartan. I really never saw a better made, or more magnificent-looking fellow, though I am not sure that his easy and picturesque dress would not have improved a plainer man.

"I remembered directly that Rolfe had said something to me about missionaries living among the Shawanees, and I was not surprised to hear that the gentleman in a black coat was a reverend, and the ladies the sisterhood of the mission. Miss Trevanion seemed rather in haste to inform me of the presence of 'the cloth,' and, in the next breath, claimed my congratulations on her marriage! She had been a chieftainess for two months.

"We strolled up and down the grassy terrace, dividing our attention between the effects of the sunset on the prairie below and the preparations for our supper, which was going on by the light of pine-knots stuck in the clefts of the rock in the rear. A dozen Indian girls were crossing and recrossing before the fires, and, with the bright glare upon the precipice, and the moving figures, wigwams, &c., it was like a picture of Salvator Rosa's. The fair chieftainess, as she glided across occasionally to look after the people, with a step as light as her stately figure would allow, was not the least beautiful feature of the scene. We lost a fine creature when we let her slip through our fingers, my dear fellow!"

"Thereby hangs a tale, I have little doubt, and I can give you some data for a good guess at it—but as the 'nigger song' has it—

"Tell us what dey had for supper—
Black-eyed pease, or bread and butter?"

"We had everything the wilderness could produce—appetites included. Lying in the track of the trading parties, Shahatan, of course, made what additions he liked, to the Indian mode of living, and, except that our table was a huge buffalo skin stretched upon stakes, the supper might have been a traveller's meal among Turks or Arabs, for all that was peculiar about it. I should except, perhaps, that no Turk or Arab ever saw so pretty a creature as the chief's sister, who was my neighbor at the feast."

"So—another romance!"

"No, indeed! For though her eyes were eloquent enough to persuade one to forswear the world and turn Shawanee, she had no tongue for a stranger. What little English she had learned of the missionaries, she was too sly to use, and our flirtation was a very unsatisfactory pantomime. I parted from her at night in the big wigwam, without having been out of ear-shot of the chief for a single moment; and, as Rolfe was inexorable about getting off with the day-break the next morning, it was the last I saw of the little fawn. But, to tell you the truth, I had forty minds between that and St. Louis, to turn about and have another look at her.

"The big wigwam, I should tell you, was as large as a common breakfast-room in London. It was built of bark very ingeniously sewed together, and lined throughout with the most costly furs, even the floor covered with highly-dressed bear-skins. After finishing our supper in the open air, the large curtain at the door, which was made of the most superb gold-colored otters, was thrown up to let in the blaze of the pine torches stuck in the rock opposite, and, as the evening was getting cool, we followed the chieftainess to her savage drawing-room, and took coffee and chatted until a late hour, lounging on the rude, fur-covered couches. I had not much chance to talk with our old friend, but I gathered from what little she said, that she had been disgusted with the heartlessness of London, and preferred the wilderness, with one of nature's nobility, to all the splendors of matrimony in high life. She said, however, that she would try to induce Shahatan to travel abroad for a year or two, and, after that, she thought their time would be agreeably spent in such a mixture of savage and civilized life as her fortune and his control over the tribe would enable them to manage."

When my friend had concluded his story, I threw what little light I possessed upon the undeveloped springs of Miss Trevanion's extraordinary movements, and we ended our philosophizings on the subject, by promising ourselves a trip to the Shawanees some day together. Now that we have had the later news that Shahatan and his wife were travelling, by the last accounts, in the East, however, we have limited our programme to meeting them in England, and have no little curiosity to see whether the young savage will decide like his wife in the question of "Wigwam *versus* Almack's."